Praise for *L*

'Cowardly, avaricious, annoying, ... tic: there aren't enough shady adj... scribe the narrator of Andrew Lips... Incredibly entertaining'   *New York Times*, Editor's Choice

'If you've ever wondered where writers get their ideas from, *Last Resort* is wicked fun. If you're a writer, *Last Resort* is heartburn in print. A deliciously absurd comedy about literary fame'

Ron Charles, *Washington Post*

'Lipstein gleefully scrutinizes the nature of success in an industry that runs as much on vanity as on financial gain . . . The book's command of contemporary-hipster details is wincingly precise'

New Yorker

'Talent is rare, which is why I let out a big yippee reading Andrew Lipstein's *Last Resort* . . . There is something in Lipstein's novel that is specific to new male novelists – their conscious sensitivity about writing sex. Lipstein takes this head on. In *Last Resort* the novel-within-the-novel is slated online for its "male gaze". This is culturally astute and a smart way for Lipstein to say: I get it'

The Times

'You won't read a more brilliantly executed literary romp this year . . . An unsparing satire of a generation of millennials who fear that their lives lack gravitas and emotional depth'   *Guardian*

'A funny, fast-paced literary satire'   *Daily Telegraph*

'A propulsive tale of American literary ambition, this novel exposes the status hunger that motivates plenty of writing – far more than writers like to admit. A keenly observed and sharp-witted debut that's assured from first page to last'

Tom Rachman, author of *The Imperfectionists*

'Lipstein asks the timely question: does one possess sole title to one's own story? A sharply written, headlong romp'

Lionel Shriver, author of *We Need to Talk About Kevin*

Last Resort

Andrew Lipstein

WEIDENFELD & NICOLSON

First published in Great Britain in 2022 by Weidenfeld & Nicolson,
This paperback edition first published in Great Britain in 2023
by Weidenfeld & Nicolson,
an imprint of The Orion Publishing Group Ltd
Carmelite House, 50 Victoria Embankment
London EC4Y 0DZ

An Hachette UK Company

1 3 5 7 9 10 8 6 4 2

A CIP catalogue record for this book is
available from the British Library.

ISBN (Mass Market Paperback) 978 1 4746 2012 3
ISBN (eBook) 978 1 4746 2013 0
ISBN (Audio) 978 1 4746 2014 7

Printed in Great Britain by Clays Ltd, Elcograf S.p.A.

www.weidenfeldandnicolson.co.uk
www.orionbooks.co.uk

To my mom,
Pamela Eve Brownstein

Part I

~~~

October 2016

Caleb, it's brilliant, he said, not listening. *Brilliant*. He was looking past my ear to the bar, where I assumed our server must be, or some other woman. That our waitress wasn't conventionally attractive didn't stop him from making a face at me after she'd introduced herself and walked away. I had mirrored it—raising my eyebrows and sucking in my lips—before taking a sip of water to break the moment.

His eyes came back to me. He clasped his hands, placed them on the table, and began talking. I could hardly listen, I couldn't stop thinking of the affectations infecting his words—*do get in touch*, *have a go*, *if I could be so daring*, unearned pauses, overemphasized *mhm*s—and how rampant it is in the book world, and elsewhere, like the café by my apartment stocked with people who dress like artists on weekends but spend their weekdays on Slack. He ended his brief soliloquy with something about Mavis Gallant, whom I'd never read and whose name I'd thought was pronounced differently. (I looked it up when I got home; he was right.) This was all in response to a new story idea, which was a response to him asking me if I had my next book in mind—*next book*, as if the one we were meeting to discuss were already in the past—which was supposed to be a segue from our aimless banter to real business talk. When I told him the new story idea—a party of thirty-somethings where everyone slowly realizes death is present, literally in the room, in disguise, and by the end of the night it will take one of them, so that the entire time they all have to prove how full of life they are—he said, a word or two before I finished, *love it*, which made me hate it and regret ever having dreamt it up.

Ah, Gallant, I said. He looked at his hand, rubbed his pointer and middle fingers together, then scanned the room. He said he wished we could smoke in restaurants, and then, *Thanks, Giuliani*, which I thought was an ironic riff on *Thanks, Obama*, which is already ironic—also the smoking ban was Bloomberg, not Giuliani—but he was apparently sincere. This tarnished some of my assumptions about him, mainly that he should be unflaggingly smooth. Ellis Buford was a quote unquote *big-shot agent*, a phrase I'd heard from too many people with too little irony. He was taller than I'd expected but less handsome in some inscrutable way. I disliked him the second we shook hands, when he apologized for being late—*please forgive my truancy*—but all of that didn't matter, nothing mattered in the face of the fact that he was a big-shot agent who was going to change my life. Yes, the phrase is ridiculous but the concept transcends ridiculousness, the concept being power. *Big shot*. Those two words were the first my lips formed the second we hung up after he called me out of the blue on the Saturday morning four days before our lunch. I was lying on my couch, drinking coffee, listening to John Wizards at full blast (my roommate was out of town), and playing chess online with my computer on my stomach, a ritual I don't normally interrupt before it fulfills its purpose, a bowel movement, when my eyes wandered to the window, catching sight of a building in the distance. I recognized it and was taken aback; the building was in Brooklyn Heights, meaning that my window didn't look south but west. That I'd been mistaken about the cardinal orientation of my apartment for the three months I'd lived there was unbelievable; I was someone who could point north any time of day. I considered finishing the game but I was going to lose anyway, so I put on my slippers and walked downstairs and around the apartment until I found my fire escape. I turned around and found the building again. I was right, I realized; I'd been wrong that whole time, and that's when my phone rang. *Caleb?* he said. *Yes?* I said. *This is Ellis Buford. I've just finished your novel. Do you have time?*

The waitress had seen him look around the room and, misinterpreting, came over with a pen and pad in hand—nothing more than accessories, surely, an ironic, kitsch addition to an atmosphere that seemed designed for readers of *Maxim*. Reclaimed wood clashed with metallic chandeliers clashed with the midcentury modern furniture and attire. It didn't make any sense, but nothing made sense anymore, and also sometimes a nice SoHo address is all you need to charge $36 for a lunch lamb shank, which was what he ordered us both, along with a Heineken for him. When the waitress looked at me I forgot I could speak, to save me from embarrassment Ellis said the place had great Manhattans, and I said, *That's great, I'll have that.*

As soon as she walked away he jumped right in, as if we'd been discussing the book the whole time. He told me how he'd position it, and me, the story behind the story, which as far as I could tell mostly meant my age, twenty-seven, which I didn't think was that young but he seemed to think it was, *And didn't you finish it when you were twenty-four?* (I hadn't, and demurred.)

That's "prodigy"-eligible. Then he spouted a laundry list of words and phrases describing the book and my style, my *aesthetic*, that he would try out with editors, some of which would end up on the back of the book and eventually in the mouths of critics and booksellers and, if all went well, Terry Gross—*and who knows, Seth Meyers?* During all this he elegantly wove in his own past successes and what they did or didn't have in common with how my manuscript might be sold. Something in me disliked this kind of talk, made me feel I should cling to the purity of Art when confronted with the vulgarities of Commerce, but another instinct, a better instinct, made me exhale, sit forward in my chair, put my elbows on the table, and listen intently as this man considered my book in much the same way he considered our waitress as she laid down our drinks.

This is all assuming we can work together, he said, and for a brief moment I revisited a thought I'd spent the past three days convincing myself was irrational: that he'd asked me to lunch only to say the manuscript wasn't for him, or that it would need considerable work. But he was staring at me. His face betrayed worry. *Jesus Christ,* I thought, *he thinks I have other offers.* The excitement passing through me felt like a vulnerability I should hide. I looked at him and smiled bashfully, and then I took a sip from my drink.

How is it? he asked.

Good, I said, as if I could tell, as if I cared. It had alcohol in it. The worry in his face was intensifying. I hadn't answered his tacit question. I asked myself what exactly I was playing at. I didn't know. *Yes,* I said, *I want to work with you.* He smiled and drank his beer, and then launched back into it. *So there are five big publishing houses, umbrellas if you will, but within them are . . .*

I didn't know if he was giving me the benefit of the doubt or if he truly believed I didn't know all of this, given I'd already admitted to having a Publishers Marketplace account, given I'd asked on our call if he thought he could sell the book in time for the Frankfurt Book Fair. He must've known how obsessively I'd researched the landscape, the editors I wanted to work with, the art that would be perfect for the cover, the typefaces. I thought again of Caslon, and deckled edges, and clothbound covers of the most subdued greens, and my mind steadied again only when he said, *Ed Pollack might like this.*

It would be a dream to work with Ed Pollack, I said, and he nodded, thinking of other names that might impress.

Rebecca Wallace, he said. *I don't know if it's for her, really, but she hasn't bought anything substantial in half a year.* I thought I hid my reaction to this but he picked up on it and passed a smile that was reassuring, or maybe playful, some mix of sentiments that combined for a flawless response. Perhaps I'd underestimated him, perhaps his sort of grace was more practical. He switched from editors to imprints, naming all the ones I expected and needed to hear and the one that I didn't want to, PFK.

Hmm, I grunted, my attempt at expressing vague doubt.

No? he asked.

I don't know, I said. *They've never really struck me as all that serious.*

He looked perplexed and mildly amused. He started balancing his beer bottle in the crook of his arm, the first mannerism of his I liked. He was taking his time to respond.

Are you sure? he finally asked, setting the bottle back on the table.

I haven't liked some of their stuff, I said. *Some of it's been a bit—*

Underedited? He gave an easy smile that said we didn't have to talk about anything I didn't want to, but I could tell he'd made a mental note of my exact words. I took another sip. I wished I hadn't said anything. The air had become thick, and now he wasn't going to continue naming imprints. Over his shoulder I saw our waitress trailed by a waiter, each holding a dish. They were flat and small, the food on it much smaller. Why she couldn't carry both I didn't know. As they laid down the dishes I smoothed the napkin on my lap and wiped my forehead. The food had been painstakingly arranged. I imagined tweezers. The meat was pink, with a layer of oily juice on top, a trail of bright red berries falling off one side onto roasted chard, all of it catching the room's best light. I picked up my knife and fork. They felt like foreign objects. I almost couldn't admit to myself that I'd lost my appetite.

By the time I got back to the office—a ten-minute walk I made in five—it was almost 3 p.m. On Ellis's urging we'd each had four drinks. *Another round*, he said each time, which was a cool thing to do but it prevented me from changing my drink; I might've just saved the bartender some time and ordered a twenty-ounce Manhattan up front. I was at the stage of drunkenness when certain footsteps surprise you, a state that also allowed me to enjoy, possibly for the first time, the modern-day Muzak that pumped through our coworking space, Top 40–esque tracks seemingly gutted of choruses, bridges, and memorable hooks, played at a volume that might be described as *enough*. I stopped by the kitchen to get coffee and saw that a new pot was brewing, which was good news—those first few drops are basically espresso-strength—and I poured a mug and took it to my desk. I had only two emails, which was also good news, except that one was from my boss, Sneha, sent five minutes after I'd left, three hours ago. Also, Sneha's face was four feet in front of mine, peering over her own laptop. She smiled and I smiled, and I said that I'd just had lunch with an old friend, that we'd lost track of time. This wasn't convincing but she passed me a new, different smile that said, *Don't worry about it, man! In our untraditional office setup we don't punch-in-punch-out. All that matters is that the work gets done. We're building something here.* What we were building was, I was beginning to understand, hard to understand. It made for a fine elevator pitch: We, Parachute, were disrupting the predatory markets of payday loans, overdrafts, and all the other ways Big Finance preys on the poor. It was a worthwhile mission, one which had made explaining my job to family and friends an exercise in pleasure. The trouble was, I'd yet to find an answer to the question that had plagued me since my first day, two months ago, which was how exactly we were planning to make money. Basically, we wired you funds when your account was low, and you paid it back within thirty days without a cent of interest. Dots might have connected if we were some nonprofit, but we'd been backed by some of the most prestigious venture capital firms in the country, meaning smart people had ventured that we'd make a fair amount of capital. Our logo depicted a teddy bear, parachuting.

I tried to read Sneha's email but I was spending all my

concentration on trying to look like I was reading it. *Ellis Buford*, I thought to myself. I hadn't told anyone about the meeting beforehand, but suddenly I had the urge to. *Louis*, I thought. And then I thought: *Geoff, Phea, Tim*. It was more fun to think of what I'd say than how they'd react. No one would match my joy, surely, and even if they understood how big a deal it was, they wouldn't be nearly as happy about it as I was. I realized I'd been holding the side of my screen with my hand, as if it needed to be held, and so I started pretending like I was testing it, the laptop's structural integrity. Sneha looked up at me, I panicked and started typing. I'd last clicked on the URL field in the browser, and it was there that I wrote, *hi hi here i am hi Ellsis Buford Ellsi Buford Ellis*. I stared at it as if I were proofreading, like nothing could ever be good enough, and then I rubbed my face, and on the tarp of skin between my thumb and pointer I smelled my breath, which had fully absorbed the stench of four $18 Manhattans, $72 worth of Manhattan. It crossed my mind that, despite how chill a workplace we all purported Parachute to be, this would not be tolerated, that if I were caught, worse than being formally reprimanded in a traditional company structure, I'd probably have to suffer a series of stiflingly awkward meetings with a variety of my coworkers covering such topics as respect, communality, and mutual trust. I got up to use the restroom, where there would be mouthwash to gargle, cold water to splash on my face.

———

This had all started—and by *this* I mean the events leading up to my first meeting with Ellis—about five months before. Five months isn't a lot of time, but it's enough for a life to change in every conceivable way. Back then I was living with a girlfriend I loved, in Gainesville, Florida, a city I also loved, dedicating myself to doing what I loved, which was writing. One night—let's say it was late May, I at least know it was a Tuesday—we'd just finished eating Mexican takeaway and were lying on our plush living room rug listening to music, and I told Julie, my girlfriend, that I was leaving her. It broke her heart and it broke mine too, maybe more than hers, because I was the one who did it. I wanted to tell her this, but it's not something you tell someone whose heart you've just broken.

Actually, no, probably this all started way before that, two years before. I was living in New York, with a fine job in advertising, when I had an epiphany about my youth—literally, I understood that I was young, and that when you're young you can do things you can't do later, like leave your fine job and move to the South to write, insofar as you have savings, which I did, from working six consecutive years at fine jobs while living with three roommates in Crown Heights. Needless to say, this epiphany happened at the end of a late night. I was waiting for the Q train, actually. I don't mean for any of this to sound flip or frivolous; at the time the decision had as much gravitas as any decision can for someone in his mid-twenties. It would be hard to express how much of a mandate I was ready to give myself to follow this dream, and I'm not someone to give myself any sort of mandate that might defy rationality. In the year leading up to my decision I'd begun to write stories, fiction, at first a few sentences on slow days at work, and then on Sunday mornings, or at night when I couldn't sleep. Then I started writing on nights after work when

I had time, and then I started making time, holing myself up in my apartment one night a week, then a few nights a week, then every weeknight and weekends too. Soon I began to resent every obligation that got in the way, from late nights at the office to dinners with friends to parties I felt I should go to, if only to feel like a social being. I can't describe those lost hours—never did I not know the time as much as when I was writing—without invoking cringeworthy cliché. It made me feel free. It let me be honest in a way I couldn't otherwise. It brought me closer to myself. I could write a thousand words an hour, but they wouldn't be my best words, because I didn't have my best hours; those came earlier in the day, when I was writing ad copy for Visa, JPMorgan Chase, or Dr. Scholl's. I figured if I had those hours back not only would I have my best words, I wouldn't have to squeeze out everything else, all those social obligations I said I couldn't make, those runs I stopped taking, those empty nights of reading and Netflix—because it turned out that I needed them, that if they were necessary to feel I was living a happy and full life they were also necessary to write how I knew I could. And so leaving New York to write became a random, bad idea that eventually turned into one I thought I should entertain, and soon enough I decided I could either go through with it or resign myself to a lifetime of lingering regret.

The day I decided to do it I called in sick. I used a Craigslist aggregator to search for subleases under $450 in every town between South Carolina, Florida, and Louisiana—the South being a place I'd never experienced and thus could romanticize as my heart desired. I ended up emailing nineteen people and received four responses. I looked up the addresses on Google Street View and various police report databases and chose a place in Athens, Georgia, but the guy stopped emailing me back, so I took my next best option, in Gainesville, Florida. It was a two-bedroom and cost $425 including utilities. It was in a brick house constructed in the sixties on a beautiful block I'd later find out was in the middle of sorority row. Over email my roommate sounded lovely, and she was, and it wasn't long after I moved in that we became best friends and fell in love. This isn't the meat of the story but I understand some facts are in order: Julie was in architectural school. She had a wonderful sense of humor and an ability to make you feel like you didn't need to speak. She had many wonderful qualities and it serves no purpose to dwell on them.

I was diligent, I kept as busy as she did, not a small feat given that she was in school all day and worked most nights until bedtime. In New York I was always cramming in writing time, rushing home from work, buying a sandwich on the way so I could have already eaten by the time I got to my place. But in Florida time didn't move until you forgot about it, I swear I could've kept it 2 p.m. forever just by lying on the couch and watching the clock. Often I'd stare at a sentence until I understood why exactly I had put down those words in that order, until I knew the thought that had tried to express itself and failed, until I knew how exactly it could be done. It was then I got to know the impossibility of writing, of ever truly transcribing the song in my head. In New York I often felt I was succeeding while I wrote, but in Florida there was only failure. Eventually, it felt like I was tearing off a piece of myself but in a good way, like there was now a small skylight in my head, and while I'd never needed the sun before, now all I wanted to do was to find that lit patch of brain and lie in it. In other words, I became aware of the fact that I'd never really written before, that writing is the act of catching an impossibility. What I'd yet to realize is that you also have to find an impossibility worth catching, a subject. Otherwise you're writing for yourself, and no one pays you to do that. This sucks to learn.

So back to that May night, or actually the months before. Around February I started sleeping poorly, so poorly I'd need ten hours of bedtime to get five hours of sleep. This could have meant only one thing: I was avoiding coming to terms with something, my life, everything. And so I forced myself to be honest, brutally so. I looked back on the past two years with a harsh eye: I had dedicated myself to writing—that is, I'd worked a full day six days a week—producing a manuscript that I'd shopped to every agent whose email address I could find. By the end of April I'd been handily rejected (or, better for all parties, ignored) by each one. There was no clear consensus as to what went wrong; it seemed only that there wasn't enough that was right, that the book didn't say enough. This, combined with the fact that I'd put everything I had into it, led me to the realization that I, in fact, didn't have enough to say. This was something I probably knew deep down even before I left New York, I'd just thought all writers share such an absence, that I would learn to fill in the hole with work, with words. I put the manuscript in the same folder as all my other writing and vowed never to look at it again.

If I was going to justify my existence in Gainesville I knew I'd need a job, and this would mean I would no longer be someone taking a sabbatical from his life to pursue his dream. I would be a waiter, or a copywriter, or a personal trainer (which, it

seemed, might be my most lucrative option). Julie was graduat-
ing in two years, at which point she'd take a job where she could
get one, and I would go with her, and this life—the one that
would unfold before me on still-sleepless nights—didn't seem
like it would move me closer to having something to say. No,
that life was beginning to feel like an appendage of hers, mostly
because hers was the one that felt like it deserved a whole body.

The night I broke up with her I wrote an email to my family—
Mom, Dad, my brother Ben—telling them the news. I should
have called but I didn't want to hear their disappointment, or,
what was more likely, their relief. (With a lack of words but an
abundance of looks, each had communicated what they thought
of me leaving a fine job in New York to move to Gainesville.) I
didn't want to see them, or for that matter anyone I knew back
home, and even though I knew I'd return eventually, to go
straight back would feel like a reversal, an undoing, so I used
that email to ask for the family car for the next few months.

This vehicle, a Nissan Altima the color of a wet dog, was a
source of contention. If it didn't hurt so much I would one day
like to laugh at all the email threads sewn around it—who got to
use it and when and how and why and what legal precedent already existed in the House of Horowitz—but really it was just
one long conversation about Justice, all three of them being lawyers, our family being what the Beastie Boys might call 3 JDs
and 1 DJ. Anyway. It was only in the context of heartbreak that
such a wish could be granted, and after Julie and I spent a week
crying and hugging and forgiving each other and crying some
more, I drove a U-Haul to New Jersey without stopping and the
next morning I was driving west without a final destination.

Though spending every hour alone in an enclosed space after a heart-shattering decision without any idea of my future might sound like a recipe for breakdown, I had two secret weapons. The first was a distraction so immediate it would make kidney stones seem abstract. Two months before I left I developed specks in the vision of both of my eyes. Some resembled cobwebs, others flies smashed on the windshield, but they all moved when my pupils did, sliding gently across the world until inertia settled them, at which point they'd disappear. *Floaters*, my ophthalmologist said, holding a light up to my eye, nodding to himself like a *CSI* detective. *They're clumps of protein that harden in the globe's vitreous and cast shadows onto your retina. Well, I can see them now, swishing around!* he said, expressing more glee than I thought appropriate. He told me they normally happen to retirees, that I was just ahead of schedule. If I thought I'd been obsessing over them in Florida, I should have waited until they were spread over the canvas of the bright blue sky for twelve hours a day.

The second way of preventing a big breakdown is something anyone can do: allow yourself smaller, more manageable breakdowns throughout the course of a few days. This might sound like a hard thing to conjure, but when you're eating a hot dog in a gas station parking lot in the middle of Indiana, watching a meth-ravaged man trying to purchase cigarettes with no money, it's child's play. Another option: couch-surf in Kansas with a stranger you found online who won't look you in the eye as they escort you to your bedroom, which is in their basement and full of Japanese erotica. Also: St. George, Utah, when you are no longer willing to couch-surf, and so you spring for a motel that doesn't have air-conditioning or Wi-Fi (and you don't own a smartphone—for reasons of sanity and happiness—which means you are all but asking to be murdered), and it's somehow hotter than it is outside, which is ninety-two degrees, and in the room next to yours you can hear an older man ostensibly making sweet pillow talk with his wife, and I say *ostensibly* because over the course of two hours she hasn't spoken once.

It was at this point I knew that if I wanted to continue avoiding the Big Breakdown I needed to be back in civilization, and so the next morning, after eight hours of pretending I'd soon fall asleep, I drove to the closest Starbucks, ordered their largest, sweetest Frappuccino, and began scouring Facebook for friends in California.

There was a lot of talk of the *work hard play hard* atmosphere when I joined—it seemed to be the unofficial slogan of every startup in New York—but what we did at Parachute was work moderately and play very little. That was okay by me. For friends at other startups it seemed *play hard* translated to *attend mandatory happy hours at Midtown bars or painfully hip places downtown*, while *work hard* meant *work hard*.

It was barely 6 p.m. and most everyone was gone. I'd canceled my plans an hour earlier—I'd been too excited to be in the company of other people, too excited not to reveal what I was excited about, which I wasn't ready to do, not in that group, not until things were more formed—but now there was still enough daylight to make me feel like I should have a night. On the subway, as the doors closed, I thought of uncanceling my plans.

After all, my excusing text—*late night at the office, sucks, have fun*—was reversible. The train pulled into darkness and I lost service, and by the time we got to the next stop I realized the night I'd passed on would serve me no better than one spent alone. My friends Geoff and Orin had invited me to be the fifth wheel at a dinner with them and their *WAG*s, a term taken from the world of soccer which meant *wives and girlfriends* (they both only had girlfriends), which was vaguely sexist but they used it vaguely ironically, so it was okay, and anyway their relationships mirrored most of those I'd encountered in my slice of Brooklyn— allergic to traditional gender norms, friendly, progressive, organic, recyclable. We were supposed to eat at a stylized diner—meaning Instagram-ready and overpriced—that I'd been reading about everywhere. I was fine missing out.

When I got off the subway I decided to go to the bar closest to my apartment, a German place, and have a beer and a curry-wurst. It was a way to celebrate, but more than that it was a way to give this day another handle I could use months, years down the road to remember it by: who I was then, the state I was in before my life would change for good.

I sat there watching baseball, eating, drinking. Again I thought of texting someone about my lunch with Ellis, and for lack of imagination I began scrolling through my list of contacts. Fourth from the top I saw his name.

Avi Deitsch.

I closed my phone, finished my beer, and ordered another.

I woke with the same thought I'd had each morning for the past week: Why did New York birds chirp louder in the fall? This morning was no different, except the thought was now full of a more earnest wonder—I was happy for it, for them, to be woken up and reenter my life. I even postponed my morning routine for a few minutes just to lie there, remembering scenes from my lunch with Ellis.

I could still taste the Hefeweizen and, preempting a hangover, went to the kitchen and prepared the French press. I went back to bed, set my laptop on my stomach, turned on WNYC, and opened my Android emulator app. This was how someone who didn't have a smartphone and didn't want to use OkCupid could date online. As a rule I only "swiped" in the morning, before coffee. That way I would not be enthusiastic about anyone I shouldn't be enthusiastic about, and would not end up on more dates with women who would tell me about their friends when I wasn't telling them about my job. (That there was a lot of "telling" seemed to be the problem, or a symptom of it.) When I saw a girl who looked like Julie but prettier, conventionally, I swiped left and closed the emulator. I was about to close my laptop when I got a notification that I had an email from Ellis. *Editors* was the subject line, and the email was a list of nothing but—twenty-four of them from all of the imprints I wanted to send to and more, including PFK. I started to type but saw that he'd just sent another email: *Sry I forgot about PFK. Ted Whistler has one of the best reputations out there, and I know he'd love this, but if you don't want to send it's up to you.* My first thought was that this one-two punch was planned. I saw that the second email had a *Sent from my iPhone* and the first didn't. I was being paranoid. Was I also being irrational? No, I agreed I was not. *Let's leave him off*, I wrote, and then, *I appreciate it.* I read it three times and then added, *Sent from my fingers*, allowing the thrill to course through me before deleting it.

By the time I got to the office Ellis had written back: *23 it is.* A minute later, another email: *I should go out with the first half today, and the second half tomorrow. I'll be calling about half the names here to gauge enthusiasm. Some substitutions may be required. Speaking of calling, do you want to talk anything out?* Yes, of course I wanted to talk it out, talk everything out, I wanted to know what exactly he'd say to editors, what he'd guess the probability was that any given one would read it, would finish it, would respond, would like it, would offer, what those offers might look like and if he would tell me everything as it happened and how he saw my career, if I was just another manuscript to sell or if he thought I was really doing something new. But this was all still so unreal—that I was even emailing back and forth with Ellis Buford—that I was afraid of interfering in any way, as if I might sabotage myself by saying the wrong thing, by revealing my desire, wanting too much. *I'm okay without a call*, I wrote. *Look forward to hearing how it goes.*

I looked around the office, how static everyone was; maybe it was just in contrast to how kinetic I felt. My toes were dancing in my shoes. Editors might be reading my words this very day, words I was proud of, words that were the best I'd ever written, words I believed meant something. They'd be considering whether to buy the book, they'd be sending it to colleagues, thinking about money. This was an idea that had been living in my head, but at that moment it was like a trapdoor released it into the rest of me, and the idea became physical, infiltrating my bloodstream, whisking through every limb and around every organ. My fingers dragged back and forth across the keyboard. I heard the wind outside. Why hadn't I ever listened to it before? It was pouring itself against the window. Wind, window. Was this a coincidence? Was I high? The feeling made me want to do something, interact with the world, except I was stuck in an office for the next eight hours. There was too much excitement, too much undirected energy inside of me, I couldn't focus it on work, I needed to use it on something that would be distracting enough to make me not think about the manuscript, and so, preempting self-reproach, I downloaded the Android emulator on my work computer, something I'd previously forbidden myself from doing. I listened to James Brown while I waited. I installed it and opened Tinder. I had a new message from someone named Mel and someone named Sandra. Mel wrote, *Howdy ho neighbor-ee-no.* She looked hot but evil. Sandra wrote, *Ginger boy.* Nothing more, like a half thought she decided to write out. Her bio was short: *Making it small in the big crabapple.* I skimmed her photos. She seemed fun, earnest. I couldn't really tell what she looked like. In fact, I didn't remember swiping on her before. In her uncanny spirit I wrote exactly that, *Don't remember seeing you.* I opened up the brand strategy document I was working on and stared at it for five minutes before a message alert came. *Is this an exercise in radical honesty or self-destructive behavior?* I wrote back, *Depends on whether or not you're my therapist.* Five minutes later:

Who's your therapist? I wrote, *JK don't need one. Had a good childhood.* After ten minutes of pretending I couldn't care if I got a response, a period I spent browsing the strategy doc and rereading Ellis's email, she wrote, *Let's get a drink tonight.* I looked at her pictures again, triangulating the three best into someone I could imagine existing, walking through a room, picking up a glass. A warm buzz crawled up my chest and out to my shoulders. When it left I checked to see if Ellis had responded.

The Starbucks in St. George, Utah, it turns out, plays John Mayer just as incessantly as the one in Union Square. I pulled on my Frappuccino again, waiting for the caffeine and sugar to wash over a night of terrible sleep. Outside I couldn't see the Altima, so I moved my things to a seat where I could. This had become a nervous tic throughout my journey, always checking in on it like it was my two-ton talisman.

I'd sent Avi a message at 8:11 a.m. and, at 8:17, got one back.

Caleb! Hello! Great to hear from you! So sayonara to the Sunshine State, huh? I've plans tonight, a glut of work actually. But if you're still around tomorrow I'd be happy to put you up for a night. Got too much space here as it is.

The unnecessary contraction *I've* and his use of *glut* were enough to make me second-guess myself. He hadn't changed. Also I hadn't said I needed a place that night. He must have barely skimmed my message. Why didn't I know anyone else in L.A.? Was that not a personal failing at my age and demographic? I started writing and stopped, becoming aware he could see I was typing. I copied my message into the URL field of my browser, which I used as a draft space. *Ah, I think we'll just miss each other. Let me get back to you.* I went down to our chat box, but instead of pasting it I clicked on his name. He was getting a Ph.D. in English at UCLA. A quick browse of his photos indicated curation with extended family in mind, or maybe in his case professors and peers. He still had very white teeth. He looked less self-conscious than he'd been in college, but who wasn't self-conscious in college? Who wasn't insufferable in college? Would I want someone remembering me the way I was back then? Maybe the reason I didn't have more friends in L.A. was because I too easily wrote people off—and who in L.A. wasn't easy to write off? *Rad*, I wrote back, hitting enter before I could rethink it. *That works.*

Avi was never a friend per se, but calling him an acquaintance would be missing the point. When we knew each other such terms didn't matter. We went to the same parties, knew the same people, probably shared a few cigarettes on nights neither of us would ever remember. We had the same relationship that many people in our corner of Haverford did; you knew very little about someone but made a lot of assumptions based on how they looked, how they acted, who their closest friends were. He dressed well, wore things I knew were cool but didn't know how to acquire myself, or how to match other clothes with, or how to wear without looking like I was always thinking about my clothes. Most days I wore white New Balances and jeans. He played tennis, was an editor on the literary magazine, was generally considered quite attractive—he looked a bit like James Dean if James Dean was a bit inbred, if I'm being mean—and yet as far as I heard he didn't sleep around. When I first saw him on campus I thought he was everything I wasn't: stylish, graceful, probably Protestant. His cheeks were ruddy and his hair was dirty blond and his forehead made me think of the forming of the Thirteen Colonies. This all hardened into an image firm enough that when he introduced himself at a party, literally stuck his hand out at my chest and said, *Avi*, I thought he was beginning a sentence about another person. This guy in front of me—a cigarette tucked in his ear, a maneuver I could not pull off except physically—could not be Jewish. And yet.

We went on like that, orbiting each other without ever getting closer or further, the years granting us an otherwise unearned informality. I once submitted to the literary magazine and was rejected from the general email address, and then later that day got an email from him saying he liked it but there wasn't enough room. In the years since college I occasionally heard his name. Each time the image that came into my head had been a bit more pruned, the small details shed but the trunk remaining—a too-easy concept of someone who didn't really exist back then and even less now.

———

When I pulled up to the house I said *Fuck*, audibly, and then took a picture with my phone. It wasn't like the L.A. mansions I'd driven by earlier that day, or even that big, really, but you could tell it was built from scratch, commissioned, an act of creativity. The driveway was set on a forty-five-degree slope, such that the front door was a story higher than the street. There wasn't ten feet of space between the house and those on either side, but the thick messy trees and brambles creeping all around made it seem like an island. I sent the photo to Louis and wrote, *hobnobbin with avi deitsch in tinseltown*.

I left my things in the car and walked up the stone steps, of which there were so many that they took two landings. I rang the bell and waited. Music filled the house and seeped outside. Talking Heads, a deep cut, very African, pulsing. Avi opened the door, a smile widening his face. This had always been a talent of his, smiling. He was wearing a white bucket hat, a light floral shirt with a recherché pattern, linen pants, and no shoes.

Quite the look, I said. *Very Hunter S.*

He looked down. *I guess I asked for that.*

Just don't go gonzo and kill yourself. It was a poor comment born out of buried nerves, but after a split second of shock his face forgave it.

Fuck you, man, he said, and smiled again. *Come inside.*

We were off to an okay start. Strained or not, I would have traded some busting of chops for informality. As much as he and I had changed—or as much as we wanted to tell ourselves we had—I couldn't ignore the reversion to our former dynamic, which was suddenly as clear to me as it had never been, that I actually cared about being liked by him, impressing him even.

It was gorgeous inside, with a vaguely Semitic feel, at least as far as Chagall prints and some decorative menorahs can take you.

Oh, shoes off, he said. *And by the way, how the hell you been?* I hadn't written to him why I was road-tripping, or even why I'd left Florida, hadn't actually talked about it with anyone even over the phone, let alone in person, and I sure as hell wasn't going to start with him. He was reading something on my face. I must've looked pained, or maybe I'd just waited too long to answer. He clapped. *Hey man, let me show you your room.* He smiled and turned and I followed him. *As I said, I've got some work to do today, probably will be handcuffed to my desk until dinner, but feel free to wander around the neighborhood and I'll just leave the door unlocked.* We came into a square room with an off-white carpet and nothing covering it. Did he expect me to bring a sleeping bag? He asked if I had his number, and when I opened my phone to check I saw that Louis had texted, *more like slobnobbin.*

I do, yeah, I said, and called it. His phone buzzed and he held it up, smiling. On his screen I saw that he didn't have mine.

They've got some great lit here too if you just want to stick around, he said, walking over to a bookshelf built into the wall. *This is technically their meditation room, but they've allowed it to be compromised with some disreputable debris.* He held up *The Adventures of Augie March* and smiled.

Real snuff, I said. *Who's they?*

Ah, right, he said. *I hope you didn't think a comp lit master-to-be could afford such a place.*

I thought you were in a Ph.D. program, I said, regretting it immediately, because it was an awkward thing to say and also it betrayed that I'd looked him up, that I knew anything about him.

He shook his head. *Technically I'm on a Ph.D. path. They don't take masters otherwise. But no, I'm going to dip out once this summer project closes.* He walked to a bare wooden wall, and then looked back at me, apparently amused. *You must have thought you were sleeping on the ground.* He pulled on a discreet strap, bringing down a king-sized Murphy bed. *Ta-da.*

I sat on the side of it, pushing up and down with my hands and butt the way people do. *It's really great,* I said. *I can't thank you enough.*

Caleb. Don't mention it, he said. *Really.* He tossed the book on the bed.

I picked it up and held it in my lap. *You were saying,* I said.

What was I saying?

About the owners of the house.

Ah, he said, his face showing what we'd both started to feel, a corrosion of the cordiality, the hollow it hid. *This is owned by— well, I think he'd like to be called my benefactor, though a friend of the family might be more accurate. I don't know. They're away to Antibes until September. Then I return to my shack in Los Feliz. And speaking of returning.*

Right right, I said, saluting. *Godspeed.*

⟨⟩

The day felt like purgatory. I didn't want to stay in the house, I feared running into Avi and having to create small talk before we could spend a more substantial time together. I wandered the neighborhood but soon felt the prelude to anxiety and returned. I killed the rest of the hours in the meditation room, I would have meditated if I'd known how. Instead I browsed the bookshelf and then the internet, I tried to nap, I listened to Avi typing, showering, living his day as if I weren't there. Around 6 he finally popped in, sighed the day's work away, and asked if I was hungry.

He ordered us pizza from a place that was *supposed to be L.A.'s best*, he said, adding an ironic raise of his eyebrows, lest he be caught handing out such a sincere superlative. He admitted to not going out that much because of the time requirements of his program and, more so, his financial constraints, which, in my chronic paranoia, I assumed to be a bid for money for the food and got out my wallet. *I only have a fifty*, I said, embarrassed, and he took it without offering change, which might have been weird but he did it fluently. And anyway, he was providing the beer and liquor, which maybe was just from the owner's stash but could I really complain, staying gratis in the meditation room of what was probably some local architect's passion project?

We set up on the back patio. It wasn't dark yet, and it couldn't have been cooler than sixty-five, but he insisted on using the outdoor heat lamps. They'd been custom-built for the space, all but invisible until faint orange lines materialized above us. He came outside holding two tumblers, each with one immense square ice cube. On the table were bottles of Campari, Beefeater, and vermouth, as well as the pizza and a bowl of oranges. He sat down and stared into the distance; it was starting to seem like we could be together without the compulsion to talk or move. Soon he made us Negronis, without measuring the ingredients, which I appreciated. He handed me my drink but then remembered the peeler in his pocket, which he used to shave off a long curl from an orange. We clinked glasses and he said we should eat before the food got cold. I thought to make some joke about the heat lamps, but in my head it sounded too harsh.

We ate and talked, each doing our part to poke up the beach ball of conversation. For the impending fear of having nothing to say we drank at a collegiate frequency. Was my social anxiety contagious? Was it all just me? The more I thought about it the more it became an issue, so I reallocated my energy into finding the next thing we could talk about, building a queue long enough to last a weekend. His classes, his neighbors, my family, Fernando Pessoa, Rachel Cusk, people we knew in college, even the stock market were all fair game under the assumption that any words were better than no words.

It wasn't until our third drink that we found our way into real conversation, when he asked me about leaving Florida. I was caught off guard. I tried and failed to find the words. I thought I was stuttering, but realized I hadn't said anything out loud when I finally did, my voice hanging in the air, *It was hard*. In retrospect I don't know how I didn't see it coming, that on the first night I was properly drunk, when I wasn't going to wake up and drive, didn't have the forward thrust of travel, I was going to break. I felt a wet film forming over my eyes, at that point one of the only parts of my face not glazed with sweat, the heat lamps now at full power, five oppressive streaks of warmth turning what should have been a nice late spring L.A. night into summer in Gainesville, and is there anything worse when you've lost emotional control than being too hot? He was looking straight at me but the grainy dusk air must've hidden those details, because when he squinted his whole face sank in horror, the horror of having to be emotionally earnest. I started crying, sobbing really, my mouth, throat, and diaphragm colluding against me to produce a truly abject noise I couldn't believe he had to hear. When I looked up again he wasn't there, I couldn't find him until he was a few feet away, taking a seat next to me, touching my back with his hand. I rested my face in my palms and the sobs only got louder, and soon his palm moved up to my shoulders and he gave a fatherly squeeze, first as if he were going through the motions but then he let himself be vulnerable too, and passed real empathy through his skin to mine, and I was surprised, mystified really, at how unalone this made me feel. *Can we turn off the fucking heat lamps?* I asked, laughing through my tears. *I thought you'd never ask*, he said, and got up.

He sat back across from me and poured me a glass, this time pure gin. Without the lamps it was even darker than before, but I could see that his face was distorted too, perhaps even on the verge of tears, and, until he spoke, I was amazed by his empathetic capacity. *I'm with you, man*, he said. *I'm there too. I mean, I know you were with her for a while, and it's not the same, but I just had my own dose of heartbreak*. I believed his pain—couldn't not, now that he'd shed a tear of his own—but there was something contaminating his words, some sort of pleasure or pride. It was as if he were already seeing his pain in the third person. That stage of my own heartbreak seemed forever in the future. It probably was, actually. My pain from Julie wouldn't recede, because it wasn't just love lost but an experience that had carved a shape out of my heart. *A few weeks ago I got back, or*— He looked up, thinking. *No, it's been a week, or ten days actually. I took a vacation to this Greek island, Paros. Sort of a last-minute thing*. I thought of his supposed financial constraints, and the $50 for the pizza, and then chided myself for being such a miser. *I just needed to get away, really, hadn't been on vacation in forever and I've been in overdrive for so long with this paper and I was, you know, burnt out. I found this cheap cottage on Airbnb and booked a flight for the next day. I didn't even pack really, I just wanted to read and swim, not speak a word if I could. Well, as I get to the cottage it's clear it's not going to be that sort of vacation.* He sat forward in his chair and flattened the cloth of his pants. He tried to look like he was thinking but I could tell he was waiting, savoring the moment. It was hard to believe his eyes had just been wet. *This place, it was double-booked, or so says the girl that's already there—like, already unpacked, living there. She's very charming, you know, very charming and beautiful.* I asked if she was Greek. *Oh no*, he said, somehow amused at the idea. *American, she's very American. Anyway, we can't figure out who's supposed to stay there, and, you know, of course it doesn't really matter because there's nowhere else to go, we know what the resolution is, and maybe I'm doing her a favor or maybe she's doing me one, but we agree that we'll just both stay. Well, there's one bed, and I bet you can figure out where this is going, and I'll say it went there the first night.*

He finished his glass and refilled it with gin. I felt like he wanted me to ask him if that was the end of the story. My instinct was to not oblige, but I found that I'd become mollified, distracted in the best way. I needed more and was willing to play the part to get it. *Don't leave me hanging*, I said. He nodded and smiled. *Okay*, he said, *so the next morning she sleeps in, but I can't, I never can when I drink, and I go for a run. Even though I'm hungover the run is exhilarating, I feel wonderful, I can't stop thinking about our night, not just the sex, which, trust me, was something else. No, it was that she was something else, I felt like I was someone else with her, excuse the cliché. Well, when I get back to the cottage she's still not awake, and so I'm just bumbling around the house and I find a couple of drawing notebooks, doodles and such. She's really talented, actually, like my first thought was that she might be an artist. I don't know if I said this but I really didn't know anything about her, we hadn't exchanged much info the night before, practically made a rule out of it, somehow we hadn't even shared our names. Maybe that was her intent, maybe we had and I just forgot, to be honest that first night was a bit of a blur. At one point later that day I admitted I didn't know if she'd told it to me, her name. I asked her what it was but she just made a game out of it, said to call her Sofia. I think she found it thrilling, this small bit of anonymity, so I played along, I was James. Anyway, before that: I'm looking through the notebook and then next to it I find a book, or a journal, or like a, you know, her diary.* He looked at me, like I could forgive his sin. I made a face, pardoning him. At that point I would have done anything for the story, the actual story, the part where meaning materializes and then the part where it gets excised, where sadness enters in, because I knew I would feel it too, his sadness, and then all of what I felt wouldn't be concentrated on my own loss. *I know, I know, a little intrusive, but I don't know who she is, and I'll never see her again, and so I decide it's okay. So I read a bit of the diary, and read some things that might imply, you know, that she's taken, but it might be in the past tense, or it is in the past sense, I mean, it's a diary. I'm only saying all this because the discovery in some weird way makes me feel even more intensely about her, or maybe it just makes me question how intensely I've already been feeling, and I understand that I, um, feel a lot, that I'm happy just being around her, that I'm even potentially, you know, falling for her, which I know is ridiculous, but, well, so what.* He rubbed his palm down his face and shook his head, resetting himself again. He was drunk. We both were. *Here's where it gets interesting. When she wakes up we go into town to a café, and seated next to us is a couple of honeymooners, Joe and Reagan, they're Americans too. We start making small talk or whatever and then out of nowhere Sofia tells them that we're from L.A., both of us I mean, together, that we live together, that she's a painter and I'm a writer. And not just that, she has this whole backstory ready, she tells them we met through my publisher, that she did the art for my book cover. I'd told her the night before that I lived in L.A., and she hadn't told me where she was from, but it was obvious given how much detail she produced that she lived in L.A. too, or used to.*

My face must have betrayed that the story was as good as he thought. He was obviously encouraged, and from that point on he spoke virtually nonstop. *And I have to say, her imagination, it's absolutely incredible, it's like she's saying whatever pops into her head but she's acting like she believes every word of it, and I'm fascinated and amazed but also kind of scared, it's like she's possessed—like, really, possessed. And not just because she's a great liar. She starts to get sort of a—well, she does this thing, I can tell she's trying to provoke the other couple—or not provoke,* provoke's not the word, *it's more virtuous than that, more good-natured, like maybe she's just trying to cut past the bullshit by going all the way. She starts asking them about their love life, private things like that, which of course makes them defensive, and things get weird for a bit, so weird that I think Reagan—Reagan's the other woman—maybe she's just trying to make things less weird, or maybe she just feels bad about being defensive or I don't know, but out of nowhere she invites us out on a sailing trip, right there and then, the two of them are going out to an island nearby and they want us to join. I couldn't believe it. I tried to say no—to be blunt, these people aren't really my type, and I would have preferred to, you know, spend more time alone with Sofia—but she* accepts for us, Sofia I mean, and I can't say no then, and all of a sudden we're all on a fucking sailboat. This guy, Joe, I can't even tell you, he's so into the whole thing, he's one of those guys who'll jump on any opportunity to perform his manliness, and Reagan, she loves it too, she can just sit there and watch her guy be a man and get enough pictures for a year of Instagram, that is after she did her makeup, which maybe took her half the ride. Okay, so we finally get to the island and we walk around for, I don't know, fifteen minutes? It's fifteen minutes before one of us, Joe probably, notices that the boat is moving into the distance, it's, you know, being sailed, it's stolen, some fucking local teens that were just hanging around when we arrived. I was freaking out of course, but nothing compared to Joe and Reagan, who were convinced we were going to get murdered. We tried telling them it was a popular island, someone would be back soon, at most we'd have to make it a night, and there are worse places to be stranded, and anyway we'd brought wine, we could have a good time. And this clicks with Joe, and he realizes that maybe here's his chance to use everything he learned in Boy Scouts, actually I was very impressed, he knew how to fish with just his shirt, he even built us a fire. So things settle down until, well, Sofia whips them up again. Apparently she's ready to come clean, except not really, all of a sudden she's telling them that she was lying before, that we're not married, only she is, to someone else, who she's cheating on with me, and this vacation is just another chain in a long tryst of ours. Well, apparently Reagan was okay with being asked how often she and Joe fuck but she has a very special relationship with extramarital affairs, and she's not okay with this. So, more conflict, more awkwardness, and maybe we should just separate for a bit but no one wants to do that, it's getting dark, and maybe we can just drink the tension away. We try our best, we finish maybe four liters of *wine, and I should say that all we'd had to eat since morning was the minnow Joe caught, not to mention a lifetime's worth of sun poisoning, and at a certain point we're no longer drunk, just, you know, in another world, and no one cares about anything, and I think for a while we stopped speaking, just lolled around, and the next thing I knew Sofia had taken her clothes off, and Reagan too, and, you know, I really don't know how we got from a to b to z but, it just, we all kind of, it wasn't like a full-on foursome but, or, I don't know, maybe it was.*

I'd had a feeling this was where the story was going, but that didn't stop my surprise, or envy. I briefly choked on a puddle of gin I'd forgotten was in my mouth. *Yeah, I know. I'd never done that before, or anything like it. It was, it felt like, maybe it was that we were all wasted, but really it was more than that, it felt completely natural, not like a, you know, a thing. It was like we were all on the same page, like it was an infectious belief that this thing wasn't a weird thing but just something that could happen, which obviously started with Sofia, her imagination, or her life force, listen I know how I sound but I don't know how else to describe it. That night was honestly the closest I think I'll ever come to paradise, and please don't laugh.* I wasn't going to. He was more earnest then than I'd ever seen him before, or could have imagined. *Well, we wake up the next day and maybe we've lost some of that feeling, the vibe, like all of a sudden it feels weird to be naked again, but when I look at Sofia I can't see anything but the paradise I felt, and I become, well, I can't look at her without thinking that I love her, and this thought is so obvious to me, and at some point I have no choice but to tell her, I really believe I'll go crazy if I don't tell her, and I do, we're swimming in the ocean and I tell her, and as soon as it leaves my mouth I realize this was a terrible idea, and not just for the obvious reasons, there's something else about it that I don't really understand. She starts acting cold, like I did something wrong, violated her, and after just a lot of arguing about nothing I find out that she knew I'd read her notebook, and she assumed that I got to the end, which reveals that she's, well, she's ill. She's sick. She looks like a young, healthy thirty-something, but apparently it's just going to be a matter of weeks before, well, she has a tumor, in her head, her brain, and it's going to start spreading, I mean, it already has, aggressively, and this whole thing, the trip, was all just a sort of, a sort of farewell tour.*

He paused. I expected him to cry, he did too, and when no tears came he looked perplexed, bereft even. But I felt them, his nonexistent tears, I was overcome. I blinked my own tears back with all my will because I felt that it would be weird for me to cry if he didn't, it would be embarrassing for him, actually, for me to feel his sadness when he couldn't, it would perhaps point to a larger truth, namely that his own sadness had been corrupted by the fact that his experience had become a story. *After the trip she was going to the Netherlands, for assisted suicide.* I winced inside, thinking of my Hunter S. Thompson comment. All I could think to say was *I'm sorry, Avi*, which was flaccid, but he took it. *Well, that was hard to hear on many levels. I felt like I'd wronged her, and also that in some way she'd wronged me, and I'd wronged myself by thinking there could be something more for us, which I really did believe, that we could meet again, in the real world, I couldn't admit it to her or even myself really but I did believe it, and I guess this was all just too much to think about, and I was probably dehydrated, maybe I had heatstroke, or maybe it was a combination of* all of that, but at some point, not too long after, I apparently blacked out. When I woke up only Joe was there with me, and he was acting weird. He was trying to be cool about it but apparently I'd been out of control. His attention left me for a second, as if he were weighing whether he'd said too much, or just then asking himself why he was telling me any of this. *Well, when we find Sofia and Reagan they're talking to a couple, our future rescuers, this pair of country singers—apparently they're rock stars but I've never heard of them— and they put us on their yacht and feed us a feast, and then, as if that weren't enough, when we get back to the main island they invite us over to their house for a dinner thing later that night. Neither Joe nor I want to go, of course, but Sofia does, which means Reagan does, and so after an incredibly distant, nearly silent day alone with Sofia we all meet up again at this guy's mansion. Well, one of the other guests there is this guy Galen, who apparently owns the boat rental shop, and it comes out that he knows the teens who stole our boat, and there's something else there, like maybe he was in on it? It's very murky, and Joe, who took all of five minutes to get plastered, starts shouting at Galen, and it's not long before things get physical between them, and as soon as it breaks up for half a second Sofia and I leave. This is her last night there, I don't know if I said that, and we're walking back, getting emotional and saying we're sorry to each other, we're trying to talk about everything at once, I'm trying to imagine out loud what it will be like returning to my life, and she's trying to make me feel better about it, she's asking me not to forget her but also to move on, to not let this experience be a snag in my life, she said a lot of things I wish I remembered more of, about the things in life that prevent us from growing, about fear. It was a lot, it was too much for me, I couldn't stop crying. She hardly cried at all, maybe she'd already cried enough. Soon we pass by the café where we met Joe and Reagan, and it's empty and the doors are open, and we just go inside, her idea of course.*

He finished his glass and refilled it, topping me off too even though I didn't need it. *We made ourselves a feast in the kitchen and ate it there over a bottle of wine each, and we left sixty euros on the counter and went home and by this point it's probably two in the morning, or later, and she chooses then to finally break, break down I mean, she's crying and crying, and things get a little weird, they get weird, yeah.* He didn't want to say what exactly that meant but he'd left the door open for too many things, and before my mind could wander he said, *She asked me to, or, yeah, she asked me to actually kill her, yeah to kill her, she asked me to kill her right there, I know, I, I didn't do it of course I didn't do it I just tried to console her and then, and then I guess we fell asleep because the next thing I know it's the morning, and she's gone, all her things are gone. She told me she was leaving at two the next day but I guess she lied to save me from, you know, I don't know.*

He took another sip.

From trying to save her, I said.

Yeah, he said. *I guess.*

As I searched for words silence stole the air, thickening it. Soon there was no instinct toward speaking, or moving, but I wasn't uncomfortable. In fact, it was the first time I'd ever felt truly comfortable around him, so comfortable that for a long time we just looked at each other.

I was calm then, centered, like I'd been exhaling for the past fifteen minutes. Suddenly Florida seemed like forever ago, a past epoch. He'd given me a distraction, and camaraderie of course, but something else too, some new—to use his phrase—life force.

⌇

I woke up lying on top of the sheets, my pants and pullover still on. My head throbbed, my mouth was parched and tasted foul, but still that feeling persisted, that I'd been lifted, or pushed forward, that I was better for it. I recalled coming into the room, chugging water, trying and failing to close the blinds, but I couldn't remember falling asleep, or even when we came inside. I opened my eyes and lifted my head and saw the sun straight on. I contemplated getting up to shut the blinds but instead just turned my head away. I listened to the rest of the house and found nothing. Interacting with another human was the last thing I wanted to do, but I had to drink water. I managed to get up and open the door. Again I listened and heard nothing. The silence felt like a virtue, and as I went to the kitchen I shuffled on my socks to sustain it. When had I put on socks? I drank two glasses of water and saw a note on the table. *I'm off to the library for the day. When you leave just click the switch on the inside of the door. As promised, I've sent you some of my own writing. Great seeing you, friend. Next year in Jerusalem. ~ A*

I read it again and once more, because there was something wrong, a word that needed tending to. *I've sent you some of my own writing. Own writing. Own,* as in, to differentiate from other writing, my writing. I remembered then that I'd told him about the manuscript, my failure of a novel. I'd told only two other souls about it, Louis and Julie. At least he, like them, hadn't read any of it—right? I excavated my memory of last night, making sure I hadn't shared it with him. I still wasn't sure. I drank another glass, fetched my laptop from my room, went to the living room, and flopped onto the couch. I hadn't sent any emails last night. I had only one in my inbox, from him, sent at 7:44 a.m. There was no subject line, the body just said, *Be kind*. I downloaded it.

When I'm hungover I cannot suffer even good fiction, fiction I normally love, and this was not good fiction. I almost couldn't read it, but I did, partly because it made me feel better about my own writing and partly because I was interested—it was the story he'd told me, or the first few scenes of it, except written in the third person. It helped me remember more of last night, which made me feel embarrassed, but what did I have to be embarrassed about? No, he was the one who'd done all the talking. I cried, yes, but so did he. Suddenly it made sense that he'd made it out of the house so early. After I finished I went to File > Properties. *Total editing time* was 3094 minutes, across ten days that was an average of five hours per. I felt wrong for knowing how to find that. The word count was 3252. I thought about him staring at his laptop for a full minute before typing each word. I drafted a nice email saying it was *evocative* and *atmospheric*, et cetera, and I made a note to send it later.

I closed the laptop and put it on the floor and rolled over on my back. Above me was another Chagall, which seemed to be a visual interpretation of my hangover. I put my hand on my stomach, slowly inhaling and exhaling, and surveyed the room. In a moment of weakness I allowed myself to lament how wonderful it would be to own a house like this, and how sharply I'd have to alter the course of my life to one day be able to afford anything like it. It was just as likely I'd find God. And yet, all of my daydreams about my future involved a house not unlike it, a house with a room for each of my three children, a workspace for me and my wife, a spacious dining room for dinner parties. All of a sudden I felt like I didn't belong on that couch, in that room, in that house. If a neighbor came over to return garden shears, and asked who I was, I wouldn't be able to answer. I had no reason to be there. But based on his mumbled deflections—a *benefactor*? a *friend of the family*?—neither did Avi, and he seemed right at home. I thought of him at the library. I replayed last night through his point of view. I stretched my legs and tightened my butt muscles. I yawned. I closed my eyes and tried to nap.

I had hoped to parlay that first night into a longer stay—surely Avi's *benefactor*'s meditation room would remain unclaimed—but as my hangover dimmed I came to accept that it wasn't in the cards; after all, his note had described how exactly to lock the door on my way out. I drank more water and ate some cold cuts and olives I found in the fridge, and then packed up and drove to the nearest Starbucks.

For the next three days I Airbnbed a windowless room in Koreatown for $43 a night. It was my first time in L.A. and I wanted to have fun but I was hemorrhaging money. If I was going to extend my little sabbatical from real life I needed to be someplace cheaper. So I spent much of those three cloudless days on my computer, back on the Craigslist aggregator, searching for sublets all along the West Coast that were under $400 a month. There was too much to sort through, so on the second day I added the filters "expired start date" and "repeat posting." By the third day I was willing to look past serial killer grammar (*great spot !! must be clean , and kind*) and still couldn't land anything. I was just about to book my place in Koreatown for two more days when I got an email back from a girl named Bertie in Eugene, Oregon. She was a senior at the University of Oregon and lived with three roommates. From her Facebook I gathered that her life revolved around ultimate Frisbee. She was in Haiti, doing humanitarian aid until the fall semester. She said as soon as I wired her two months' rent the room was mine.

I left at 6 the next morning because the drive was fourteen hours nonstop and I had texted Bertie's roommates that I'd be there *before bedtime*. When I reviewed the exchange in the morning I regretted using such a creepy phrase, especially because no one responded. I thought to call but feared that would be even more unwelcome, so I just started driving; at that point I saw Los Angeles as a black hole for my checking account, and all I wanted to do was get away from it.

I had heard Route 1 was beautiful, but that would have added hours to my trip, so I took Interstate 5 instead. New Jersey turnpikes get a bad rap but I would have taken an endless string of Best Buys over that abyss of visual information. By hour three I was seriously struggling. It was as if all of the trip's podcasting caught up with me at once, all of the cute phrasing and mouth clicks and contrived affectation coalescing into one amorphous host who seemed to always be so surprised by what his guest had to say, who played dumb too often, who laughed too hard too close to my ear. I didn't have much else downloaded to my laptop so I switched to Top 40 for fifteen minutes before deciding silence was best, was needed, was natural—for millennia man had subsisted on nothing more. This paved the way for a nice meditational period, which quickly turned into an audit of all my past failures, which narrowed to my manuscript, which by then was a well-worn topic with predictable ruts: all the strokes of genius that turned out to be pretentiousness, all the emotional depth that was actually sentimentality, all the wasted hours. It was a dimly lit cave I'd slept in for many nights, but all of a sudden there was a hidden passageway out, a failed manuscript I could dwell on that wasn't mine: Avi's. I gripped the steering wheel and gave a little jerk to either side. The thrill of circumnavigating emotional pain.

His story was bad, yes, but why exactly? Tolstoy's epigram on families could just as well apply to fiction, but inverted: each successful story succeeds in its own way, but all the bad ones fail for a short list of reasons. For starters, he'd tried to make objective something so obviously personal, starting with the point of view. A switch from third person to first would not only have opened up a lot of emotional doors, it would have let him tell the story truthfully, allowing the protagonist's flaws to show, if not unintentionally. But flaws need sympathy, and there was hardly anything to feel sympathetic about. Sofia is going to eventually reveal her plans for euthanasia. Avi's narrative, on the other hand—to recap: a comp lit postgrad feels compelled to take a vacation—would need to match the emotional depth of hers. He would need some sort of breakdown of his own—not a postgrad breakdown but something real, a divorce. Yes, and more. A lost child. Some pathos to spend all that serious writing on. And god, the writing, so humorless, down to his title, *Jouissance*. I'd looked it up. It's French for fucking, or not really, something from Lacan, save me. And speaking of fucking but not really, where were the sex scenes? Two strangers fuck on a lawn at night and all we get are their *moans, dissolving into that dark, that salty air.* Knowing Avi, I'd bet my life that his foursome scene kept the men apart. Surely he'd fail to see the opportunity to make Joe, who was already way too passive, an active character. One impulsive man-on-man hand job and Joe's regret could be the motor for most of the denouement!

When the sun set I was still moving pieces around, reimagining lines of his I was surprised I could even recall. I only stopped three times—for gas, a bathroom break, and a late lunch at Subway—beating Google Maps' prediction by forty-five minutes. The girl who opened the door was surprised to see me, and a bit put off. I got the impression she didn't love the idea of Bertie subletting her room to a man. When she let me in I stopped myself from making a joke about bedtime, and generally managed to transmit my harmlessness. She gave me a perfunctory tour of the house and showed me my room, which was bigger than I imagined, with wide windows on two walls, wildflowers and ferns shooting into view. I took off my socks, brushed my teeth, and plugged in my laptop. I cracked my knuckles, exhaled, and opened a new Word doc. I wrote:

As I walked down the dock, my eyes still needed to adjust—I'd spent the ferry ride hunched over a newspaper—and I couldn't understand the source of an unusual sound, a sort of sticky thwack. A few moments passed and the world resaturated with color and I found it: men hoisting dead octopuses over their shoulders and slapping them against wooden boards, over and over, each tenderizing swing giving the meat a second's grip on the lumber. I stood there for a minute and watched, and they didn't notice me, or maybe they were just used to tourists gawking.

I read it three times. I changed a word and then changed it back. So much is decided in the first paragraph, the first sentence, really—point of view, tone, texture, velocity. And now that all that had been decided I didn't really have to think, I could just imagine the story in my head and put it on the page, and for two months I spent most of my waking hours doing exactly that (and all the better to evade the breakdown that still occasionally threatened to surface). I'd wake up and write in my room and then go to the Eugene Public Library for a change of scenery and at 6 I'd drive back, picking up dinner on the way. I'd eat in my room while I wrote, something I was never able to do—eat and write—but it didn't really feel like I was writing, it felt more like I was watching a TV show, one which I just had to occasionally pause and put down on paper.

Since returning to Brooklyn I found myself wincing every time I opened a menu. But here the prices weren't bad. This I took as just another sign that things were going my way, would continue to. I checked the time; I had twenty minutes. I ordered a beer, figuring I could get half a glass of relax in me before she came. Normally for first dates I needed a push in the opposite direction, to be more extroverted, excitable, talkative. But over the past few days it seemed I had a new reserve of energy. And there was something else too: somehow this didn't feel like a normal first date. I actually looked forward to meeting her.

Café Rue Dix was not three blocks from where I used to live, and yet for some reason I hadn't been once. It was Senegalese, a culture I knew nothing of, but I believed the food would be authentic because they had no flags or any other discernible signifier. The facade was open and I sat facing out, watching the diners, who all lounged comfortably, sharing fluid conversation, and I wished such good fortune on myself. Actually, I felt nothing but good fortune. For the past few days it seemed the universe was finally in my favor, doling out rewards in bits and pieces that were only getting bigger. This theory was tested when, about midway through my beer, I made eye contact with the woman two seats over and realized she was Sandra at the same moment she realized I was Caleb. She was nearly done with her drink, must have already been there when I arrived, which made me wonder if I'd done anything embarrassing in her presence. No, I hadn't, but had I already let the worry show on my face? I suggested we move to a table, and when we did I searched her for signs that she was displeased by me, by my appearance, it seemed like she wanted to leave, surely I was projecting. The waiter came and gave us menus and we both smiled at him the way uncomfortable people do. She had shorter hair than she did in her photos, a longish bob, a great bob, which somehow made her look younger. Her eyebrows were thick and a bit wild in a great way. She had beautiful shoulders. She was wearing a sleeveless brown blouse and simple black pants that were perfect together, and it occurred to me that I should stop thinking about how nice she looked and speak, and for my grand opener I said that I used to live around the corner, and then amended it to four blocks away, which actually was wrong, so I said it was three, and this all should have confirmed that I'd hired one of those services that write your Tinder messages for you.

She looked straight at me and asked if I really was this boring, her eyes conveying such easy kindness I almost said, *Your eyes convey such easy kindness*. Instead I said yes, I was in fact this boring, and she had no choice but to sit there with me for an entire meal, and if she didn't I would go home and write about the night to my incel friends on 4chan. She didn't know that *incel* stood for "involuntary celibate," and she barely knew what 4chan was, and that impressed me greatly. She started telling me about a computer science course she took in college. I was slowly becoming mesmerized by the way she spoke, literally how she produced language, which seemed to be completely improvisational, it wasn't just that she said interesting things but that she never seemed to know the next word until it came. I'm not doing a good job of explaining it. She wouldn't say *first and foremost* but *first and final*, or she'd use *ebb* without *flow*, *jetsam* without *flotsam*. That she could produce novel syntax at such an alarming rate, I have to be frank, was arousing.

Her accent seemed to be aspirationally upper-class, or maybe just middle-class with academic parents. I asked what she did for a living. She was unemployed, which I should have guessed by the lack of a profession in her profile. She had worked for the United States Mission to the United Nations, as an assistant policy advisor on the Human Rights Council, but her role had been made redundant due to budget cuts. I made a few informed comments about the Human Rights Council and she asked me to rate, from one to ten, how proud I was to subscribe to *The Economist*. I said eight, and then changed it to seven. She asked why I changed it and I said that the covers are so bad, it would make me feel better about reading it on the subway if I knew the person across from me was looking at a nice cover. She smiled so beautifully, like she was trying not to. The ease I felt between us, which for me (and I'd wager anyone on Tinder) was a one-in-a-thousand miracle, only faltered when she returned the volley, asking me what I did for work. I gave her the elevator pitch, literally what I told the other people in our building in the elevator, with about the same amount of enthusiasm. She asked what exactly I did at Parachute and I told her, and it wasn't what I said but how I said it, that I was passive, and reluctant, and maybe she'd been joking before but now she really looked like she was wondering if I was this boring, and suddenly all I wanted to do was tell her the one fact that would prove I wasn't, that I had lunch yesterday with Ellis Buford about a manuscript of mine, and that she should Google his name, and maybe we should reschedule for a month from now, when she could Google mine.

Eventually, we recovered. There was too much time not to, and I really liked her, and I could feel she liked me. We split beef stew and empanadas, and had a few rounds of drinks. We talked about our families, seeded some inside jokes, laughed a lot. We did all the things you're supposed to do on a first date with someone you think you have real potential with, down to the brief, somewhat awkward but thrilling kiss. And yet, after we said goodbye, as I was walking home and reliving our best moments, I couldn't help but feel that the whole time I'd given her an outdated version of myself, that the real me was being recalibrated and there was an upgrade on the way.

———————

The next day, Friday, at 3. I was killing time, looking out the window to the wedge of Manhattan skyline visible from our office, trying to pretend I hadn't seen it ten thousand times before. I still hadn't heard anything from Ellis. I wanted to email him or God forbid call him but I knew it would only bring bad news, or no news, which was the same as not calling, except for the desperation. I was feeling desperate enough as it was; since I'd installed the Android emulator and Tinder at work, my eye ticked down compulsively. Against all rationality, I had the growing sense that the two unknowns—the future of the book, and my chances at love, specifically with Sandra—might just be cosmically aligned, that success with one would augur success with the other. And so, left with no updates on the book front, I sought out the next best thing.

I went to Sandra's profile and saw that she'd been active fifty-four minutes ago, which made me think I should swipe through some more people, but I didn't want to. I was too excited about her to want to talk to anyone else, maybe even too excited to want to talk to her; really all I wanted was to exist in the wake of our date, remembering moments of it and thinking of things she'd said and things she might say, things I might say to her, our possible futures. My right knee was shaking. I had too much on my mind and needed to empty myself of some of it. I texted Louis.

He had farther to walk and I'd left immediately, but by the time I got to the café he was already outside, smoking, looking up at the sky with one eye closed. He wasn't supposed to smoke, he'd promised me that, so I grabbed the cigarette from his mouth, took a drag, and stepped on it. As soon as I lifted my foot a calm surged through me and I regretted putting it out. *Goose*, he said, our utility salutation; like *shalom* it could mean *hello* or *goodbye* or *don't take things from my mouth*. These days our relationship seemed to exist only in two modes: something bordering on nonsense, and transcendent earnestness. I don't know when exactly this started, but it was sometime after college (we shared housing in three of our four years at Haverford), when our communications shifted from in-person to Google Chat. Throughout the day we might send each other random assortments of letters (*gurjj, druff, fridj*) or information meant to set a new bar of banality (*tall eyebrow guy wearing red pants 2nd day in row*) but then share our most vulnerable thoughts—personal failings, a falling-out with a family member, herpes scares. I loved him, and he loved me. We'd never say it, but there it was.

We went inside to get coffees and brought them out to a bench. We talked about his therapist, a Freudian almost as devout as Louis. I am a rabid atheist on the topic; when no one in your circle is religious or even a registered Republican it can be thrilling to find such fundamental opposition. For a few minutes we argued for and against the merits of psychoanalysis, and once we started talking about dreams I changed the subject, asking him if he remembered Avi Deitsch, *that guy from Haverford.* This was a weird question to ask; of course he would. When he looked at me I betrayed myself even more, and he knew something was up, that perhaps this meeting wasn't as impromptu as I'd led him to believe.

I hesitated. I hadn't thought things through. Louis was also a writer, currently in a program at NYU, thankfully nonfiction, criticism. I told him that I'd signed with Ellis Buford, that he was currently shopping a manuscript to editors. *The Florida manuscript?* I nodded, which was a lie (but maybe not because I didn't use words?). He hardly flinched. I reminded myself that his dreams consisted of bylines, not book deals. I told him to look Ellis up and he took out his phone and I waited. *Nice,* he said. *Looks legit.* I took his phone to see what page he was on. *What about Avi?* he asked. The diversion hadn't worked. *Oh,* I said. *Nothing.* He gave me a dubious look and pulled out his cigarettes. *Well, he works in publishing now. He's at a good imprint, PFK. He's like an editorial assistant, or an assistant editor.* Louis took back his phone and lit a cigarette. *I told my agent I didn't want it shopped to PFK, which might have been kind of weird, but I just—* Louis was holding his phone so close to his face I thought the cigarette might burn it. *Are you listening?* He nodded, and squinted. *Says here he's at Quartz.* I leaned in to see the screen but there was too much glare. *PFK,* I said. *Geoff told me PFK.* Louis showed me the phone, which showed Avi's LinkedIn profile. I grabbed it. *If you had a smartphone you'd know this,* he said. *You don't need a fucking iPhone to access the internet,* I said. *Then why didn't you look it up?* I told him I did, that Avi didn't have a LinkedIn profile a week ago, or maybe I just hadn't found it, or maybe I actually didn't check LinkedIn. Who has LinkedIn? He took out another cigarette without me having to ask. Louis was amused and I couldn't blame him. From his perspective I was being paranoid. Wasn't I publishing a book so the world would read it?

After ten seconds of silence it was clear his thoughts had moved elsewhere. We finished our cigarettes and talked about recent dates. His had been duds, *commercial successes but critical failures*. I tried to convey my excitement about Sandra but it was dampened. When I finished he said, with vague irony, *Sounds promising.*

On the walk back to the office I took the long way. Actually, I circled the block four times. My mind was racing, literally trying to outpace itself, as if thinking through everything fast enough would put it all in the past. I imagined Avi at his desk, opening an email from an editor, a new manuscript. He'd see my name. He'd open it, browse through, see his name, and Sofia, and Joe, Reagan, even Galen. (Why hadn't I changed the names? I tried to while I was writing it, but it didn't feel—what? Authentic? Maybe I planned to sub them out once I finished, but, well, I hadn't.) If I were Avi I'd read it as if someone had handed me my life story, which was sort of the case but not really. Yes, he'd have to realize that right away—that this wasn't his story at all. No, if he were to cross out every sentence that wasn't factually accurate, wasn't his life as he'd lived it, how many would be left? A thousand? A hundred? Twenty? None? This was a work of fiction the same way historical fiction is fiction; the truth is just scaffolding, something you throw away once the thing's been built. If Vermeer read Tracy Chevalier's *The Girl with a Pearl*

Earring, would he feel like he was reading about himself? Would Sylvia Plath even care to read or watch any of the supposed reenactments of her life? And those were actually trying to be faithful. I took so many liberties with his story, how could he read mine and see anything but the differences? I couldn't help but wonder what he'd think about those changes, if he understood why they were necessary, that it wasn't just to make it my own but because his story was reality, and thus not good enough for fiction. His characters didn't have backstories that could illuminate their present selves. His plot had no arc. I wondered if he realized all this, if he recognized the thought behind my manuscript, the craft—above all I wondered what he thought of it as a whole.

～～～

I was still mulling this thought when I walked into the office, and was startled out of it by a loud clap—and then, equally as loud, *There he is!* Dan was standing in the middle of the floor, his arms up above his head. *Sorry to catch you folks so late on a Friday, but we've got some good news—nay, great news. To the boardroom!* Dan was Parachute's founder, though his official position, as noted on LinkedIn, his business cards, and elsewhere, was CMIHO, for Chief Makin' It Happen Officer. Before I started I thought this was at best ridiculous and at worst evidence of a personality disorder, but once we'd met I became utterly incapable of deriding him in any way. He had a gift (or perhaps it was pathology; in the startup world the two could be inseparable) for infusing every interaction with enough bonhomie to bottle and sell, and even I don't have the reserves of cynicism required to render his idiosyncrasies into humor. Years of collegiate wrestling and then CrossFit had made him almost as wide as he was tall, and when I watched him waddle I scolded myself for even noticing.

The boardroom was shared by us and three other startups, but it was meant for real companies, so we only took up a third of it. After the team shuffled in, someone suggested we all sit on opposite sides of the table, a joke repeated with enough frequency to have become our de facto pledge of allegiance. Dan began ambling around the room, and launched into a thoroughly prewritten speech about how far we'd come. He said his one goal for the past four months had been to raise enough money to keep our doors open, and that his one goal from the beginning of Parachute had been to find a way to be financially sufficient, *to no longer need to raise money.* He said that we'd just accomplished both goals. Then he put his fist on the table, a foot on a chair, and said, *Ladies and gentlemen, goats and geese, we're being acquired.*

Very few of us were surprised. A third were on the management team and had been primed. I myself should have known. Weeks ago, on a hunch, I'd done some detective work, stalking Dan's calendar and timing bathroom breaks to align with intriguingly titled meetings—*Next Steps,* or *Operation Genghis.* (He took these calls in the office's only relatively soundproofed room, the lactation room—or, as the sign said, *Mother's Room,* as opposed to *Mothers' Room,* an error that brought Norman Bates to mind—which shared a vent with my favorite bathroom.) Still, I wasn't prepared for the news, the details, the reality of it. The acquirer was Wells Fargo, and they were buying our options in a cashless exercise with accelerated vesting schedules. (Usually you have to work years before acquiring all of your allocated shares; in this case Wells Fargo was giving them to us all at once. This was great for everyone and wonderful for me, as my two months of work would have otherwise qualified me for nothing.) The one detail Dan took his time with was the sale price. I wanted to give him the benefit of the doubt, but what he did for the next twenty minutes amounted to nothing but an abuse of, as he would call it, *informational asymmetry*. With our attentions held hostage he told the complete Parachute origin story (he'd come up with the idea while helping an underprivileged mentee do his taxes), recited a litany of inside jokes, and praised each and every one of us. He promised things wouldn't change (and then implied that if they did, which they surely would, we were each contractually safe for a year), and then, finally, as if it were an afterthought, told us the sale price was $45 million. I watched as the rest of the team briefly closed their eyes or looked at the ceiling, carrying ones and recounting zeros. I didn't need a second to calculate my own stake. I'd been given ten *bips*, or 0.10% of our total worth. $45,000. Not a fucking bad two-month bonus. More words were said about preserving the essence of our company and the passion behind it and blah blah, everyone was now taking furtive glances under the table at their phones, texting spouses or verifying calculations. In solidarity I took mine out and stared at my home screen, a calendar of the month, the individual dates almost too small to read. My eyes rolled over next week, and the week after that, and the week after that, guessing the exact day my life would actually change. Dan wasn't relenting, telling some story about his high school gym teacher, who had scurvy. I didn't think he was going to cry but I wasn't certain. People had put away their phones and were nodding sympathetically. *That's great, Dan*, Sneha said. *You should be proud.* Apparently the story had ended. Dan thanked everyone and told us we should go home, give ourselves a *long weekend*, a true-to-form abuse of the phrase.

———

When I got home I put a Thai bowl in the microwave. I promised myself that when I sold the book I would stop getting frozen food from Trader Joe's. Not that I could be sure of any sort of meaningful payout; in fact, the advance would likely be less than the $45,000 I was getting from Parachute. But it wasn't about the money, I was fully employed as it was and could afford whatever I wanted to eat. No, it was about who I was, what life I allowed myself, and right now I was still just an employee of a future subsidiary of Wells Fargo, the type of person who might eat mass-produced pad thai at 6:15. But when I sold the book, I'd be, what? A novelist who works at a subsidiary of Wells Fargo? Who eats a baguette with cheese and marmalade at 9? What the hell was I saying? My head wasn't straight, that was the problem. I went to the living room and made a gin cocktail but it tasted bad so I poured it out in the kitchen sink and got a beer. I went to my room and took a Xanax from a supply of twenty I got that summer when I had chest pain and a doctor suspected it was anxiety (it was). I waited for it to kick in, I figured I could indulge my anxieties in the meantime. I went on

Twitter, where I discovered that Avi followed Bill McLean but
not Meg Cantu. Both were editors at Quartz specializing in literary fiction but Meg had my manuscript. I found a site that de-
tects plagiarism between documents and I uploaded Avi's story
and the most recent version of my manuscript. I waited for the
results and wondered why I hadn't done this before I sent it to
agents. Louis would ascribe subconscious intent but actually
sometimes people just make mistakes. I'm not the type to dot my
i's or even fully dry my back after a shower.

The day I finished the manuscript, decided I was done, as
happy with it as I'd ever be, I took a ten-minute break to jump on
the trampoline in the backyard of the house in Eugene and then
I read through all of my past emails with agents to see which
ones didn't completely hate my last submission. I remember the
day well. In Oregon, apparently, fall feels months away until the
morning it comes, and that was the morning it came. The wind's
chill started to seep into the house and the trees' rustling dropped
an octave, and I could no longer ignore the reality that I was
going to move back to New York, find a job, once again inhabit a
relatively stable existence. This is all to say: I quickly moved on
from worrying about the manuscript to worrying about everything else in my life and even what shape that life might take.

The page reloaded with the results: *1% Identical, 2% Similar,
2% Related-Meaning.* Considering we were fundamentally telling the same story I considered this an acquittal. There were ten
or so unique phrases (out of seventy thousand words!) that could
be traced back to Avi's manuscript. This was fine, they were not
important. In fact, I changed them right then, highlighting the
new text so I'd remember to update it in my first draft with the

publisher, whoever that might be. I was feeling better, which was rational but probably chemical too. The pad thai had gotten cold in the microwave so I reheated it and smoked a bit of weed. I finished my beer and got another and ate at my desk. Avi's story was still on the screen and I read random lines. Some of the descriptions were so distinct from mine that they seemed like lies, like he was the one getting it wrong.

At this point I was in a wonderful place. I might even have laughed out loud, which I do when I'm alone maybe twice a year. I texted Sandra, *I had fun yesterday. I'd like to see you again soon.* It was nice to text someone exactly how I felt, and not just try to figure out the best thing to say. I took a picture of my toes and wrote, *my toes,* and then deleted it. I was inebriated on four substances—relief the most potent, and organic to boot—all colliding inside me, having their own little UN, agreeing on the resolution that I should be very tired and happy, and with such consensus I crawled into bed. I began yawning so much I was interrupting one yawn with another. It wasn't long before I fell asleep, which was good, because if I'd been awake for another hour I would have received Avi's text, and no chemical on hand would have put me to sleep then.

———————

One thing about my phone is that sometimes for no reason messages appear without the sender's name on top. On group texts this happens one hundred percent of the time, on non-group texts maybe twenty percent. I open the phone and see *1 new message* and click *View* and only the body shows. I have to go back to the home screen and then to the messaging submenu to see who it's from. This was the case when I opened my phone Saturday morning, around 9 a.m., not a minute after I woke up. *Are you around to get coffee tomorrow or Sunday?* I texted back, *Yes :)& the sooner the better.*

I put the French press on and started trimming my mustache and right before I got the last few hairs I had a flash of paranoia that the text wasn't from Sandra. I finished and went into the bedroom and then to make a point to myself about how calm I was I did twenty push-ups before checking my phone. I had another text: *OK. Let's meet at Sit & Wonder at Noon.* If the *OK* wasn't enough, I knew by the business-casual uppercase of *Noon* that I wasn't in courting company. I checked just in case—*From: Deitsch, Avi*—and began pacing around my room. I reread the message I'd sent him. *Yes :)& the sooner the better.* Disastrous. Even if Sandra was the recipient, why had I used a smiley and why hadn't I put a space between it and the ampersand? This happy guy looked like he had a bad chin beard, or a sloppy bow tie.

But this was all a blessing in disguise, I reasoned, mustering conviction. I'd have to meet with him eventually, let him air his grievances (surely in some overembellished way) and then respond with gravitas (not going so far as to formally apologize). Maybe I'd admit that I wished I'd approached him first. If he believed, somehow, that something needed to be done, that I'd actually *wronged* him, I'd have to set him straight. It would be uncomfortable (having to appease him, the possibility of confrontation) but it was better to get it all over with now. If we'd planned this a few days out I'd just be putting myself through some needless anxiety, possibly a night or two of bad sleep, and I wouldn't be as well rested as I was now. I could have done without the Xanax, which I could still feel, but that could be cured by a perfectly timed coffee on a relatively empty stomach. I poured a small bit of the French press into a tea saucer and the rest down the sink. On the table were two bananas with a day of life still in them and I had them both.

———————

I got to Sit & Wonder thirty minutes early, just enough time to get fully jazzed on single-origin and the weekend *Times*. It was the end of October but still warm enough to sit in the backyard, which would afford us some privacy and just the right amount of background noise. I grabbed a few slivers of the paper and brought them to the back with me, but when I sat down I saw one was the Book Review, which felt too on-the-nose, so I got up and exchanged it with Small Business. The big story was about the dominance of Amazon, which didn't seem like news or even about small businesses. I started to read but my phone buzzed. It was Sandra, finally. *Yes, me 2. Are you free tonight?* I texted back, *I can be. Pick the time & place & i'm there.* I reread it and cringed. *I can be* was a half lie because it implied I had plans, which I didn't, and what happened to saying exactly how I felt? I was on tilt, I realized, despite how well I'd convinced myself I was taking this meeting in stride. And then, as if the whole world were colluding against me, just as I took a gulp of coffee I saw through the café, at the register, Avi, bantering with the barista. I averted my eyes. I checked my phone and saw it was twenty minutes to the hour. That Machiavellian psychopath. I drank the coffee as fast as I could, and by the time he saw me and made his way back I'd nearly finished the cup.

Hi there, he said. I looked up, feigning surprise. I was pleased to see that he too was on tilt, and much worse at hiding it. *Avi*, I said, standing. *Good seeing you, my dude.* I heard my words and winced inside, but forgave myself once I saw his smile, as wide as it ever was, his forehead creasing beautifully. Yes, we were both trying to outdo the other in courtesy, sunniness. To appear serene meant you were at peace, that you knew you were in the right. We hugged and sat down, filling a few moments with the pretense of finding our chairs, giving us enough time to appraise one another. He had an unfashionable haircut, a buzz cut plus two months, which on him felt in fashion, made the idea of fashionable haircuts seem, for a moment, ridiculous. The same could be said of his clothes, baggy and shapeless, blue jeans and a green-and-yellow plaid shirt. I glanced down and saw he was wearing Timberlands. As if neither of us could deign to bring up the reason we were there, we forced pleasant small talk, about how twee the name Sit & Wonder was, and Amazon's effect on small businesses, and soon momentum had taken us into medium talk, about dating (he'd found success a few months ago—a furniture designer named Francesca) and us both being back in New York, and how the fall here can make you feel more vulnerable, more realistic, a vestige of secondary school surely. We talked about the anxiety of having full-time jobs again, which I didn't feel so much but went along with since he seemed quite earnest. He said he'd been on anti-anxiety medication for years and had recently gone off them, which was a struggle, since the withdrawal induced its own anxiety, along with, as he put it, *a night or two of psychosis*. The withdrawal anxiety was orders of magnitude worse than any of the original symptoms, he said, plus he'd gained twenty pounds, which I couldn't see but maybe that explained the clothing. Instead of all of those pills he was taking one, a microdose of LSD. A month ago he'd met an *off-the-grid psychiatrist* who prescribed it, and since then he'd been doing it habitually. This was a topic I was intensely curious about and had no primary sources for, and I asked him what exactly *habitually* meant. *Two days on, one day off*, he said. I asked him what the dose was and he said it was fifteen micrograms and then, gauging my ignorance, told me that a real dose might be ten times that. I asked if it helped and he said it did, that it was like hitting a reset button, et cetera, et cetera, using all the analogies I'd heard before and then one I hadn't. *It's like at the beginning of each day, we start at the top of a mountain, ready to ski down. We're so used to living our life the way we live it that we always go down the same way, following the tracks from the day before, and the day before that. Microdosing is like a new snowfall that covers all our old tracks, so each day we go down a different way.* I thought this was elegant and wondered where he got it from. I remarked, half to myself, that if each day we ended up at the bottom of the mountain, what was the point of skiing at all? He shrugged and I felt I was being negative so I made a joke about sleep and ski lifts, which wasn't particularly funny but he allowed it and even smiled. The only other person in the backyard, a man who was ostensibly reading but, I noticed, hadn't turned a page since Avi arrived, picked up his phone. *Hello?* he said, standing, putting a hand over his other ear. *Wait, I can't hear you, wait, wait, just—*

He walked inside and Avi made a vague face and said, *If it's okay I'd like to discuss things now.* The transition wasn't fluid but it wasn't trying to be, in a way I found both expert and adult. I was impressed. *Sure,* I said. *Let's.* He took a sip. *So, as you must know, a manuscript crossed my door the other day.* He pretended to think about what day it was, and then said *Thursday.* It annoyed me that he used the phrase *crossed my door* when he clearly didn't have an office, and then I told myself to calm down and bring a positive energy to the table. I took a sip of my coffee. *I'm sure you must have felt a lot of different emotions,* I said. *Perhaps I should have prepared you. Maybe that would have made things easier.* His head tilted and gave a small jerk back, a display of disagreement, one subtle enough to appear organic but it wasn't. I could feel my reserves of positivity beginning to drain. *Ah, well. I think it might have been even more useful to get in touch a while ago, don't you? Like, even before you started shopping it.* I nodded, and then regretted giving in so easily. *Why's that?* I asked. He shook his head slightly. *I thought we could hit the ground running here but I guess we'll have to agree on some basic facts first.* He looked at me sternly and nodded, asking for my approval. I stuck out my hand, palm up. *Okay, well, shortly after you visited me in May, after I told you what happened to me in Paros, and after I sent you the story I wrote about it, you went and, without my knowledge, wrote a novel retelling my story. Now you are attempting to sell that novel to a publisher.* I tried to find fault in a single word but couldn't. *Okay,* I said. *That's one way of looking at it.* He asked if I saw things differently. I noticed his phone on the table and said, despite my better judgment, *Are you taping this?* He laughed like he couldn't help it. *Jesus Christ,* he said, putting in his password and sliding me the phone. I slid it back and he held it up so I could see it being turned off. *It was just a question*, I said. *Okay*, he said. *Well, do you see things differently?* I rubbed my face. *I'll say I think there are similarities between my novel and the story you told me and the story you wrote, and I was inspired by some of it, but of course there are other elements from my own life that I was also inspired by.* I was suddenly aware of the caffeine lifting me, and grateful for it. *And to be honest, Avi, the story you told me took all of twenty minutes to tell. The story you wrote was a few thousand words. That's not a novel. It's not even an outline. I could have gotten in touch with you, sure, but the thought didn't come to me then because I couldn't see a reason to, and I'm struggling to find one now.* He readjusted himself in his seat. *Well*, he said, *for starters, you could have made sure I was okay with it, made sure that, you know, I wasn't working on my own novel.* I could tell this was a lie, or rather a half lie, since he was only suggesting it, and before he could hedge or say another word I asked if he was working on a novel. *Sure*, he said. *I haven't made as much progress as you have with yours. I mean, I haven't had the time.* Now he wasn't even trying to lie; he was just letting empty words drop from his mouth. *Okay*, I said, pushing my chair back. *Well, I wish you luck in the endeavor. I'm going to head off now.* I stood up. *Caleb*, he said. *I think it would be beneficial for us to come to an agreement, to get on the same page.* I didn't want to look him in the eyes but I knew I'd have to before I left. *Okay*, I said, *Look. I'll change all of the names and identifying details, and you keep on writing your novel, and when it comes out please send a copy.* I leaned over to grab my bag. *Do you understand the gravity of the situation?* he asked. *Sure*, I said, walking away. My feet crunched the gravel and I couldn't hear what he said but the one word that was clear, *Ellis*, was enough to stop my step. I wished I hadn't turned around, because my face betrayed the answer to his next question before I had a chance to consider it. *Does he know about this?* He reached for his coffee and took a sip and then turned back to the table, shaking his head to himself. *Well, maybe he should. Maybe I should call him. Or maybe my boss can, they have lunch every now and again.* We stayed in that position for ten seconds, or more, me standing, looking at his back, him with both hands around his mug. I sat back down. He was trying to look calm. I wasn't. *What do you want me to do?* I asked. *Call Ellis and tell him to trash it because I forgot to have a heart-to-heart with everyone who's ever inspired anything in my writing?* This was a throwaway line, much the way his was, uncool and a bit melodramatic, but I'd apparently struck gold. In one microexpression that he corrected immediately I saw that the thought induced nothing less than terror. Whatever outcome he'd been hoping for—if he actually had a specific resolution in mind, which I was beginning to doubt—the last thing he wanted was for the manuscript to disappear. At first I could hardly believe it, but then things clicked, I had an unusual bout of empathy. I could sit in his head. He needed it, the book. As much as his life suited him—a highbrow degree, a job in the arts, a partner paving her own interesting path—it lacked something exceptional, some remarkable facet that he'd always expected from himself, that anyone who knew him did. As trite as it is, it was his very way of being in the world, his grace, that implied and necessitated something more from him without helping him find it.

I know you've spent a lot of time on this, he said, *and it shows. After all, you've landed a great agent. I don't want to have to interfere with the whole process of you two selling the book, I'm just suggesting we come to some sort of agreement.* The guy with the phone came back outside, now carrying a pastry in a napkin. *What does that mean?* I said. I picked up my phone to look at the time, which I forgot the moment I set it back down. *I think we should be fair,* he said, his eyes wandering over to our new witness. *I just want to reach a conclusion.* He was watching his words, which of course would be obvious, would only make the guy aware he should be paying more attention. Somehow this seemed like my advantage. *Be straight with me,* I said. *What exactly do you want?* He nodded, his eyelids flickering with thought. *Do you want a portion of my advance?* Now his head turned completely to the guy, catching his stare and sending it down. *I think you're making an interesting offer, but that's not really*— He held his hand up, making some unidentifiable gesture, his pointer and thumb stuck out, his wrist swiveling back and forth. *What is that?* I asked. He smiled and nodded, yet all he could do was continue making that ridiculous sign, too afraid to put words to the thought, and that display of cowardice gave me just enough assurance to figure out what he was trying to say. *Jesus fuck,* I said. *Avi.*

His face was practically writhing, terrified that I might explicitly say what he couldn't, so I did. *You think your name should be on the book, that* you *should be giving* me *a portion of* your *advance.* His mouth produced soundless words and then he started over. *Or both of our names,* he said. *Both of our names on the book. I really don't see how it's different from a ghostwriter relationship.* Now it was my turn to laugh. *You don't?* He finished his coffee, swallowing slowly, prolonging the pause. *Well, I do,* he said. *Of course it's a bit different. But as far as how we each contributed value to the*

book, it's the same dichotomy. There's the story and there's the writing.
I shook my head. I couldn't believe it. *Except that I provided both.*
He leaned in and lowered his voice. *Caleb, how can you think that?*
I kept my posture and my volume. *Avi. How much of what's in the
book did you tell me? Realistically, how much of what I wrote actually
happened to you?* A moment passed, a few did. There was a mutual resetting, like it was the end of a round. *I would need to read
it again to answer,* he said. *And anyway, it's beginning to feel like
we're really getting into the weeds.* As if the conversation served
any other purpose. *I see this discussion as a starting point,* he said,
one that I'd love to continue, but I really should be going. He checked
the time on his phone. *You did that in the wrong order,* I said.
You're supposed to see what time it is and then say you should be going.
He gave a good-natured laugh, as if it had been a good-natured
joke. *This has been productive, but it might make sense for us each to
have some time alone to think about things.* Some time alone. To
think about things. He was out of ideas but knew to quit while
he was ahead, or at least while he thought he had me on the hook
with this whole idea that he'd call Ellis or have a fucking execu-
tive editor at Quartz do it, which he wouldn't, not that the idea
didn't bother me, it did, because it pointed to a larger truth,
which was that Ellis should know about all of this—that he
didn't was Avi's entire advantage—except I couldn't tell him, not
now, not on the eve of the sale. He stood and stuck his hand out
and I didn't take it but that didn't satisfy my animus or even a
portion of it so I backhanded my mug off the table. It shattered.
I refused to look down at it. He kept eye contact for a few seconds before breaking it with one of his award-winning smiles.
The pleasure's all mine, I shouted after him. Maybe it wasn't really

a shout but it must have been categorized as such in the mind of the guy sitting there and the few people now staring at me from inside the café. In this neck of the woods a simple show of aggression is too rare not to be a story to tell later, and I became hyperaware of their attentiveness, that they were memorizing all of the scene's details, what I was wearing, what he was, our hair.

I took a deep breath in and then out, and I got to my knees, and began gathering the ceramic shards. Once I found all of the big pieces I carried them to the table and, seeing that he'd left his mug, put them inside, one by one, as gently as I could.

The waiter poured me another glass of water, the third in ten minutes. He was surprised at my thirst and I was surprised to be getting such good service. Normally the staff at Sisters prefers maintaining their ethereal vibes over waiting on customers. An hour earlier I'd finished a fifteen-mile run, south to the Hasidic community in Borough Park. In some ways it was the happiest place to be in New York on a Saturday, kids screaming in the streets and not one business open. I was hoping to lift my mood, or at least reset it. I'd spent the preceding hours staring at my laptop, researching libel and defamation laws. He had no case, there were no identifying details besides his name, and I'd change that before publication. I drafted emails to him and Ellis and one to both of them and then deleted them all. I decided he was right about us needing time to think about things. He had needed to bounce his ludicrous idea off me to understand it was ludicrous, and now he would need a few hours to let it sink in.

Can I help you along with the menu, or are you still waiting for your other? The one requirement for working at Sisters was a perfect head of hair that could work on multiple members of Fleetwood Mac. *I'm still waiting, thanks.* I flashed a smile. He left and I checked my phone: 8:27. She was thirty minutes late, which worried me, though it was nice to be preoccupied with something other than Avi.

The place was popular for good reason, it was stunning inside, with high ceilings and good wood everywhere. There was a snaking marble bar, cane-back chairs and parquet tables, the right amount of greenery and an enormous white pyramidal liquor shelf built with a degree of grandeur normally reserved for church organs. It had the same orbs of light as every bar in brownstone Brooklyn but it seemed earned here, all of the features combining to evoke the seventies without having to have a disco ball. I was in the back, a small space anchored by a fish-eye mirror behind the bar that captured everyone in the room and made you feel like you were in a submarine. Against all odds the room also had a stage, where men in brown woolen suits with exceedingly large instruments were setting up. They'd been threatening to play their first practice notes for the past ten minutes, and just as this finally happened—a baritone saxophone farting melodically—Sandra appeared, waving with both hands, mouthing *Sorry sorry sorry*, and then giving it voice as she wrapped her arms around me and kissed my cheek. She wore a white dress with blue flowers and she was more beautiful than I'd remembered. People were looking at her and I could feel myself smile; I became aware that I hadn't done that in earnest the entire day, not since the night before, and that didn't count because I was high.

The waiter came and Sandra ordered a cocktail and I got a beer. We tried to talk but the band started playing, first a wandering alto sax solo that coalesced into the melody of "The Girl from Ipanema," and when that petered out the rest of the players joined in. They weaved through each other seamlessly, the collective sound thready and brittle but soporific too. And yet the second I made eye contact with Sandra I could feel my cheeks tightening, because hers were, there was something upsettingly funny about the song, or maybe it was the band or actually the place, like it had always been an inch away from taking itself too seriously and this crew with their fedoras and snapping fingers took it well past that point. I was briefly amazed not just by the disappearance of my anxiety, but by how much joy I felt in its place; all it had taken was a few minutes in her company. I glanced back at her and saw she was having a hard time controlling herself, her eyebrows tenting more every second, and it wasn't long before her hand found her forehead, shielding her eyes. The waiter came with our drinks and then, out of nowhere, a man emerged onstage, as if he'd been hiding behind the bassist. He was a short and slender Brazilian-looking fellow with a Little Richard haircut, and he began to sing the original Portuguese lyrics, his voice as high as a fourteen-year-old's, and it all became too much. Sandra put her hand fully over her eyes and her other palm fell on my leg. Her hand was shaking, passing the vibrations of her body, which was practically convulsing.

In that moment I abandoned all the day's mess. I couldn't care about Avi, care about anything at all. I put my hand on the far side of her back and put my lips to her ear and starting singing along, my working knowledge of Portuguese being eighth-grade Spanish, and this she loved, I knew because when she looked at me there were tears in her eyes, and she squeezed my leg so hard I yelped and kicked it up against the table, knocking both drinks over, our glasses shattering one after the other, and still the band played on. I got up to collect the pieces but our waiter came over with a broom and Sandra had the right idea to just put money on the table and leave.

Outside, she finished laughing, and we watched through the window as Brazilian Little Richard concluded the song and gave a great big bow and we laughed some more. We started walking and I suggested having ramen at Chuko but she said she'd been there a thousand times. I asked her if she lived in the area but then remembered she'd told me all that on our first date: she lived in Fort Greene, she'd moved in with her dad after he had a stroke. I apologized and she put her hand on my arm. She seemed eager to change the subject and said, *We could have an incredible dinner for free but there are conditions.* I asked what they were and she said I'd have to agree to the whole package before that was divulged. I asked if this was how the UN worked and she said yes. I asked her where I should sign and she took my hand and we started walking. *We're going to a party hosted by my friend Franny. It's not a dinner party per se, more of a party with enough hors d'oeuvres to make a dinner out of. There'll be meats and cheeses you've never heard of and everything in between, we'll be served what real adults eat at home because Franny is a real adult.* She looked at me for confirmation and I nodded. *So, on to the conditions, which I'll remind you you've already agreed to. The first is that, when asked, you will say you're my boyfriend. We've been dating for a few months, we met on Tinder. I understand how creepy this is, but trust that you'll feel creepier if they think I brought you there as a second date. The second condition, if you can't already tell, is that I might intermittently act weird. Franny is my oldest and most successful friend. She owns her own business doing exactly what she wants to do, and she's ambitious and fearless and I've been unemployed for four months. You can understand.* Her honesty and vulnerability, it goes without saying, made me adore her, made me want to show her just how honest and vulnerable I could be. *The good news is that there are no more conditions. If you have any questions you should ask now because it's just up there.* She pointed to a beautiful brownstone featuring large bay windows with maroon trim that I'd taken notice of many times because it was the first thing I saw when I left my apartment. *I live there*, I said, pointing to my building. She asked if I was serious and I asked if she'd feel better if she had some weed and a drink, and she said yes.

I wasn't in the right mind to clean up before I left, and honestly I'd have done a perfunctory job anyway. The point is, at that moment my apartment was a realistic version of itself. In my living room was a completed Settlers of Catan board, magazines strewn among mailed notices I didn't know what to do with but didn't want to throw out, glasses full of water that probably tasted dusty. Most of the furniture was Frank's, my roommate, the platonic ideal of one, a laid-back patent attorney whose one true talent was finishing up in the bathroom fifteen seconds before I needed it. (He might have had other talents, I wouldn't know.) It was good furniture, mismatched but that was an okay style for me at this point in my life. I was glad she wouldn't see my bedroom because I have a belief-based system about not making my bed, and also one about where clothes should be laid in lieu of using my dresser. Then, without asking, she walked straight into my room. I followed her in and she asked if I was planning to ever get rich enough to have a maid. I told her if she waited in the living room I would make her a drink.

I mixed tequila, guava juice, and lemon, it was simple but with a peel of lemon and ice it looked nice. She loved it, her mood perked. I went to get a joint from my bedroom and by the time I got back she was done with the drink. She rattled the ice cubes in the empty glass, asking for another. *I'm not an alcoholic*, she said. *Just when I'm around successful friends.* I mixed gin, seltzer, elderflower syrup. This time I used an orange garnish. She tasted it and gave me very kind eyes. We each took a hit and waited a minute and then kissed. It was wonderful, unrealistically fantastic, sailor-home-from-duty good, and I was briefly amused and a little saddened that chemicals could so easily replace a more naturally grown fondness. She said she was hungry and I became paranoid she was just looking for an excuse to leave, and then she laughed at me because my face looked worried. She stood and held out her hand and I took it, and we didn't unclasp them for the entire time it took to walk down four flights of stairs and across the street and up three flights of stairs through one of the most beautiful apartments I'd ever had reason to be in. The girl who greeted us at the door looked far too young and happy to be that successful but alas, she introduced herself as Franny. She had a celebrity lookalike, but I couldn't figure out who it was. I noticed she was staring at me, and then I realized it wasn't staring, really, I'd just forgotten how humans act, and Sandra said my name for me. *Caleb*, I repeated. *Sandra and I have been dating for a few months, and we met on Tinder.*

Franny looked at Sandra and Sandra admitted we were high. Franny tried to show she thought this was funny but she was obviously a bit annoyed. I realized that she looked like Minnie Driver in *Good Will Hunting* and stopped myself from saying so. We went into her living room, joining six or so attractive people whose ease and blond hair made me feel Jewish.

Sandra quickly fulfilled her promise to intermittently act weird, directing me to sit in an empty chair and asking me what I thought about it. It looked like a normal expensive chair. I noticed it had no visible seams. People watched in silence as I sat down. It was apparent that I was supposed to have a good opinion of the experience. Actually it felt great, but also to be fair I was high and the environs really put things together. I pretended to think about it, really tried to move around in a refined way, like my ass was tasting wine. *It's very ergonomic*, I said, but then realized they use that word in ads so I said, in a moment of inspiration, *I feel elevated*, which really struck a chord. There were hums of approval. I had made strides for both Sandra and myself. *Franny built it*, Sandra said. I asked what else she made and a guy on the couch said, *A fortune*, and everyone laughed. *She makes other kinds of furniture*, Sandra said, which was by that point obvious. People looked at me like I was a disaster for needing that explained. Actually I was being paranoid again, but with so much attention on me I felt I should speak, so I said that I lived across the street. This was met with some encouraging eyebrow lifts, so I continued with it and told the story about how I discovered my window faced west instead of south. This was a swing and a miss, and my next trick was to say that Olivia Wilde and Jason Sudeikis lived a few doors down, which was true, and if people found that interesting they were hiding it, because it was gauche to know anything about celebrities. Franny handed me a cocktail and I took a sip. It was well made, I tasted cognac, citrus, Byrrh. I thought to say something along these lines to gain back social capital but then decided I'd rather be daft than a prick. Instead I asked what wood the chair was made of. The answer was more complicated than I could have guessed. I had a hard time listening because it was boring but also because something was going on in my brain, it was like two little inchworms were trying to find each other, both worms were about Franny, one was her name and the other was her profession, and a second before the worms were going to connect Avi walked in the room. (*Francesca's a furniture designer, actually*. Fuck him for using her full name.) He put his hand on the small of her back and they kissed briefly. He waved to the group, his eyes passing over mine without hesitation. He must have been listening from the other room, even slyer than I knew. And where was the schlub I had to put up with earlier? He'd changed into a claret-colored button-down tucked into ankle-length black slacks, his feet sockless in black dress shoes. It was certainly the lighting but I could've sworn he had makeup on.

He took a spot on the couch and started making conversation with the guy who'd said *A fortune*, and slowly everyone found a talking partner. Sandra was talking with Franny, which left me with the girl to my right, a blond Brit with short hair who was appealingly ugly, she had the sort of facial bone structure that only comes from generations of wealth. Her name was Patricia and I missed her profession because it seemed made-up and also I was busy thinking *Patrician Patricia, that'll be easy to remember.*

We discussed the Trump *Access Hollywood* tape, Bruce Nauman, and favelas. She'd just finished *The Alchemist* and we talked about it for far too long. I was losing concentration but then she said something interesting about how in the years after college before people get married and have children we have a need to define the smaller stages we pass through—new jobs and partners, a loved one's passing—and we often do this by changing our look, especially our hair, thereby announcing our new phase to ourselves and everyone we know. She said we often feel desperate not to be confused with earlier versions of ourselves, and this leads to some irrational and ultimately regressive behavior. We sat with that thought for a few moments. It felt nice to be comfortable in silence, to have forged such easy intimacy with a stranger. Franny put on music, the Dirty Projectors, and I told Patricia that we listened to them all the time in college. I regretted this a little because it might have implied, vis-à-vis her comment about past selves, that I was sticking my nose up at the choice. But I regretted it a lot more when she asked where I'd gone to college. I tried to evade the question by pretending I didn't hear her, and quickly looked over at Sandra, who sat with a plate of meat and cheese on her lap. I wondered when she'd gotten it. I turned back to Patricia; it was obvious she knew I'd heard the question. I said, *Haverford*, and she took a second to think and then looked at Avi, who had picked up on the word and was looking at us.

Avi, you went to Haverford, no?

I did, he said.

Everyone was paying attention. If this group had one talent, it was apparently snuffing out latent tension.

We know each other, I said, watching as they all replayed in their heads the moments he first walked in. There was no point in letting things simmer, so I said, *We're having a bit of a spat, which we've chosen to ignore, along with each other.*

Without missing a beat, Patricia asked what the dispute was about. Her candor struck me as not very English. She crossed her legs and took a sip of wine. Like everyone else, she was doing the best she could to pretend this wasn't the most exciting moment of her week.

Property, I said.

Is that all I am to you? Sandra joked. This wasn't bad but of course no one bit, and after a moment of silence Patricia tried again, literally imitating herself, recrossing her legs and taking another sip. *So what's this dispute about?* The comic effect of the repetition gave her some slack to ask again, even more adamantly: *Jesus, just come out with it.*

Caleb took something from me without asking, Avi said. *We're trying to figure out how best to make things good again.*

And let's stop being coy, Patricia said. *What exactly did he take?*

I took the story of a foursome he had on Paros and wrote a novel about it, I said. *Paros is a Greek island.*

Avi looked at Franny and so we all did. Her face couldn't hide ignorance of such a story, just as his couldn't hide its truth. But as regretful as he was, he couldn't help but momentarily bask in the glory of having this fact broadcasted, the pleasure seeping out of him in a grin he caught a second too late.

Well, that's not exactly it, he said. *With Caleb I've learned that things aren't always what they seem. For example, he told me just earlier today that he hasn't been on a second date in the past six months.*

Now Sandra was the reluctant recipient of the room's attention. She was fidgeting in her chair and my heart leapt for her. I started to speak but she held out her hand. *I don't know anything about you*, she said, staring daggers at Avi, *and I have the greatest respect for Franny. But from the second you walked in I got terrible vibes.* I didn't know exactly how, but this breached something that hadn't been breached yet, something still sacred. Perhaps it was that she'd judged all of him at once. Or that an actual friendship was hanging in the balance. Most likely it was her violation of the one rule required for navigating social currents like these, which is to always hold something back, to never be ruthlessly honest.

Franny told Sandra that she should leave, *and take him with you*, an addendum I had to applaud for its unapologetic haughtiness. I knew then that one day Franny would be a real success, a name to know, and I took a moment to capture everything I could about the scene. Sandra stood and I followed. I could feel a fart and wanted with all my life to punctuate our exit but knew such irreverence would be in the wrong direction and also I'd laugh, I was practically laughing thinking about it, and that would ruin our whole thing. Sandra had a better idea, on the way out she took the bottle of wine she'd been drinking as well as a stick of salami, as if to say, *We'll be making our own festivities.* I was looking forward to trying the wine because when the opportunity arises I like to really ask myself if the expensive stuff tastes better—not to mention that with Avi back on my mind I needed some more drink—but by the time we got to my place she'd already downed it.

As we were riding the elevator up she looked at me coyly, or not coyly, she wasn't at all hiding what she wanted. You can bring me your best aphrodisiac—your juiciest oysters, your most potent horny goat weed, your most remastered Marvin Gaye—but nothing will hold a candle to anger, which is fundamentally horniness without secondary sex characteristics. As soon as we were inside I glanced into Frank's empty room and she pushed me against the front door. She put her mouth to my neck and I rubbed my hands on everything I'd wished I could touch since I'd met her. We went like this back and forth against the walls, making our way to my room with all of the efficiency of a Roomba. In the doorway she took a step back and ran her fingers through my hair and we kissed again, softer, suddenly remembering how nice it could be to do that not for fury's sake. She walked us into my room and took off her clothes but I hesitated to approach her, a part of me didn't want to have sex, wanted to prolong it so that when it happened it would be more than just fucking—at the very least it would have been nice to be somewhat sober—but when I tried putting words to it they all sounded like a poor translation of *I have chlamydia*, and so I took off my clothes and joined her in bed and tried to pretend it all wasn't some release that really had nothing to do with us.

I never sleep well with new people, especially if I'm enamored enough to have already imagined what our kids might look like, but with the help of the weed I made it to 8. My first waking thought was that I couldn't believe I'd allowed myself to wear my sleeping mask. I pulled it off and pushed myself up until my back rested against the headboard. Sandra was wearing my threadbare teal shirt, which still reminded me of Florida. Her breathing worried me, it was unnaturally slow, so I put my hand on the top of her pillow and moved it a bit but nothing changed. I coughed and still she didn't move, and I was about to try the pillow thing again when she said, quite loudly, *Do not disturb*. I was startled by this, which she apparently enjoyed; she was stifling laughter, I could see her back shaking. I got up and went to the kitchen and made us coffee and breakfast: eggs, avocado, and kale, which I sautéed in olive oil, coriander, and a splash of mirin. For a minute I lost my thoughts to Avi and burned the kale, though she didn't seem to notice. We ate in bed in silence and then cuddled, tangling our legs in as many ways as we could, finding all of the positions our bodies could lie in comfortably together, as if we were doing research for years of mornings like this.

At one point she said, *What do I have to do for you to tell me everything?* which I took to mean my secrets, or my insecurities or whatever, and so I said, *You don't have to do anything*, and I started talking about how my mom made us take fluoride medication when we were little and how that gave me and my brother irregular enamel lattices, which explains the slight mottling of my teeth. She waited patiently for me to finish and then said, *I mean the whole Avi thing*. I told her she'd have to tell me something of equal importance, and she replied, reasonably, that she didn't know how important it was because I hadn't told her the story yet. *It's very important*, I said, and she sighed. *Okay*, she began, reluctantly, *When I was fourteen my uncle touched me inappropriately a few times*. I couldn't believe it was through this stupid deal that I'd earned that information. *I'm sorry*, I said. *It's okay*, she said, *I'm over it as much as I will be. Thanks to a wonderful therapist and three shitty ones.* I thought back to our Tinder conversation, when she asked who my therapist was and I said I didn't need one because I had a good childhood. *Have you forgiven him?* I asked, and knew immediately from her expression that this wasn't something you ask, that it would have been better to say any other stock thing. *No*, she said, *I haven't. Your turn.* She clearly wanted to change the subject. I told her the entire saga from the beginning, which I decided was when I moved to Florida. I said it all as if I were writing in my diary—noting the facts and my feelings about them as objectively as possible. She took a minute to digest it all, silently mouthing parts she wanted to pass over again, letting out a few sharp, fleeting laughs. Then she asked a question I had surprisingly or not surprisingly failed to have ever asked myself: *Why do you think this manuscript is good and the one you wrote before wasn't?* I said, *Hm*, and then, *Well, it's not that the other one wasn't good, it's just that it wasn't publishable.* She rolled her eyes, which was fair, because this was a cop-out, and I really thought about it. I mean I really, really thought about it.

I went to the kitchen to get more coffee and watered the plants by the window and then those in the living room, and there I saw that the screen of the window was off its track and I fixed it, and I finally hung a birdfeeder I'd bought months ago, and I filled it with seed, and I sat on the couch with my coffee and waited for the first bird to appear, which took ten minutes. When I got back to the room she was, impressively, doing nothing, just lying with her hands behind her head, staring at the

ceiling, her phone nowhere in sight. I wanted to tell her something straightforward and cheesy, like, *I like you*, or *I want to
spend a lot of time with you*, but I didn't, because I was worried it
would seem, in context, like pandering. *In the old manuscript I
was the protagonist*, I said finally, *but in this one, since I both know
and don't know Avi, I think I had a footing but also room to explore*.
She asked if I didn't think there was room to explore my own self
and I said I didn't know the answer or really how to answer. She
nodded, the moment began to pass. I felt uneasy. There was the
faintest flicker that I hadn't been honest with her, that in all that
time I was mulling over her question I was really weaving in and
out of two answers, one that made sense but was easy—what I
told her—and one that wasn't coherent, something that should
be kept inside until it coalesced enough to be put into words.

She moved down the bed and kissed me and I couldn't believe how good her mouth tasted, and I realized that while I was
putzing around the living room she'd brushed her teeth. I wanted
her to leave that second because I felt easy around her and wonderful and I was perhaps falling in love with her and it would be
so nice to spend the rest of the day with that thought. I was going to find a way to make that happen but when I looked at her
there was something gravid about her mouth, the top lip just
over the bottom, and also her hand, lying on the corner of the
bed, palm down, as if she were holding it back. *I'm not telling you
anything new*, she said. *Maybe it will sound new, but I bet you won't
be surprised to hear it, which means you knew it all along*. She waited
for confirmation and I nodded, even though I wanted anything
but for her to continue, because if I didn't know what was coming I at least knew it would be something I'd immediately want

to unhear. *You created this thing. It's yours. Of course it is. But there's a reason you haven't told your agent about Avi's story. I think you think you'll get Avi to realize he doesn't deserve anything more than an apology, and maybe he doesn't, but unless he thinks that too, the problem isn't going to go away.* I said that I was the one who wrote it, as if this were an interesting angle, and I told her what I'd found online, that he had no legal basis to sue, and she let me go on and on, saying the same things twice, or three times, probably because she trusted I'd stop eventually, because the truth always settles, and when it does it doesn't move again, and soon enough it had found the bottom of my stomach. She put her hand on mine and I shoved my face into the bed. She started rubbing my back and I rolled next to her and lay in the crook of her arm. *I should head out,* she said, and sat up. She began searching half-heartedly for her clothes, maybe she was waiting for me to ask her to stay but I didn't say anything. I wanted her to go but for the opposite reason than before, so I could have the rest of the morning to be alone in misery.

———

On Monday I got to the office an hour late. I struggled to care. Actually, that was the reason I was late. Coming in to work was the last thing on my mind. Still, when I walked into our section of the floor, it was hard not to be aware of my truancy: the air was thickly diligent, they all stared deep into their screens and sat palpably upright. I'd never been so conscious of the sound of keys being pounded. I felt like it was everyone's first day but mine. Was this all because of the acquisition?

Dan was nowhere to be found, neither was Sneha. I stared at my login screen. My username was "Calawag" for no reason I could remember. How long was it before it would have to be "Caleb Horowitz," before Wells Fargo would make us trade our Macs for PCs, before my email address was c.horowitz.3@ wellsfargo.com?

For an hour or so I scanned a customer data sheet Beck from sales had sent around. Would my productivity ever return to suitable levels? Even if I sold the book, even if I didn't have that or Avi or anything related to it sapping my concentration? It didn't seem possible. I went to the bathroom and sat on the toilet, my pants down even though I couldn't shit. I took out my phone and began browsing my conversations. The sixth one was with Ellis: One lone message, sent after our lunch. It was marked as *Read* even though I hadn't seen it before. *LMK if you need anything.* A wave of anxiety passed through me as I considered my coffee with Avi, and then my conversation with Sandra. I checked the time, it was just short of noon. I workshopped a text for five minutes and ended up with: *Updates?* I sent it and closed my phone. Fifteen seconds later I felt it vibrating in my pocket. I flipped it open. He was calling. I went back to my desk, grabbed my coat, and took the elevator down. He picked up on the seventh ring.

Caleb, how goes it? There was background noise, music, clinking. Was he always in a restaurant?

Not bad, not bad, I said. *What's new?*

Listen, Caleb, I'm in a sort of meeting now. To update you, we have an offer from Filigree. It's nothing serious but it's helpful, it'll help me put some pressure on everyone else and push through some more serious conversation.

Oh, I said, refusing to let my mind wander, afraid that it would find a number greater than what I was about to hear. *What is it?*

Forty-five, he said. *It's, you know, immaterial. They won't go much higher I bet but I never thought we'd end up with them anyway.*

Right, I said. I could feel something rising in my stomach, something wonderful. I entertained telling him about the coincidence of $45,000, of Parachute's sale, but thought better of it.

Listen, trust that I'll keep you up-to-date. It's going to happen fast. I wouldn't make any cardiologist appointments this week.

What?

Okay, Caleb. More soon. He hung up on me. I wasn't offended. He could spit in my mouth if we were leapfrogging $45,000.

I remembered that I told him I preferred emails to calls. Did the fact I'd just called him negate that? And actually I preferred text over everything else, I wanted to be updated wherever I was. I opened my phone and reread his text and then I thought, *Be chill.* I went back to my conversations and scrolled up to Sandra's, then my brother's, then Avi's. *OK. Let's meet at Sit & Wonder at Noon.* I texted Sandra, *What should I do about Avi.* I walked to the café and got a coffee while I waited for her to text back. I finished my coffee and filled the cup back up with milk and Sweet'n Low. The barista saw me do that so I bought a croissant and walked back to work. I Googled the editor at Filigree he'd sent the manuscript to. He looked like Topher Grace if Topher Grace hated his family. His last tweet was some lame joke about Trump. I pitied him for lowballing us; it was great to feel power over someone who just yesterday had had all the power over me. $45,000. It didn't feel real, that number, a number that apparently was pennies, or so Ellis thought. That it didn't feel real made me feel like I should do something to make it more concrete, so I went on StreetEasy and started browsing apartments I'd soon be able to afford. Sandra texted me back, *Be honest with yourself about what you want and what you're willing to give up to get it.* I read it a few times. I liked it. I even mouthed it softly to myself. I texted Avi, *Be honest with yourself about what you want and what you're willing to give up to get it.* I switched from studios to one-bedrooms.

By 6 Avi still hadn't texted me back. Two hours earlier I took my phone off vibrate-only, a mode it had been on for at least two years. I couldn't go ten minutes without opening it. I tried turning it off and on. I sent myself a message to make sure texting still worked and then one to Louis: *Text me back.* Ten minutes later he wrote, *No.*

When I got out of the subway in Brooklyn I stopped by my café. The last thing I needed was coffee but I never run without it; apparently I was going for a run. At home I changed clothes and skimmed Google Maps. I had never been to Roosevelt Island, which was seven and a half miles away. I knew I could probably do a fifteen-mile round trip but that assumed I would take all the right roads, and that assumption was wrong, and by the time the sun was gone I was desperately lost in Sunnyside. When I asked people how to get to Roosevelt Island they laughed, or gave a fun guess. I dared go into a restaurant to ask, an old-school red sauce joint, my white shirt transparent and my hair dripping. The host just looked at me. I asked if I could at least use the bathroom and he said, *I am sorry I cannot do that.* By the time I made it to the island I'd already run fifteen miles at least and couldn't fathom running back. I wished I'd stayed home and taken half a Xanax. I waited outside the subway turnstiles begging for a swipe and vowed to never turn down the request when I was on the other end. I had to take the F back through Manhattan, a thirty-minute ride just to get to my work stop, and thirty more minutes from there, and if there was any consolation in all of this it would be the killing of time, that when I got home there would be a text waiting for me, which there wasn't.

Against my better judgment I took no Xanax, smoked no weed, threw sleep hygiene to the wind, and started browsing the internet with my screen not six inches from my face. I thought it noble to take the inevitable insomnia in stride, that perhaps this punishment might be the moral rebalancing needed to set karma right again. At midnight I put the laptop away and stared at my ceiling and waited for the ritual to begin: just as sleep seemed near I'd be swept into a parade of recursive thought and self-exhortation, a long, knotted question that never reached punctuation because it always found its way back to the beginning. Mostly I thought about wrongs—wrongs I'd inflicted on others, wrongs that other people had inflicted on me, wrongs I'd inflicted on myself (my forte). My mind kept returning to Avi, of course. As much as he talked about wanting to reach a conclusion, he'd made the conscious decision to punish me with silence. Perhaps texting had been a fraught choice, with each message kept in perpetuity. Yes, I probably should have called, but I knew he wouldn't have answered. No, he preferred for me to feel this way, desperate for information, because that was a form of power, albeit a weak one. To my irrational sleep-deprived brain it didn't seem like a coincidence that the machinations behind the most important moment of my life, the selling of the book, were also completely hidden. Yes, it all seemed to be going on just out of sight, and out of reach.

At some point I couldn't take it anymore. In an especially irreverent mood, I decided to leave my apartment. I put on my slippers and grabbed my phone. My roommate was staying with his girlfriend, so I went into his desk and borrowed a cigarette. As soon as I stepped outside I regretted not bringing a sweater. The night was already hinting at winter. I decided feeling cold was part of the moment. I lit the cigarette and sat on the steps. I wished I had a stoop, and decided my next apartment would be in a brownstone. I took another puff and felt a notch better. A few lights were on across the street. I looked at Franny's building, not sure which exactly was her unit, and tried to recall how we'd got up to her apartment. Squinting, I made out the gold-lined molding of the ceiling of her living room, which was lit. So was her kitchen, where she appeared not a minute later. She was washing a dish, I could tell by the way her head jerked. In an especially honest moment I admitted how jealous of her I was, which shouldn't have been a revelation; everyone was. She'd carefully laid the tracks of her life to arrive at the most coveted prize imaginable: doing what she wanted to do for a living. It didn't matter if someone had some glaring flaw, if she was obnoxious or annoying, self-destructive or inhibited, underappreciated by her partner or single against her will—if her paycheck was her passion she should earn the envy of all the rest of us compromisers. I was sure her business required ungodly amounts of bullshit, of course it did, but that was a different category of compromise. This, I understood then, was how I felt about writing, why I had pursued it with such irrational perseverance, why I was more at peace with myself failing at it than succeeding at anything else. All I'd ever wanted was to do it, really do it, make a life of it, and there was no fucking way I was going to let anything stop me, let someone even threaten to interfere—especially not someone who should have been entirely inconsequential to my life, who said one thing and did another, who pretended to want mature dialogue but was really just a petty shithead. I opened my phone, read my last text to him, and drafted a new one. *Avi, we need to talk about this eventually. I believe there's a resolution out there that we'll both be happy with.* I read it a few times. I finished my cigarette. I entertained going up and getting another but felt like I might be able to fall asleep. I read the text again, deleted the second sentence, and sent it.

I woke up at 7:55, seemingly on my own, but I saw my phone on the bedside table, its outside screen lit, and realized its buzz had broken my dream. I was too tired to make sense of the text, and needed to read it over. *At this point I'd like to discuss with Ellis present.* I started to write back but my phone buzzed again. *Rather, I'll be discussing with Ellis. Whether you are there is up to you.*

I made myself coffee and had a protein bar. I brought my laptop into the kitchen and went on Slack. Our office manager Derek wrote, *I think flu season is already here. Going to need to WFH today.* Dan responded to this with a frowning face and a *Feel better!* so I wrote, *That makes two of us. See y'all tomorrow (hopefully)!* I closed my laptop to think about things. It didn't take long. It seemed I no longer had a choice. My anxiety was immediately transformed from indecision to dread, of postponing the inevitable. If I didn't preempt procrastination the angst would only accumulate. I got my phone and called Ellis but I couldn't do it, I hung up after a ring. I started texting him but he called back. I didn't answer and didn't want to text him because then he'd know I was near my phone, so I wrote him an email, asking to set up a call in a few hours. I took a shower. He wrote me back, *Happy to. And I have more good news: Offers from Seabrook ($55,000) and Perry Books ($85,000), a pre-empt (as I said we might get) which we're going to turn down (can discuss if needed). Wouldn't be surprised if we get another today. I'm setting our deadline for Friday. Give me a call at noon to talk through all?* I wrote back, *Sure,* and played online chess. I lost four times in a row and then checked my work email. I only had one message, a note from Sneha about holding off on the messaging project *until we can circle back with the Acquirers.* I did push-ups, then tried calming myself with music. I once read that listening to high-tempo music doesn't necessarily make you run faster, it's all about where the beat subdivides in relation to your own pace. I measured my

heart rate, which was eighty. Normally it's in the fifties. I tried
searching for music with a tempo in the fifties but it was too
slow, so I Googled *110 beats per minute* and found that that was
allegretto. I searched Spotify for *allegretto* and ended up on an
aria by Mozart. I tried to appreciate it but I couldn't, it was te-
dious. My knee was bouncing repeatedly. The microwave clock
said it was 8:24, which was 216 minutes from noon. I called Ellis
and he picked up immediately. We made small talk. He asked
how excited I was and I said I was very excited. I'd meant to
bring it up right then but I couldn't even begin to form the words,
and besides, he had a lot to tell me and maybe once I delivered
the news he wouldn't, maybe he would punish me, withhold information from me for withholding information from him—no,
of course he wouldn't do that, but still my instinct to delay was
right, yes, it should be framed as an afterthought, something I
was only adding as a sort of *by the way*. He started giving me
background on the editors at Seabrook and Perry, and while he
was telling me some of the books they'd edited I tried to find the
same info online. The editor at Perry was named Terrence Copeland and he didn't have a Twitter account. On further research I
realized this was because he was sixty-three. Apparently he had
edited two of the books I read in my creative writing class in
college. Ellis started explaining the rationale behind setting the
deadline for Friday, and I let him talk though I could hardly listen. I wanted to say, *However the hell we can get the most money*,
but really I wasn't supposed to care only about that, there were
other considerations like finding the right editor for the book, et
cetera. Soon I could no longer pay attention for five straight
words, all I could think about was what his face looked like then,

and what it would look like as I told him the story. When he said, *And we'll just have to wait and see*, I knew the call was winding to a close, that this was my last chance, so I told him I wanted to discuss something. I said this so nonchalantly he probably thought I was going to suggest cover options. Then I told him everything.

Well, not everything, not all of what I told Sandra but all of what he might have to hear from Avi. At first he didn't quite get it, which was my mistake, I led with the fact that my novel was based on a real incident, real people. He stopped me to ask if I'd changed the names. I said I hadn't but that wasn't the point. I started over from the beginning, the real beginning, Los Angeles. From then on he hardly said anything except when I asked if he was there, to which he replied, *Yes*. When I finished he said my name, *Caleb*, and then he paused and said it again. When I responded he produced a short, mean laugh that made me feel terrible, like I was a seven-year-old in trouble. He asked why I hadn't brought this up earlier. Before I could answer he asked if I knew how much of a limb he'd gone out on for me. I couldn't help but think of the logical fallacy built into the question—if it assumed that when he signed me he knew all of what I just told him, if he knew what he was getting himself into, then not a long limb, and if it more practically assumed he knew only what he could know, then still a very short limb, not a limb at all. I realized my toes had been curling up in my slippers since I started telling the story. *This guy*, he said, *is he in New York?* I realized the one detail I had left out was what Avi did, and I told him. The silence lasted more than ten seconds. I thought to ask if he was still there but I could hear white noise so I just waited. I took the time to look out the window and see how bad my floaters were; they were pretty good but probably just because it was overcast. *Okay, Caleb,* he said finally, *okay.* He sounded friendlier than normal, upbeat even, condescendingly affable. *So let's, uh, let's do this. Let's have you come into the office today at two. And I want you to have Avi come at three, if he can. I mean, I'm sure he can, tell him it's the only time I can meet all week. I'll send you an email with the address and how to get in, which you'll pass on to him. He can't be getting in touch with me directly. And listen, also, it's very important you don't say anything more to him, besides about the meeting. Okay?* I confirmed. *I also want you to forward me every exchange you've had about this, emails and texts and whatever else, and his story, of course, just forward me the email that he sent with it.* I told him that that was a brilliant idea, that once he read it he'd understand what a lunatic Avi was, that there was nothing to worry about. He didn't respond to that, instead he said not to be a second late and then, his voice unrealistically calm, *I can only help you if you help me, Caleb. When I take on a new client, my assumption is that they are telling me everything. We've made it too far now. Anything that happens from here on out, well, you'll only have yourself to blame.*

The receptionist took my name and directed me to a burnt orange couch, mid-century modern. She smiled and watched as I found a comfortable position, which made the task impossible; eventually I just forced myself to stop moving, my right ass bone kissing the wood beneath the cushion. I smiled back at her and she returned to her computer. The office was well lit, filled with gray cubicles. The carpet was like brown noise. Everything seemed out of touch but it worked, lent it an old-fashioned vibe, publishing perhaps one of the only industries that treats deference to tradition as a stylistic virtue. I watched a few people milling about and immediately regretted my outfit. They wore silk blouses, wool sweaters, nice pants, leather shoes without socks or socks that were smart, somehow. I knew most agencies didn't operate under such a code, but I hadn't signed with most agencies, I'd signed with Willet Damsey, Ltd. That morning I had picked out my outfit to say, *Yes I'm contrite because I have made a mistake but I'm also, foremost, an artist.* This idea was expressed through an ill-fitting large green sweater and old black jeans, argyle socks, and leather brogues. I rolled up my sleeves and picked a book from the coffee table. It was *Cloudsplitter* by Russell Banks, which, according to the sticker on its cover, had been a Pulitzer finalist in 1999. I hadn't heard of it. I opened to the first chapter and read, *Upon waking this cold, gray morning from a troubled sleep, I realized for the hundredth time, but this time with deep conviction, that my words and behavior towards you were disrespectful, and rude and selfish as—* The receptionist called my name. I wanted to finish the sentence but she was looking at me intently. I stood up and followed as she escorted me to what must have been the farthest office on the floor. On the way I remembered to switch my phone to vibrate mode, which is illustrated by a cartoon of a speaker with a bow tie, which I found funny, because I was incredibly nervous, or maybe it was funny, that today people who wear bow ties aren't very polite, they work for

Goldman Sachs or appear on Fox News. Before I saw Ellis I saw what he saw every working hour: a view of all of Manhattan, or at least everything below 57th Street. It looked like a miniature version of the city, one you could destroy with the press of your thumb. He was speaking to someone, a young man I gathered was an assistant by the way he failed to look Ellis in the eye or even hold his shoulders square to him. He must have been 120 pounds. His sweater was grungier than mine but looked expensive, his pants tighter than mine but better fitting. They were talking about a manuscript, apparently. Ellis told the assistant that he had to look past stylistic tics to the story, that if the latter was there the former could be ironed away. It wasn't until the assistant walked out that Ellis acknowledged my presence, first with a palm out to the chair on the other side of his desk, and then with a word, *Please*, spoken as if it were the last of a soliloquy. He offered me a drink and hardly waited for me to decline before moving on. It was a snub, small but certain. I stopped myself from swallowing. I heard the cars on the street eleven floors below. Something had been pulling at me since we first made eye contact, and suddenly I saw it in all of its horrible simplicity: I'd been wrong. I'd miscalculated, badly. I'd made assumptions I shouldn't have, not just that Avi's story would all but exonerate me, but that Ellis would be, to his grave, my dedicated handler, my perpetually positive advocate. When I looked back up at him it seemed that he was making a show of his anger, performing it.

Did you remember to get in touch with Avi? he asked. This wasn't a fair question but it was also quite fair. I almost hadn't. I remembered just as I hopped on the subway on the way here. Luckily Quartz's office was a ten-minute walk away and he responded immediately: *Sure, see you soon.*

Of course, I said. *He said three worked well.* Ellis again asked if I wanted coffee, said it would be a long meeting and, *You should have your wits about you.* I accepted and he called in the receptionist and told her to bring two. When she walked away he looked at me for a protracted moment and then asked for a description of Avi. I reiterated how we met and our relationship in college, which was hardly one. He looked like he wanted more and I said he was a good dresser and generally kind. He swatted a fly away from his face and made an annoyed expression. I didn't see the fly and entertained the thought that he was playing mind games, which I appreciated in some small way; if he could do this to me I could only imagine what he'd do to Avi.

Jesus Christ, he said. *Caleb. Don't be careful. Three o'clock is when we're careful. Now tell me what he's like, like you were, you know, describing him to a friend, writing him in a story.*

I thought for a moment and then said he was the type of person to worry about saying the right thing, the type to see himself in the third person and be socially inhibited by this fact. I said that I didn't know a thing about his family but I'd bet they were nothing like him. The receptionist came in with our coffees. It seemed to me she was extending the process in order to catch some gossip. Apparently Ellis did too. *Ruth*, he said, *please.* She nodded and smiled at me and walked out. When I couldn't hear her footsteps on the carpet anymore I said that I couldn't imagine Avi thinking basic carnal thoughts like *I want something sweet* or *I have to use the restroom.* Ellis nodded along like I was doing a good job, and when I ran out of these weird oblique descriptors he smiled, finally. He took a sip and then I took a sip, and he told me that Avi could sue. I said that I'd done my research, that he had no basis to sue, and Ellis said it didn't matter. *The very mess of it would be enough to scare away even the most enthusiastic editor. And if we don't say something until we have a contract, they'll be able to negate it under false pretense.*

Avi wouldn't sue, I said.

Maybe not, Ellis said, seemingly in agreement. *Not that it matters.* He took another sip and took a second to think to himself. *Why do you think he wouldn't sue?*

I don't know, I said. *Maybe because he wouldn't want to drag himself through litigation?* Ellis wagged his head back and forth, asking for a different answer. *Well, I don't think he'd get much out of it.*

Mhm. He picked up a blue stress ball, inspected it, and then threw it up in the air to himself. I didn't know what that *Mhm* meant and was building up the courage to ask when a knock came at the door. I was expecting Ellis's face to fall again into irritation, but it lifted with delight. He waved in a tall pale man in a fitted gray suit and a forest-green tie. They shook hands and the man sat next to me. At that angle I had a perfect view of the curve of his dome, which was long and mesmerizing, like it adhered to a very simple formula. J. K. Simmons, that's who he looked like, except he had more hair above his ears, and also his features didn't make sense the way movie stars' do. He was choosing not to acknowledge me until Ellis introduced us.

Caleb, Ellis said, *I want you to meet our counsel in this matter. This is Rupert Paul. He's an expert in this sort of stuff, and also a friend.* It was an unfortunate name; he looked about RuPaul's age too. I wouldn't believe the two of them were friends, and as I tried to imagine them getting a beer he turned to me and offered his hand. I looked in his eyes and saw nothing. I asked what *this sort of stuff* was, exactly. Rupert was about to give me what I assumed would be a very literal answer when Ellis interjected. *The absolute best thing that can come out of the meeting today is for all parties to agree on a resolution, so Rupert can write it up and it can be signed, sealed, and delivered before the whole business of the book wraps up. I'm talking tomorrow end of day. At the latest. After that point things get a lot trickier. To be clear and up-front with you, I'm not going to sign this off to a publisher without that contract.* He looked at me for confirmation and I nodded. He gave a hard knock on the table and said he wanted to use the rest of the time before 3 for any questions Rupert might have. Rupert folded his hands over his knee and turned slightly toward me. He asked for the entire story from beginning to end and I told it to him as I'd told it to Ellis, except this time I had to stop every other sentence for the sake of a clarification. When I'd gone to L.A., was I a resident of New York or Florida? Was Avi on a state scholarship? As I was writing my manuscript did I reopen his? Would there be any record of this? How did I pay for my apartment in Eugene? Had I told anyone about what I was writing? Did I alert any institution—a bank, for example—that I was living in Eugene? Who did I spend most of my time with there? In Florida? Before Florida, in New York? I hadn't even gotten to the point in the story where I finish the manuscript when the receptionist called to say Avi had arrived. Ellis told her to bring him in after she had four more coffees ready. He looked at me sincerely and said, *Be careful what comes out of your mouth and what doesn't. Decide what you need and what you want and, most importantly, the difference.*

Minutes later Avi walked in with the receptionist. Apparently he'd gotten the memo about attire; he had on the same outfit he was wearing at Franny's. He took the only available seat, which was next to Ellis, facing Rupert and me. Anyone walking in would assume he and Ellis were on one team, and Rupert and I on the other. I had a feeling that this wasn't an accident on Ellis's part, that in fact his plan wasn't to intimidate or cow Avi, but the opposite—to draw information out of him, make him think he had a partner. Ellis thanked him for coming, and then introduced Rupert only as *a bank of information for all of us to draw from.* Rupert instigated a handshake but they were obviously too far away so he turned it into an awkward wave, a chance for us all to laugh the nervous energy away.

So, to start us off, Ellis began, his tone too pitch-perfect not to have been rehearsed, *let me just say that the reason we're all here is because something great has happened, is happening. We shouldn't lose sight of that. Caleb has written a book that the world wants to read, and I know that we can overcome any barriers in the way of that happening. There's no real reason to reiterate all of what's occurred, because we'll only get stuck on the details. I don't want to get stuck on details. I want to have a truthful, earnest discussion. I know we all agree on a basic outline of how things unfolded, and I want to work from that.* He looked to Avi and then me, capturing a nod from both of us. *So, now that we've gotten the first two hours of this meeting out of the way, I have some thoughts of my own to share.* He turned to Avi and placed a palm on the desk. *Caleb forwarded me your story, which I've read, which I hope is all right by you. I think it's a fact that we have two tremendous writers in the room.* He looked at me and I nodded. I'm usually repulsed by such unapologetic dishonesty, though I couldn't help but admire Ellis's nearly psychopathic ability to communicate, both verbally and otherwise, something he knew to be false. I briefly wondered if people like him were born with such ruthless guile or if they only came to acquire it as a necessary tool for success—that it's actually ambition that makes them exceptional, open to sacrifices of the soul that others deny themselves. *Honestly*—he took a moment to nod to himself, agreeing with what he was about to say—*if you were looking for representation down the road, this is something I'd love to discuss—down the road, as I said. But this story you've written, when I'm comparing it to the manuscript we're currently shopping, well, it's not the same story. It has similar characters and a similar plot, but it doesn't have the same*—he rubbed his fingers together, almost like the gesture for money—*texture. To put it bluntly, it isn't drawing from the same well. To put it even more bluntly, this isn't a case of overlapping intellectual property. These two stories exist as separate entities, and I don't think anyone, given the full case, would disagree. Now what I—*

That's not my concern, Avi said, staring unflinchingly at Ellis, who had apparently never been interrupted before; his lips continued to move but produced no sound. *You seem to be suggesting that Caleb's manuscript doesn't impinge on my ability to use my story, which it does.* He coughed without breaking eye contact. *Though I don't mean to imply that's my fundamental intent for this meeting— to be able to use my story for my own purposes.*

What is your intent? Rupert asked.

My intent is for justice to be served, he said, the rhapsodic phrasing redeemed by a sincerity I found impressive.

And how might that be achieved, in your view? Ellis asked, and then more to the point, *Do you mean financial remuneration?*

Avi made an awkward face meant to convey the transition was gauche, but I could tell by his expression he'd also actually taken offense. *Financial remuneration*, Avi said. *I don't even know what that would look like, what type of money we're dealing with, what's on the table and—*

Please, Ellis said, holding up his hand, serving the interruption back. *We're not there yet. And if we were going to talk numbers they'd be in the form of percentages. How my discussions with editors play out shouldn't distort what we agree is fair today.*

Wait, I said, unsure what I would follow with. Actually, that's all I wanted—for everyone to wait, to just stop talking so I could think. *I never agreed to talking about percentages. I never agreed to anything.*

Caleb, Avi said, looking at me for the first time. *This book wouldn't exist without both of us. If you're not willing to admit that and have a discussion, then I'm happy to walk out right now and find my own lawyer.*

Instead of answering I chose to take a sip. But as I waited for Ellis or Rupert to pick up the conversation I realized they were both expecting me to respond. *I think*, I started, and then stopped, looking at Ellis. His head was down but his eyes sprang up to meet mine for a fortifying instant. *Right, you're right. It wouldn't have existed without the both of us, not that we both contributed equally.*

And isn't it as simple as that? Avi asked. *If it wouldn't have existed without both of us, then any step forward has to involve both of us. And that alone should imply equality across the board—in everything, I mean.*

You don't mean everything, I said.

Yes, Avi said. *I do.*

Okay, Ellis said, leaning over his desk. *Let me put terms to your words so, well, you know what* exactly *you're suggesting.* He widened his eyes playfully, letting us know he didn't put too much stock in what he was about to say. *You split everything. The book has two authors, you each get half the profit.*

Okay, Avi said, not confirming or negating that this was what he meant. *I mean, how would that work? It would be like we wrote it together?*

Sure, Ellis said, shrugging jovially. *You're a tag team writing duo. You wrote this together every night, side by side, and during the day you sent notes back and forth. Or, alternatively, you can just be honest. Avi came up with the idea, and Caleb wrote the book. All that matters is that whatever story you land on, you stick to it. Remember, you two would be doing interviews together, and readings, and signings. With any luck you'd go on tour together.* My instinct was to glance at Avi but I could tell he was looking at me. I briefly wondered how easy it was to undo hate, to be okay with someone you'd once believed was the bane of your existence. Then I considered it from his point of view.

So we'd be, like, photographed together? he asked. I found the question embarrassing, but of course I also wanted to know the answer.

That would make sense to me, Ellis said. *It would be like you're a band. Like Simon and Garfunkel. Or Macklemore and what's-his-name.* Now I took the chance and looked at Avi. Even steeped in consternation he looked effortless, at home in the world. There was no question who, of the two of us, would be what's-his-name. I imagined Avi fielding questions at readings, smiling at even the dumbest ones, being the one who people come up to afterward to talk more with.

What are the other options? I asked.

He took a moment to forge eye contact with both of us. *Let's try this. How about each of you takes a moment to think to yourself, silently, about what you hope to walk away with today. Really think about it. And then we'll see where those visions overlap.* I nodded and looked at Avi, who was already in thought. I felt Ellis's eyes on me and looked up. We exchanged a look I didn't quite understand, but which seemed to punctuate what he'd just said. What did I want to walk away with? I was amazed at how hard it was to even penetrate the question. I could only think about minimizing my loss, preventing Avi from taking what was mine—not what *I* actually wanted. The harder I thought about what to say, the blurrier the words became in my head. Really I wanted to strategize, plan three moves ahead, but the reality was I couldn't, and before I could think myself into some contrivance I couldn't dig myself out of, I spoke the truth. *I see writing a book as bringing something into the world. What I did is bring this story into existence.* It felt good to be so honest, it gave me confidence, and as I continued I no longer kept my head down. *Without me it would still just be an experience someone had. The only reason we're discussing it now is because now it has value attached to it. And I know that I've created that value myself.*

Ellis nodded at me and turned to Avi. *Do you agree with that?* he asked.

Avi had clasped his hands and put them on his chest, a position that let his arms transmit the rate of his breathing, which was slow. *I see a book as the delivery of a story, a medium for it, and the story is mine.*

Great, Ellis said. *That's great, really. Ostensibly you're disagreeing, but I think because of it we have a much better idea of what you each expect.* He was right, somehow. The air in the room was clearing. It felt like we were standing on top of a hill, but didn't know in which direction to advance. He looked deep in thought, and then turned to his laptop and opened it. As he began to type and click around, his brow furrowed until it slackened entirely. *Ah, that's right,* he said. *Solomon's baby.* He closed the laptop and set it aside. *It's a story from the Bible, where two women each claim a baby is theirs.* In laborious detail he told the whole parable, finishing with the obvious lesson: *What I'm getting at is that neither of you seems okay with splitting the novel, and from this I can tell that you each, rightfully, feel it's yours. And if I'm also implying that splitting the thing would kill it, well, so be it.* In my pocket I felt my phone vibrate, just once, a text. *I don't mean to get too personal here, but I sense that the two of you don't really want to spend any more time with each other than what's necessary.* He looked at Avi and then me, his eyes suddenly carrying something intense, they were widening, barely. As I stared back his lids began to fall, a small show of annoyance. At me? For an instant he peered down to the table, no, to beyond the table. I looked down to my pocket and he started talking again, continuing on with the Solomon bullshit. Slowly I took the phone out and, pushing it close to my stomach, opened it. *30 min ago Carrington offered 220k.*

Hey, Ellis said. *Attention in the room, please.* I swallowed and apologized, and he cleared his throat and continued. *You two are different people. You want different things, and you seem to have irreconcilable convictions about what you deserve. But that just might be, well, it could be our big advantage here. In fact, I think the answer is already on the table, and I think you each had a hand in putting it there. What I'm about to say is a bit outlandish, I know, but I want you to think about how I got there. Caleb, you believe you deserve the book's value, and Avi, you want the recognition. I say we make that happen.* We all knew what was being suggested, but Rupert, after some verbal throat-clearing, put it in terms only a lawyer could. *What Ellis proposes is that Caleb retains all profit created by said manuscript and the exploitation thereof, while Avi retains the right to put his name on the work and all others derived therefrom.*

That's interesting, Avi said, too easily betraying his own satisfaction with the proposal.

It might be, I said, *if only every publishing house in New York hadn't already seen my name on it. After all, you don't just buy a book, you buy the writer.*

This thought was apparently so idiotic that Ellis could hardly contain a guffaw. *Jesus Christ*, he said. *I mean, Caleb, you're an unknown debut author. And yes, there'd be some clearing up to be done, but the explanation's ready-made: it was shopped under your name because Avi was worried editors would know him. He was embarrassed to be connected with it, especially given the graphic nature of the plot.* I looked to Avi, catching his glance before he sent it back to Ellis. *The truth is this wasn't a collaboration. One of you picked up where the other left off. We have to find a way of representing that.* Again I looked to Avi, who had now decided to hide all emotion. Rupert tapped his pen against the table and said some encouraging words that I couldn't hear because I was approaching tunnel vision. Then Avi spoke and I came back into the room.

You might not think it's fair. I can understand that, he said, eyeing the edge of the table. *I don't think it's fair, either, which is why I agree with Ellis. It's not that I think I deserve more or less than you. I just think we deserve different things.*

Deserve is such a good word, Ellis said, looking at me, passing the same intense stare as when he'd sent the text. *I think you should really think about what you deserve.*

I swallowed. *I'll need to*, I said. *Think about it, I mean.*

I'd be fine giving you creative control, Avi said, *if that's what you're worried about. All of the edits and all of that.* Was he just pawning work off on me? I didn't want to look at him to see.

Thanks for that, Ellis said. *That's helpful, though to be honest I don't anticipate there being much in the way of edits, except of course the names, which I'd like to come to some agreement on.*

The names? Avi asked.

Ellis nodded and then looked at me. *As I'm to understand it, these characters are based on real people, and*—

The names have already been changed, Avi said.

Great, Ellis said. *Another item off the list.*

I turned to Avi and saw, beneath a stony stare, embarrassment, vulnerability. At first I couldn't find its source, thought that maybe he was only self-conscious about the names he'd picked for the characters, a fraught exercise if ever there was one.

But then I thought back, recalling when he told me what actually happened. Yes, even then he'd used the new names, was thinking in terms of the story he was writing, not of the people he'd actually spent time with—the woman he was once, supposedly, heartbroken over. It struck me that I'd underestimated how much stock he'd put in that story, how much potential he thought he had as a writer, how sensitive he must be to the facts of the case: that I was more talented, that I had brought to life something he couldn't.

It wasn't long before talking became perfunctory. I racked my brain trying to find a new solution, but couldn't; in fact, the harder I tried, the worse my ideas were. Other arrangements were offered by the group and briefly entertained. Mostly they gave Avi some of the profit and me some of the authorial stake. But *stake* never meant anything more than being labeled a ghostwriter, and I didn't care for that, care enough to give Avi a cent of what should be mine—what was, at the very least, three times my salary.

As we wound down the meeting—reiterating what had already been said, scattering easy jokes where we could, reverting to small talk—I felt the fulcrum of the decision bearing down on me. They had all made it clear in word and tone that the new arrangement worked for them, that if I wasn't happy with it I should be the one to suggest something new. As I watched Avi smile, loosen up, betray his relief, I had to continually remind myself that he had no idea just how much he was giving up. Not that I had any real idea of it either. How much was $220,000, really?

Postcoitus. Sober sex, at last. It was supposed to be meaningful and of course it was, not to mention wildly exciting and, well, I began to feel like I was falling in love, I came close to telling her so as I was close to coming but didn't, thank God. Yes, it was meaningful, but that isn't to say it couldn't have been more so—it could have, if I'd had a clear mind, for example, if I could have been sure I could close my eyes and not think of Ellis's office, Avi's smirk, the weakness in my legs as I stood to leave.

We'd met outside my apartment. She wanted to hear all about the meeting and I wanted to do anything to avoid thinking about it, and when we kissed in the elevator I conveyed the distraction I was thinking of, and it wasn't three minutes before we were in bed. But once it ended—an eventuality I should have foreseen—there was nowhere to go. She asked about the day again, nicely, twirling my hair, smiling at me in that way which would have been manipulative if it wasn't so pure. I told her. It was recent enough that I could recite dialogue, the exact arc of the conversation. I hardly even needed to think about it.

Minutes passed before she spoke. *Two hundred and twenty thousand dollars*, she said, finally.

It's a lot, I said.

And that's just the minimum.

I'd assume it caps around there.

She opened her mouth but closed it. Instead she just watched me, her head turned away but her eyes tracking mine.

What? I asked. She didn't say anything. We'd hardly known each other a week and already she could see through me. *What?* I said again.

Do you really believe that? That it won't go higher?

Maybe. Sure.

You don't. She sat up on her knees. *You fucking don't, and you should think about that.*

No cussing.

I'm being serious, Caleb. Follow that thought. Why'd you lie?

It wasn't a lie, I was just—

Fine, whatever. Why won't you admit it's going to go higher?

I don't know.

You do know. It's because you don't want to sound like you're being bought, that your principles might possibly be corruptible. But they are, everyone's principles have a price. That's why they're called principles. To be completely honest, it sounds like you're only protecting yourself from what you actually want. To want money doesn't mean you want, like, a nice car or clothes or whatever, it can mean you want freedom, time—time to write, space to write. You want to be a writer, Caleb. But a writer isn't someone who writes one book. You have more in you, I know you do, and you have a great agent willing to represent you. She seemed to have just caught herself, that she'd long relinquished the pretense of impartiality. Her expression said that she wasn't going back, she would no longer hide her opinion, but that I had to stop pretending too.

I let myself listen for my roommate in the apartment, the sounds I'd trained myself to perpetually ignore. By the noises coming from his room, I could tell he was watching *Family Guy*. By the TV's volume, I knew his door was open. How often had I thought of his existence while having sex? How many pubic hairs on the toilet seat were his? How much more frequently would I clean—or, more realistically, have my place cleaned—if I didn't live with him? Was this the life I imagined for myself in three, five, ten years? And if my current "career"—as a soon-to-be Wells Fargo lifer—was going to get me all the things I wanted (my own place, some savings for a house, kids, their education), was it really how I wanted to get there? By Sandra's face I sensed these thoughts were showing themselves on mine. I felt exposed, ashamed even. But for what exactly? For knowing what I wanted? Wasn't that the very thing I was trying to figure out?

———

When I woke up I forgot Sandra was in the bed. I offered to cook breakfast but she said she should go, her dad's aides were switching shifts soon and she liked to be there for that. After she left I made myself eggs, which I never do alone but I already had it in mind. I watched NY1 to continue the theme of doing things I never do. It seemed odd that every other man-on-the-street segment was conducted under scaffolding. If I hadn't been so tired I would have found the metaphor there. I started playing chess and opened my email. There were two messages from Ellis. The first contained a contract, with Avi and Rupert cc'd, sent at 6:13 a.m. He requested signatures from Avi and me by the end of the day, noting that if he didn't have them then, we'd have to consider withdrawing our manuscript, which could *significantly, meaningfully impact our chances of a later sale.* The second had been sent at 8 on the nose, just to me: *Seabrook upped the ante, topping Carrington at 250,000. Not to get you too excited but I'm getting the feeling this is going to hit even higher. Just something to think about.*

I just missed the C and had to wait fifteen minutes for the next one. The F, my transfer, was down, there had been a *switch*

malfunction, also known as force majeure, so I waited to get back
on the next C and transferred at West 4th back downtown. At
the office I got in the elevator with a man who was holding a
pack of silver balloons. Right before the doors closed a woman
came in who looked fussy, chronically. She squealed when she
saw the balloons. *Oh my God, Den is going to be so freakin' surprised*, she said, and squealed again. She was so enraptured by
the balloons she didn't notice her handbag was over the door
sensor, that it had tried to close three times now. She pushed the
button for floor five even though it was already lit and then she
poked a balloon. I put my hand between her bag and the entrance and she looked at me like I'd exposed myself. For the rest
of the ride everyone was silent, which turned out to be an apt
segue into the office atmosphere. Again I was the last one in,
except this time no one said hello or even looked up. Like the
day before, they were all working industriously, faces awash in
the glow of their screens. But something was wrong; there was
an eerie emptiness. It took me a few minutes to realize what it
was: there was no music playing. I scanned a few faces and understood the mood wasn't due only to the silence. On Slack I
wrote to Derek, *what the hell is going on*, and he wrote back, *check
your email*. There was a message from Dan, subject line: Acquisition Documents—To Be Signed By 5 PM. The email itself was a
long-winded congratulations I could tell said nothing of import.
I opened up the contract, which was thirty-nine pages of ten-
point legal type. I wrote to Derek, *help*, and he wrote, *go to page
9*. The header was "Entitlements Regarding Acquisition of
Shares." I started reading and then went back on Slack but Derek
was already typing so I waited for him to send his message:

they're accelerating stock vesting which is all well and good but what D didn't tell us is that we're only for sure entitled to a quarter of it. for the rest of the shares we as a company have to "earn out," meaning hit goals which are usually crafted to ensure we won't hit them. and not just that, the portion we do get is being doled out in four fucking "tranches," one a quarter. A quarter of a quarter of $45,000 was not even $3,000, pre-tax. *ah,* I wrote. *thanks.* I searched the contract for the term *earn out* and found nothing and then gathered all the concentration I had and figured out where it was, on the third-to-last page. It took up no more than ten lines. There were three goals, the first being the only one we could possibly achieve. It was to grow by fifteen thousand users in a single financial quarter, something we were projected to accomplish in a year, but that projection had been made only to pitch investors. I went to the kitchen and grabbed a handful of chocolates. I ate them ravenously at my desk, and then signed the acquisition contract. I went back to the kitchen, got twice as much chocolate, returned to my desk, and opened Ellis's email. I started reading the contract, trudging through Rupert's turgid legalese. I thought of him writing it, saying the words out loud to himself. I imagined he punched the keys with one finger of each hand. I imagined he had bad breath but in a unique way. It was eight pages but all of the salient details were in a boxed paragraph on the last page, spelled out quite clearly and with surprisingly minimal jargon. I'd only have to check a box and write my name next to it in a text field that automatically converted my letters to a signature-style font.

I went to the kitchen to get a glass of milk, a treat I rarely allowed myself, considering it was whole and meant for the coffee. Only after I took my first sip did I realize Dan was sitting at the table, peeling an orange. I tried to conceal my surprise. He said, *Hey there, bud*. I laughed like it was a joke and he asked me how I was doing, gesturing for me to sit across from him. Beside his large veiny forearm was a bottle full of murky brown liquid with a logo that looked like rage, illustrated. We made conversation about the differences between whey and casein protein, and he implored me to amp up my workout any way I could. I wondered if he noticed that people were upset. Maybe he was just programmed not to. It seemed to me then that what might have been a flaw fifty years ago—a lack of concern for the emotional states of others—was now a required trait for his kind of success. He asked me if something was on my mind, tilting his head and narrowing his eyes just enough to let me know he was reading all my thoughts just before I was. Maybe I was completely wrong about him. I asked if he was nervous to be giving up something he worked so hard on. He paused, as if he were really thinking about it. I waited with bated breath, expecting some succinct but brilliant epigram, one that would put to rest both of our problems and maybe all of the world's. He smiled and said that he was optimistic nothing would change. *We've got some great partners in Wells Fargo. Can hardly think of better hands to put my baby in*. He excused himself and left.

I sat back at my desk and realized I'd forgotten the milk. I opened up the contract and skimmed all eight pages, doing my due diligence without really reading. I checked my phone and saw that I had no messages, and I signed.

Part II

~~~~

May 2018

Can we go a little higher this time? Like this? I tried mimicking something I couldn't even put into words, but he knew what I meant. Mario always knew. He reached for a tool he'd once described to me as *thinning shears* but then thought better of it, paused, and picked the scissors back up. I'd never before had a barber who contemplated.

Is there a special occasion, then? he asked, scouring the back of my head. *You're normally in here monthly.*

I felt a lurch of annoyance even though I knew I shouldn't. *A friend's book launch*, I said, which wasn't exactly true.

Very cool, he said, his eyes flicking up to the mirror. Had he caught my ambivalence?

Yeah, I said. *I'm happy for him.* He gave a genuine smile. He was great at his job, which was not just to cut hair to look expensive but to be as socially fluent as a diplomat. I tried to imagine how well he'd control his expression if I gave him the whole story, not just whose book it actually was, not just that I hadn't even been formally invited to the launch, but that I'd only made the appointment with him today—not, say, yesterday, which would have been ideal, as everyone knows you need to give a haircut a sleep and a shower—because I needed something to do to prevent me from sitting at my laptop, continually refreshing the *New York Times* Books page. Last week Ellis had forwarded

us a note from the director of publicity at Perry Books, who inti-
mated that they expected the *Times* to post their review on the
day of the launch event. I didn't know it worked like that. Maybe
it didn't usually, but Perry's publicity team struck me as quite
capable. (This was either in spite of or because of an apparent
lack of hierarchical structure; I never knew who did what, could
only imagine one superhuman sending emails from three different accounts.) They managed to get the launch—a talk between
Avi and his editor, our editor, Terrence Copeland—in *Time Out*
and the front section of *The New Yorker*, not to mention a good
deal of retweets from publishing bloggers and randos. I can't say
it didn't hurt a little each time, seeing his name. I frequently reminded myself that it would go away eventually, it had to, I only
needed to feel the feeling enough to get numb to it, let it depreciate until it was nothing at all. Yes, *depreciate* was a good word,
the operative word; money doesn't depreciate, or it shouldn't.
No, my accountant had all but guaranteed steady appreciation—
not counting the "fun money" we agreed to throw into some
more volatile bets. (I was now a stakeholder in a company that
used "commercially reared bees" to pollinate crops in the Pacific
Northwest. Even though my stake was quite minor, it was still
exciting to get the quarterly reports.)

I won't say money doesn't change you because this isn't a
commencement speech, and anyway, it does. Of course it does.
How could it not? It's money, liquefied value you can trade for
maybe not everything (love, a good childhood, a good adult-
hood) but by god most things. Like food. No longer was I allergic to anything on the menu that was *market price*. Also, having
good hair, as often as you liked. Sandra and I had monthly ap-

pointments with Mario. I'd get an undercut with layering and something else, I have no idea what. Each time I told him it was the best haircut I'd ever had and it was always true. Sandra would get something even more arcane that adds volume or reduces it, I don't know, but it made her look like she was always on vacation or in an ad for one, and every time she met up with her friends they'd touch it.

The sound of the Nespresso machine filled the air, louder and more mechanical than the Keurig we'd had at Parachute but somehow better, more authentic. *You want?* Mario asked, and I nodded. *Yes, please.*

Of course, there's food and hair and clothes and whatever else, and then there's another category, a higher category. There's money and then there's *means*, as in the means to free yourself from the most fraught love-hate relationship in modern society: a man and his paycheck. If money can't exactly buy you happiness, it can at least buy you out of a certain kind of unhappiness. Actually, money makes the idea of work much more appealing, because it becomes optional, and things that are normally punishing tend to become attractive once they're made voluntary— physical labor becomes going to the gym, taxes become philanthropy, the bad sort of therapy becomes the good kind. And so I considered whether to continue working at Parachute (which was now technically "Parachute, powered by Wells Fargo"), I really gave it some thought, and then more or less politely declined. One week after the deal with Perry (two months before I'd receive my first check of $207,500, or a quarter of my advance; more on that later), I asked Sneha for a meeting. I told her that with the acquisition money I wanted to take some time for myself. Her eyes conveyed that she knew how much stock I had, so I told her the truth, or a very distant cousin of it, which was that I didn't believe in Parachute's mission anymore. Her face first betrayed that she agreed with me, and then that she couldn't believe I was giving up such a cushy job. Finally there was only resentment, because I obviously had money, somewhere. She told me to take my things, and by the time I got home even my Slack account had been disabled.

It took all of two weeks to confirm what I'd suspected since I started my life as an employed person, after a brutal post-college summer when the only thing I wanted was work. It was something I hadn't had the chance to understand in Florida, because the idea of not having a paycheck weighed on me every single day; after Gmail, Bank of America was my most visited website. The realization was that working for a paycheck was a fine way to spend your days but certainly not the best way. The best way was to pursue what you wanted to pursue, on your own terms. (In my case this was writing, something I was slow to pick up again—afraid to, possibly—but recently I'd begun spending the belly of my days on it, had even sent a chunk of a manuscript to Ellis a week ago. He'd yet to respond, but I understood he was busy. I preferred he get a good read in anyway.) Maybe this insight isn't quite at the level of a Chinese proverb, but it goes counter to what most people fundamentally believe, have to believe. I wanted to spread the gospel to Sandra, but I was worried she'd have a knee-jerk reaction against it, or misinterpret me—I didn't think she should *retire*, just think about things. Having been steeped in unemployment for some time, she needed a job to, if nothing else, scrub away the plaque of self-doubt. She'd begun interviewing for positions she clearly didn't want, didn't really want, maybe she wanted them more than other jobs but not more than a career she could be passionate about, something she admitted had eluded her. Her interviews were mostly at consultancies that helped global companies navigate changes in international relations. No doubt these were prized posts, a great way to leverage UN experience, but mostly because of the money, which wasn't something we jointly needed, which was how we were beginning to see ourselves, that is, joined together. Maybe we hadn't said it out loud to each other but we clearly wanted to spend the rest of our lives together. Add to all of this the fact she was taking care of her dad, or helping to, at least; he had a full-time aide but they never did anything exactly right (and occasionally failed to show up on time). I knew the issue of her taking some time off would be a touchy subject. So, one night before we fell asleep, I said, as if it were an afterthought, or a funny thing that happened that day, *You should take time to figure out what you really want to do.* She nodded. I pushed. I told her what my mom had once told me, that your career is like a tree, once it grows in a certain direction it's very hard to turn back. She sat up so she could look me in the eyes. *I'm taking the time I need. And I don't need your consent to do so. Also, no offense to your mom, but careers aren't trees.* By morning I'd forgotten about the exchange, only remembered it because she was being distant. We hardly spoke that week, we barely made eye contact; tension was new to us and, accordingly, fed on itself. In this temporary isolation I began to understand what should have been obvious by then: that as much as we celebrated it together my achievement was not hers, that the happiness it gave her would always be somewhat second-order, that perhaps it even contributed to the mounting pressure she felt to realize her potential. The week-long cold war ended with her telling me, over breakfast, about her mom's career in politics, as a campaign manager. (She'd passed away twenty years before I met Sandra, from breast cancer.) Her mom missed the chance to work on a senatorial campaign when she became pregnant with Sandra, and was still clawing her way back when, five years later, she received her diagnosis. We never spoke of that week, but the memory of it saved me from ever again giving her unsolicited career advice. The day after we reconciled, her first job offer came in, which she declined. Apparently she'd decided to apply to graduate school, in international affairs, and had already started her essays.

Mario placed a cup and saucer on a chairside table meant for that very purpose. He stopped working, waiting for me to take a sip, and another.

Even as we were living in it I knew this period of our lives would always be some sort of golden age. Our apartment was continually well kept for guests, the flowers alive, the pantry filled. Friends came more days than they didn't, for cocktails and parties, lunches and dinners, book clubs and board game nights, but also the best sort of event: the laissez-faire, sprawling, all-day drink-and-eat-and-smoke-and-do-nothing thing. My instinct is to use that dreaded word—*salon*—but even if that hadn't been co-opted for pseudo-intellectual gatherings overstuffed with MFAs and cheap wine, it wasn't exactly right, because it implies a focus, and this type of get-together was wonderful for its lack of one. Someone would be reading a newspaper alone, two people would be playing chess, three would be out on the fire escape smoking, a few eating leftovers in the kitchen and the rest collapsed on couches and chairs, talking about whatever, hopefully contradicting each other and themselves. All that mattered was that the right people were there, and that's really where the effort was. We were never not on the lookout for new faces, and no relationship was too tenuous to prompt an invitation. It wasn't about how someone looked or if he or she fit in in any definable way; I'd fill our apartment with investment bankers from the Upper East Side if I knew they and everyone around them would have fun and feel at ease. And this—the having fun and feeling at ease—was where Sandra shone most. In her I'd unwittingly found the best possible partner for such an endeavor. She thought things out before they needed to be, knew what should be perfectly in place and what should be left to serendipity, had a way of making everyone feel included while instilling an air of privacy—but most of all she let people let their guard down. (Even when I had invited someone into the group, it was she who knew how to fold them in. She could sense who anyone would click with and, more importantly, who they wouldn't.) She gave you honesty and expected it back, and beyond that she passed no judgment. Between our walls there was no pretense or posturing, not by rule but by intuition. A friend of ours once said that most socializing involves people waiting to go home; we believed our events to be successes only if our guests dreaded leaving.

Here we are, Mario said, holding a mirror to the back of my head. My instinct was to ruminate, as when a waiter has you taste the wine, but Mario knew better. *It's perfect*, I said. *I wouldn't change a single hair.*

When I got inside I pretended to have patience. I'd done the same thing in high school when my college admission letters started arriving. I'd put the letter on my desk and start my homework, or read a magazine, knowing that no matter what my fate was I had decided on its delivery. My laptop was in the bedroom, so I went to the living room, not sure what exactly I'd do there. It had just been cleaned, so I made an honest effort to appraise the cleaning. I walked up to the window and inspected the glass. It was my first bay window, something I'd always wanted, a constant in all my daydreams about a vaguely successful future. Outside the trees were blooming, my block full of the ones that smelled like semen in the first few weeks of spring. I breathed deeply. All I could smell was the apartment, its natural scent, something that delighted me and yet I still had no idea what it was. I walked over to where the couch was going to go. I'd never bought an unused couch before. And this wasn't just any couch, it was a couch that *could make a room*, as Sandra said, quoting a nameless friend who was obviously Franny. Most of Sandra's opinions about furniture I knew I was getting secondhand, but we had an implicit agreement not to say her name. In the first of our interior design planning sessions Sandra floated the idea of buying a chair or two from her. I immediately said no and then regretted it, told her later that night she should buy what she wanted, I just didn't want to know where it came from. Then, a week later, two of them materialized in the living room, beautiful cane-back chairs with tapered legs, their wood a light brown that reminded me of human hair. I'd put them in the corner facing the wall, like they were in time-out, and they hadn't been moved since. They did rhyme with other aspects of our place, though, the molding on the ceiling and my wonderful maple desk that was left by the previous inhabitants, and the lobby of course and even the building's facade. All these components were of the same time period, though I couldn't say exactly when. *Victorian* seemed right, but so did *pre-war*. (Then again, as Ezra Koenig once sang, aren't all apartments pre-war?) Franny would know the time period, she could apparently time-travel there, how else could she manufacture something so seemingly entrenched in history, something that probably cost a fortune and yet didn't make me feel guilty? This not feeling guilty was apparently an acquired talent, one I hadn't yet mastered but I was getting there; I no longer felt self-conscious as I wrote our rent check. We chose Fort Greene to be close to her dad, who lived in a rent-stabilized apartment a block away. Our broker told us rental prices were triangulated among location, building/amenities, and size. He said that if our budget was $3500 a month we could probably choose two of the three, so we ended up paying $5200. (I figured we were still paying $3500, just every twenty days.) Thinking of all of this usually sent me directly to my bank account, and before I remembered what I was doing, or rather what I was not doing, I left the living room and walked into the bedroom.

In the doorway I counted to ten, delaying each digit more than the last, and on ten I darted to my laptop and flung it open. On my browser bar I typed *Avi Deit* and it autofilled the rest, *Avi Deitsch Last Resort*. I hit enter and clicked the *News* tab and there it was. *Introducing: The Highbrow Beach Read.* The text was previewed: *E. L. James, meet E. E. Cummings. In this day and age, it's hard to find a true crossover*—Crossover? This was already too much. I needed to stop, think about what I'd already read. I clicked on the article and saw that it was by Dwight Garner, a reviewer whose opinion I had possibly never agreed with. I decided I needed to work my way up, starting with the opinion of reviewers I valued less. Much less. I typed *goodreads* into the browser bar and it knew exactly where to take me; I'd been to the page five, ten times before, though on each occasion I could never stomach more than a couple of reviews. The book was still two days from release but there were already 191 ratings. The advance copies had been apportioned wisely: there were only seven one-star ratings, and just three of those came with written reviews. The most recent: *This was like being at a party and having the most obnoxious person there tell you a story for 2 consecutive hours! At least that's as far as I made it before I decided to save myself.* I thought this was sort of funny but then when I reread it I felt annoyed and a little sad. I went on Twitter and found the tweet I'd read yesterday, from an editor at *n+1. We don't need more sex novels.* It had twenty-one comments, seemingly all in agreement. I was beginning to understand that for a book like this—that is, a debut with a reportedly outsized paycheck—not having read the thing didn't preclude you from having an opinion. There was already a narrative taking shape, one that wasn't altogether positive. Part of me felt like I should have expected it, that it was inevitable. Sometimes I even suspected that Ellis not only foresaw but helped bring about the bad publicity (the cliché goes without saying), starting with the decision to sign with Perry.

They'd offered us $830,000 (and a two-book option at $1.5 million, which Ellis insisted we decline), though Carrington had come in, at the last second, at $880,000. Ellis, Avi, and I had been having frequent calls to discuss everything—hourly during the last two days. (Ellis had stipulated that all communication be done over phone, presumably so there wouldn't be a paper trail.) On the last call he introduced Carrington's offer but said he felt *Perry is the best bet, if not just for Copeland.* He admitted that Copeland likely wouldn't be doing much of the editing himself, it was his name that counted. I mentioned that I'd heard from a friend (Louis's classmate) that Copeland had something of a mixed reputation—that he was, at best, a cad. (She'd specifically said that Perry female staffers of a certain disposition had learned to ignore his *lingering leers.* I remembered that phrase verbatim because, a year later, it appeared twice on the Shitty Media Men list, a widely circulated, anonymous spreadsheet of men in media reputed to have been abusive to women. Copeland's name, the first I searched for, was absent.) Ellis, through silence and mumbling, confirmed that he thought this side of Copeland's reputation wouldn't hurt.

Without thinking I went back to the *Times* review, letting my eyes come out of focus. I scrolled down, past the author photo—it looked harmless enough but still I couldn't bear to linger—until I found the cover image and refocused. Initially I'd thought it was too on the nose, but seeing all the clever abstractions of other new releases made me understand the choice. It didn't need to do too much; the hype alone would lead people to it. It was all but a background, a bright, saturated beach scene devoid of people, the sun almost at the horizon and a palm frond poking in from above—are there palm trees in Greece? I was told the photographer was French. I scrolled up but stopped; my eye had caught something: *#metoo*. I repositioned in my chair and didn't stop squirming until I finished the paragraph: *Those craving another #metoo-friendly addition to their bookshelf won't find it here. If the male gaze isn't omnipresent, a male glance (or two) still abounds.* I wanted to defend myself, but I had more integrity than that. Dwight wasn't wrong. At moments, there was a certain, if slight, objectification of Sofia and Reagan, not just by the narrator but baked into the narrative itself. It wasn't essential to the story, and I would have edited it out then and there if I could have. I searched for *#metoo* and found only one other mention, in the teaser for a different piece. I exhaled. I wanted to move on, I searched for *reclus* and found one result. *Deitsch, a former assistant editor at the imprint Quartz, seems fine letting* Last Resort *speak for itself. Since the announcement of the book's nearly seven-figure sale, he hasn't given a single interview, adopting a reclusiveness that might put Salinger or Pynchon to shame.* This was the other element that I, in my most paranoid state, assumed Ellis was behind, had conceived of even before the four of us met a year and a half ago. I'd compared a boilerplate contract I found online with the one we finalized with Perry. (As per Rupert's recommendations, it stipulated Avi and me as "writing partners," such that Avi was the "public face and name" of our operation, with all profits going to Avi Deitsch LLC, of which I was the sole proprietor. The contract also obligated Perry to keep our arrangement private; I speculated that even some members of the publicity team were in the dark about my existence, given that Ellis looped Avi into email chains but kept me bcc'd.) Our contract had been gutted of any of the usual requirements regarding author appearances and promotions. After researching more thoroughly, I understood this was no small victory; for a sale that large (for any sale today, really), the publisher expects the author to pull his weight. But Avi's absence seemed to be doing more work for *Last Resort* than any interview with Terry Gross could. And what could a writer say, really, that was more interesting than a flat-out refusal to appear? Avi had always kept a scant online presence; those few public crumbs would have to be magnified to feed those who wanted to know who, exactly, he was. All his Facebook photos were private, but his profile image, a shot of him in a rowboat wearing a goofy wide-brimmed hat, had been used in virtually every publication that wrote about the deal. On a shoddy but popular blog run by a guy known for his antagonistic Twitter tiffs, one post featured only his profile picture, with the words *SELLS BOOK FOR A MILLION DOLLARS* on the top half, and on the bottom, *ROWS GENTLE INTO THAT GOOD NIGHT.*

Of course, this all helped grant the launch a kind of special buzz that rarely surrounded literary events. In fact, last week one of the Perry publicity managers suggested we switch to a larger venue. But Greenlight felt right, and the info was already all over the place.

Just before I finished the article my phone buzzed, terrifying me. Sandra. *Pretty positive NYT review huh?*

tl;dr

I know you probably think he missed the point, but that sort of review is guaranteed to bring more people in. By this she meant that the review made the book seem like literary fiction for people who only read romance—or maybe like a romance novel for people who only read literary fiction.

Garner, of all people

You sure you still want to do drinks tonight? The Danes should be over ~ 8

I am certain

& you're sure you don't want me 2 come to the talk?

Who says I'm going? I turned the air conditioner off and was surprised to hear the patter of rain. You couldn't see a light drizzle from our bedroom, the oak tree caught the drops before they hit the window. *I don't want to get wet.*

You probably believe you're not going & yet you KNOW you'll change your mind 10 minutes pre

The sign of a first rate intelligence is the ability to hold two contradictory ideas at once

Jes christ. Have fun but not too much.

<hr>

The rain hadn't deterred anyone, apparently; by the time I arrived Greenlight had already hit capacity. The girl at the door told me I could wait outside for someone to exit. I asked if there was a guest list, and she looked at me like I was unhinged. Maybe I was. I considered how I might take advantage of her wariness to get inside but then I saw Ellis. We connected eyes for long enough that he couldn't pretend he hadn't noticed me. In fact, in that first moment he looked like he'd seen a ghost. I waved and he came over. He said something to the door girl and she simpered and moved aside. After we walked in he turned left, guiding us to a cranny of space by the magazines.

I didn't expect to see you here, he said, hearing his tone and adjusting: *So glad you made it.* His head bobbed up and scanned the room, squinting. *I'm sorry to say your bud's not here yet.* Bud. The last image I had of Avi, the last time I'd heard his voice, had been our meeting in Ellis's office. *Listen, I've been meaning to get back to you about your new thing. Haven't had a chance to give it a thorough read, but I really can't wait to.* The comment was perfectly perfunctory and vague, like I was some MFA he'd met at a literary conference. He looked into the crowd again. *Here, let's get you settled.* With his hand on my shoulder he shepherded me through the crowd to the back, where they were serving wine. He made some inane upbeat comments about the turnout and then asked me how I'd been. I said I was fine in about as many words because he was hardly listening, since we started walking together he'd been searching for someone else to talk to and finally found her, a short woman with an elaborate hairstyle I couldn't begin to classify. He said he had to *circulate, as it were*, adding, *Do keep in touch*, which pissed me off immensely.

As I was waiting in line for wine someone turned to me as if to say something but then didn't. I was suddenly conscious of my facial expression, that my mood had taken a sharp dive. I saw my reflection in a window, but couldn't make out what I looked like, only my haircut, which now embarrassed me, that I had paid $120 for it just to stand by myself in the back with everyone else. I remembered that I hated book talks, even when the book in question wasn't one I'd surrendered authorship of. There was the interviewer who was usually an (at least somewhat) well-known writer, performing her writerly awkwardness to the point of charm, speaking in a tone of voice that was so gentle it sounded passive-aggressive, lobbing softball questions that would give the interviewee a chance to expound on his creative process, to divulge his own quirky habits, to display self-effacement worthy of the breakdown stage of a cult. In response to these answers the interviewer would give an encouraging nod on every fifth word, even before a cogent thought had been said, as if she couldn't agree more with *I just think that the*.

I asked for a glass of red wine and then another for a friend. The woman couldn't have cared less but still I turned to the crowd and smiled at a make-believe pal. I walked back to the front of the store, hoping to grab a seat but of course they were all claimed; even those without a human held a monument of belongings instead. One chair was empty but it was being claimed—molested, practically—by a woman who eyed me carefully. I retreated to the wall of books, where at least I could lean back.

Already passersby outside were looking in at us, getting their friends' attention, as if they'd never seen a congregation of people dressed in Everlane and Eileen Fisher. I finished one cup of wine and placed it on the bookshelf. I tried convincing myself I had more patience than I did. I checked my phone: 6:35. It was supposed to have started already. I watched the two empty stools up front, praying Avi wouldn't sit on the one that faced me.

Soon it was 6:45, and then 7. A good portion of the crowd was now reading, a lot of them *Last Resort*. From what I could see they'd mostly just started. This gave me an ill feeling, a sort of twisting in my stomach, which took me a minute to figure out: if they hadn't even read the book, then maybe the small satisfaction I was allowing myself for such a turnout was unfounded; it really had nothing to do with me or my words. Maybe it was just the money that had been paid for those words, or the marketing, Avi's elusiveness, a few well-placed event listings. In a brief but darker swing I even allowed that the money itself wasn't only my doing, that it was Avi's marketability that had inflated the sale price, that editors wanted a piece of this up-and-coming, handsome, suave young man—someone who was even one of their own.

At 7:15 the door girl finally walked in front and thanked everyone for waiting. Her tone was apologetic, which was good, except that it augured bad news. She put on an I-feel-you frown and said, *I am very sorry to report that Avi Deitsch will not be attending tonight's event. He's come down with the flu, and regrets his absence.* The crowd began murmuring, and then talking at full volume. There were some groans. She clearly had no idea of what a lie she'd been party to—that Avi wasn't sick, he was absent for the same reason he'd been absent all this time, he had nothing to say about the book because he'd had nothing to do with its creation. I felt like I was being driven mad. I wanted to laugh. I tried to find Ellis. He'd probably made Avi believe he could do this, had enough hubris to think he could lead a horse to water and then make that horse talk intelligently about something he knew nothing of. I couldn't find him. The girl was quieting the crowd. *Please, please*, she said. *We're still going to have the event. Please. We have a special guest, please.* She lifted a piece of paper from her pocket, raised her voice, and read a brief biography of

Terrence Copeland, listing the books he'd edited and the awards they'd won. Copeland walked in and waved off spattered applause. I'd never seen him in person before. He seemed a lot older than in the pictures I'd found online, and an interview posted on YouTube two years before. He looked like Steve Bannon if Steve Bannon had better skin and took more vacation. The door girl could feel the expectation and was milking it. *Our other guest tonight,* she said, *is an accomplished novelist, and a proud Fort Greene local.* The New York Times *called her first novel a . . .* The muttering began again and I couldn't hear the rest. People were disappointed, audibly. In walked Natasha Miller, whose debut *Mise En Place* had been out for five years, not too long in the history of literature, but still it was pre-Trump and felt like an epoch ago. The book's story had aged it remarkably, so much so that I couldn't imagine it getting attention today. It follows the waitstaff at a prestigious Manhattan restaurant as they fuck, do drugs, host elaborate dinners, and go to the sort of parties people who've never lived in New York dream they'd go to if they moved here. I didn't doubt why she'd been chosen to fill in (besides the fact that she probably lived around the corner): to accompany Terrence Copeland. Her presence and the sort of writing she was known for would work to reframe the ill repute that still shadowed him. Next to her, his vaguely prurient, devil-may-care aura seemed rakishly, refreshingly old-fashioned. Miller was in her mid-thirties and wore a form-fitting maroon dress. His thick baggy red sweater and khakis conjured up a long-tenured English professor. Together they were like a Reagan-era casting director's idea of a realistic couple. She started by asking a few thoroughly obvious questions, but then said she wanted *to pivot to the elephant in the room*. This briefly piqued the crowd, as if she might ask anything of interest—Avi's reclusiveness, Copeland's reputation, claims that *Last Resort* inhabited the male gaze. *There are some pretty steamy scenes here*, she said, panning the room like a kindergarten teacher reading a picture book. He didn't really react, which was awkward but also momentarily interesting, as if he might riposte with something pithy. The guy next to me picked up his phone and discreetly started taking a video. *I gotta admit*, she said, *I'm not one to read a book more than once, but I'll say that there are some dog-eared sections in my copy*. I admired her for admitting she didn't reread books. He was silent for five whole seconds and then demurred. She laughed though nothing was funny, and then reframed her question to instead ask for any information about anything, and this established the template for the remaining thirty minutes: question, demur, pivot to open-ended lob, self-regarding yet imprecise answer. Eventually she took questions, which mostly alternated between anodyne inquiries and accusatory statements with question marks at the end. *Did you anticipate the book would so easily find an audience? Do you find it odd that almost all reclusive authors who end up in the canon are male? How did you arrive at the cover art? Have you considered how the protagonist might be seen differently if she were female? What writer that you've worked with before does Deitsch most resemble? Some have noted that the book's homosexual scenes are couched in a strictly heteronormative narrative—was this taken into account in the editing of the manuscript?* None received a straight answer, except for the cover art question and, *Does Deitsch have another book in the works?* to which Copeland replied, *Not to my knowledge, but I'll have to hunt down his agent at the bar*. This received a spate of chuckles, and turned out to be a great time to call it. Miller thanked everyone for coming and Copeland waved.

I stayed in the back, watching as he found his way to a corner beside the register, soon to be joined by Ellis, his assistant, and a few others. They stood there uncomfortably, trying to pretend they weren't being watched, and it wasn't long before they gathered their belongings and left. I went to get more wine but there was none left, just a few cubes of cheese and crackers, which I gathered in a napkin and took with me to the front. I sat down because my legs were tired and also because I didn't want to leave yet. People were leaking out and I wanted to see who had come, not that I recognized more than a couple of them, but I thought I should memorize the moment, which was ostensibly mine, or not ostensibly—the opposite of ostensibly. I'd been using that word too much recently but maybe too much of my life was ostensible, or its opposite. Soon there were just a handful of us left, and we were getting glances from the employees. They wanted to close down, to them this was just another too-late night. There would be a reading tomorrow or the next day, maybe not as big but eventually there would be one bigger, there'd always be something new. Perry would continue to publish, the *Times* would continue to review, Twitter had no off switch. I could already feel time crystallizing around me. One day the book's cover would look outdated, a relic of 2018. On my way out I bought a copy as an apology to the workers, as if they'd get anything out of it. They rang me up without acknowledging my presence, lost in a heated discussion about undergraduate English syllabi. I wondered if *Last Resort* would ever be assigned in a creative writing course. I wanted to ask them if they'd read the book but thought better of it. I went outside and sat on a bench and dragged my thumb over its pages. Then I opened to a random passage and read a sentence and closed the book and smelled it. The rain had stopped but the streets were wet. Everyone seemed to be walking home faster than usual. I saw that the cover had a "Signed by the Author" sticker. Certainly someone else had done it, he had too much of a backbone for that. And yet, when I opened to the title page I knew it was his, instinctually—no, I knew it from the contracts; I'd stared at it for just as long then. I couldn't help but admire it, the confident, narrow loops, the way they all blended into each other in an unbroken dance. My handwriting was always terrible, my signature looked like a feral child's. I knew a signed copy would sell better, but what a cowardly thing to do, to not say no—it was just as cowardly as not saying no to this event when he knew in his heart of hearts he wouldn't do it. What could he possibly say for himself? Really, what *would* he say for himself? I imagined texting him, *you are an invertebrate*. I took out my phone and scrolled to our last conversation. He'd written, *Sure, see you soon*. This was before our meeting with Ellis, a year and a half ago. Just to see what the words would look like on the screen I wrote, *Missed you tonight. You alright?* I thought of what sending it would do, mostly it would dissolve our tacit agreement not to contact one another, but wasn't that also just an act of cowardice? Was I just as complicit, just as craven, in my own way? I hit send.

I thought of going home. I looked down the block and then the other way, remembering the bars in the area, trying to guess which one Copeland and Ellis had ended up at. I allowed myself to entertain the thought that I should be there, at the bar, which wouldn't be whichever lame one they chose but that stuffy

Japanese cocktail place in the back of Walter's because it was the only spot in this neighborhood with any flair or pretension. I imagined being there, having drinks bought for me on a corporate card, surrounded by Copeland and Ellis and some random assistants and Sandra and Louis maybe, and if no one there recognized Copeland or Ellis they could at least tell something was going on, it might not be a vision of the Weimar Republic or Gertrude Stein's Paris but for me it would be a moment in time, a night that would serve as a marker in my retroactive life, a memory that time could distort and inflate so it could be exactly what I'd need it to be when I was no longer having nights.

My phone buzzed. It couldn't have been him, and yet. *Ah, just a bit of food poisoning. Congrats on the Wood review by the way. Hope all's well.* At first it was impossible to home in on any of the three thoughts: the vulgar cordiality at the end, the bold-faced lie (which it now obviously was, if you're going to use one of the two easiest excuses in the book—flu, food poisoning—at least stay with the one you choose), and finally, the casual revelation of a review by James Wood of *New Yorker* fame. If I had to choose one person in the world to review me, it would be him. I checked the time: 8:04. We'd told our guests to be over at 8—as if anyone would show then—and our reservations were at 9:30. I had twenty minutes, maybe. I thought for a second, maybe five. I ripped the title page from the book, let it fall to the wet sidewalk, and began power-walking home.

Congrats on the Wood review, he'd said. Congrats? What I was reading, my laptop screen no more than four inches from my face, was possibly the snarkiest review the guy had ever written—albeit snarky in a slightly endearing way, a way that made the book seem intensely readable, that might even, as Sandra would say, *bring more people in*. In recent years, a negative James Wood review was a rarity, only even possible when consideration was obligatory, when a book of literary fiction had entered (or was perceived to soon enter) a certain stratosphere of hype—George Saunders, Zadie Smith, Emma Cline. The first third of the review didn't even mention the book, was just a long muse on the lost art of subtlety in contemporary fiction—*If all of today's relevant novels can be made into film, what is the point of books to begin with?*—a great big setup to introduce *Last Resort* as the trend's new touchstone. *If it's meant as a gateway drug for fiction, written for those who haven't picked up a novel since high school—acting as both a book and its SparkNotes, replete with symbols alongside the map to find them—then so be it. But one doesn't get the impression this was Deitsch's intent.* After the long preamble Wood conceded that it was *atmospheric* (i.e., it took place on a Greek island), that it had an *ambitious plot arc* (i.e., an overambitious plot arc), that it was *charged* (i.e., there were sex scenes). Actually, for someone who didn't care for *writing that tries to do what pornography does better*, he seemed to care an awful lot about the sex scenes—what books they supposedly drew on (I'd read none), what they asked of the reader (*not to undermine taboo but ignore it entirely*; I was on board), and what they distracted from (*what once-in-a-lifetime experiences can actually do to us*; this was an interesting point). As a Wood review often did, it opened my eyes to how the book could, possibly would, and probably should be read.

But this all wasn't the real problem with Avi saying *Congrats on the Wood review*. The real problem was that *he* was saying congrats *to me*. I wasn't the one peering out from the pages of *The New Yorker*, looking so silently proud, solemn, brooding. Shot in black-and-white, the photograph showed Avi sitting on a countertop in a sparsely decorated apartment, kitchen cabinets in the background, an orchid drooping by his side, his hands holding the edge of the counter, knuckles out, arms straight, the musculature of his forearms in relief. One leg was folded over the other, his feet balancing on the edge of a wooden chair I recognized as Franny's. His shirt was crumpled, his hair recently cut but not kempt. His face was inscrutable, opaque, keeping the viewer at a distance. I couldn't have looked like that, I know because I've tried, in the mirror. It was perfect, as long as you ignored the content of the piece, and, well, most people would. I couldn't help but think of Ellis, and what hand he might have had in the review, how hard he would have pushed for it to go to Wood even though he knew how it would turn out. A terrible review by James Wood was still a review by James Wood, and that would only inspire more conversation, give more people more reason to have an opinion, to post, to buy. I wondered if the irony was lost on him, on Avi too—that Avi's mug absorbed all of the article's damage while helping to build a mythology that would boost sales, and my bank account.

Sandra came into the room and I minimized the browser. When I'd walked into the apartment she was busily getting ready; we didn't have enough time to talk about the launch so we agreed to do it later. (Really I knew discussing it would only sour my mood for the night, ditto the review.) She walked up to me and put her hands on my shoulders. *You know I don't care if you look at porn*, she said. I unminimized the window. She asked what it said and I told her and she rubbed my back as I read her passages. She asked how I felt about it and I said that I felt like shit, that I couldn't decide which part I should feel worst about. A knock came at the front of the apartment. *I'm sorry*, she said, kissing the top of my head. *I'll let them in, take as much time as you need.*

I imagined interacting with people I barely knew. Why hadn't I taken Sandra's offer and bailed? I tried putting myself in better spirits. I let my vision go out of focus, scanning the blocks of text. Even if it was generally negative, even if Wood was a bit liberal with the punches, there was consolation in the fact that the article had been written, that it would always exist. Thirty years from now, no matter if *Last Resort* was still in print or completely forgotten, it would be proof of what I'd done.

———

Sorry sorry, I said, bursting into the room, as if I'd gotten there as fast as I could. Sandra glanced at the clock above the couch and I followed; we'd need to leave in ten minutes. I gave hugs and went to the bar cart, pouring myself an hour's worth of scotch. I settled down by Asger and Jeppe, across the room were Sandra, Freja, Mikkel, and his wife, whose name I always forgot. The five of them were Danish, met through a string of connections starting with Jeppe, who had met Sandra through the UN Human Rights Council. Asger and Mikkel's wife were also in the UN.

Mikkel and Freja were journalists. I'd met almost twenty Danes in New York and they were all either diplomats or journalists, which made me wonder if anyone in that country baked bread or sold insurance.

I was happy to sit with Asger and Jeppe, I was curious about their friendship and eager to distract myself. They were apparently very close but quite mismatched. Jeppe seemed to be at peace with everything in the world, while Asger was the type to remember who said *Bless you* so he could reciprocate accordingly. As Jeppe told me about an unnamed nation's application to be on the council, Asger watched silently. After Jeppe said that the mystery country would *completely shift the dynamic*, I said, *At least tell me what it rhymes with*. Jeppe gave a nice laugh, a laugh for two, perhaps anticipating his friend's sobriety, and sure enough a beat later Asger suggested we change the subject. *What's their GDP?* I asked. *Ballpark*. Asger turned to me and asked what I did for a living, which I thought was a fine transition but there was something in his face; he looked regretful, like he'd gone too far. I replayed his question in my head and now it seemed like a taunt, though I couldn't figure out how exactly, and before I could get there Sandra stood up and clapped. *Time to go*, she said, which might have been true but I wouldn't believe she hadn't noticed us. We quickly downed our drinks and retrieved our coats only to amble all the way there, turning a fifteen-minute walk into thirty.

Miss Ada was an Israeli restaurant between Fort Greene Park and the basketball courts Louis and I played at, loved by Sandra and me for its chicken liver hummus and atmosphere, which I personally attributed to the clientele and waitstaff. It was as if they sourced unconventionally attractive people, people who had one feature that would have made them an easy target in seventh grade—a hawkish nose, a facial birthmark, gap teeth—but which now served them well.

As we were being seated I went to talk with the sommelier— or rather, a tall thin man waiting by the kitchen who told me the restaurant didn't have one—and by the time I got back to the group my seat had been chosen for me, between Asger and Mikkel's wife, whose name I still couldn't recall. Sandra and Jeppe led the conversation, arguing over Trump's foreign policy. When Jeppe mentioned Israel, Sandra deftly shifted course—it was a topic I hated discussing because I knew where the group stood; my defense of Israel was instinctual (and, admittedly, a bit irrational). She brought up Brooklyn's Hasidic neighborhoods, and we talked about that and biking, Scandinavia, Sweden, Stieg Larsson, and, finally, Knausgaard. *The man is everywhere*, Freja said. *His books of course but his fingerprint too. It's like every male novelist now knows he can indulge himself as long as he's just a bit vulnerable. I've got a friend who works at Lindhardt og Ringhof*—I could hardly understand her, and looked it up later—*the Danish publisher. They've just acquired the epitome of that trend, an American debut. It's called Skillevejen*—ditto; it means "crossroads," which sounds lame but apparently there's a double entendre there—*I don't know what it's called in English.* I looked to Sandra, who had been watching me and diverted her eyes. I tried to swallow but there was no saliva. *I think they're even trying to get a blurb from Knausgaard, which would of course just guarantee that the book will never match the hype.* I wanted to say that that was the point of hype, to exceed the actual thing, but I just sat there, listening as she gave a summary of her friend's appraisal—the sex scenes came far too often and were far too gratuitous, the whole thing stank of the male gaze, it was unapologetically commercial—a rant which, somehow, ended with, *She said it was very good, and obviously she reads quite a lot. In fact she believed the author was something of a genius.* She thought for a second. *Avi Dench, he's called.* I readjusted in my seat, feeling how hard I'd been pushing my back into the bench. *Deitsch*, I said, unable to stop myself. *It's Avi Deitsch.* Then without thinking I added, *I know him, the author. We went to college together.* I saw Sandra stiffen. I'd chosen precisely the wrong tone. If I'd really wanted to get it out there and move on I would have said it like I could talk hours about him, that I wanted to. But I'd uttered his name like I had in me a world of gossip that just needed to be pulled out. *Well?* Asger asked. *What is he like?* I smiled at him and said, *He's a nice guy, kind of quiet*, which is just the same as saying, *Please, ask more.* Asger raised his eyebrows. *Come on*, he said. *What does it rhyme with?* No one got this reference, and even Jeppe looked confused. I should have taken the opportunity to move on, or do anything else, but I just absorbed his awkwardness, let it travel through me until it blossomed on my face. *It's a sensitive topic*, Sandra said, which again worked exactly against us. *We had a sort of falling out*, I said. *But I wish him all the luck in the world.* It seemed like I'd almost pushed us past the topic but needed to clinch it. *Him and his highbrow lowbrow fuck fiction.* Now that we had a common enemy, things clicked into place. Mikkel said, *A book should be more than pussy and pretension*, and Freja said, *The Bible didn't have either and it's a bestseller*, and as the conversation moved on I finally unclenched my hands and feet.

The waiter came and we ordered food and wine, a job we all agreed was Sandra's. After some deliberation she ordered two of the cheapest bottles, which I knew she'd do and was the reason I'd tried to find a sommelier. We were mindful that our means were not others', and this tab, like all of them, would be divided evenly among the group. Even though it was assumed we were well off, everyone's instinct was to let it stay an assumption. In fact, I found that being rich only sent friends for their wallets faster than they had before.

The wine was gone by the time the food came, at which point Mikkel ordered two of the most expensive bottles. (Along with check-splitting, conspicuous consumption was something people were now eager to partake in.) I noticed I was getting looks from Sandra, the kind that meant I was drinking a lot, which I was, I realized then; hadn't seen it myself even as I ordered my second beer to drink alongside the wine. Suddenly I could feel it too, that I wanted to drink. It made it easier not to think about the things I didn't want to—the launch, the reviews, the version of the *Last Resort* conversation we would have had if it was known I was the author. Yes, someone at the table knew someone else who called *me* a genius; to have accepted such a compliment in public would have been a highlight of my year, possibly even more than a post-launch drink with Copeland and Ellis.

The incessant din made it hard to talk to anyone but those you were sitting next to, and Asger practically had his back to me. Mikkel's wife must have been the first diplomat I'd met who was willing to talk about her job without reserve, which she did endlessly. I tried eavesdropping on Asger's conversation with Freja, which was in Danish but still they used English phrases, and when they did I jumped at the opportunity. Eventually my efforts became desperate enough that he begrudgingly sat back and opened his shoulders to me. Freja explained that they were talking about the rise of leftist podcasts that mocked liberals— *Chapo Trap House, Red Scare*—a subject she was currently writing a piece about. She said that downloads spiked during office hours, and guessed that a lot of people yearned for something irreverent but stimulating while at work. I said something inane and Asger, in nearly the same tone as when he first posed the question, asked what I did for a living, and then amended it to, *How do you spend your days?*

In the past year and a half I'd found myself becoming less socially inhibited and, even more so, less self-critical, shedding the habit of the party postmortem, held the morning after (or at 4 a.m.) to rebuke myself for all the brutish and insensitive things I'd said while inebriated. This didn't mean I said fewer of those things; on the contrary. But it did seem like a positive that I was potentially freer, less self-censored. Except there was one topic I'd become wary of to the point of conversational paralysis: what I did all day. A substantial topic, to be sure, but one I'd become especially deft at evading. The truth was that recently I'd been spending my *working hours* (that is, the hours everyone else spent at work) writing—really, finding ways not to—but I couldn't say that, because anyone who knew me knew (or was led to believe) that I'd made a great deal of money from the Parachute acquisition, which would make me a certain (New York, L.A.) stereotype: someone who'd earned a fortune in business (or hadn't earned it at all) and used it to support their "passion." The contract I'd signed with Avi and Ellis mandated mutual confidentiality—should our arrangement become public, the person at fault would be liable for *the resulting financial loss suffered by all other Parties*. I didn't know how exactly the dissemination of the details of the agreement would lead to financial loss, but the thought of having to repay what I'd already received, let alone lose what I was owed, was too much. (Impossible, actually. Not including rent I'd already spent about $25,000—on trips to Israel and Seoul, on clothes I'd since not worn that filled me with guilt every time I went to my closet, on Jesus Christ I don't know what, things add up; espresso machines aren't free and neither is furniture.) And so, only Sandra and Louis knew that I'd written the book, that I was profiting from it. I hadn't wanted to tell Louis, but he was bound to put it together anyway. Not telling my parents was a much harder decision to make, but I understood their limitations. I'd once told them of the manuscript I was working on in Florida, after getting them to promise not to tell a soul, and for years after I'd had to endure grilling from relatives and family friends.

My answer to Asger was the one I'd given many times before: *Planning my next move.* Of course it was fair to need time before jumping into something new, I had supposedly spent long hours earning a supposedly big payout. Usually I delivered the line so limply that no one asked a follow-up, but Asger was drunk enough to be forthright. *Not everyone needs a second act*, he said, delivering it so easily that it took me a moment to feel its edge. It struck me that some version of that sentiment must have been shared by many of the people I surrounded myself with. I picked up my beer but there was none left. Asger saw this and couldn't hide his small pleasure, and I momentarily despised him for resenting me, because it was such an easy dumb thing to resent someone for, their money, and on top of that it was money I had earned, not that he could know that, know that I'd made a fortune in the one field you are virtually guaranteed to earn nothing in. *That's true*, I said. *After all, some people don't even get a first.* He didn't respond, but instead held his head like someone taking the higher ground, and I realized that the others had let their conversations trail off and were now paying attention to us. I called over the waiter and asked for two more bottles of the wine we'd just finished, as well as another beer. Jeppe took a conspicuous glance at his watch and was about to speak, surely to say they should be going soon and maybe we didn't need more wine, but before he could I said that the meal was on me and Sandra. Asger took this as a dig, which was exactly what it was, and said, *I really shouldn't have any more, after all I've got work in the morning.* I asked him if the world order would remain intact if he woke up a bit hungover. By the looks of Sandra and Freja and everyone else I understood that I was the bad guy, that out of context his comment had seemed innocent, mine incredibly rude. This upset me even more—the elegance of his snub—but Sandra was shooting me daggers. It took all the pride in my body to tell him I was sorry, that I was a bit drunk.

Eventually the tension dissipated and banter resumed. Again Asger turned his back to me, and Mikkel's wife picked up right where she'd left off: her email signature. I could see that only a glass or two had been taken from the new wine. I didn't want it to go to waste, especially now that I was paying, so I gave myself a significant pour, and then another one five minutes later when there was a distraction, some commotion at another table. It wasn't too long before people stopped eating and conversation slowed and then came to a lull, and when Sandra asked for the check there were still a couple of glasses left. At this point the room had fallen under a fuzzy numbness. I wanted more but could hardly produce a coherent sentence, even Mikkel's wife had given up on me, had turned away to talk to Jeppe. On both sides Danish singsong gibberish filled my ears, as good as a lullaby, and when the waiter came with the check, which was intercepted by Sandra, I told the group I was going for a walk, that I needed some time to think, and hoped to see them all soon. With her eyes only Sandra asked me to stay. She had a talent to make them melancholic at will, at any moment she could turn herself into a young Charlotte Rampling. I stood and kissed her on the cheek, and told her I'd see her back at the apartment.

As soon as I stepped outside I was glad for my coat of alcohol. The wind whipped through the trees, fizzing their leaves, none more than those on the hill at the top of the park, and I started walking in that direction. On my way I saw a cook smoking outside a wine bar and asked him for a cigarette. He brushed me off in a way that felt justified, maybe he appreciated not having to be polite on his break, maybe I was just visibly drunk.

I walked through the park, up the path to the only lit area, the memorial monument, an obelisk erected in honor of American POWs who died on British prison ships during the Revolutionary War. I tried reading its inscription but didn't have the concentration. I made my way down the hill and sat on the grass, facing a row of brownstones. I could see inside a few, their rooms full of soft yellow light. In one a man slouched in a chair, reading. Until I saw him I didn't realize how sad I felt. I regretted being an asshole at dinner but knew that wasn't it, what the sadness was about. It was more enduring, it had been with me for some time, so I thought about it more, recklessly, drunkenly, I allowed myself to be brutally honest, and I saw that what I was feeling wasn't really sadness but an absence of its opposite, happiness, which was surprising, I thought I had been happy, or at least I thought I should be, deserved to be, after all I'd done the one thing I always thought would finally give me happiness: sell a novel and have my days to write another one. The phrase *life-changing* came to mind. It struck me that the term itself implies a life that needs to be changed. Yes, my life had transformed, it had become something that was, from the outside, worth admiring, envying even. And yet here I was, inside it, and still it needed to be changed.

Even without the lights on I could see around me, the lawns normally taken over by children and canoodlers. I looked up and saw a plump moon perfectly intersected by the silhouette of a naked branch. I thought of a book by Norman Mailer that I didn't finish and couldn't remember the title of. Early on there was a passage about the moon, written with such candid verve, and I remember saying to myself that that's what I wanted to do with my writing. I could hardly pick up *Last Resort* these days for the sake of my anxiety but when I did that's what I saw, that I'd put myself in it, that I'd used it to express things in me that would not have come out any other way, and for that I should have been proud. It didn't matter what people assumed about me, it didn't matter what happened when you Googled my name, because I knew what I'd accomplished, and I knew I could do it again, I was doing it again, I needed to. Yes, I needed to. This couldn't be what my life settled down to.

———

I woke up, grabbed my phone even though I knew I shouldn't: 6:34. I put my head down and closed my eyes for a minute. No, I was permanently awake. I slunk out of bed and made my way to the living room. It was hard to gauge how much of my malaise was from drinking, how much was from lack of sleep, and how much was from the thoughts I'd let pass through me in the park. I sat on the couch and let those thoughts take hold again, but then decided I should stop. What was important was the conclusion, that rare moment of clarity. Knowing you're unhappy is half the battle, the other half is finding your way out, and I knew the way out: it was writing, it was another book, one I could claim as my own. Only then would I fuse the life I lived with the life inside me, only then would I be happy.

I snuck into the bedroom to fetch my laptop, earplugs, and noise-canceling headphones. I made coffee and set up shop in the living room. I turned my Wi-Fi off, put the earplugs in and my headphones on. I opened up my Word doc and started reading from the top. *That day wasn't just any spring day. This was a—* I stopped. *That day wasn't just any spring day.* I read it again, I swallowed, I read it again. What sort of psychopath would even think that to himself? I rewrote it. *If there were clouds in the sky they weren't here.* This seemed better. I closed my eyes, I read it. It was much worse. I jumped down to another sentence, I couldn't make it halfway through. My skin became cold and clammy. How could I have sent this to Ellis? I rubbed my face. I should relax, I thought, he knew me, what I was capable of, he could see the forest for the trees.

The story I'd been working on was the one I'd told him about in our first meeting, the party of Brooklynites, where the characters realize death incarnate will, at the end of the night, take one of their lives. Three months ago I'd sent him four story ideas, this not one of them, and he gently nudged me back in this direction. *To me it feels more fresh*, he'd written. *More of a risk.*

I looked outside. Since I sat down the sun had already gained on the horizon. I scrolled ahead, scraping off plot details, abstracting scenes, seeing for the first time the shape of the book. From start to finish—28,931 words so far—the narrator seemed to be roaming around, mingling, collecting potential conflicts, narrative arcs. It was meta, of course it was, albeit unintentionally, but maybe that's the only way meta works. I needed to think about this. I got up and lay down on the couch and tried to gain perspective, I imagined it was someone else's book. Soon it became hard to focus, I was too tired to think. I didn't resist.

I woke to a room full of light. The radio was on in the kitchen, a British man interviewing someone in Myanmar. I got up, walked into the bedroom, and sat on the bed. Sandra was at the mirror, putting her earrings in. She sent a smile that said she wasn't going to mention last night unless I brought it up first. I wanted to say that I loved her, but didn't, because I didn't want it to seem like an apology. She wasn't exactly hurrying, but she was being efficient. We had someplace to be, I couldn't remember where but didn't want to ask. I got up and went to the bathroom.

In the mirror I saw that my face was a bloated mess. I showered and then ate breakfast, a plate she'd left for me, two eggs, an avocado, and fried kale. Based on its temperature I guessed she'd eaten her portion half an hour ago. Sticking out of her purse I saw an audio splitter and remembered we were going to visit Emmitt, her dad. She brought it when she went to see him so she and he could listen to comedy specials together, which they couldn't do out loud because most of his aides, who were usually from Ghana or Namibia, were devoutly Christian. Perhaps they had to put up with much worse in other homes, but given all they did—helped him use the toilet, adjusted his pillow a hundred times a day, did his exercises with him for hours on end—Sandra was wary not to offend. The one time they listened to Dave Chappelle without headphones she was careful to make it clear to the aide, by talking loudly to Emmitt, that the comic was black.

We were thirty minutes late (my fault). As soon as we arrived we began our routine: she inspected the house and cleaned, because it was never as clean as it could be, while I sat with Emmitt and the aide, talking about current events and my life. Sandra said that Emmitt hadn't been much of a talker before the incident, and he certainly wasn't after. It wasn't until a year ago—six months after we'd been seeing each other—that Sandra even allowed me to come with her. I never knew if she was worried I'd be uncomfortable in his presence, or that I would in some way fail to engage with him. He was legally blind though he could usually make out who was standing in front of him, unable to get up on his own but could move enough to give you a hug, push up his glasses. He usually couldn't speak more than a sentence without taking a break, and in general tired very fast. But for all his physical handicaps the injury had barely touched his cognition. He might not speak for minutes but then offer a joke that riffed on all of the preceding conversation. Sandra had told me that a few weeks before at the ophthalmologist's, after the doctor had put a drop in his eye, he exclaimed, *Would you believe it, I can see!* Over time he and I had established a rapport, one that was propped up by humor and gentle ribbing, though the conversations were mostly sustained by me and the aide, this time a shy Zimbabwean named Billy.

As I tried generating banter, my mind kept reverting to the story I was writing, whether I was on the right track, or on a track at all. I brought up Tesla, then Mike Pence, then Chinese sanctions, and stopped there—I could tell I'd hit on something when his eyes began to pace around the ceiling. He wanted to hear more, so I grabbed the *Times* and read an article to him. When I flipped the paper over I noticed, on the table, the Arts section. I couldn't help myself. I slowed my reading pace and teased it out. There, below the fold on the front page, was the Garner review, along with the photo I'd avoided yesterday. It was more of a headshot than the *New Yorker* photo but had the same essence: Avi's mug right in the center, framed by a black turtleneck, à la Steve Jobs, except Steve Jobs never smiled like he was in love with, and possibly courting, the photographer. Actually he did, but, well, Avi did it better, somehow merging the passivity of James Dean with the confrontational seductiveness of Truman Capote, as if to say, *Here, take me.* The word is worn thin but it was surreal seeing him there; it was hard to believe this was real life. *You already read that sentence*, Emmitt said, jolting me. *Right*, I said, and put the Arts section away.

When Sandra came back in we made sandwiches and ate silently in the living room, Billy scooping the food from the plate and leaving the utensil on the side for Emmitt to take into his mouth. Sandra ensured his life was as autonomous as it could be, instructing the aides on what they shouldn't help him with as much as what they should. (Of course she knew that when she left, Emmitt convinced them to do much more for him.)

In those quiet periods of eating I would often take in the apartment, which was beautiful, with its parquet floors and chandeliers and the subtle smell of century-old wood, the sort of place realtors could sell in minutes. Sandra often told Emmitt what nearby apartments sold for. Sometimes she was more straightforward, urging him to consider downgrading to somewhere more reasonable so he could use the extra money for other needs; it wouldn't be too long until the cost of the aides required a liquidation of some of his assets. He wouldn't hear of it. He'd say he appreciated the place more than any possible buyer could. It wasn't just that he'd lived there for twenty-five years, he had a fundamental understanding of its worth. This was true, he'd made a life constructing homes (no matter that his units were a bit more pragmatic than brownstones). It often struck me how cruel it was that he couldn't see such a remarkable space—as if that were any crueler than him not being able to see his own face, Sandra's, the rain.

When I finished my food I found that everyone else was only halfway done. Normally I paced myself so this wouldn't happen, but I'd forgotten, or I just didn't want to. All of a sudden my legs were restless, I didn't want to sit there but doing something else would have been rude. I went to the kitchen and got orange juice, and when I sat down I couldn't help continually readjusting in my seat. Sandra was watching me, following my coltish movements. *Do you want to take a walk?* she asked. I could see that she was bracing herself, hoping not to be disappointed in me. I thought of how I'd left the table the night before, how it had been more of a social failure for her than for me. *No*, I said. *It's okay.*

After lunch we tried again to engage Emmitt in conversation but he wasn't interested. He asked to listen to his book instead. Sandra told him he could do that anytime, when we weren't there, but he didn't respond to that, so it was decided. It was a biography on Ulysses S. Grant. I couldn't keep my concentration for two straight sentences. I began walking around the room, and soon came to the oak buffet, where I saw an old photograph of him and his brother. Emmitt asked me what I was looking at and I told him. His mouth started skewing to the side, a sign he had something to say but was weighing it against the trouble of speaking. I pointed at the speaker and Sandra stopped the book. I asked him when the photograph was from and he said 1983, that it was the first project he was the lead on, and probably his best, because he was too scared to get fancy with anything, could only imagine the building's future residents wondering why some curve was this way or that, and so he vowed to only make intentional decisions he could explain to a layperson. I had never heard him speak so much without stopping. I knew that grin, I'd caught it on myself once or twice before. In Eugene, in Florida. I imagined how my face had looked then, how happiness had lifted every muscle. I wondered what it would take to keep him smiling like that, what it would take to put that smile back on me. The background seemed oddly familiar, and I asked him where it was. *The Rockaways*, he said, *96th Street. The Boulevard and 96th*. I looked to Sandra: she couldn't tell what I was thinking but Billy could, he was already frowning. It wasn't in his agency agreement to leave the apartment.

The Uber driver was just about as happy. It took us five minutes to get Emmitt into the car and another ten to get him out and into his wheelchair. Also, we'd accidentally ordered a car for just three of us, by then it was second nature to consider the aide as an extension of Emmitt. (I wondered if the mistake was obvious, I wanted to apologize to Billy but thought it better to simply swallow the guilt.) When we arrived there was no one else around, it was still too early in spring for the beach to be crowded, the driver would likely have to make the trek back without a fare. We told him if he waited for an hour we'd pay him $75 in cash, and he agreed.

Trash and detritus lined the block, with piles of dirt and sand placed seemingly at random. The sky was overcast, chillier than it had been in Fort Greene. Planes landing and taking off from JFK intermittently filled the air with their metallic crescendos, but in their absence seagulls could be heard, as could the faint crashing of waves, Top 40 blaring from cars speeding down Rockaway Beach Boulevard. I closed my eyes and experienced it as Emmitt might. I couldn't imagine the soundscape had changed much in the past thirty years.

He said he wanted to touch it, the building. I wished the

driver would circle the block a few times but instead he just sat in his car, playing on his phone and taking indiscreet glances at us. We pushed Emmitt over and helped him stand as he put his hands on the brick. Against the structure he seemed small, hunched, scared, like it could hurt him, but when I looked at his face I saw that he was, in no small way, thrilled. He said they'd redone the facade. I knew this was true because of the bright shade of the brick, nearly lurid compared with the salt-worn complex across the street. I asked him how he knew that and he said, *These bricks fit right.* I didn't say anything but it looked like a lot more had been changed. The windows had been installed not long ago, as had the entryway. From what I could see the lobby was all new, mimicking those of the buildings around us that had been recently redone. Still, it was the same structure he'd once imagined, drawn, seen built. Those walls were still coterminous with people's lives, the distances between still set the stage for childhood memories.

Soon he had to sit but asked to stay in his chair by the building, where he remained for the rest of the hour. Occasionally he would lean to his right, closer to the brick, like he wanted to hear it. At one point I joined him, sitting on the ground with my back against it, listening, but the only sounds I perceived came from outside.

When we got back in the car he was unusually chatty, telling us about the process of getting the building approved but also everything else, about New York City nightlife in the eighties, what his brother was like when they were young, what it was like when sushi first came to town. He seemed happier than I'd ever seen him, and I wondered why we hadn't done this before.

Before we left he asked me to take a lap around the building. He wasn't sure if there was a cornerstone, not with his name of course but maybe his company's. I did as I was told and saw nothing. I hesitated to tell him, but when I did he didn't seem to care. It wasn't so important that the world knew who built it, just that he could claim it as his own.

~

I minimized the document, opened my browser, and, without even having to think about it, typed in *Last Resort Avi Deitsch*. The page said *No internet*. I'd forgotten my Wi-Fi was disabled, thanks to a productivity app I installed on my laptop. (The app's timer showed I still had two hours and forty-three minutes left; I'd apparently only been "writing" for seventeen.) You could end your session, but you had to hit a cherry-red EMERGENCY STOP button.

When we'd gotten back to Emmitt's, Sandra told me she wanted to spend some one-on-one time with him and that I should go home. She said it in a way I couldn't decipher, like she was annoyed but worried, like she herself wasn't sure how to feel. Perhaps it was obvious that I was hungover, or distracted. Being in front of my computer didn't make me any less so. The problem was I could no longer read a sentence without trying to inhabit Ellis, guessing what he'd think, what he'd say. It was certainly *more of a risk*, as he'd put it. I decided I didn't need to wait for him, he wouldn't advise it anyhow. To be a writer, as Dorothy Parker put it, meant "applying the ass to the seat." But after I'd put down another hundred words a buzz came from the kitchen.

I'd never heard the sound before. Right next to the light switch was a console, apparently there for when Bruce, the doorman, wasn't, which never seemed to happen. On a little screen above three buttons—TALK, LISTEN, DOOR—I saw Louis, rendered in too-high-definition for such a small device, holding his hands to his eyes like goggles. In the crook of his arm I saw a basketball, and realized I'd forgotten our plans. Louis was preternaturally good at the game, specifically shooting three-pointers. I was bad but tried on defense (a rarity in local pickup games) and was also willing to test the limits of our opponents' foul-calling. It was a pastime of ours to go to the courts, get underestimated as a pair of geeky-looking five-foot-ten Jewish boys with running shoes, and put the local teens to shame.

When he came inside he immediately started dribbling—asking me to ask him not to do that, which I did, and he did. He took a look around and said, *Love what you've done with the place.* He was being ironic. He hadn't been over yet, had consistently made excuses to hang out elsewhere, to miss the get-togethers Sandra and I hosted, to meet up at the courts even though they were just around the corner. Louis was weird about money, regular money, not to mention $830,000 (pre-tax, pre–Ellis's fee) money. I had tried explaining that I'd only see half that number, but it didn't matter. As a card-carrying member of the Democratic Socialists of America, he declared vulgar any conspicuous sign of wealth. To him, a doorman with a hat was the poster child of slavery in a late capitalistic society, *another sight in this modern-day zoo*, a phrase that ignored the existence of actual modern-day zoos. Maybe I didn't totally disagree with the sentiment, but the bar for ostentation seemed set at any salary above his, not a difficult threshold to overcome given that he was a freelance journalist.

He touched the wall and pretended to be scalded. *Dance with the devil ya bound to get burned*, he said, which didn't mean anything, but then, *Heck, I'd put in two months at a startup to get digs like this*. He was trying to provoke me. He knew he wasn't supposed to say a word about the arrangement, not even to me, not even when we were alone.

Stop, I said. *I'm serious*. I heard my voice and understood just how poor my mood was.

Sorry, he said, zipping his lip. *So we ballin'?* He dribbled once more, the piercing echo negating all attempts to quell my irritation.

I can't, I said. *I'm writing*. I felt bad but, to be fair, the plans we'd made were not the most binding. He'd texted me the day before, *Cud ball 2m @ 3*, and I wrote back, *Cud*, and that was it. I could see his disappointment, that he was trying to hide it, which was worse; I knew he'd turn it into something more antagonistic. *I'm sorry, man*, I said. *I've hardly been able to get a second to just sit down and think*.

All right, he said. *I mean*—here it was—*it would seem that unlike most functioning adults you have a lot of time to do exactly that*.

Says the guy down to play basketball every day at three.

Okay. You can't play. Got it. He turned to walk away.

I'm hungover, I said. *I'm sorry*. This seemed to slow his step. *Stay for a bit, we'll have a drink*. I shuffled down the hall to the kitchen, and shouted from there. *You want mango juice? Lychee?* I heard myself, and made a mental note to tell him lychee juice was only $3.99 at the store on the corner. *Something harder?*

There wasn't an answer, so I got the mango juice, a Diet Coke, and two glasses. He wasn't in the hall, so I brought them to the living room. As I set them down a glass slid between my arms and shattered, spreading shards across the floor. I didn't want to pick up my foot, I wasn't wearing shoes and was worried I'd lose my balance. *Can you grab the broom?* I asked, but there was no answer. I called his name, and then again, though I already knew I was the only one there.

———~~———

I ordered coffee and a soup I'd hardly touch, because if you only ordered a coffee at Mike's the waitress tended to give you a look. I'd been there for five minutes and was trying not to regret leaving home. On the screen in my kitchen console I'd watched as Louis left and saw that he ripped a begonia flower from its tree, right in front of Bruce, I'm sure, who knew which unit he'd been to, had the records to show it. Suddenly it felt like my apartment had been poisoned, that there was too much ill will there, so I left.

Except for an elderly couple everyone was alone, but still there was enough noise to distract me. They all seemed local, the type of people who lived in Brooklyn when everyone still wanted to live in Manhattan, people who kept to themselves, didn't buy clothes unless they had to, voted in local elections before it was cool. In other words, they were people who weren't likely to end up in my novel. But why shouldn't they? Maybe I just needed to leave my comfort zone. I finished my coffee and flagged the waitress. As she poured me another cup she said, *One more of these and you won't be getting to bed tonight.* I imagined her at home, taking the pin out of her hair, looking at her face in the mirror. *She placed the pin on the table and considered her day,* I thought, and had to stop already. It was a lie, every word of it. I checked the productivity app: one hour and forty-six minutes left. I hit the EMERGENCY STOP button, and my laptop searched for Wi-Fi, finding it at Pratt, across the street. The signal was weak but after a minute I could load Gmail. I had an email from Ellis, a response to mine, *Re: New story.* I didn't want to click on it, I sensed what was coming, but I had no other choice, did I? *Sorry for the lag bud. And great seeing you last night! Not the event we promised but I think we gave them a show nonetheless. So, I won't beat around the bush. I know I've kept you waiting long enough so I got some help from a reader here (Ophelia; she's whip smart, really— she'll probably have my job in a couple years). We had a good talk about it, and think you brought some real gusto to the table, and you have some GREAT ideas speckled throughout, but to be honest I'm not seeing the sort of originality that's really going to make an editor enthusiastic. And trust me—you want them in love or not at all. I think (part of) the problem is the ideas themselves. They're not talking to each other, and without that the project's not going to cohere into something larger than its parts. This just doesn't seem like the same writer that gave us* Last Resort—*all that feeling, and emotion, and* immediacy. *I don't mean to say you should scratch it all, surely there are some salvageable parts. So think on it. And please Caleb, don't rush! You've got time. And speaking of, I've been a bit short of it, with all the arrangements et cetera. So for the time being I'd rather not review anything until it's a bit further along. Thanks for sending!* I put my hand on the mug and held it there until it was too hot, until my palm burned so much it felt cold. Nothing hurts like the truth. I pulled my hand away; it was throbbing, I could feel my pulse. I submerged it in my water glass.

I hated him then, Ellis, for taking so long and for telling that to me with such artificial warmth. But what did I prefer, really? That he be rude? And what did I expect; he was a master of geniality. I thought of my meeting with him, Avi, and Rupert, how he'd praised Avi's writing, lied to his face to lubricate the conversation. That whole meeting had started to warp in retrospect. For example, when Ellis asked me about Avi, what the guy was really like, was he preparing to defend our case, or was he sizing Avi up for something more? I was surprised to find a small bit of consolation there: if I felt manipulated, out-duped, used—at least we'd both been, Avi and I. Suddenly it seemed absurd that we weren't on speaking terms. I went back to his text. *Ah, just a bit of food poisoning. Congrats on the Wood review by the way. Hope all's well.* Perhaps I'd been too critical. Maybe it was my own bitterness, my defensiveness that had gotten in the way. It wouldn't be a first for me. I took a large gulp of coffee, I thought for a bit.

With my phone under the table I memorized his number. I went to the counter and asked to use theirs, a corded block colored eighties taupe. I didn't expect him to answer, given all that I'd heard—even journalists whose job it was to get in touch with him couldn't. And yet on the second ring he did, and a small *Hello* came through the line. I was paralyzed. I had no idea what to say, but there was something else—I couldn't believe it, didn't want to, but it was the aura of celebrity, as if he were anyone else than the person I'd once loosely called a friend. *Hello*, he said again. *Hi*, I said, just to stop him from hanging up, and then, *It's me, Caleb.* There was silence, or a sort of silence, ambient sound, but then that suddenly disappeared and then there was nothing. I thought he'd hung up, I was waiting to be reminded of what dial tones sounded like when the background noise reentered, and then *How's it going?* came vibrating through, like the phone itself had produced the voice, was the thing I was conversing with. *I'm good, you?* I asked, my question just another attempt to sustain the conversation, keep us both there without having to say anything real, and we continued on like that—*I'm well . . . Good . . . Nothing new? . . . Not really, everything good?*—and as soon as he broke the cycle I wished I'd been the one to do it. *I heard I missed out last night.* Heard? From who—Ellis? *But even in your absence you were the main attraction*, I said. He gave a good-natured laugh. *There's one attraction*, he said. *The book. And for that you should be really proud, Caleb.* To hell with voice making it easier to discern tone. He was either being entirely earnest or mocking me. *Anyway, how's it going?* which meant, this time around, *Tell me why you called or let's call it a reunion.* I didn't know exactly, and so against my better judgment I was honest. *I don't really have a reason for calling. I just thought it would be nice to connect, to see how you were, and, well, I'm not doing too well myself.* I stopped. My eyes had become wet, barely, but I was mortified to think of it coming through my voice. I got my ground and continued. *I just think we should trade some notes.* He allowed himself another pause, long enough that I got to know the background noise, some children talking, wind coming into the receiver of his phone. *I would be okay with that*, he said, his voice distant at first but then it became loud, he had turned his head away and was bringing it back, there was someone there with him. *I mean, we're bringing something into the world together, why shouldn't we talk shop? I'll tell you what. I'm upstate right now, at Storm King, actually—but I'll be back late tonight.* I said that I heard Storm King was beautiful and we made small talk about it. I proposed meeting tomorrow morning someplace private, and then offered my apartment, which I immediately regretted as soon as I tried seeing it from his eyes, how well-appointed it must seem, luxurious even. *Let's meet at my place at eleven*, he said. *If you're willing to make the trek.*

———————

On Tuesdays Sandra hosted a women-only book club, but she'd asked to move it elsewhere. Then, an hour before it started, she told them she wasn't feeling well. She didn't say it but I knew she was staying in for me, that she was concerned—or at least wanted to find out if she should be concerned. This didn't help. From the moment she walked in, giving me a big hug and thanking me for the idea of going to the Rockaways, I was trying only to make her think I was fine—smiling when I could, manufacturing jokes, forcing myself to act silly—a self-defeating strategy if ever there was one. It was the first time I'd witnessed her unsure how exactly to handle a situation. When I told her about my call with Avi she listened blankly and then said, almost as a question, *That's great.*

She'd brought home a carton full of orange wine, as well as a few copies each of *The New York Times*, *The Washington Post*, and *The Wall Street Journal*. (These she left on the living room table without a word.) Really, I wanted to spend the night reading reviews online (I'd already read the ones from the *Times*, *Post*, and *Journal*, each at least twice over), of which there were now almost twenty, not counting blogs. She'd sensed as much, so we sat in the living room, each absorbed in our own activity. She was transcribing a conversation she'd had with her dad that afternoon; it was the first time he'd opened up about a lot of things, including her mom's passing, which she was too young to really remember. Ostensibly we were sharing the wine—when I refilled my glass I also topped her off—but I was drinking at twice, three times her pace. I spoke only to comment on the glass in my hand, wearing my limited vocabulary thin—phenols, tannins, skin contact, et cetera—as if the more I *appreciated* the wine the less conspicuous my drinking would seem. And it was conspicuous. Each new review was like opening up a fresh wound, and I was bent on hunting down every last one. For the first time in my life I read *The Charlotte Observer*, the *Orlando Sentinel*, the *Pittsburgh Post-Gazette*. I bought a digital subscription to *The Dallas Morning News*. It was hard enough to come upon a criticism I disagreed with—or found patently absurd. Harder still was the aperçu I had to agree with. But the more I read (and the more I drank), the more they all blended together (can twenty reviewers really describe a novel in twenty distinct ways?), the more I began to see past the commonalities to the disparities, the way they each connected with it on a personal level. And it was, in many cases, personal. A reviewer for *The Sacramento Bee* said it was *like reentering a recurring dream I never knew I had. The*

Baltimore Sun included the line, *Deitsch isn't asking us to live vicariously through the characters, but to just live vicariously.*

Shortly after we opened our third bottle (she'd had, at most, two full glasses), she said she was going to bed. *Don't be up too late*, she said, which meant, *Don't drink too much.* I did, of course, I finished the bottle and contemplated opening another one, but by then I'd started to feel distraught in a way I knew another glass would only amplify. Reading reviews in such a state (or rereading them) produced a nearly out-of-body experience, like that of attending my own funeral, hearing my own eulogy. The metaphor may be trite but it was apt; after all, a eulogy is written for someone who's done with living. It was hard to stop myself from crying and soon enough I didn't, I let it all come out, tears that were dumb and drunk but also completely logical. I'd failed in a very big way, I'd been wrong to make the decision I did, to take the money, I'd been wrong about why I wanted what I wanted, wrong about what getting it would do. I was in a torrid state, a hopeless state, a state that allowed me to fully admit that my current manuscript wasn't going anywhere, was as good as nothing, or worse, it was like a plot of land with a rotting house on it, which is worth less than the plot would be if it were empty because it'll cost you to tear it down. And yet, even if I trashed it and started over again, I didn't believe I could build something that wouldn't also need to be destroyed—no, in my heart I knew that I didn't have and wasn't close to having what I had when I wrote *Last Resort*, which was a great deal of pain and, more so, a story I believed enough to get free of it through.

The stack of newspapers loomed as the focal point of the room's only light, a golden arcing lamp. It was like I was standing in front of a monument constructed in my honor, one I'd be able to visit whenever I wanted to—in ten years, twenty, forty—but it didn't have my name on it, I could never point to it, I could never say it was mine. What I had instead was this apartment, this haircut, the clothes in my closet, the fine wine rotting my gut. What I had was the freedom to write empty words all day.

I didn't want it anymore. Any of it. I'd be a middle manager at Wells Fargo for the rest of my life if it meant I could rewrite history. I'd give every cent I had to have my name back. I would. And in twelve hours I'd have that chance, I'd be meeting with the name on my monument.

⁓

As a point of pride I still took the subway when I could. I liked seeing a cross section of the city, and besides, it was a hassle to call a car without a smartphone. But I woke up late, and the address he gave was deep in Red Hook, a twenty-minute walk from the nearest stop, and I was worried the subway would make me nauseous—I'd slept off most of the hangover but certainly not all of it—so I had Sandra call me an Uber.

When I arrived I was self-conscious about pulling up in a car, so I told the driver to drop me off at the end of the street. The building was the same sort of big bright brick block you find all around the neighborhood. It stood across from a large, densely wooded park that I found creepily still. I buzzed, and half a minute later I got a text that said, *coming*. I wondered if he now regretted inviting me over, that perhaps we'd take a walk instead, but when he opened the door he greeted me with a quick smile and told me to follow him in. He explained that visitors invariably got lost there, and I could see why. To get to his apartment we traversed three separate sets of stairs and two corridors long enough to make a wrong turn a major setback. I told him it reminded me of a middle school and he said it was a converted luggage factory. I said, *How Red Hook*, which came out wrong, barbed, but he produced an easy, forgiving laugh. His sudden charm reminded me of how I felt when we first met in Los Angeles. That felt like forever ago, and I said that, and he nodded thoughtfully, like he knew it all too well. We came to his door and he warned me about the state of the apartment. He said that he mostly lived at Franny's now, and then something I didn't understand about privacy issues.

It was a loft, unbelievably spacious, more or less a cube, the ceiling at least forty feet high. It would have been quite a task to make the room feel cozy and he hadn't even tried. What little furniture there was I could tell was from Franny, which worked well in our apartment but here it made the space seem somber, austere. Against blank walls he'd placed a few ferns and a fig tree. They seemed like shrunken, bonsai versions of themselves.

He began leaning against a counter I recognized as the backdrop of the *New Yorker* photo. The orchid was missing, replaced with a bowl of wrinkling apples. In the light of a long lamp dangling from the ceiling I could see him better, all of the details left out of that image. There were new creases on the sides of his eyes, an uneven line stamped into his chin. He had lost weight in his chest and arms and gained some in his face. I noticed the distant sound of vacuuming. I wondered if it had just started or if it had been there the whole time. He asked me if I wanted coffee, which I did, desperately. I'd had a cup when I woke up but it had hardly done anything. He prepared a French press, grabbed a bag of bagels, and then a container of whitefish salad from the fridge. *Stomach all better, then?* I asked. He glanced at me, registering my own sincerity before responding, *Much.* It seemed he didn't even care to be convincing, but then, after he got a bagel from the bag and began cutting it open, he said, *No, I wasn't sick. You probably understand why I didn't go.* I thought this admission took character, not as much as saying, *I couldn't bear to lie to the faces of strangers, to pretend someone else's work was mine,* but still. *Yeah,* I said. *I think I have an idea.* He took a bite. *Look,* he said, his mouth full of bagel, *I've got a career to consider. I go to events like this, I'm on shaky ground. I end up saying something I don't mean to, someone quotes me on it, and it's there forever. This is a tricky book, Caleb. It's not exactly progressive, there are some things we maybe should have changed.* I had a hard time looking him in the eyes, I needed to stay amicable. He pushed the bag of bagels over to me. *I didn't mean to be rude,* he said. *But I'm starving.* I grabbed a bagel, eager to put my attention anywhere but on him. *Are you still at Quartz?* I asked. I knew he wasn't, he probably knew I knew. *I mean, I heard you might have left publishing but I couldn't believe it.* He nodded enthusiastically. *I quit, yes. I mean, it wasn't totally my decision. Or, it was, but—I wanted to edit literary fiction, Caleb. And now I've published a book that's ostensibly literary fiction but, because it's immensely commercial, everyone with an MFA hates it. Hates me.* This seemed like a bit of a stretch. *It's fine, really. Editing's not what I was meant to do, I was meant to be on the other side of the page.* I thought I understood him but needed to clarify. *Writing,* I said. *Sure,* he said, glancing over to a table across the room. It was scattered with pages, which seemed inked, not printed. As if he couldn't have cleaned up a bit. *Not quite ready for a novel, but I'm starting small. I've got a few pieces lined up, in NYRB, the New York Review of Books*—like I didn't know the acronym—*and the Believer. Oh, the Paris Review too. That's a column, actually, just not sure on what, exactly.* A column without a subject could only mean they'd approached him. As if he could read my mind, he said, *Ellis has been great at these opportunities. He's relentless. I mean, consider all the coverage we've already got.* Did he know it wasn't just Ellis? Did he even read the emails from the Perry publicity team? *And congrats, by the way. I've only read a couple of the reviews but they seem generally positive?* I finished applying the whitefish and took a bite, making sure to talk through the food. *He emails you a lot too, huh?* He nodded. *Definitely*, he said. *And always under a new thread, for some fucking reason. It's like my inbox is half him. I wish he kept to a single chain, or at least had one for all his random ideas. Yesterday he tried telling me we should collaborate again, me and you I mean. He says I'm your muse, can you believe it? I said those days are over. He says you're heading in a sort of a—let me think—"heady" direction?* I swallowed. *Right*, I said. He sized me up. *I see, don't want to give too much away. I feel that.* He went to pour the French press and I looked back at his writing desk, the entire apartment. *You said you're living with Franny now?* I asked. He handed me my cup. *Yeah, this is mostly my place to write. Cheers.* He lifted his cup and I followed. *To Ellis*, he said, *and everyone else we couldn't have done it without.* I swallowed my pride, I needed to be game. *To the Perry publicity team*, I said. *And Joe and Reagan*, he said. *To Joe and Reagan*, I said, *whatever their real names may be.* He didn't pick up on this. *Their real names*, I said. *Right*, he said, taking a drink. *Their real names are Joe and Reagan. Joe and Reagan Carr.* I swallowed. *Are you serious?* He wagged his head from side to side, letting an impish smile creep on his lips. *Yes, I lied a bit, a small lie.* He took a second to think about it. *It was a bit impulsive, I know, but it was an impulsive time—for both of us.* He scoured my face, which I was trying to keep stoic. *Well, see it from my point of view*, he said. *You wrote every word of it. I needed to keep something of my own. You change Joe and Reagan, then why not change Avi too?* I felt the coffee widening my veins. *And you didn't think that might be a problem?* He shook his head and picked up his bagel. *Well, I'm sure Ellis and what's his name, Rupert, would have a conniption, but really, in what world would these people say something, assuming they even know about the book, which I doubt they do. And if they do, well, he's a fucking ad exec at Arnold. He's got a career to maintain, she does too, actually. It's not exactly a flattering plot to be part of.* He took a bite.

The fucking pomposity. The ego. Yes, it was ego that had blinded him, was blinding him now. *We* this and *our* that, "All the coverage *we've* already got." Was he kidding me or kidding himself? I tried sizing him up again as objectively as I could. Was he actually delusional? He said he was meant to be "*on the other side of the page*," but the only time he'd succeeded on one was when he was staring out of it. I sensed his eyes on me, I looked up. Could he tell what I was thinking, or at least how I was thinking? *Look*, he said, *the book's not actually based on them, you know that. The author wasn't even there.* For the first time what he said made sense. I nodded thoughtfully, I didn't want him to dwell on it. I took another bite and decided to extricate myself from his apartment as soon as I could. Avi wasn't my road to authorship, he was savoring every inch of it. And besides, I had nothing to offer him; he clearly didn't need money with this fucking pied-à-terre. He looked up at me, possibly reevaluating his own conviction. *This whitefish*, I said. *It's great. Where can I get some for myself?*

It was surprisingly easy. Maybe it shouldn't have been surprising at all. Using LinkedIn, with confirmation from Facebook and their wedding page on Zola, it took me all of ten minutes. Joe and Reagan Carr, Jersey City. I'd tried to look them up once before, back in Oregon, except I didn't have their last name, nor that other crucial detail—*he's a fucking ad exec at Arnold*. I browsed their social media profiles, just as Avi must have done. Yes, I did all of what he'd think to do and more, I unearthed every public image and mention of them, scoured their college yearbooks, their friends' Instagrams, reverse-image-searched their Facebook profile pictures.

They deviated in a few ways from how I pictured the characters—they looked younger and a bit more realistic; they had blemishes, their bodies were shapes that didn't jibe with the ones imagination produces—but all in all I wasn't so off the mark. I went back to the manuscript, recalling two paragraphs that detailed their appearance. I searched for "nose" and found the first.

Reagan was beautiful in a way that made her a catch for Joe, but not so much that her looks would spill onto her personality. The two of

them taken together clashed in the anachronistic way some couples do;
Reagan was modern, cherubic, with light skin and big clear eyes, but
Joe's slicked thin blond hair, tapered jaw and slim, pinched nose were
straight out of the eighties.

I searched for "Marilyn."

The early brightness washed away their edges; at a distance they
looked stylized and simplified, like they were in a cruise ad. Joe had on
a black square-cut bathing suit, a white towel around his shoulders,
and sunblock on his nose, which could have been earnest or ironic, but
most likely was somewhere in between. All but the trim of his blond
hair was hidden by a once-red baseball cap, now bleached pink, sitting
backwards on his head. His stomach aged him past thirty, with a
broad shallow mound growing from its center, yet somehow it suited
his grown boyishness. Reagan's head was tilted down and her face
was concealed by a wide-brimmed floppy hat, white polka dots on red.
Her off-white skirt bathing suit, gladiator sandals, and the silver
band around her bicep all suggested Marilyn Monroe, and her body
matched—legs slight at the ankle and knee, thickening at the thighs
into wide-set hips, leaving a vast valley of stomach before her breasts
perked apart, a quality of the suit's design or hers I couldn't tell.

I couldn't believe they'd had a foursome. They looked so normal. And maybe they were. After all, Avi suspected they
wouldn't come forward. Perhaps he was right about that. He was
right about a few things, actually—like the fact that Ellis would
have a conniption if he found out. Yes, there was no doubt about
that. It would probably be the first time in his fairy tale of a life
he'd lose his temper. He'd have to recalibrate his perspective,
admit that Avi wasn't such a golden goose, in fact he was de-
luded, he'd mindlessly risked everything for everyone else but

himself. Maybe Ellis would even cut him off from some of those magazine opportunities, throw *me* a fucking bone every once and again. I went back to Ellis's email from yesterday, scrolled down so I wouldn't have to read a word of it, and then wrote, *Can you talk?* As soon as I sent it I regretted not saying more, not mentioning the story, acknowledging his feedback. God, he probably thought I wanted to talk it through. His reply, no more than fifteen minutes later, indicated as much. *Bit stacked on the calendar as it is, though I'd love another one of our long lunches someday soon.* (Had we ever had a second?) *Happy to talk feedback but let's make it a phone date instead. Does 2:30 or 2:45 work for you today? I've got another appointment at 3.* It did work, except I wasn't going to wait an hour, I couldn't. I picked up my phone and called, knowing he wouldn't answer but I could leave him a message, tell him it wasn't about the story, convey urgency. But he did answer. *Ellis Buford speaking.* Apparently he didn't even have my number in his phone. He was unreal. *Ellis, it's Caleb.* In real time I could hear him controlling his tone. *Caleb, what's up, bud?* I skipped pleasantries. I asked if he had a few minutes and hardly waited for him to respond. I told him the truth as efficiently as I could. I reminded him of our initial meeting, of Avi's lie, his deception. Throughout I could hear him writing, with pen, which could have either meant what I was saying was important or he was multitasking. If he was upset he didn't bother letting me know. Whenever I caught my breath he confirmed my information with a simple *Mhm*, or a *Right.* When I finished he waited a moment, as if to make sure I was done, and then said, *Thank you for coming to me with this. I admit it's quite a surprise.* I asked if he could believe that Avi had done such a thing. *Unfor-*

tunately I can, he said, which filled my heart with glee. *We're lucky this hasn't turned into anything.* I was struck by that word, *luck.* I wanted him to say more. I asked if he could imagine what would happen if Joe and Reagan went public. He coughed, lowering the pitch of his voice. *Well, sure, it would really blow the fucking lid off everything. Perry would be furious, they'd be scrambling. We would too.* I waited for him to thank me, to give some sign of alliance, even just to throw some more dirt on Avi. But there was nothing. He said he had to go. The call had taken less than ten minutes. I got up and lay down on the couch. Perhaps I'd overestimated Avi's mistake, everything. The guy had some points, didn't he? Well, not that they probably didn't know about the book. If they hadn't seen a review, certainly someone they knew had, someone who perhaps didn't know about their island orgy but thought the name coincidence was too funny and sent along the article. Either way, I sensed Avi was right, that they wouldn't come forward. I mean, they hadn't. And even if they did, well, he was right about that too. How could a novel be based on someone if the author had never even met them? If Joe and Reagan did go public, *Perry would be furious,* as Ellis put it, *they'd be scrambling,* they'd use everything they had to defend themselves.

All of a sudden I felt an intense kinship with them, Joe and Reagan. We were all victims of Avi's lies and deceit, weren't we? They deserved the truth, just as I deserved my name back. Sunlight was the best disinfectant. Yes, they needed to know about the book if they didn't already. And if they did, they needed to understand that they'd been wronged, that they deserved something for it, financial remuneration, something that would be Avi's liability if not Perry's—no, I'm sure the contracts would put the financial burden on him. These contracts were circumspect, they were brutal. Maybe he'd end up needing some money after all.

———————

I should have known he'd respond so quickly. He was, after all, a "Senior Account Supervisor." *Hi Caleb. Thanks for reaching out. Yes, we wouldn't mind meeting up. As it happens Reagan is working from home today and I can be there in an hour or so, if you're willing to come out to greater Jersey City. Give me a call, # under signature. And how did you say you knew Avi again?*

I hadn't. In my first draft I had, but then I realized there was such a thing as too much information. I couldn't distract them from comprehending the magnitude of the situation. If they knew who I was, my place in things, the story would be too convoluted. And they'd probably think I was a madman. So I'd simply told them that I was *on the team that helped produce* Last Resort, *which I'm sure you're aware of,* and that I hoped to discuss *the ramifications of the book*. No more, no less.

I started to write back but stopped. I should just call, I thought, except my phone was back in the bedroom, where Sandra was, reading. She might already be suspicious. When she got home, half an hour ago, and asked how seeing Avi was, I struggled to speak coherently. I wasn't used to lying to her. And yes, for now I needed to lie. She was too good at poking holes in logic, and maybe I knew my logic was poke-able, but that was okay, I knew that what I was doing was right, that I was on the right track at least, that I was, at the *very* least, unraveling things, pulling the thread I had miraculously teased out from the tangled ball of yarn that was the bane of my life.

As if on cue I heard her shift around in the bed, and then get out of it. She walked to the kitchen and then, a minute later, came into the living room, banana in hand. She sat across from me on the green velvet armchair, slumping and crossing her legs. *Please just tell me what's going on.* Her tone made her sound worried, because she was worried, but still she tried to compensate. *I know that if you were cheating on me you'd be more discreet than this.* At that point it was just a matter of time before she drew everything out of me. I asked her if she wanted to come with me to Jersey City for a lunch. She took a bite, swallowed, and said, *Yes, I'd hope you'd be much more discreet.* I told her I was going to meet with Joe and Reagan. She squinted at me, trying to recollect the names, as if they were a couple we'd met once at a party, and when it clicked her eyes lit, and then narrowed. When I told her that those were really their names, that Avi had lied, she closed her eyes, allowing herself a moment without having to respond. I knew what she'd say, so I told her that I'd revealed nothing, only that I was part of the team behind the book, that I wanted to discuss the matter. She wanted to say too many things at once, and for a few moments couldn't say anything at all, and I took the opportunity to say, *Avi really fucked up, it was entirely selfish,* which really wasn't the card to play, so I paved that over and explained that I only wanted to talk with them and see how they felt about everything, if they understood what a big deal this was, that they were entitled to something, surely, for such an egregious, flagrant violation of their right to privacy. Now she could see what I was trying to do, or maybe what I hoped to gain from it. She looked disappointed in me, which sucked. I told her sunlight was the best disinfectant and she shook her head and I said that it was true, these people deserved to know the truth, and also, we should imagine how they feel, given all of the excitement around the book, the press. *Please*, she said. *Don't pretend that you're considering them even for a moment.* She stood up. *These are real people, Caleb, not characters.* I tried to speak but she cut me off. *You're using some ridiculous notion of the truth as an excuse to do what you think benefits you.* I was also standing, suddenly. *No*, I said, *not benefits me. Benefits them too, possibly. And besides, you're pretending that what benefits me isn't what benefits you.* Maybe I regretted saying that, but she was pretending not to know what I meant, which she never does, which is good, because I detest that and all forms of nonverbal dishonesty. *Look around*, I said. She rolled her eyes, or did something else I can't describe but that's what she meant: *I'm rolling my eyes.* I crossed my arms and she turned her shoulders so she wouldn't have to look at me. *No, come on*, I said. *Look around and tell me how much of what we have, we have only because of the sacrifice I made.* Now she rolled her eyes. *It's not something I ever asked you to do*, she said. *No*, I said, *sometimes we do things because we want to, and we know our partner will support us. You, for example, have decided to take some time off, and I have supported you, in more ways than one.* She swallowed and shook her head. *Tell me if I'm wrong*, I said. She didn't, because I wasn't wrong, but that wasn't the point, which I knew, except when she said, *That's not the point*, I became angry, because, well, I was angry, mostly at myself, but her holding a mirror up to me wasn't helping anything, in fact every time

I looked at her I became more furious, because her face looked how my face would have looked if I could have seen myself at that moment, and then, all of a sudden, when I had apparently seen her face for a millisecond too long, I stopped being able to control myself. *The point is that all of what we have, we have only because I PAID for it. Except I did not pay for it with money, or time, or anything I can get back, no, Sandra, I PAID FOR IT WITH MY NAME!* I knew I was shouting because I heard my own echo, which had never happened in that room before. *All of this, Sandra,* I said, leveling myself, *it's all here because of what has only benefited, apparently, me? You think I haven't hated it? Having to lie? Having produced something I'm finally proud of and not being able to own it? Only I have to bear that weight, only I do. We both live like this, but only I have to bear it.* She wouldn't look me in the eyes, which was fair, but it made me want to yell again, and that made me scared of myself. I breathed in and exhaled so she could hear it. I tried to speak but now she was trying to not look disappointed in me, she was possibly disgusted by me, and that was infinitely worse than how I'd ever felt in her company. I wanted her to cry, I let myself think about how I could make her do it, what I could say that would push her there, and with no better ideas I reflected her expression, her disgust, I could believe I was disgusted by her long enough for my face to get the right configuration, and when it did she looked bewildered for a moment but then she understood, she could see past me, and then she looked only sad. *Do what you want*, she said, and walked out of the room.

Before I could think about it any more, before I'd have to see her again, I did it, I emailed Joe. Then I took a shower. When I came out she was on her computer in the bedroom. I quickly got changed, grabbed my things, and left the apartment.

⌇

I took five copies with me, one for each of us and, well, two extra. There was a lot of traffic, I tried passing the time by rereading key passages featuring Joe and Reagan, but each time I couldn't go more than three consecutive sentences without having to stop. Much of it I had no memory of writing, which was fine. Not fine were the parts I could recall writing in great detail, how inspired I'd been, how confident I'd been of my flow, balance, truth-telling, realism. No one should ever be able to see his own ego with such clarity. I left a book in the car, a gift to the driver, who didn't return my *Thank you*, but I guess I wouldn't be too thrilled to be stranded in "greater Jersey City" in the middle of the lunchtime rush hour either. It was Bayonne, really, or so said the driver's GPS when it corrected the address. I couldn't ask Sandra to call me an Uber so I'd had to catch a cab, an endeavor that took me all the way to the Barclays Center. The first two I flagged refused to go to New Jersey, and so I told the third an address in Hell's Kitchen and then, when we were two minutes away, pretended to get a call redirecting us to, apparently, bumblefuck Bayonne.

When the driver pulled over I asked if we were there because I didn't believe we could be. It was a street of town houses, each with aluminum siding and a chain-link fence. Thick telephone wires drooped above the curbs. This was the sort of New Jersey neighborhood I grew up in, where the richest people had fine, normal jobs as middle managers at companies no one's ever heard of, where the kids went to public school and then Rutgers if they could get in. It wasn't for senior account supervisors at Arnold Worldwide, especially those whose lives could be the stuff of bestsellers.

I got out of the car and noticed the blinds—a few of the vertical slats had been disturbed. They were waiting for me to arrive, had been watching. I reminded myself that to fully understand the situation and what needed to be done I'd have to get out of my own head and into theirs. This would take careful observation but it would also require empathy. I again reminded myself, chanted in my head, really, that they'd been wronged—*they've been wronged, they've been wronged*—and that they might be too afraid to act on it, but I could, I had to, give them courage.

The door opened and Joe came out, followed by Reagan, who was pregnant, and now the housing situation made sense. They were wearing work clothes—slacks and a button-down shirt for him, a long-sleeve floral wrap dress for her. She was wearing makeup, his hair was flawlessly gelled and combed to the side; they both had clean parts. I waved and then, before I made my way, reminded myself that I was not the author of the book, that in no way could I say so, that I was simply there to listen to them and guide their thoughts.

I hopped up the steps to their door and we passed pleasantries, the exchange apparently interesting enough for the driver to wait in his car watching. When we walked inside I apologized for being late and they effusively told me I wasn't. The house was well kept or had at least been recently cleaned; there were vacuum lines in the carpet. They took me to the dining room, which

I could tell had also just been tidied by the stack of folders and loose papers temporarily leaning against the wall in the living room, ten feet away, a recurring image from my own childhood. The walls were white and the room was full of light, and I had to stop myself from flicking my pupils back and forth to gauge the state of my floaters.

Reagan offered me coffee and I accepted. Before she went to make it she placed plates and a deli platter between Joe and me, cold cuts arranged in a circle, turkey and corned beef. *Sorry for the fare*, he said. *If it were up to me we'd have every meal delivered, but we're trying to be better "financial planners."* He added air quotes, making sure I understood he didn't take financial planning too seriously, which made me feel he took financial planning so seriously he lost sleep over it. *Oh*, I said, *it's nothing*. He shook his head and then garbled something about a mortgage, nodding to a new stroller in the corner with a large tag still on it. I laughed vaguely, struggling to come up with a coherent response. He motioned for me to take some of the meat and then called out, *Honey, did you not bring out bread yet?* I winced inside, praying they wouldn't be the sort of couple that uses passive-aggression as a mode of communication. (They certainly did in the book.) She brought out a plate of rye, along with mustard and Russian dressing. Joe was about to say something but instead he sighed, shook his head, and got up. He returned with utensils and a face that said *What does a guy have to do?* I wanted to die. Actually the term *disembowelment* came to mind. I wanted to punish my-self, because deep down I knew that this wasn't how they were normally—if it was, they wouldn't be so grating, would have learned more subtle ways to deliver contempt—that it was my fault, my presence.

Not wanting to jump into it but unable to think of anything else, we strained to make conversation. Soon he said, apropos of nothing, *Reagan's pregnant*, and I understood just how ill at ease he was. I told him I'd guessed that and I asked the requisite questions and by the time he'd answered them—their first, a girl, name TBD, due in July, grandparents nearby—Reagan had returned with my coffee. The second she sat he clicked into gear, wasting no more time. *Remind me how you were involved with the book*, he asked, his voice carried by a forced ease that reminded me of what he did for a living. I repeated what I'd said in my second email, that I was on the team that produced the book. With barely any movement he made it clear that wouldn't suffice, so I said, *I worked on the writing side*, which seemed to earn me some trust but his brow remained furrowed. I panicked, I struggled to find any other way that could explain how I'd know what I'd have to end up knowing. *I helped him write it*, I said. *I was a ghostwriter of sorts*. This was a mistake, according to the rules I'd set for myself, but it did at least encourage them to lean in and open up a bit. *But I should be clear that, during my time working with Avi, I had no idea that the names we were using were real. I wouldn't have proceeded otherwise*. They nodded solemnly and then shared a glance, each apparently waiting for the other to say something they'd agreed on beforehand. In my paranoid state I expected them to ask for proof of what I'd said. I was already formulating my answer when, after they'd passed enough volleys of eyeball ping-pong, she asked if Avi would sign some copies. This didn't bode well. *Of course*, I said, and before I could add that I'd have them shipped later that day, she pulled out five books from the chair next to her and pushed them across the table. Right as I put my hand on top of them Joe reached for a copy and pulled it back. I assumed they'd bought them that morning, at most two days before, and asked if they'd had a chance to read it yet. Joe laughed, he said he got one months ago from a friend, a *publishing insider*. The rest they'd pre-ordered on Amazon. I asked how he'd first heard about it and he said he'd read an excerpt online. I said I didn't think it had been excerpted that early and Joe laughed again. He was either a great liar or a terrible one. *I forget what site it was on, a friend sent it to me.* He said he probably wouldn't have read more than a few words but Reagan's name caught his eye, because it was relatively rare, and then his own did, and so he jumped ahead and read a random sentence and knew instantly it was their story. He smiled at me and picked up the book and began riffling through it and within ten seconds he'd found the line. *Reagan's hand rose in the air and snapped away on the penultimate syllable, a mannerism I recognized as Sofia's.* He looked at Reagan, who pretended not to understand what he wanted. Her feigned confusion broke into a bashful smile, but there was also scorn there, and again I wanted to leave my own skin. Finally she did it, the motion so perfunctory it hardly registered, and I wondered if she herself actually thought Sofia had once done that, that she'd once copied her. Maybe she did believe it, the mannerism was relatively common, but still, I'd seen enough to confirm a feeling I'd had since we started talking: her instinct was to avoid seeing herself in the book, while his was the exact opposite. I couldn't help but think of

James Salter's *Light Years*. The novel is an account of a divorce, and it was apparently (not so subtly) based on the lives of a couple Salter knew. The day it came out, he was walking on Lexington Avenue when he ran into one of the protagonists, a woman named Barbara Rosenthal, and handed her a copy. It wasn't long before the Salters and Rosenthals stopped speaking. While the husband, Laurence, resented his portrayal (in the end, a failure in life and love), Barbara liked hers enough to name a dog after her character—and have a quote from the book etched on her gravestone. Though it's hard to hear that story without feeling some pity for Laurence, you have to wonder at Barbara. What kind of instinct is it to want to define your life by another's fictionalization of it?

As we continued talking, Joe read more passages, all of which involved his character. He spoke rapidly and with no consideration of what might be interesting, like a punctured balloon caroming around the room, and I could only wonder when he'd run out of air. I'd easily believe that they'd agreed not to tell anyone about the whole thing, had only the vacuum of their relationship to discuss it in. They both emitted a prudish vibe, an uptightness that seemed to define every microexpression and turn of phrase. This clicked with the presence of Reagan's stomach, which seemed to expand each minute. Their combined caution made them ripe to be parents, or maybe it was just that the impending child primed them to be this way.

It was clear he thought his character represented him well, that the dialogue in the book matched his own, that he was just as witty, eloquent, and vulnerable. *It's so funny to read yourself on the page*, he said. And then, later, *I feel like I've started seeing myself in the third-person.* I thought of Avi, how much he'd pretended to resent the book while I could sense, buried deep inside of him, the same sort of pleasure. It was similar to pride but different, it was relieving in a fundamental way, and desperate, not just about being seen but consecrated, preserved.

I had the urge to bring up Joe's last scene, in which he makes a drunken exit, humiliated and on the cusp of a breakdown. He's unable to come to terms with a brief homosexual incident with Avi's character, and also admits to Avi that he's afraid the trip has made Reagan unrecognizable to him. But I decided not to, because the more Joe spoke the more Reagan seemed to be shrinking into herself, and I knew that I needed her. Even if she didn't identify with her character, she was evidently the more rational of the two. Yes, she would see that a crime had been committed, what they could be owed for it.

In all of his talk of the book, Joe had failed to bring up that scene of intimacy between him and Avi (which I, of course, had fabricated), or anything else of a sexual nature. This was a feat, given that a fifth of the book is fucking or the prelude to it. I picked up a copy and flipped through, reading fragments at random until I found the exact page I was thinking of. *I'd turned this bridled excitement into stares that caught her, that she tried to break but couldn't, that sent her thumbs into her thighs and her mouth to the side.* I stopped speaking but continued along the page, mouthing the words to myself. *Oh,* I said. *This scene.* I could hardly look up at them, their discomfort was so palpable. *I didn't mean to bring up something so* . . . I pretended to search for the word. *No, it's nothing,* Reagan said. *Literally nothing.* She swallowed. *It's a book. A novel.* Joe nodded, wanting to agree but he didn't. *It's fiction*, she said. I wondered how many synonyms she might find. *Sure*, I said, turning to Joe while tailoring my words for Reagan, *I mean, it's fiction, yes, but the story's based on your lives.* Joe let out a hollow laugh and put his hands behind his head, performing nonchalance. *Maybe*, he said, thinking, and then suddenly he sat forward again and planted his palms on the table. *Well, I think the characters are based on our lives. The characters*, he repeated, *not necessarily the story.* I asked if he really believed that, that the story was invented. I was combing through my memory, trying the impossible task of separating what Avi had told me nearly two years ago from my own imagination from what ended up in the book. He gave a smug shrug. *Let's just say—* he began, but Reagan put her hand over his. *The story*, she said, *it's not what happened. I—I'll put it that way.* She gave a concluding smile and placed her hand on her stomach, the move reflexive. *What?* she asked me. Apparently my face was leaking doubt. *Well, doesn't that make it worse? I mean, I get the impression you two haven't told a soul.* I looked at Joe. *And I bet you told the friend who shared that excerpt with you that it was a wild coincidence. But the truth is, stuff like this leaks, it's bound to, it's—it's too interesting. And if it does, leak I mean, if people know you're in this novel—your family members, your friends, coworkers—they'll only assume that what happened in the book actually happened. I don't mean to be so harsh, really. There's a bright side, I think.* I took a second to read their expressions, which, in spite of all their apparent apprehension, were only begging me to go on. *The bright side is that, well, no one reads anymore. Not everyone you know is going to work through a whole novel just to read lines of dialogue their friends did or didn't say. No, they'll get what they need by reading about it online, and they'll take whatever narrative's out there at face value, and be satisfied. But this narrative, the one that ends up being* the *narrative, well, it's kind of up to whoever helps break the story in the first place. For example, if it leaks and the reporter goes to Avi first, maybe the articles are, you know, this sex novel's characters are real, they live in Jersey City, and of course they'll use a photo of you they found online, and you can bet they'll outline the novel's most lewd scenes. On the other hand, if you get the story out, well, maybe they'll say Avi infringed on your privacy, he stole your names and identities, he made you into puppets, and all for the consumption of the public.* Almost in sync they trained their eyes on the book on the table, and then shifted them to each other, and then back down again. A silence rose. I could hear what sounded like a tricycle making its way down the street. A plane's engine tore through the sky. It was so quiet that when I looked at my coffee mug I expected it to start shaking, to hear the rattling of ceramic and glass, the opening scene of a sci-fi thriller. *You have to ask yourself why your names weren't taken out to begin with. Just two find-replaces—it would have taken ten seconds. Honestly, if I were you, even if you weren't worried about all this becoming public, even if you just felt you were owed something for the crime committed against you, I'd do it. If I had a kid on the way, a mortgage? Definitely.*

The air changed, barely, but we all noticed. Suddenly I was being appraised, my own presence was being questioned. I'd been inhabiting them for too long and had forgotten that I too could be inhabited. I had planted the seed, and now I needed to step away, let the sun and rain run their course. *I didn't mean to say anything upsetting,* I said. *You have to understand that I also feel personally wronged here. I feel guilty, even. I mean, I helped write a lot of the book, never knowing what I was really contributing to.* Joe took a long drink of water. He looked at Reagan, who now had both hands around her stomach, as if to keep the baby inside, keep the world away. *Look,* I said. *This whole thing could obviously cause you both a great deal of anxiety.* I looked straight at Reagan. *But it shouldn't. This book isn't about you.* Her face was softening, or at least I imagined it was. One hand left her stomach and landed on Joe's leg. He looked at her. *I just hope you two get what you deserve.*

A metal clank came through the door, echoing around their foyer. *Mailbox,* Joe said, and gave a smile, one more genuine than any I'd gotten so far.

I started to make myself a sandwich and they followed. We ate in near-silence and at a hurried pace, eating the tension until it was gone, and when the sandwiches were gone too we nibbled at a box of almond-flavored pastries. We didn't make much conversation, partly because they were both drowned in thought, partly because I wanted them to stay that way. When we started talking it was just chitchat about their work, how they met, about Sandra and her dad and apartment prices in Brooklyn. I told them the story about visiting the housing complex in the Rockaways. Our time together was nearing its end. I explained that I didn't have a smartphone and asked them where I could flag a taxi. As expected, they offered to call a car, which I accepted.

The cab company said it would take around an hour. Luckily they had an excuse to leave the table, they were now both working from home and had to get on with it, and so I sat on their couch and read an old *GQ* while they separated to opposite ends of the house. I listened as they rapped at their keyboards, ostensibly to catch up on work but to me the noise sounded like something else, like progress. There wasn't a doubt in my mind they were only messaging each other.

———— ～～ ————

The driver and I had a good rapport. His name was Florin and he was a first-generation Romanian immigrant, born and raised in a small town near the Danube. He had three girls, the oldest sixteen, which was exactly how long he'd been driving. He had a side business, he said. It's why he supported Trump, no matter that he wasn't a citizen and couldn't vote. When I asked what the side business was he said *Lotion*, and then changed the subject, asking me what I did for a living. I told him I was a writer. *Like books?* he asked, and I said, *Yes, exactly.* I told him I wrote fiction and he said he heard a lot of fiction writers had mental problems. He was half joking but when I responded, *It does involve talking to yourself all day*, he seemed to take me very seriously.

I didn't normally talk to cabdrivers, and when I did I rarely got much back. It could have been Florin, who might have been especially amicable, but I believed it was something else, that I was radiating some positive energy, finally. I congratulated myself on my handling of Joe and Reagan, I possibly could have pushed them further, but I'd have risked showing my hand—rather, that I had a hand at all. No, when I left I was sure that they believed, at the very least, that they were morally entitled to compensation for what Avi had done. The problem was that it wasn't a matter of believing, but taking action, and this I wasn't so sure about. I could hardly imagine the two of them even deciding on a name for the baby. No, they weren't likely to take the first step, I had to account for that. They'd have to believe it was already public, or would be soon, and it was up to them to make it theirs.

We'd been submerged in the Lincoln Tunnel, thick in traffic, but soon, as the cab crawled forward, a slit of light appeared. I flipped open my phone and watched as it regained service. I began composing a text to Louis. *If I ask you for your help, you have to promise—* I stopped. Was I being prudent? Couldn't he be traced back to me? I erased it and wrote, *who was the best journalist in your class?* As we were driving under the High Line my phone buzzed: *me.* I took a second to admire the terraces jutting out of the Whitney. I wrote, *who's that girl you still keep in touch with.* After we'd turned onto Canal: *i keep in touch with all of them.* I wrote, *it was a euphemism.* A minute later: *anya.* I asked for her email and he asked why I needed it. *i have a breaking story,* I said and he wrote *!?!?!?.* I asked for her email again and he sent it.

Even though there were no lights on and no discernible noise, I intuited Sandra was there the second I came in. It was her smell probably, though I couldn't detect it consciously, only my lizard brain could extract the requisite data. I knew the second I saw her she'd fill me with guilt, perhaps even sap me of my conviction. Luckily, she wasn't in the living room, and my computer was. I approached it on the heels of my feet. With the lightest taps of my fingers I created an account on ProtonMail, *LastResort429*, and composed the message. I wrote everything I needed to and more. I did so without subtlety, without conjecture or hedging. I said things as they were. I was an unbiased, objective narrator. Third-person omniscient. A crime had been committed. I was informing someone who could report on it. I didn't reread the email. I was afraid of catching myself, of being too rational. I almost hit send but then added, *I've written to a few other journalists. I'd love for you to be the one to report on it, but I just thought I should be transparent.*

I walked past the office and saw her sitting at my desk. *Our desk*, I corrected myself, already primed for diplomacy. It was, technically, ours. She was wearing an outfit we called her *white-collar pencil pusher*, because it was a cream collared blouse and a pencil skirt. She only wore it for work events and interviews. I hadn't seen it in over a year. I stood in the doorway and waited for her to stop typing, which she didn't do for quite some time. I imagined she was pounding on random keys just to keep me waiting. *What have you been up to?* I asked lamely. *Nothing,* she said, waiting a beat before continuing to type. I walked up to her and saw she was in Word; it was a cover letter. She looked up and asked if I could give her a minute. I said sure and walked to the bedroom and lay down on the bed. I picked up a book she'd left on the nightstand, *Eichmann in Jerusalem*. I tried reading but couldn't keep focus.

Fifteen minutes later she came in and sat on the bed, her back to me, her arm extended to her side, propping herself up. The silhouette of her beautiful jaw broke the yellow rectangle of the doorway. It was clear she wasn't going to ask me about the day. *Are you applying for jobs?* I asked. *Yes*, she said. *I've had enough of a break.* I put my hand on her back even though I knew she wouldn't react. I asked what happened to grad school. She said she did more research, she needed more experience, she could get into a program but not a great one. This logic seemed a bit truncated, I made a mental note to bring it up later. I waited for the air to clear and then said I was sorry for what happened before. She said, *It's okay*, in a way that made clear just how hurt she was. *Truly*, she said, which isn't a word she uses, *I'm glad we had that chat. It was clarifying.* She seemed to be waiting for me to ask what exactly it clarified, but before I could gather the words she gave an answer so succinct I was left in awe of its efficiency. *What I assumed was ours you see as yours only.* This was hard to argue with, not that I didn't want to. I admit the thought crossed my mind to deny it, to pretend I didn't understand what she meant, but that would have been a waste of time. In that moment I could see all of what had happened with terrifying clarity: I'd made a sacrifice, the reward wasn't as great as I thought it would be, and the cost was much greater, and I had become bitter—bitter with myself, of course, but it wasn't that simple. From her point of view our lives were just as we expected them to be, or better; she suffered no doubt or regret or anxiety. For some time I had made every effort to believe that too. I'd escaped my own truth by latching onto hers, but I could no longer, and now there was a gulf between us. I not only envied her position—enjoying what I couldn't—I resented her for it. As if the choice hadn't been mine. As if she could have known what I was thinking when I'd deceived myself for so long. I had even started to believe I was owed something for this discrepancy—that what was ours should be mine only.

You're right, I said. *I do see it that way. I did, I mean. And now I can see how fucked up that was. How wrong I was. I'm sorry.* I thought to give her a hug to show I meant what I said but it was clear she didn't want that. No, her face said: *I don't want to be in the same room as you.* I decided to save her the effort, I told her I was going to take a walk and think about things. She couldn't even look at me as she said *Okay.*

It was a balmy night, there were intimations of summer. I walked east, in the direction of Bed-Stuy, snaking through the streets named after presidents, almost into Bushwick, and then I turned around, trying to retrace my exact path. I replayed the conversations we'd had that day over and over in my head, seeing it from my side and hers, trying to live in the space between. I regretted everything I'd done to make her disappointed in me, I hated her disappointment, it was worse than my own, but it was a small price to pay to make things right again. Yes, even if she wouldn't agree with what I'd done—what I still had to do—I knew of no other way to bridge the gulf between us, to finally rid myself of the regret I feared would never go away.

The apartment smelled like weed. I imagined all the cortisol I'd made shoot through her veins, the dopamine she'd tried to replace it with. I found her in the bedroom, watching *The Crown*, a glass of something clear in her hand. When she looked at me we had a silent, instantaneous conversation about whether we wanted to talk about what had happened earlier; we didn't. I sat next to her on the bed and took a sip from her glass: Cointreau.

She told me I could have it, that she'd had enough. Her breath confirmed. She grabbed her sleeping mask and I asked if she was going to brush her teeth, in the nagging way I do, and she shook her head. Before I went to brush mine I lit the joint on the table, just a small hit; I had a feeling I'd sleep well but wanted to make sure of it.

~~~~~~

I was right, I slept beautifully. I slept how I imagined normal people slept, how the religious slept, like I wasn't on my own. I was the first to wake up, a rarity. It was nearly 10. I sat up and slid my legs over the 1500-thread-count Egyptian cotton. I realized I was enjoying the physical comfort they provided in a way I hadn't before. The last time I'd actively enjoyed the sensation of sheets was probably before I went to college. My squirming woke Sandra. She moved her head onto my chest and put her hand on my stomach. *Breakfast*, she said. I liked that she wasn't polite, she was never polite unless something was wrong, it was a return to normal. Perhaps it was only that she hadn't fully woken up yet, hadn't remembered the state of things, but I was happy to work under the assumption that everything was all right if she was. I went to the kitchen and poached eggs and fried plantains and put the eggs on the plantains with some basil leaves and hot sauce. We ate in bed and then, through a conversation between our legs, agreed to have sex. It was slow and a bit insecure—we didn't talk or make eye contact—like we were new lovers, each at risk of invading the other's privacy. After we'd lain in silence for a few minutes she picked up her computer and we did the *New*

York Times crossword puzzle. It was Thursday so it was doable, for her at least. I contributed at most three answers but gave it my full attention. It was nice to try and fail at something for a prolonged period of time. It felt like I was in middle school. She got up to shower and I lay there, happy to be bored. When she came back she changed into a business casual outfit, the pencil skirt with a colorful silk button-down that looked like an abstracted scene of buffalo grazing on Neptune. I asked if she had an interview and she nodded, but then amended, *Not an interview. I'm getting coffee with Nathan. He's working at a consultancy now, and they're hiring.* I remembered that she disliked working with Nathan, that he was maybe personality-disordered, but kept my mouth shut. Suddenly I began to see the next chapter of our lives, that it contained unpredictable turns and conflicts, opportunities and needs, daily life of a different texture. This satisfied me in such an immense and diffuse way I didn't want to think of anything else. I imagined her getting a new job, all that excitement and celebration and worry. I saw her preparing for the first day and I even envied her, briefly. Maybe our lives had become too slack. Maybe we both just needed to step through new doors.

I picked up an old *New Yorker* and read it until she left. On her way out she told me to have fun at the dentist, an appointment I'd completely forgotten about. This only confirmed my belief that she should be working, should be putting such a steel-trap mind to use five days a week. Nonetheless, it was bad news. I hated going to the dentist. I liked *him*, I had to, he was handsome and had perfect teeth. But he continually tried to upsell me, an annoyance I came to see as morally corrupt. I once told him my brother had crowns put in and he must have written it down somewhere because each visit thereafter he reminded me of this fact, that I too might need them, *and with these things I always say better now than later.*

When the door closed I went to the living room, lay on the couch, reached for my laptop, and pulled it onto my chest. I didn't even bother checking my personal email, went straight to ProtonMail and found two messages, the first time-stamped at 7:04 a.m., which was encouraging. *Thank you. I will follow the lead and see where it takes me. If I need anything else I will be in touch.* The second was sent at 10:55. *Your sources were amenable, thank you. I have a potential publisher, and we're working together to connect the dots. Also, I'm sure you looked me up, but you can find some of my recent stories at anyapaulson.com.* In fact, I hadn't read anything she'd written, and this made me feel momentarily negligent. I knew from Louis she mostly did political writing, and that she was even further to the left than he was. I brought my mouse over the URL, a hyperlink, and saw at the bottom of the screen that it linked to *grabify.link/track* and then a string of letters. I Googled Grabify and found that it was a site you rerouted traffic through to grab someone's IP address, which put to rest any doubts I had about her diligence.

I left the apartment just before noon, and when I got out of the subway I had a text from Louis: *so THIS is why you wanted her number. you knave!* I wrote, *tell me what you know.* By the time I got to the dentist and signed in he hadn't responded, still hadn't after twenty minutes of leafing through a year-old copy of *People.* When they called me in I kept my phone in my pocket so I could feel it vibrate but when they started preparing me for X-rays I was paranoid it would explode, or at least make me infertile, and I put it in my bag. When the dentist came in I wanted to retrieve it but was too embarrassed. Soon he was telling me I should really do this or that, I hardly listened, I navigated my way out of that conversation more brusquely than I'd ever been capable of, and by the time I paid and left it was only 1:13. I still had no response from Louis so I called him. He didn't pick up but texted me a minute later, *crunching hours*, which could have meant anything. I wrote, *update, please*, and he responded, *check your email*. I turned around and walked back to the dentist's and asked to use their Wi-Fi.

It was a Google Chat conversation between him and Anya. She'd remembered that he went to Haverford and asked him what he knew about Avi Deitsch. He gave typically ironic answers, the one time this habit of his might be beneficial. She said she had *something in the works, potentially v juicy* and then, a few minutes later, that she was *meeting with a crucial source*. Louis hardly responded—*nice*, or *sweet*—and it wasn't long before she said she had to go, that she was *hoping to get it out ASAP*.

All I wanted was for the day to pass, for the article to come out so the world would be closer to knowing the truth, but also so I could no longer do anything to stop it. Only then could I begin the process of smoothing things over with Sandra. This would take an indeterminate amount of time. There would be a moral reckoning, a new low point in our relationship, but, with work, we would reclaim everything we'd had and more.

I needed to pass the time. I considered shopping for clothes, but at that hour the stores would be empty, and I'd likely have a bored salesperson watching over me. The Cobble Hill Cinemas

was just a ten-minute walk away. All that was playing was *Rex &
Ruby*, a kids' movie I didn't know much about except that it featured a gay teenage rhinoceros. It had gotten a ton of press for
being the first major motion picture to present homosexuality to
kids. I bought a ticket even though it had started twenty minutes
ago. It was me and about twelve other people, all in groups of
two or three, none without children. I sat in the back and hoped
no one would see me. On-screen was a teenage rhino, Rex I assumed, trying on his mom's earrings. For such a supposedly en-
lightened film this seemed a bit trite. Also he had long eyelashes.
Actually, when I was a kid I'd tried on my mom's earrings a few
times and when I later heard this made me gay I cried myself to
sleep more than once, so maybe a movie like this could do its job
without winning the Palme d'Or. Still I couldn't watch another
minute of it. It was only 1:29. If I went home, got changed, went
to the gym, and ran ten miles, by the time I got back to the
apartment it would be 4, at least.

Before I started running I texted Louis, *no email, pls text with
updates.* He wrote back, *all this work no pay,* and then nothing
else until 3:42, just after I'd hit seven miles. I was so excited to
see his name I dropped the phone on the treadmill, launching it
into the mirror behind me. I kept the treadmill running and
went to get it: *green means go.* I wished desperately he'd choose
this one time to say things straight. A second later: *has someone at
the times.* I couldn't believe it. I wrote, *the Times??? of New
York????* and he wrote, *prob,* and then, *it is being fact-checked. could
be out by rush hour.* I wrote, *nyc rush hour or mid-america rush hour?*
He sent an emoji that my phone couldn't interpret. I texted, *no
emojis,* and he wrote back, *it was a cow.* I closed my phone and

looked ahead, forgetting I was inches from the mirror. I saw more blemishes than I'd normally care to notice, a few bumps along the side of my mouth and stray hairs my razor missed. I was too close to see anything but pieces of myself, didn't even recognize the shape of my face. I stepped back gradually until my identity cohered, and I stood there, hands at my side, sweat stamping a few curls onto my forehead. Looking at myself suddenly felt like it had when I was young, not young young but young enough, when I could see my own potential, the lack of defined form.

I checked my phone, 3:44. I decided to see if I could finish ten miles by 4, except on a treadmill it's never a question of can or cannot but set it and forget it. I had enough adrenaline to kill a small animal, and handled the first minute fine, but then, on a stride like any other, my right leg landed and it felt like there was only jelly inside. I caught myself before the tread did, and hopped off, falling to the floor. I clutched my leg with both hands, as if that might stop the pain radiating from within. It seemed as though some pulleys had snapped. A woman power-walking a few treadmills away was staring at me. She asked if I was okay and I said I was in a way that conveyed I wasn't. She looked sympathetic enough so I asked if she had Uber.

I'd been able to make it down the steps of the gym by myself, but when I got out of the car I found that the muscles in my leg could not expand or contract, and so from the street I called for Bruce to come and help me, and I used him as a crutch to get up to the elevator and then into the apartment. I could tell Sandra was home, so I began preparing my case against going to the hospital. Fortunately, she didn't come into the bathroom until

I'd had the chance to retrieve a stool from the kitchen and bring it into the shower with me. I couldn't understand how she couldn't see my silhouette, that I was sitting, as I could see her shape fine, gesturing wildly as she told me how well the meeting went. When I finally pushed aside the door she asked, calmly, *What the fuck are you doing?* I told her I'd pulled a hamstring, which was certainly possible and my story for the time being because as far as I knew that didn't require medical intervention. I asked her to help me to the bedroom. After she dumped me on the bed I convinced her I wasn't in pain, which was a lie, and then to help me find my phone, which wasn't near the pillow where I usually left it or on the bedside table or the dresser. She looked in every conceivable spot, and with each minute it became harder to ignore the grim reality, that I'd left it in the Uber, of course I had, the one time I'd been in one without being able to contact the driver. She called my number, texted it, and then left a voicemail. *It's okay*, she said, turning me over so I was prostrate, so she could examine my leg, which was apparently quite swollen. She went up and down, grabbing it in clumps, asking me what hurt and what didn't, though none of it hurt now, in fact I could only tell something was wrong when I consciously tried moving it, and then the pain was so agonizing I couldn't keep my eyes open. She suggested going to the hospital, citing the $775 I pay per month for the health insurance I hadn't used once in the past sixteen, but when I protested she let the idea go. She went to get painkillers but only found Tylenol. She said Advil would work better. I didn't think any OTC painkiller did anything but I agreed with her, because—I am not proud to admit this—I knew she would leave the apartment to get me some, and that would allow me to go on my laptop, which I wanted many times more than I wanted for the pain to go away. She gave me a kiss and said she'd be back soon and I asked if she would also pick up a pizza from Mario's, wasn't it getting close to dinner?

As soon as the door closed I rolled to the side of the bed, threw my legs off, and planted my feet on the floor. I tested them with a bit of weight. It wasn't promising. I knew I'd end up falling but gave it my best. When I hit the floor the thud was loud enough that I waited with bated breath, making sure she hadn't heard and wasn't coming back to check on me. I crawled by throwing my forearms out back and forth like they did in war movies, because I didn't know how to crawl and this at least felt less pathetic. By the time I got to the office my arms were covered in dust; I made a mental note to have the place cleaned. I pulled my laptop off my desk, opened it on my chest, and Googled *Avi Deitsch*. I always thought covering one's mouth to show surprise was just cinematic tradition, but there I was. From *The New York Times*, twenty-seven minutes ago: *Bestseller a Bit Too True to Life, Find Main Characters*. The copy underneath: *Some novels make you feel like you're there. Rarer is one that makes you feel like you* were *there. One married couple in Bayonne claims this spring's hottest* . . . I clicked and found a picture of Joe and Reagan in their backyard, him sitting in a lawn chair, her standing, peering off-frame, a Saint Bernard between them, the only one looking at the photographer. How the hell had they already done a photo shoot? Where was the dog yesterday? Hadn't they needed to get the story straight, fact-check? Apparently not; the article was written in the we-have-just-one-source tense, each statement wrapped in conjecture, hedged as if the copy came straight from legal. The only parts stated as fact were about Reagan and Joe, and the book itself. The byline was credited to both Anya Paulson and Alexandra Alter. My instinct was to delay reading it. I scrolled up and down, it couldn't have been longer than five hundred words. Just enough to set the scene (*a pretty if not well-off New Jersey suburb*), give the backstory (*The couple met Mr. Deitsch on a brief sojourn to the Greek island of Paros. The circumstances of their time together are unclear, but, according to the Carrs, what happened there was nothing close to what the novel asserts*), make the claim (*appropriation of name and likeness*), and lay down a few juicy quotes. The longest of which was by Reagan, a rant about the book's story not being what actually happened, which ended with, "*We are deeply dismayed to have our privacy infringed upon, and to have been used in such a pornographic plot, and we will not sleep until we get justice.*" Only in the last paragraph was there explicit mention of legal action. *The couple didn't comment on whether they plan to take the matter to court, but Mr. Carr did note that they've already reached out to the publisher. "We should hope Perry Books is ready to speak to what, exactly, happened," he said. "And we'd hope they're ready to make things right again." Yet to respond are Mr. Deitsch and his representative, the power agent Ellis Buford.* I went on Twitter and searched *Deitsch*. In between retweets of the article were mostly inane comments, but a couple of posts had caught fire. One featured an image of the book's "all persons fictitious" disclaimer, with select words crossed out and replaced: "This is a work of ~~fiction~~ **nonfiction**. Names, characters, places, organizations, and ~~incidents~~ **orgies** either are products of the author's imagination or ~~are used fictitiously~~ **absolutely happened**. Any resemblance to actual events, places, organizations, or persons, living or dead, is ~~entirely coincidental~~ **spot on.**" (209 likes, 34 retweets.) Another was a meme with Avi's face on a stock photo of a man eating salad and the words *CRUNCHY TOMS, LITTLE SOURS*, which I didn't understand (114 likes, 41 retweets).

The elevator dinged and I froze, waiting for whoever it was to go into their apartment, but then I heard the key slide into the door and I shut my laptop and put it back on my desk. She walked past the office without noticing me and went into the bedroom. She said my name and I didn't answer, because I wanted a moment to think, which I got and which produced nothing. She came into the office and asked me what I was doing. For some reason I thought she'd be mad, but all her face showed was pity. She told me I looked like that Wyeth painting. *Christina's World*, I said, and laughed a weird little laugh that wasn't mine. I could tell she could tell something was up. And of course she knew exactly how to play it: wait, prod lightly if at all, let the guilt rip itself out of me. *I didn't want to leave you here alone*, she said, *so I ordered the pizza to be delivered.* She smiled and went to the kitchen and got me a glass of pear juice to take the Advil with. She watched as I took it, as if I might not, like I was an asylum patient. *Thank you, nurse*, I said, and she didn't respond. She lay down on the couch above me, which I took as a blatant power move, probably because I was paranoid, I was literally guessing at the number of seconds that would pass before she had the information everyone I followed on Twitter did. I needed it to be over. I reached up, grabbed my laptop, and handed it to her. She didn't take it, she just let it hang in the air until my wrist couldn't bear the weight any longer and I set it down by my side. *How mad am I going to be?* she asked. *That's up to you*, I said. Very carefully she bent down and picked it up and set it on her lap. She gave me one last look before lifting its cover, spraying herself with light. Her face stayed blank as she scrolled down the page. She must have only skimmed it; she closed the laptop not a minute later. It was obvious how carefully she was modulating her breathing. *Don't look at me like that*, she said. I wanted to say the same thing back. She didn't look disappointed as much as she looked like she didn't know me. I thought of our first date, when I knew there was the possibility of love, when she didn't know I was a writer and every stereotype of one, and how badly I'd wanted to tell her that I'd signed with Ellis Buford, because I actually believed I needed her to know that to know I was special the way I knew I was special. *Look at you like what?* I asked. She hesitated. *Like I'm your—* She stopped. She might have cried or screamed but did neither. After a few moments she said, *Like I'm your fucking compliance department. I'm not. I'm not going to do this anymore. The choices you make from here on out are your choices, they're only yours. And just to be clear, I think the ones you've made recently make you seem like a self-centered asshole who is helplessly driven by—by nothing! By selfishness! By your own fucking ego!* Before I could respond she got up and walked out of the room, fully aware I could not follow her. I listened as she not so much packed her bag but did what she could to make the sounds of packing a bag. A few minutes later she came back into the office with a duffel I recognized as my own, and I said as much. *I don't have my bag anymore*, she said. *Remember? You told me to get rid of it. You've bought everything we have, which apparently lets you control all of it.* I laughed a laugh that probably sounded ugly and pathetic. *And the chairs in the living room?* I asked. *The ones we bought from Franny? In what world would I decide to get those?* She looked confused, which at first I thought was a petty tactic. *What chairs?* she asked, and I asked her if she wanted me to crawl to the living room and show her, and then she knew what I was talking about, and her confusion melted into sadness. *Those aren't from Franny,* she said. *I got them from Sisters. They were selling them for cheap because they got new furniture. I thought you'd recognize them, but you didn't.* I knew what was coming, almost said it before she could, so she would know I knew. *They were the kind we sat in on our second date.* I hated that we were both thinking the same thing, how distant that night felt, how far away it seemed from the one we were in. *I'm going to stay at my dad's for a few days,* she said. *That way I won't be an obstacle to your crusade. I won't even have to witness it.* She picked up the duffel and said I could call her if it was critical. Before I could remind her I didn't have a phone she said she'd be checking her email, and then she left.

I sighed, laughed, cried a bit. I had to piss. I crawled to the bathroom and managed. I wished I'd brought the laptop with me because the bedroom was right there. It took me twenty minutes to change, smoke a bowl, and get in bed. It looked beautiful out. I wished it would start raining. I checked the weather and then ProtonMail. There was an email from Anya with a link to the article, this time not through Grabify. She wanted to set up a call. I could have complete anonymity if I wanted. It could be off the record. It seemed she'd learned a few things from the *Times*. I opened my personal email. I had five messages but my eye knew where to go first, the one labeled *Rupert, Avi, Ellis*. I heard the buzzer from the kitchen. I thought it might be Sandra, that maybe she'd had a change of heart—and forgot her key? No, it was the pizza. I crawled out of the bedroom and then climbed up the corner of the wall where the hallway met the kitchen and hit DOOR on the console. I tried hopping on one leg, using the wall as support, but by the time the knock came I was only halfway. I shouted *BE RIGHT THERE*, and then again when I was halfway closer. When I finally opened the door the guy looked struck with fear, as if he might have to help some poor soul to the hospital. I told him I was fine, that I'd just need to get my wallet from the bedroom, which might take a minute but actually he could just go and get it. He hesitated, which I understood. I said I'd give him an extra-big tip, which didn't help my case, or helped it all the way; he placed the food on the floor and left. It smelled wonderful. I was high. I ate right there, three slices and half the salad, my Diet Coke and her Barq's. Ten minutes later I was in bed again. Avi and Ellis had each already responded. Ellis thanked Rupert for *putting this together*, and Avi wrote only, *Yes, I will be there*. I scrolled up and read the original email. Our *presence* was being *requested*. A chill overtook me, alerting me to the presence of the follicles on my head and the skin of my scrotum. We were to meet tomorrow at 8 in the morning, this time at Rupert's office. The hour struck me as aggressive. We would be joined by Perry's publisher as well as the general counsel at Seymour Group, the conglomerate that owned

Perry; these two were not included in Ellis's email. After I finished I read it again from start to finish two more times, and then the ending twice more. *This is not a meeting any of us wishes to have. Your attendance is absolutely imperative.* I believed the words until I remembered I didn't. No, this was a meeting I not only *wished to have*, I'd nearly orchestrated it myself. And yet I felt uneasy, I could think only of my second-grade teacher's voice saying, *Be careful what you wish for.* I wanted to think about anything else. I masturbated, which was nice but left me exactly where I'd been, alone and anxious, angst pulsing in my body like a dull pain. It was dawning on me that I was not at all done with making decisions, being strategic, performing. I had gone so far but there was still the final mile: putting my authorship back on the table, showing it as an exculpating solution. Not that I would be so obvious, ideally I wouldn't even be the one to suggest it. No, I couldn't let on an inch, show too much of myself, let anyone see through me, especially not Ellis. With every bone in my body I feared that he would know what I'd done, have an intuition about it, ask me. If that happened, if he could in fact see through me, I'd have no choice but to own up to it, show them all just who I was and how much I was willing to sacrifice.

It had been a long time since I'd had to wake up as early as 5:30. I dreamt the sort of dream I always have before a highly anticipated day, one where I go through every mundane step of waking up and getting ready except at half speed. In this dream I'd made it to entering a taxi and closing the door when an especially brassy version of "Call Me Maybe" began. Last night in the absence of my phone I'd quickly downloaded an alarm application onto my computer. (I hadn't wanted to waste time choosing the ring option; of course it took me an hour to fall asleep anyway.) I hopped out of bed, forgetting the state of my leg, and would have fallen if not for the wall. I pushed myself away and found that I could stand, walk even, as long as I did it deliberately enough. I made myself coffee, played chess, and listened to NPR. I shat, showered, and shaved. The night before, I'd laid out an outfit, but opted for the silver suit I usually wore to weddings. Downstairs I waited by the doorman desk as Bruce called me a car. *Big day?* he asked, straightening the lapels of my coat. *I hope not*, I said, and he chuckled, and it occurred to me that I'd never before questioned whether the laugh he gave me was in any way real.

The office was in the Financial District, the building and those around it all at least thirty floors. I couldn't believe how much everyone looked the way they should—the scene would have made fine B-roll for a boardroom blockbuster—but then again I looked like them too, with my suit and briefcase, which held only my laptop, headphones, and a banana, but still. I had thirty minutes to kill, so I went into a Starbucks and reread the email from yesterday, and then went on Twitter. I had thirty-four notifications, which was about thirty more than I'd ever had. Random people had started following me and liking my posts, ones I'd made years ago. I searched for *Caleb Horowitz* and nothing material came up, and then I searched *Avi Deitsch* and saw everything. The top tweet was by someone named Rhett Webster, who was apparently an editor at Moonlight, an imprint

212 · Andrew Lipstein

that had made an offer for *Last Resort* but exited the auction early. It posted last night at 12:17 and already had 141 likes and 30 retweets. *It's industry scuttlebutt by now, but: LAST RESORT was originally shopped under the name Cal Horowitz, a real person who is friends with Avi Deitsch on Facebook. Were Buford and Deitsch trying to avoid trouble from the beginning? WHY NOT JUST CHANGE THE NAMES OF THE CHARACTERS?* The first comment, seven minutes after, was by Jules Stafford, an editor at Carrington: *Beat me to it.* My hand was shaking. I pushed away the cold brew I'd bought only to look like I wasn't loitering. I closed my laptop and twenty seconds later reopened it. I scrolled through more of the comments. I couldn't focus on any one of them, I always wanted to see the next response. I Googled *"Cal Horowitz" "Last Resort"* but nothing came up besides Twitter. It seemed wise to temporarily reduce my digital imprint. I went on Facebook and made my photos private. I went back to Twitter and scrolled through my old tweets. I stopped on one that said, *i before e except after c or if you have spellcheck just use that.* The embarrassment I felt could not be put into words. I deleted my account, closed my computer, packed up, and left.

As soon as I walked in a security guard beckoned me over. He took my driver's license while another guard sent my briefcase through a scanner. He shepherded me through a metal detector and then waved a wand around my body. I watched as people streamed in and out of the building unchecked, and wondered what I'd done wrong. It was fifteen minutes before my license was brought back to me, along with a sticker featuring a grainy rendering of my license photo. The atrium seemed to have been designed to produce as much echo as possible, ditto the shoes these people wore; so many footfalls could be heard in a single second that it was impossible to latch onto a single beat. The elevator maître d' glanced at my sticker, now firmly planted on my chest, and directed me to the appropriate shaft. In my cab was one other person, a man holding his phone as far away from his face as he could, frowning. He didn't move an inch in the five seconds it took us to go twenty-eight floors. I got off and entered through a glass door etched with the name *Holder, Baron, Moss & White LLP* in a tasteful serif type. I was struck by how poetically those names semanticized; it made me think of *Hamlet*. Behind the desk a blond woman with a may-I-speak-to-the-manager haircut asked if she could help me in a tone that implied, *Who the fuck are you?* The room smelled of lavender. Actual lavender? I looked around. Her eyes widened continuously, as if they'd explode if I didn't answer her non-question. *I'm here to see Rupert Paul,* I said. She picked up her phone, hit a number, and asked if he was expecting me. I said *Mhm*, and she did the *come-hither* thing with her finger so she could see my name, which she said into the phone. She hung up and told me to follow her, though it was only a ten-second walk. When we got there she held her arm out right to the open doorway, as if I'd never chanced upon a room before.

The five of them were sitting around a table. Only Ellis was facing the door and he didn't look at me, so I just stood there, waiting to be summoned. There wasn't much of a view; beyond the window was another skyscraper, its windows tinted. The room was vast and comically empty. Besides the table and a desk there were just some chairs, a few ferns, bookshelves full of matching maroon and indigo volumes. The space reminded me of those *New Yorker* cartoons where a CEO is being approached by one of his serfs. I realized I still had the sticker on my chest, I pulled it off and put it in my pocket. Rupert sensed my presence and turned around. *Caleb*, he said, *you're late*. I was ready to give a heartfelt apology but his tone was light. In fact, despite the room's aseptic feel there was a certain ease—mirth, even. As I approached I was surprised to find that he was its source, actually he was in the middle of a joke, something about a friend getting a wedding announcement in the *Times* just to advertise his law firm. They all laughed, none louder than Pauline Fell, Perry's publisher. I knew that laugh from a YouTube video I'd watched the night before, where she was interviewed by Hilton Als at the New Yorker Festival. She reminded me of an English professor I had in college, the same wryness that never fully revealed itself; I liked her immediately. Not so Dennis O'Halloran, the general counsel at Seymour Group. He stared at me as if I couldn't stare back, which was self-fulfilling; I don't know if I made eye contact with him again. I noticed their outfits were all decidedly business casual, and I shoved down my self-doubt—but really, why could I never get it right? After Rupert asked what happened to my leg—*Torn hamstring*, I said, *got it running*—he made the requisite introductions, modulating his tone from congenial to legal with every word. As he spoke he continually twisted his wedding ring around his finger, a habit I hadn't picked up on before. I sat in an outsized chair next to Avi, and when I gave him a wave he barely looked back at me. I found this coldness peculiar, and couldn't help but entertain the thought that he

knew everything, all of what I'd done to make this meeting happen. But the more I inspected him the more I knew this wasn't
the case. He was slouching, his arms resting on the chair as if he
were keeping himself above water.

Well, let's not waste any more time, Rupert said. *We have no reason to let it be noon without a statement.* He looked to Dennis, who
nodded, and then back to Avi and me. *I'd like to make clear that
what you two say here today will not incriminate you, this is not on the
record. But we do need the absolute and total truth, it's the only way
we'll know how to proceed in the most prudent fashion. So.* He sighed.
*Everyone in this room is up to speed on all of the arrangements among
Ellis, Avi, and Caleb leading into the sale of the manuscript.* It
dawned on me what that meant, what should have been obvious
before: everyone in the room knew I was the author. I couldn't
help but glance over at Pauline Fell, expecting, well, what, exactly? That she'd graciously bow her head? She kept a steady gaze
on Rupert, and I swallowed my expectations. *And I can assume
we've all read the* Times *piece,* he said, scanning us, collecting our
nods. *Now, what we need to know is what happened.* He looked to
Avi, waiting for him to speak, which he didn't, so he said his
name and then concentrated his stare. Avi sat up, crossed his legs,
and folded his hands together, a good show at confidence if not
for his voice, which was just a bit too high to match. *I am not going
to sit here and say that I didn't do anything wrong.* He'd practiced
these words, surely. *I made a mistake, which was to assume it
wouldn't be a problem to use the real names of the people involved in
the story the novel was based on.* Rupert sat forward in his seat,
waiting for Avi's next words, but they too would have to be pulled
out of him. (*Why not?* I wanted to say, *Why didn't you think it*

would be a problem? I hoped with all my heart someone else would ask that, I even looked to Ellis, who wouldn't return my gaze.) *Avi*, Rupert said. *What else?* Avi scrunched his forehead. *And I'm sorry*, he said, almost like a question. *That's not what I meant*, Rupert said. *What I meant was, how much of what happened in the book happened in reality?* Avi glanced at me, as if I were somehow more qualified to answer. *Well*, he said, *as you know, I didn't write the book, I only lived the outline of the story, a story I told to Caleb, which was accurate.* This completely disregarded the question, seemed to suggest, if anything, that Avi hadn't read the book. Dennis pushed forward in his chair. *And I'd like to ask Mr. Horowitz, Caleb if I may, whether he knew that the names being used in the book were factual?* I didn't, it was an easy question to answer, and I did, with pleasure. Except that this was met with averted eyes; no one believed me. Avi should have, of course he did, but he only mimicked the adults around him, tacitly communicating his disapproval. *That's fine*, Rupert said. *It isn't of consequence. As my dad might say, the toothpaste is out of the tube.* He got up and went over to his desk, returning with a few one-pagers, which he passed around. Right as he sat down his eyes twitched to the door, which was open. He paused, seemingly contemplating whether it was worth the walk. It wasn't. *Here's a statement we've prepared, please take a moment and have a look.* In the first sentence I saw the word *I* and glanced at the bottom, it was written not by Perry but by Avi himself, supposedly. I looked around, everyone else was reading, I needed to catch up. The top portion was a straightforward admission; it stated the dates he went to Paros, summarized his interactions with Joe, Reagan, and Sofia (calling them *pleasant people and enriching interlocutors*), and noted that it was his own negligence that had *led to the use of their real names and identities*. I tried to read the rest but couldn't, my concentration was being spent on stopping the fingers of my right hand from pushing too hard into the paper, and anyway I felt like I'd read it a thousand times, it was a boilerplate apology—*In retrospect I understand that I've hurt . . . if I could go back in time . . . recognize my own errors and am deeply ashamed*, and so on. Rupert watched over us as we read, and when Avi finished, the last to do so, he said, *This is all just a suggestion, something we've prepared for your benefit. Whether you agree to use it or not is completely up to you. But, I will say that if you aren't prepared to release this or something like it, it is in Perry's interest to release their own statement, and it will not be nearly as amenable.* Avi eyed the paper again. He was going to accept it, obviously. If I didn't speak, everything would be settled. *Isn't this a bit premature?* I asked. *Wouldn't it be prudent to get in touch with Joe and Reagan? Before we issue a statement? Perhaps something could be worked out, or—* I watched as Ellis looked at Dennis, and then Rupert. He seemed worried, in a sort of secondhand way, like he was a spectator to something tragic. His eyes dragged back in my direction but didn't make it all the way. There was something I'd missed, was missing. *No*, Dennis said. *We won't be getting in touch with Joe and Reagan. The statement will be out there and then they can decide what they want to do.* I glimpsed an opening, the opening I'd been waiting for. *But wouldn't we run the risk of them suing? Shouldn't we use this statement in some strategic way to head that off?* Ellis opened his mouth but then Pauline interjected. *Yes, Caleb, they will sue. If they haven't found lawyers yet, someone who knows more than they do will instruct them to do so, and that lawyer will serve papers to Perry.* I nodded as if I understood, which I did, technically, except I didn't in the way of implication, the logic girding everything else. *It seems like we're rushing,* I said. *Actually, I feel like we're missing something, which is that, yes, Avi made a mistake, but the book didn't actually violate their privacy. How could it? I mean, besides just using their names, it's not like he recorded what actually happened. I wrote it and I was never even there, I'd never even met them. It seems like if that fact was known, if it was revealed that Avi wasn't the author, that I was, if we acknowledged all of that, how could they sue?* Pauline's eyes were narrowing, not in concentration or anger but confusion. *We won't be doing that,* she said, *for a few reasons, starting with the fact we'd have to pulp at least three printings of the book. And then there's the press, which would be hard to predict but ultimately confusing and probably negative, negative in the bad way, in the sell-less-copies way, not in this way, which, honestly, is probably going to move us into another three or four printings by the end of the month. But most of all, Caleb, and I am speaking very honestly with you, probably more honestly than I should, you have to understand that this isn't our battle to fight, or, well, it is, but we won't end up with the bill. This is a textbook indemnity clause violation.* She could tell the phrase meant nothing to me, and was evidently disappointed. *In the event of a lawsuit by a third party, the party to blame is the party responsible for the damages, which, in this case, would be you.* She inhaled and exhaled. I waited a beat. *Avi,* I corrected her. *Avi was in violation of the indemnity clause.* Her lips skewed to the side, and she turned to Dennis, asking him to take the reins. *Yes, perhaps it was his fault,* he said. *But the "party" in this case, per your contract with Perry, is both yourself and Avi.* He closed his mouth, he bounced his head to the side. He wasn't going to say something but then he did. *And Caleb, you might not want to*

*hear this from me, but you will hear it from someone, eventually, and
I'd feel negligent if I didn't say something, which is this: I cannot imagine a judge who wouldn't take the profits of the book into account when
assessing the extent of the privacy infringement. You are, after all,
making money off their identities. And, to be clear, those damages will
be paid by Perry, but they will be taken directly from your earnings.
Moreover, if the damages happen to be greater than your earnings,
which is a distinct possibility—that would be my guess at least, and
please don't misconstrue this for legal advice—then I would presume it
would be the profiting party who would be liable to pay. That's a guess,
of course, to be honest I haven't spent so much time with your subcon-
tract with Avi and Ellis, which seems a bit unprecedented in itself.* I
looked at Avi. It struck me that I should hate him but I couldn't,
most of my animus was directed at Pauline, actually. They were
all twisting the knife together but she was the only one whom I
connected with on a personal level. It seemed that, out of respect
for me, no one was going to speak. Dennis's words echoed in my
head, out of order and at varying volume. I kept on returning to
party and *profit*, there was a phrase there I already knew, *profiting
Parties*—yes, *any damages done to all other profiting Parties*, it was
from the agreement between Avi and myself, which was, apparently, *unprecedented in itself.* If I went ahead and made the contents of that agreement public, I would be liable for any resulting
damages. But what would these damages be from, exactly? Making public the nature of the book, that it was based on real people?
That ship had sailed. Did I have anything to lose? No, I didn't, I
shouldn't—the opposite, in fact, at least if my earlier hypothesis
was correct, that my authorship would weaken Joe and Reagan's
case. *What would happen if I made public the agreement between Avi*

and myself? If I outed myself? If all of what you say is right, then do I really have anything more to lose? Dennis and Rupert exchanged looks. Maybe my logic was firm, maybe it wasn't. *This is very complicated*, Rupert said. Dennis nodded in agreement. Ellis sat forward in his chair and connected his palms. *It might not seem like it right this second*, he said, *but everyone in this room shares interests. If you went ahead with what I think you're suggesting, you should know that you'd be isolating yourself, you'd be relinquishing all of the support you've had so far. I would terminate our contract, and you would no longer have access to Rupert as legal counsel.* I nodded, as if I were considering his words. I wasn't. His tone, and the fear it concealed, was just what I needed to give the idea all of my conviction. *Okay*, I said, *but to be honest, I'd be surprised if you still considered yourself my agent anyway. So perhaps it's better that we just make it official. Actually, you're fired.* Rupert nodded. *Sure*, he said, *but for that to hold up in court you'll really want it in writing. Email is fine. And speaking of court, I would offer a suggestion, which isn't to be confused with legal advice, and that's that you find yourself legal counsel.* He was right. I needed a lawyer. My instinct was to ask him if he knew anyone, because I'm sure he did, knew the exact right person, but I swallowed the thought. I asked if they needed anything else from me. *Not if you don't have any more questions*, Rupert said cordially. *I don't*, I said, and he smiled, as if waiting for me to leave, so I continued. *I assume you thought this meeting might take longer, but I won't waste time, clock more hours on his bill.* I nodded to Ellis without looking at him. Rupert simpered. *That's not how it works. Actually, if I was compensated every time someone wasted my time I'd be rich.* This seemed like a joke. Because he *was* rich. I got up from the chair, careful not to put too much pressure

on my leg, and, realizing I was still holding their prepared statement, let it fall from my hands. Up front I wished the receptionist
a good day, which caught her so off guard she could only respond,
Yourself, which gave me more pleasure than it should have. This
time I had the good fortune of riding the elevator down alone,
five seconds of solitude before I reentered the echo chamber.

Back at Starbucks I treated myself to a Frappuccino, even
though the caffeine from earlier had hardly dissipated, was just
mixing like old friends with the new rush of adrenaline. I took
out my laptop and put on my headphones and listened to "Tomorrow Never Knows" by the Beatles. I'd once heard that Mat-
thew Weiner paid a quarter of a million dollars to use it in an
episode of *Mad Men*. Money does wonders, doesn't it? Have
enough and you can bring any artistic vision to life. But it can
also be blinding, it can distract you from what you actually want,
what's worth having.

I went to my email and downloaded my agreement with Avi
and Ellis. I drafted the message from my personal account but
then realized Anya would sooner read one sent from *Last
Resort429*. I copied it over, cc'd myself, and sent it. I exhaled.

Part III

October 2019

I *want to use language the way Klint used gold. I want to feel like I'm choosing words that just aren't available to other writers.* I took a seat. Glen's rants usually lasted no more than three minutes. It wasn't long before I'd stopped stopping him, having realized that if I did he'd just pick up where he left off later. If it had been my first day I might've made it clear who was running the class, I might even have corrected him, that it was *Gustav Klimt*—Klint was *Hilma af Klint*, who also used gold leaf but she wasn't who he was thinking of. Recently I started actively trying not to be an asshole, which I feared was becoming my professorial persona. Glen was a junior chemistry major, and while I'd guess he was taking An Introduction to the Novel for the same reason most of my students were—to satisfy a humanities requirement—he differed from them in that he actually cared, though *cared* might not be as descriptive as *had a personal mandate to wring every minute from the credit he could, including office hours*. Actually, his approach to writing—that a writer should constantly be demonstrating their skill—was a perfect foil for my *POP*, or *point of perspective*, a take on *point of view* that did nothing to alter the original phrase, as coined by Don Garnett, the department chair. Garnett encouraged all of us adjuncts (and there were only adjuncts) to double down on our own perspectives, ignoring whatever pedagogy was currently in style;

at seventy-eight years he'd seen many come and go. He'd earned his status in part by being loosely associated with the Beat poets, and I say loosely because his age didn't exactly line up with the era—he would have been twelve when "Howl" came out.

When Glen ran out of gas I brought the conversation back to my POP, which is that in a successful novel the writer disappears. The book I was couching that thought in was Charles Jackson's *The Lost Weekend*, which I had the feeling half the class hadn't read—or, at best, had only skimmed. That was a shame, because it was a superlative display of realism written in third person limited, and semi-autobiographical to boot, a very hard environment for the writer to disappear from, but he does. When eyes finally started succumbing to the gravitational pull of the clock and I knew salvation was near, I swiftly summarized my lesson and dismissed the class.

I left the building through the faculty entrance, so I wouldn't run into any of my students, and rode my bike to my apartment, which was not in the faculty housing complex but a garden-style condo off campus; this way I avoided conversation with my colleagues too. Every day when I got home I threw myself on the couch, and every day I remembered that I'd been meaning to move it so it would face the window and not the three bare walls of my living room. Who had the energy? Perhaps I did not too long ago, but a lot can change in just a year and a half.

I'd since moved to a small town in upstate New York to work at a school that had just cracked the top seventy-five in *U.S. News & World Report*'s list of liberal arts colleges. I'd grown my hair out, shaved my mustache, and put on some weight. I'd accepted I was in a sort of intermission from life, one that would allow me to slide a bit. Maybe more than a bit. Drinking wasn't exactly a problem but making sure it wasn't had become a task. I was seeing a woman whom I had no future with, Frau Lehmann I liked to call her, which I found funny and she didn't because she was actually German and that was what she was called. She and her husband were separated but she planned to keep his name for reasons I found vague. Her first name was Gabriele. If she had a sense of humor it was very dark, and her self-involvement eclipsed narcissism. She was a tenured professor, teaching the language that was her first, which seemed to me like cheating, albeit an honest form of it. Our sex seemed to involve anger. We were each one of maybe three viable mates the other had in a ten-mile radius. I don't even think she'd object to that term, *viable mate*. Actually it sounds like something I would have stolen from her, that she'd be proud to have coined. Really I suspected that she was always playing a part with me, that she even embraced the caricature of a humorless, slightly sadistic, blunt, militaristic, hyper-efficient German fembot, as if by hiding her other selves from me—i.e., the person who had the capacity for connection—she made sure to keep me at a distance. This was something I was surely guilty of in my own way. We were both coming off something serious and emotionally wrenching and needed something not either of those things. She was my first lover in a year, since I'd last slept with Sandra, a sort of goodbye sex that involved both of us crying and neither of us coming. The end was complicated and heartbreaking and protracted beyond reason, and I'd rather not talk about it because it hurts to the point of numbness and I'll likely just become ironic about it. But I will say that it was my fault. I had become a person even I didn't want to be with, and I probably wouldn't have stuck around either if I'd had the choice. *But.* But. I will also say—and yes, I am bitter—that if someone really loves someone else, and they can see that their partner is going through something, they stick it out with them, they help them through it. That is all I need to get out there. Also I want to say that she moved out quite soon, and made kind of a big show of it, all the while knowing that I too would have to move out, that I'd have to break the lease, and it would have been nice of her to help me pack and clean.

So yes, a lot had changed. What hadn't changed was my celebrity, the lawsuit(s), and my writing. Yes, the world knew I wrote the book—it's how I landed such a prestigious post, teaching prodigies like Glen. With enthusiasm and diligence Anya published a piece in the *Times* (where she is now a staff writer) detailing the contents of my agreement with Avi and Ellis. It made clear—with quotes from me, no comments from Avi and Perry, and a few anodyne remarks from Ellis (*this is quite a complex issue*, and *matters belie easy interpretation*)—the genesis of the book, who wrote every word, and why the chips settled as they did. But she also continued to write about every new kink in the story, the real story, which was not about the shifting of authorship (a phrase that cannot hold a candle to *breach of privacy* or *pornographic plot*), but about Joe and Reagan's lawsuit. Ellis was right, apparently, all that happened between Avi and me was *complex*, too complex for virality or a catchy headline, unlike the other side of the story, which was complex but in a way that made you want to learn every last detail (down to what Avi's seatmate on his flight back from Athens had to say).

It would be hard to exaggerate the legs of that whole saga, or the effect it had (and has continued to have) on the performance of the book, a break not even Ellis could have orchestrated. Yes, as the story unfolded the book was catapulted out of the arena of novel-reading folk into the arena of, well, regular people. Coverage moved from the book section to the arts and culture section to the front page (In *The Wall Street Journal*, the headline "Fiction or Non? A Dewey Decimal Head Scratcher with Legal Implications"), albeit below the fold. I knew we were in uncharted territory when my brother texted me to say his high school buddies were asking about the book. (It was in this group that I'd once witnessed someone refer to *Tallahassee Coates* without anyone offering a correction.) Despite decidedly "mixed" reviews, the book's legacy seemed to be that of a literary accomplishment— probably owed to the fact that its popularity frequently put it in more commercial company. When I saw it for sale in an airport store it had been labeled not just "sexy" but "cerebral," lest some unsuspecting traveler be left unprepared for characters with introspection.

Joe and Reagan weathered a great deal of attention in the beginning, but it seemed they were all too real, too much like normal people (they'd given birth to a healthy girl, Amelia, with another one on the way), and thus it was depressing to linger on their actual lives (as opposed to the steamy scenes that featured their avatars). Sofia was dead, either from a brain tumor or euthanasia, and it was perhaps this ambiguity that, unfortunately, prompted some curiosity about her. I guess we all pretend we're above something until it becomes a "topic" and then everyone gets in on it. It started, not surprisingly, on Reddit, where commenters figured out who she was, ten different times. She was a lawyer in Chicago who'd gone missing and never returned, but actually she was this waitress in L.A. who supposedly moved to Japan and never spoke to her family again, and then the consensus landed on a writer from Thessaloniki who had died from cancer in 2016 and had, somehow, shed her accent. A small headline in the corner of the cover of a supermarket tabloid (I think it was *In Touch*) claimed there was a draft of the novel that revealed her identity. It's with some shame that I confess to having followed all of it, half expecting and fully hoping the world would figure out who she was before it got bored. And so, because Avi was the story's protagonist, and because he was better-looking than Joe or Reagan and no one knew what Sofia looked like, and because he was still so secretive and his digital presence nil, he remained the public's focus, the celebrity, the lead photo of the article. Although the public knew who wrote *Last Resort*, who *really* wrote it, the only term that clung to my name was, inexplicably, *ghostwriter*. All I got out of the entire thing was a short interview in *GQ* and a longer one in *Publishers Weekly*. Maybe I would have had more but my lawyer started fielding all requests, and by fielding I mean denying, which brings me to the lawsuit(s), a topic which, as I am doing right this second, forces my pointer and thumb onto the bridge of my nose. This gesture is often accompanied by an insult, aimed at myself, muttered under my breath, out loud if alone. This time it was, surprisingly, *you pathetic also-ran*. I didn't know I knew that word.

Every time I met with him, my lawyer, a guy named John de Chirico who worked out of a decent office in downtown Brooklyn, he'd say he had a lot to catch me up on. But it was all legal throat-clearing, more or less, the acquisition of documents and *other case-building activities*, as he'd put it, activities which had so far cost around $68,000. (He was only tangentially involved in the main lawsuit, which Perry was legally allowed to conduct. His main purpose was to build a new suit against Avi, who was represented by Rupert, in the hopes of negating our prior agreement or at least establishing that Avi would be liable for some of the damages incurred by Joe and Reagan's suit.) I'd found him through a family friend, or maybe it was someone that family friend's friend knew. He'd worked on a relatively high-profile case of literary plagiarism a few years ago that settled out of court, which didn't seem like a victory per se but maybe it wasn't a loss? I don't know if I'd necessarily recommend him myself. At the very least he answered every question I had from a place of informed confidence. Also, he went out of his way to answer questions I didn't ask. Mostly on the topic of money. Mostly to say I should stop spending it any way I could. (All payments from Perry were frozen, and there was a lien on the bank account that held all my book money.) He often implied I might end up owing all of what I'd earned. If it came to it, he knew a wonderful bankruptcy lawyer. Part of me thought: *If I'm going to have to declare bankruptcy, why not spend every cent I have?* But I never said that and for the most part I was frugal. The college paid me peanuts but provided a housing stipend. I hardly went out, and even if I did it was impossible to spend $100 in that town. My bike cost $85. I ate in most every meal. This was usually done at my desk with my laptop open to the story I was working on. By being physically occupied with eating I could read what I wrote the previous night and be unable to edit or, better yet, delete anything. In this way the idea of eating one's shame became nearly literal.

The story I was working on, had been working on since that summer, was about me, or someone like me, except I was a businessman of sorts, an oilman. What exactly I did was vague, which was a persistent problem, though not my biggest. The manuscript failed in many ways but primarily because the characters couldn't forge honest connections between themselves. This was unfixable. I hated all of them, the characters, often it felt like they hated me. I wrote at a torrid pace. In fact, some nights I wrote five thousand words. In total I had more than two hundred thousand, enough for three books. My theory was that if I so rarely struck a chord, I would need to heap on as many hours as I could to string together a good enough song. (That I constantly held *good enough* as my standard was its own problem.) The only person I talked to about the manuscript was Frau Lehmann; she agreed it was not good but still read whatever I let her. When a passage made her laugh I knew it was only because one of the characters was being cruel, but still I allowed myself pride and committed the feeling to memory.

That night I was supposed to make her dinner. We usually stayed at her place because it was bigger and she had furniture. I sometimes wondered if she used her cooking to troll my stereotypes of Germany; mostly she served bratwurst or one of the associated sausages, along with sauerkraut and mustard. I wanted to eat more healthily but couldn't tell her that because she would ridicule me, so I'd decided to invite her over more often. She professed to dislike Mexican food in a way that seemed racist, so I made pozole in an effort to trick her. She would eat it and love it and then I would announce the dish's provenance and watch her suffer cognitive dissonance. But there'd been a mix-up, she'd ordered delivery to my place: Thai, drunken noodles, and dumplings. She told me I could eat my flaccid soup for lunch. We drank beer and watched *The Wire*, which she loved for being *an indictment of America*. I found that being with her made me feel sad and lonely, which made me eat too much. By the end of the second episode I just wanted to sleep, but if we didn't have sex then the entire night would have served no purpose, so we did. When it was over I wanted to ask her to leave, go stay at her place—she had once done the same to me, albeit at an earlier hour—but I didn't, because I was a coward, and also I needed a ride to Amtrak in the morning.

On the other hand, she did make the best eggs. It was more butter than egg but I tried not to notice. Her watching me delight in her cooking was the closest we came to affection. When we got in the car I pretended to be interested in the story airing on NPR so I wouldn't have to hear her rant about New York, something she did without fail whenever she drove me to the train. It was an interview with a playwright and she wouldn't have it. She turned it off and started telling me how autumn was the worst season to be in the city. *You've only been once*, I said, and she said, *Ah, but I know it*. She and her husband had taken a vacation there two years ago, during the most turbulent months of their marriage. I'm sure they stayed in some miserable Midtown hotel and ate overpriced steak au poivre surrounded by other miserable tourists. Against my better judgment I asked her why fall was the worst season and she said, *Everyone is so brittle, and afraid of losing something.* I told her that that was certainly how I felt and she turned the radio back on, lest we share a moment of intimacy.

It was four hours to the city and another to downtown Brooklyn, a period that I used to swallow nearly three hundred pages of *The Power Broker.* Only in misery and mild depression was I such a diligent reader. I waited in the lobby for forty-five minutes. I tried to read more but couldn't stop checking the clock. Each time I did I had to remind myself I wasn't paying for these minutes, something de Chirico would surely remind me of too. At the beginning and end of each of our meetings he wrote the time very legibly on the top of a page and circled it, a gesture clearly done for my sake, so I'd know he was billing in good faith, which made me lose a bit of it and also question the value of my own time. For his thirty minutes I would spend $687.50 (he charged $275 an hour and usually added two hours of *preparatory work* to the bill), but also eleven of my own hours, at least, a period I could have used to produce value, hypothetically, if I'd chosen a vocation that enabled me to produce value at will. He came into the reception area through the front door, wiping his fingers with a napkin; I knew from its colors he'd gone to Subway. He gave me a firm shake and led me to his office, throwing an open palm out to everyone he saw, occasionally adding a sort of bow. *We have some good news and some bad news,* he said, simultaneously finding the right spot in his chair and sorting through his mail. He picked one letter from the stack and threw the rest out. *Good news first. The book is doing fabulous, still.* I was no longer receiving the sales reports, but de Chirico had access to them by means of legal discovery. I already knew it was doing fabulous, it had over 180,000 ratings on Goodreads, a number that increased substantially on a weekly basis, which was about how often I checked. (Mostly this was to see if the author's name had been updated, which it hadn't. Apparently all metadata is up to the publisher. When I'd ask de Chirico about how we could legally enforce a change he'd invariably reply, *One thing at a time.*) *And so the bad news*, de Chirico said, doing this thing with his fingers and cheeks that I can't put into words (massaging? pleasuring? checking for cancer?) that bothered me instinctually and made me regret our relationship, *the bad news is that both of the Carrs have, apparently, been made redundant at their respective firms, and have amended their suits to include loss of income.* As usual, he alternated between intense eye contact and none at all, and I wished for once he'd settle on a middle ground so I could better infer how severe this was. Then, as if he were reading my mind, he said, *I don't doubt they'll secure this claim.* By this point I spoke his language and understood him to mean, *They will win*, but I wanted him to say it, because I was angry and annoyed. *Secure?* I asked. *Secure*, he repeated. *Such a public episode would, no doubt, have hindered their chances of employment.* I knew not to bring up the fact that they'd helped make their story public; this wasn't relevant, legally. Instead I mumbled. Again he reiterated to me, with no economy of words, that this particular lawsuit was technically between them and Perry, and also that, despite the fact that we had little influence over the case, we (most likely) had everything to lose from it. I asked what exactly their *loss of income* might amount to and his head became a pendulum. *This is hard to approximate*, he said, and then, without enough of a pause, *one to three and a half.* I heard someone cough in the hallway. *Million?* I asked. *Sure*, he said. *If you put them at a hundred thousand each over ten years, plus health care, et cetera, well, yes, maybe even more than that. After all, they've got kids.* Before he could say it I added, *And this is in addition to emotional distress, of course.* He nodded. *Exactly.* My instinct was to find humor in this only because I had no other sane way of digesting it. I was smiling, a smile I assumed was deranged based on the smile he was giving me— careful, pinched, flat. I asked how these damages might hold up against my expected earnings and his face didn't budge. *It's hard to know. I want to say it'll be neck-and-neck.* I looked at his neck, which was thick, red, and splotchy, and wondered if it had been like that when he was my age, if I still ran the risk of having a neck like that. After a swift montage of my recent dietary choices I decided to become a health freak from here on out—gluten-free, paleo, the whole shebang. *Neck-and-neck*, I repeated. *About equal*, he said with a nod, as if I'd never heard the phrase. So it was: one of the greatest commercial literary successes of the year, of the past few years, could barely hold a candle to the financial worth produced by two ad execs. Being a believer in the open market, I could draw no other conclusion than the most obvious one: as far as value is concerned, using the term's most base, direct definition, fiction has very little use. This might have been a depressing thought—that I'd spent much of my adult life trying to produce something meant to be consumed by the public that did not actually provide the public much in the way of value, or at least not as much as the management of various banner ads, billboards, and podcast sponsorships—if it wasn't so absurd, too absurd to even try to understand.

I felt a pulse of anger travel from my chest out to my arms. It wasn't often I blamed Joe and Reagan for their lawsuit—I couldn't for the obvious reason, that I myself had set those gears in motion, but also because I believed they were owed something, in America no one can be criticized for trying to monetize justice—but in that moment I indulged myself, I saw them as I'm sure anyone comes to see his adversary in a protracted legal battle: as an endless string of invective: corrupt, crooked, reprobate, venal, base, bent, profiteering, greedy, ill, a folie à deux of felonious decadence. Alas, the anger I felt for them was never as long as its apex was high; sooner or later I'd slide into the next stage, retrospective bargaining, the *if only*s, *if only* I'd done this or that then none of this would have happened. The easiest hypothetical was, well, me not having written the book in the first place, to have used my time in Oregon to write something that was completely my own, that was completely fictional, but what reason did I have to think that that wouldn't have turned out like everything else I'd written, that is: bad, sentimental, pretentious dogshit? The only fiction I'd written since *Last Resort* that wasn't abjectly terrible were random passages from a sort of sequel, which was only for fun, I couldn't turn it into anything serious, no publisher would touch it. I allowed myself to return to it only to prove I could still produce decent work. There was something about the story; reentering it and putting it down on the page didn't feel like labor the way writing felt like labor, but an experience instead: one I found compelling, meaningful, true even, because, well, it was true. Yes, the act of writing that story felt like recording reality. I *was* recording reality, I was taking an imprint of it, that was the whole point, this I realized in an exceedingly rare window of clarity. I needed to know my protagonist was a real character, one with real flaws along with real charm, who was tragic in a way that was hard to explain, just as real people are hard to explain—not like the characters my imagination produced, who were all inevitably logical, understandable, neat little puzzles.

No, there was no escaping any of this. The reason I could write *Last Resort*, the reason it wasn't slop like everything else I'd written, was because it centered on someone who was also in the real world, he was the channel that made my fiction real. (In some way Avi must have known this too, or felt it, how fiction could preserve someone in amber, he'd tried to preserve himself in his own shitty story and then when he'd read my manuscript, and knew I'd done a better job, he'd not only wanted it to be published, he'd made sure we kept his name in the fucking thing.) And of course this had also been my fatal problem: I had finally found a character worth building a story around, one who would breathe life into everything else, but it was a character I couldn't lay claim to.

I had the urge to tell this to de Chirico, I wanted to put these thoughts into the air, but he was speaking, had actually been doing so for some time, another soliloquy meant only to assure me of the value he provided, I could tell by the amount of legal jargon he was feathering in—*alternative verdict, heretofore, statutory audit, summarily, exemplary damages*. He ended with an off-key joke: *At least we can thank our lucky stars Sofia won't sue.* I couldn't hide my distaste. *You mean her family*, I said, giving him an out. *No*, he said. *I mean her.* He squinted, trying to extract something from me. He started searching through a manila folder on his desk. *Perhaps I took for granted your understanding of the precipitating events*—his term for what happened in Greece. It must have taken him a full minute to find it. *Here we go.* He pulled out a piece of paper, put his glasses on, and lifted his head to read. *According to an interview conducted by Perry's legal team, Mr. Deitsch believes Sofia is alive.* At first I struggled to make sense of the sentence, to consider it outside the reality of the book. *No*, I said. *He told me she had a brain tumor.* He wagged his head while he began mouthing the words on the page. *She said she had cancer, that it was terminal*, he said, playing the part of Avi. *But I had the feeling it wasn't true, that she was, um, I don't know—ellipses—It was just a feeling.* He looked up at me. *Can you make me a copy of that?* I asked. *Take it*, he said, sliding it over. I asked him what else Avi had said about her and he pointed to the page. *That's our entire file on Sofia. Or rather, the party known as Sofia.* Surprising myself, I appreciated that little flourish. I looked back down to the page. Reading his dictated interview, I saw Avi as I hadn't seen him in over three years: as Avi from *Last Resort*, his character—someone more vulnerable, surprising, likable even than the Avi I knew. *But I had the feeling it wasn't true, that she was, um, I don't know . . . It was just a feeling.* No wonder he'd lied to me. It was all too embarrassing: him off in L.A. writing saccharine fiction about their time together, she off who knows where, probably thankful he can't track her down, that he doesn't even know her real name.

He asked if I had any other questions or concerns. I said I

didn't and he looked at the clock and wrote the time on a page and circled it. When I stood up I felt dazed. I had too much to think about. I could barely get my head around the news about Sofia—what type of person lies about dying?—but something else was bugging me, a thought I'd discarded too soon and needed back, and it wasn't until I made it outside that I found it again: the thought of the two Avi's, the one I knew and the one I'd written. But it was more than that, or it became more than that, it was also the idea of her, Sofia, who possibly still existed in the world, who was distinct from my Sofia in not just a few ways—I'd never met her, didn't even know her face—but most crucially she'd done something significant my Sofia would never have done: she'd lied about dying to someone she cared about, or at least someone who cared about her. I felt compelled to adjust her character, to see her anew. I closed my eyes and did, see her I mean, the image as clear as any my imagination drew: she was in a resort in Mexico, a tourist spot past its prime. It's cheap but not dingy, just neglected. On the plane ride she'd concocted a full identity—a name, job, small preferences that weren't her own (men should never wear shorts, it's important to journal every morning, fruit juice is repulsive). It was all coming to me, scenery descriptors and scraps of random dialogue and even burgeoning subplots, all of it setting the stage for Sofia to perform. Why was I letting this sift through my fingers?

Across the street I saw a Panera. For 4:30 it was surprisingly full but quiet enough; the music was acoustic and I had my noise-canceling headphones. I knew I should look up train times and plan accordingly but to let a second of typing go to waste would be to miss a crucial detail, a thought that could be nurtured later, a phrase that had to be said at some point. I'd typed more than a thousand words when I noticed the tomato soup I'd ordered was on my table, waiting for me, its surface already congealed. When I went to the bathroom and came back I read from the beginning. It worked. Not all of it, but for the most part it felt true, there was the delicate balance of a distinct reality. I had not felt this feeling—of reading my own words and not just not hating myself but even liking myself, being proud of myself, believing in myself—in years. I checked the time, 5:14. I thought about writing on the train. I could probably move through another two thousand words, three maybe. But then I'd be upstate with this short story on my hands. And then what? I'd wake up in my same bed and smell the same smells I couldn't even imagine now, the smells that told me in the first moment of morning where and who I was, and I'd get up and make do with the same food in my fridge and, well, I'd return to myself. And then I'd be myself. And then I'd be the person who couldn't write what I was writing now—in a fucking Panera, no less: fiction that was, undoubtedly, worthy. No, I needed to get down enough pages to build the scaffolding, to set the overarching tone, to establish a vision that was so strong even the regular me could execute it.

I entertained putting feelers out and staying with a friend, but everyone I thought of would expect conversation, would patiently wait through a grace period and then gently ask how things were going, how the lawsuit was coming, how far I was into my next book (I had, regrettably, mentioned it to a handful of them). Louis was my best bet, the one most likely to provide alcohol and allow for evasive non sequiturs and let me do my own thing if I wanted to, but the last time we met things had been weird in a way I couldn't quite understand and didn't want to confront now.

I ate the soup systematically, just to get it down. I drank my Diet Coke and went to the bathroom again and walked out into the cool October air. Nine-to-fivers were commuting home, mindlessly retracing the steps they'd set that morning. In a new burst of optimism I didn't regret my vocation at all. All things considered I'd made decent choices, they were reckless choices but ultimately genuine. I breathed in, and out. A woman with a deep purple skirt suit walked by, she was talking on her phone but smiled at me midsentence. It reminded me of a Mentos commercial. I felt young, or more specifically, I believed that the day I was going to die was very far in the future.

I looked in the distance and then turned around and looked the other way. I closed my eyes and recalled the surrounding neighborhoods, contemplating which would have the cheapest hotels. Gowanus had a La Quinta Inn or something, a Fairfield Inn. The R train could have me there in fifteen. I texted Frau Lehmann that I'd be spending the night after all, that I'd be home tomorrow, maybe Sunday.

~~~

Not a block out of the subway I came to a Holiday Inn. I could tell I was acting frantic by the way the woman at the front desk looked at me, or wouldn't. It wasn't as cheap as I'd wanted, $139, but I reasoned that it would be less than $20 an hour for Wi-Fi as long as I used it for seven hours, which I would, because I had hours of writing in me that I would need thesaurus.com for.

I went up to my room and showered. Frau Lehmann had texted me something long with a period at the end. My eyes passed by *selfish* and also *your own personal nursemaid* and I closed my phone. I ordered delivery from a cheap sushi place I used to frequent and forgot the name of but Seamless remembered. I set up my computer at the desk in the corner and made myself coffee in the little machine hotel rooms have that always smell like mold. As it spurted out the drink it made dying sounds. I briefly considered the mortality of machines and made a note to work that into the story.

I'd never pulled an all-nighter, a proper one I mean, sober and for the sake of productivity. I expected myself to hit a wall, to need coffee. I'd penciled in a bodega run for a 5-hour Energy. But it turned out I didn't need sleep at all, it was like the first sixteen hours of wakefulness was only a prologue to a more meaningful mode of thinking. Things made more sense, abstracted themselves. Everything was funnier, easier, luckier. I kept the TV on to muted infomercials, which made me feel like I was living in the past. I made it a goal not to masturbate and lasted till 3 a.m.

For most of the night it seemed I could write whenever I put my fingers on the keyboard. I only needed to think back on how wrong I'd gotten Sofia before, and then I would feel the presence of this other person, this person who was not that Sofia, this person whose existence baffled me. It reminded me of black holes: the closer you get to the perimeter without being sucked in, the faster you're spun out in a new direction (this may have just been from a movie). The black hole itself was the real Sofia, or, rather, what I didn't know of her: how she could have done what she did. The more I asked myself that question—what type of person feigns death to ensure her own privacy?—the more my imagination produced. Except at a certain point, call it 4 a.m., the trick began wearing off. The more I circled the black hole the less I believed there was anything inside, and the less its pull affected me. Soon I found that I was just floating in space, not a word in my head, and used whatever momentum I had left to put myself in bed.

For a few seconds after I woke up I had no idea where I was, who I was. That this liminal space was more enjoyable than the status quo depressed me. I saw my computer on the desk and remembered everything. I got up to see how much I'd written. 6818 words. I read a few random passages, half expecting to come face-to-face with my own manic delusion, but I didn't. A lot of it was good, would be great even after some serious editing. It made sense but not too much; I understood why I'd done things that I had no idea of in the moment. I thought to sit down and continue right then but I couldn't, I was depleted. For lack of sugar or sleep or something else I was soaked in malaise. The sky didn't help, a gray blanket that made it impossible to intuit the time. I went to the window and tried to guess. There was barely a moving car in sight. A pack of twenty-somethings wearing bright festival colors walked lazily down the sidewalk. I gave up and checked my phone. It was 11:22. I went back to the window. Across the street was a nondescript red-brick apartment building. Only one unit had lights on, the room hidden by a white satin curtain. I imagined a couple with a young child, careers that were just fine, a fridge full of food past expiration. I continued packing on unappealing details to see when I'd stop envying them, but I didn't. I needed to eat, I needed coffee. I grabbed my wallet and went downstairs.

The woman at the front desk told me I was thirty minutes past checkout, which was fine, there was a one-hour grace period, but also did I know about their special promotion? $49.99 for another night, they could just use my card on file. I agreed to it and signed and then asked her to direct me to the nearest bodega, where I got a corned beef sandwich, a bottled Starbucks coffee, and a six-pack of Heineken.

In my room I realized the fridge wasn't cold so I put the beers on top of the AC and turned it on high. The bottled coffee was terrible so I made one in the room and drank it at the desk while I ate and typed. My mind was miles away from where it had been last night, but still I was able to pick up right where I left off. The problem was, well, that I was picking up right where I left off: gently orbiting the black hole, which hadn't become any more forceful in my absence. I stopped. I didn't doubt that I could, over the next few months, write the book to the end. No, that's exactly what I was afraid of, that I'd finish without getting any closer to the heart of the matter: who she was, why she did what she did. If I didn't find a way into that impregnable question, the person on the page would end up no richer than my own imagination, that is: not good enough.

Not thirty minutes after I sent my first message my phone buzzed: Thanasis had replied to my inquiry. Twenty minutes later Catherine had. And then Nikos. I had to turn off text notifications. By 5 p.m., midnight in Paros, I had received twenty-two replies to thirty-nine inquiries. They would all be happy to help me out, and had I heard they were just a ten-minute walk from the town center? That their apartment's magnificent view would give me unforgettable moments? That they spoke always great English? I could immediately rule out about half of them, and replied to the rest. I updated a spreadsheet I'd created for the process, and then helped myself to a congratulatory beer. Within minutes I was calm, at peace, in some state I suspected Eastern philosophy would do a better job naming. I watched the muted infomercial on the TV, I considered going to a bar or taking a walk, but really all I wanted to do was write, even if it wasn't at some torrid pace, even if I was just coloring between the lines. It wasn't often I could do this thing I supposedly loved without harboring a small but constant bolus of self-disgust.

I'd been at it for another hour when my phone buzzed. It was nearly 6:30, 1:30 a.m. in Paros. *Impressive*, I thought. But the text was a photograph of a container of lavender honey goat cheese. The message below said, *They didn't go out of business, they just rebranded.* When someone sends me an image, I have to go back to the menu to see who sent it. It couldn't have been from anyone but Sandra but still I checked. Seeing her name spelled out made my heart lurch. This cheese had been a guilty pleasure of ours. We used to get high and finish the package in a single night, pairing it with whatever we had in the fridge; it was a culinary stem cell, capable of making itself useful with anything, savory or sweet. One day it was no longer in our local bougie grocery store or anywhere else. We couldn't even find it online, we didn't know the name, only the wispy illegible font it was written in. I wrote back, *Might not be in my budget these days*. I closed my phone and set it by my leg, watching it. I knew she'd text back soon. Nothing in human evolution could have prepared us for the thrill of waiting for a small block to vibrate. I imagined her deleting words and starting again, I'd watched her do this many times before. A small happiness swept through me and then evaporated. Buzz: *Maybe a salaried friend can buy you some. LMK when you're back in civilization*. Before I could think myself out of it I wrote, *Actually I'm here for the weekend*. She asked where I was staying and I told her. She wrote, *I thought you said you were in civilization*, and then, *It would be nice to meet up*, and then, *No pressure*. I texted, *I'd like that too*, and then, *When?* Now that I was sure to see her, every second was excruciating. I wanted to call her but knew I wouldn't. *Now?* she wrote, and then, *Or whenever—my plans are flex til Monday*. I checked the time, 6:26, and wrote back *7 30?* She said, *Yep*, and then, *Feel free to crash*, and then, *Unless you prefer room service*. Before I knew it I was pacing around, having nothing better to spend this new energy on. I did push-ups and then took a shower. When I got out I looked at myself in the mirror. I'd never noticed a change in my body because I saw it every day, but now I tried seeing myself through her eyes, recalling what I looked like the last time we slept together. I remembered how she used to tell me how much she liked my torso, and I was struck by the urge for her to see me naked, for her eyes to confirm that I'd gained weight and for her hands to touch me in the same way they always had, so I would know that her desire wasn't for an aesthetic value but for me. I wished I'd brought my razor. I even entertained getting a haircut. I imagined her choosing an outfit, the way she'd hold something up and frown at it until she decided it would do.

I shut my laptop, packed my things, and went down to the lobby. Just as the automatic doors opened I realized I might as well try to get a refund for the extra night. The woman at the front desk told me she couldn't. Her apology was effusive and when I abruptly ended the conversation she seemed offended. I hailed a cab.

I didn't recognize the address, Clay Street, and was surprised when it became apparent we were going to Greenpoint. Sandra and I hadn't considered the neighborhood when we looked for our place. Even though it was one of the hippest in Brooklyn—it seemed that every few months another friend moved there—we decided it was too out-of-the-way. We pulled up to a newish building, three floors, each one apparently its own unit, the top two with a light orange glow that seemed antiquated somehow. All of the windows had identical boxes of simple red geraniums, probably provided by management.

I rang Unit 2 and she buzzed me up immediately. I climbed the stairs to find the door open and her waiting, with jeans on and a black T-shirt about three sizes too big. I tried to remember if it was mine. When I saw her face I knew that I loved her no less than I'd ever loved her, that fact so evident it seemed willfully naive to expect otherwise. My body began filling with pain and I hoped hers was too. As we hugged I was overcome by her scent, which I could never recall from memory. I saw past her to a spacious studio, its "rooms" delineated not by anything in particular but emptiness; clothes and books were strewn across the bedroom and then there was a clean strip of floor and then the living room started: an area rug and floor pillows, a long plush couch and a coffee table. It wasn't a beautiful place, not the way our place had been beautiful, but it felt like a home. I asked myself how much of that feeling was just her. We pulled away and I saw that she was tearing up, which made me start to. She made a wordless joke out of it, a funny face, it all killed me. She said my breath smelled like beer and I asked if she was going to call the cops. We walked inside and she asked me if I wanted a drink. On the kitchen counter I saw an opened bottle, its label pulled off, and said I'd have whatever she was having. She went to the fridge and opened it but stopped, suddenly, and looked back at me. I tried seeing what she did, I even turned around to take in the background, the lighting. *What?* I asked. She didn't answer, just bent down to get the beer, but when she stood up she continued staring. *You think I look different,* I said. I could tell from her reaction that wasn't it. *Come on, Caleb, you look exactly the same.* She was never a good liar, at least to me. She walked over and handed me the bottle. In her face I saw that she was trying to create conversation but was still stuck on whatever it was she'd been thinking. *How's being a prof?* she asked finally, sitting on the couch. I sat on the chair beside it, and it all felt too formal, or the opposite, too domestic, like we were an old married couple each with our own place in the living room. I told her about the school, about Glen and Don Garnett, about eating in the cafeteria to save money and playing pickup soccer with students and being confused for one. I asked how her dad was doing. (From the few texts we'd exchanged since our breakup I knew he was now living in a facility, on Long Island.) She said *fine* in a way that meant *worse*. I felt responsible for the room's sudden shadow, I put on a grin and asked if he still referred to me as *Horrorwitz*. She didn't need the levity, she said she wished that was the case, it would surprise her if he remembered me at all. To change the subject she started telling me about her job, she worked at a consultancy that helped multinational companies adapt their foreign offices to local regulation and custom. She seemed to like it enough, she got to travel to Singapore and Caracas, Mumbai and New Delhi. She took out her phone and showed me pictures of herself at an Indian wedding, in a sari and face jewelry, looking helplessly white. It soon became clear we could talk forever, fill days just sitting there, we had missed so much of each other's lives, but also it was as if nothing had changed, we could still lock our heads together, talk as fluently as I talk to myself, almost transcending the need for full sentences, verbs. Except the more time we spent catching up—discussing families, friends, jobs, the lawsuit—the less it seemed like we might broach anything serious—us, our breakup, our love lives—and at a certain point, maybe midway through my second beer, I promised myself I'd wait for the current topic to taper (a mildly flirtatious comment Mikkel, the Danish journalist, had made one night while his wife was in the room) and then ask if she was seeing anyone.

When I finally pushed the words out she laughed. She even took a sip before answering, which was cruel, especially because the answer was yes, she was, a guy named Austin who worked in textiles, whatever that meant. I asked where he was from and she said, *Why don't I make the stalking process easier and send you his Social Security number?* I said, *I don't need it, you know I'm a Googler nonpareil,* and then she laughed but not as hard. To say anything, I asked if they'd been on any good double dates recently, which was a stupid, awkward question, and also my tone came out a bit sour, because I was sour, and before she could answer I amended it to, *With anyone I know? Avi and Franny?* No, she said, they'd only been dating for a couple of months. And also Avi and Franny broke up. This was supposed to surprise me but didn't. She saw as much and agreed. *It's not that they weren't good for each other,* she said. *It just always seemed inevitable.* We both thought about that, which felt true but impossible to express why. I asked how he was doing and she said she didn't keep in touch, only got updates from Franny. The last she heard he was teaming up with some guy, a restaurateur he'd met through Franny. They were starting a coffee place in Williamsburg, a sort of homage to Vienna's historic café culture, a place for writers to work and meet and have caffeinated arguments. The thought of it didn't sit well with me, not because it was all just a genuflection to trendiness—it was so fucking Williamsburg— and not because he was selling his status on the open market— surely he was—but because it helped me make sense of the future, I could begin to imagine the person he'd become, how in the intervening years he'd turn into someone who, if you'd just met him, would make for a convincing proprietor of hip establishments, someone who was part of the "industry," who would dress and act and vacation accordingly, and in that same period of time we'd all become someone new, some of us would change more than others but we'd all have changed enough to look back on the present with something like condescension. We'd miss some things about being our age, sure, but there would be the arrogance, the self-satisfaction time encourages, the knowledge that the problems we were dealing with today were, in fact, not problems, really, at least they shouldn't have been. Maybe this was all something humans have always had to live with, or maybe it was actually just an overly abstract dumb thought, but with her sitting in front of me it took form, I felt the moment's mortality, that it was something of a miracle for us to be in the same room together because such a scene would make up such a small fraction of our lives; eventually, in retrospect, the two of us together would feel like an impossibility.

She told me I looked sad, and I said, *Sorry*, and then, *I was just thinking about things*. I noticed it was dark, the night was complete. She followed my gaze to the window. She stood and, as she walked toward it, asked if I was seeing anyone. I knew she'd planned that, so she wouldn't have to look at me when I answered. She started lowering the shades. *Yeah*, I said. *I'm seeing a German woman I have no future with*. Despite this neither of us laughed. She straightened a painting that hung on the wall and then came over to my chair and stood over me. The ceiling light was just beyond her head and I couldn't see her face. Her hand floated a few inches from my knee, and I put my fingers against her palm, and I was surprised at how little pain I felt, that the only visceral feeling I had was comfort, if that can be visceral. It all felt so normal, being with her like this, it was as if we'd never been apart, and yet I couldn't help but think I was indebting my future self all the pain I wasn't feeling, along with a great deal of interest, and this made me hesitate, she was hesitating too, and for a minute we hardly moved. Finally she slid her palm over the back of my hand and wrapped her fingers around mine. I got out of the chair, careful not to move my hand too much. In the new light I saw every grain of her face. We kissed, one small kiss and then a longer one, and then we were kissing. She pulled us together so our stomachs were touching and she put her hand around my head and her fingers pushed my hair against its inclination, which hurt in a way that didn't matter. This was something she'd always done, I realized, must have done even during our first kiss. At every stage what we had was enough, I would have been satisfied with just touching hands, and then just kissing, and then just touching her body through her clothes, and then seeing it without any, and her seeing me, us attaching ourselves to each other in all the familiar ways, calmly passing each other pleasure and taking in the scents and tastes we were no longer accustomed to. At every stage it was enough and maybe I even wished we wouldn't go further, because each time we did it became less intimate and more sexual; we were still too used to each other for the thrill of unfamiliar friction.

When it was over we lay nearly motionless in diluted happiness, our feet touching and nothing else. I thought about how easy it would be to live here. It would take a day, maybe two, to figure out our nighttime ritual, how to navigate each other in the morning, where to leave important mail. I didn't even have to find the images for the montage—us getting back together, moving in, continuing our lives together, marrying and having children and raising them and being happy—I just had to close my eyes. I didn't want it, not yet. I would, eventually, but I needed time, more specifically I needed the time to change, there were things I still needed to do that would temporarily turn me into someone she didn't want to be with, but I needed to do those things to become someone she would want to be with, specifically someone who wants to be with himself. I told her I hadn't changed in any of the ways she hoped I would and she didn't say anything. A minute later she got out of bed and turned on the ceiling fan. I listened as she locked the front door, rinsed the beer bottles, and put my clothes in her washer-dryer. She turned off the lights and when she came back to bed I could hardly see the silhouette of her head, let alone her face. She got under the covers and put her head on my chest and her hand on my stomach. I wasn't tired but knew she'd fall asleep soon, so I waited for that to happen and then got out of bed and, using the light of my phone, read on the couch. I couldn't see anything but the page, yet I could place myself in the room, I knew where the walls were, the furniture. I was already used to being here.

———

Men with gravelly voices were shouting. *Hey! Higher and in, in more! Like this!* I could hear in their coughs how cold it was. Every minute a truck door slammed. An engine seemed to be constantly running. There wasn't a clock by the bed, so I went to the living room and found my phone. 6:15. On a Sunday. I opened a shade and saw a horde of workers outside the adjacent building. They were smoking cigarettes and drinking coffee, passing around white Dunkin' Donuts bags. I wanted to wake Sandra like I used to, alert her to some problem neither of us could solve. She never minded. I sat on the bed, hoping she'd wake up, but she just rolled over and covered her head with the pillow. I went to the couch and lay down with my laptop. I went to her Face-book page and searched her friends for someone named Austin, but there was no one, which was annoying, that either he was too cool for Facebook or they were too cool to friend each other.

By habit I opened Gmail, assuming I'd have more college spam to read and delete, and saw I had six messages from Airbnb. I opened them, barely reading three consecutive words at a time, but on the second-to-last message my eyes went straight to the most pertinent string. *Yes he stayed with me.* I couldn't believe it. It felt like the whole world was tilting my way—or it had been, and I'd just started noticing. *Mr Deitsch is a friend of yours? Yes he stayed with me but never left rating. If the place he enjoyed, can he give me rating?* It was years ago, how could he leave a rating? I went to her profile. Her name was Theofania Loukas but she looked Polish. She had fourteen reviews. Her bio read, *One day I will explore the world but today this world comes to me! I enjoy a beautiful place, sun settings and lively performance!* I wrote, *He is a friend of mine, in fact. He asked me to get in touch. I'll be sure to ask him to give a good rating. But he needs the contact information of a woman who stayed there around the same time he did. He apparently has something of hers, or vice versa. Thank you!* I reread the message

and then again, and sent it. Twenty minutes later—enough time
to find three people named Austin who lived in Brooklyn and
worked in textiles (one of whom was fifty-five and, well, not
Sandra's type)—Theofania responded. It only struck me then
that my screen was facing the bed, which was paranoid, but still
I moved to the other side of the couch. *WHY DIDN'T YOU SAY
HE IS FAMOUS WRITER? Yes, happy to help, of course I will. Mr
Deitsch stayed May 16, 2016. That month we have two other visitors
only we have Annabelle Flynn who stayed one night May 14 and
Gerry Wilkiams who stayed one week May 21. Sorry I cannot give
personal information.* I went back to the listing to see if there was
a review by anyone named Gerry or Annabelle. Only Gerry. I
clicked on her profile and dragged her picture onto my desktop.
I uploaded it into Google's reverse image search, and found her
on Twitter—Gerry Williams, a middle-aged woman who pep-
pered her feed with retweets from a local ministry. I Googled
Annabelle Flynn. I found the website of a real estate agent in
Connecticut, the Instagram of a surfer from New Zealand. I
went to the Images tab and didn't see the same woman twice. In
fact, most of the results were for a dress named the Annabelle-
something from a company named Flynn-something. But in the
fourth row my attention stuck to a picture of a woman in a venue
of some sort, a club. She had long brown hair, green eyes, and a
pinched smile. She looked uncomfortable, caught in the head-
lights of a party photographer. I clicked on the image but it was
only 150-by-150 pixels, so I zoomed in until she filled most of
my screen. In her tight grin I saw someone who was self-
conscious, neurotic even, but ultimately artless, disorganized. I
closed my eyes, thought of Sofia, and reopened them. The

woman in front of me could have been a version of my Sofia, maybe—maybe my Sofia could have been some form of her. If not just physically, she could've played the part in the movie. I clicked on the link and was taken to a website that was mostly black and neon with a banner image of bartenders doing shots; this was not *Town & Country*. The page was titled *Tappan—Soft Opening Friends & Fam, 3.2.19.* I scrolled down until I found the picture, which was captioned only *Annabelle Flynn*. She was in the next one too, her back to us, a foot away from a guy mugging for the camera. He had cultivated stubble, teeth an unlikely shade of white, he reminded me of early-aughts pop punk. It was captioned *Chef Ty Letting Off Some Steam*, which didn't seem exactly right. I looked up Tappan, it was a new restaurant, "Native American Nouveau," in the West Village, naturally. I went back to the picture of Annabelle. I was surprised by my attraction to her; she was beautiful in the conventional way, a way I'd spent my adult life learning how to see past. I searched the name on Facebook, she was one of the first results, as she also lived in New York. I could only access two photos, profile pictures. In one she was with her family—parents, siblings, cousins, I assumed—around a picnic table. In the other she was in a red cocktail dress, holding a glass, wearing a goofy hat with a swan on top. Both were low-res.

I heard Sandra squirm and looked over at her, watching as she brought the clump of blankets she'd been hugging over to her other side. I knew her well enough to know that she was trying to convince herself she could go back to sleep, that in a few minutes she'd twist and turn some more and then straighten each limb and then finally remove herself from the bed. By the time this happened I'd exchanged my computer for an oversized book I found on the coffee table, which was about Tamara de Lempicka, a twentieth century Polish artist I hadn't heard of. She painted highly stylized, robust, arresting women with hair like ribbon, women who, in some inexpressible way, presented an idealized form of feminine autonomy, a thought which I would not express to anyone except Sandra, because she'd know what I was trying to say and also how to hone it. I watched as she got up, wrapped herself in a fleece blanket—we'd kept the AC on all night even though it was fall outside, an old guilty pleasure of ours—plodded across the room, and sat on the couch, her legs curled up against my side. I asked her where she got the book, it looked new and I didn't know her to shell out $75 for coffee table art books. She gave me a look that said *Austin*, and I looked back at the book in a positive way so as to not seem resentful. After a measured pause I asked if she planned to tell him about what happened last night. Her face bloomed into a guilty, pained expression that meant, *Yes, because I have been meaning to break up with him, and this will be part of that conversation.* This should have made me happy but it didn't, it made me acutely anxious. Her being romantically involved, I realized, had saved me from having to reconcile the fact that we should be together with the feeling we shouldn't be at this exact juncture. We made eye contact. I had the urge to tell her that last night was great, that it made me feel whatever the opposite of empty was, empty being my de facto state for the past six months, but I didn't, I couldn't, because that would be unfair, any meaningful exchange would eventually be converted into hurt. Just as I let this thought settle she said, *I really enjoyed last night.* I squeezed her foot. *I did too.* I looked at her and felt horny, ineradicably so, perhaps as a conscious effort to divert all emotional thought or maybe I was just horny. I put the idea away by standing up, and then justified standing by asking if she wanted me to make coffee. Instead of answering she asked if I wanted to try the best lox I'd ever had in my entire life, and then, indifferent to my answer, went back to her bedroom and stared at a pile of clothes. I asked if we were going outside and she said, *No, stay put. I'll be back in twenty,* and in three minutes she was out the door.

I heated water and ground the coffee and once I got the French press gestating I figured I still had some time, so I went on my computer, back to the Airbnb listing. Theofania had changed the title of the page to *BEAUTIFUL COTTAGE—SETTING OF FAMOUS NOVEL.* The second image featured the book with Avi's author photo overlaid. I skimmed each review—after all, she'd spelled it *Gerry Wilkiams*, maybe it was *Anabelle* or *Amelia* or anything else—but found nothing.

I went back to Annabelle's Facebook page. It was hard to come to terms with the fact that, if she actually was Sofia, she existed outside my imagination, that I couldn't just will into being the facts of her life. There was nothing besides her favorite bands—Tegan and Sara, St. Vincent, Sleater-Kinney, all of which she'd probably "liked" more than a decade ago—and similar jetsam. She last changed her profile picture in 2014 (and good for her). I couldn't find a Twitter or Instagram. Soon I'd exhausted all possible leads and began reentering my body. I could feel that I'd been in full-blown computer mode. In a small mirror leaning on her bookshelf I saw that most of my hair was on the right side of my head, and I decided to take a shower.

I couldn't get the water right, or else her boiler was broken. The whole thing lasted three agonizing minutes that were more invigorating than any cup of coffee. When I came back into the living room Sandra was unpacking the food. I hadn't dried my back or head, and needed the towel around my waist to do it. I noticed her looking at me. She always used to tease me for being bashful about my body, and it seemed she might say something, a joke, or whatever that joke had sublimated into over the course of our relationship, but she didn't, and all of a sudden I was reminded that we weren't together, and it felt like I didn't belong here, that I shouldn't be casually naked in her living room, that soon she would ask me to leave and it would be a relief for us both. As she turned around I quickly toweled myself and got my clothes from the washer-dryer and then joined her in the kitchen area. I saw that she'd picked up coffee and told her I'd made some. In a stilted exchange we each made the case to have the other's offering, which was even more distancing, that our relationship was tenuous enough to require politeness. We ate standing around the kitchen counter, drinking her coffee. She told me the lox was flavored with beets and I pretended I could taste it. Outside a light rain began, punctuating our silence. The lines of water looked like jail bars. I wouldn't believe it was only last night's alcohol that had made things easy between us. And yet. It was quickly becoming too uncomfortable to even look each other in the eye. I asked to move to the couch, where we wouldn't be standing across from each other, and she readily agreed. We finished our bagels and then the rest of the lox. I decided I should leave, or at least offer to, maybe she wanted me gone but felt too awkward to ask, but when I turned to her I saw that she was crying, had been for some time, the slick strips on her cheeks broad and even. I asked her what was wrong and she shook her head, and then opened her mouth, and eventually she said, *Last night you said that you haven't changed in any of the ways I hoped you would. What the fuck does that even mean?* She allowed herself to wipe her cheek. I said her name, limply. *Caleb*, she said. *You're the one who always wanted to change.* She paused and then said, *You always want something more, you always have, but it's never—you can never—it's not going to make you happy, happiness is a noun, and you're driven by verbs, desire and want, and I don't care how corny that sounds, it is corny, I literally got it from a book my therapist gave me.* She let herself laugh but it quickly evaporated. I didn't know she was seeing a therapist, nor could I imagine her doing so. I said I was sorry, which I meant, but that only seemed to disappoint her. We let a protracted moment of silence overtake the room, and then she asked me what I was thinking. I told her all of what she said was right. She looked at me for more. *Yes*, I said. *I am driven by what I don't have.* She started staring at the greasy white paper where the lox had been, and soon her eyes glazed over and her mouth bent into a frown. We stopped speaking in a way that seemed final, and a few minutes later the rain suddenly increased, and it didn't feel like morning anymore. *I'm glad we did this*, I said. *But I feel like it's time for me to go.* Her eyes were still, like she hadn't even heard me. It took me packing up all of my things and putting on my shoes before she finally got up. She asked how long I was going to be in town. I said I had to go upstate today, that I had a mandatory department dinner, and

I had to prepare for class tomorrow morning, and the second the last word left my mouth she said, *There's a film noir cinema nearby. Most of what they play is unwatchable but if you're high, especially on a day like this.* I waited for her to finish the thought but she didn't. I said that if I stayed it would just make things worse when I left. She nodded, like she understood, like we were both adults who would make the right decision.

⁓

Don Garnett was understanding, he pretended to make a note of it, but really he didn't keep records. Frau Lehmann less so, or I assumed as much. She never answered my text.

If I'd written down what we did that day, from the time we left her apartment to when we fell asleep, at a very domestic 10:45, and read it years later, I might have thought it was from the thick of our relationship. We walked hand in hand for most of it, or didn't, it wasn't of consequence because the whole time it felt like we were touching in some way. We were only apart when she went to the bathroom at the theater; in the apartment we peed with the door open, like we used to. The film was Italian, about a murderous fugitive who meets a beautiful nightclub singer. They work together to rob jewelry stores and mug johns she finds in her sister's brothel. By any standard it was bad, but because I could never tell what was coming or even which characters to root for, I felt a sense of presence that's hard to come by even in good films. Also I was stoned. Someone stole our umbrella from the lobby and by the time we got to the lunch spot, a seafood restaurant, we were soaked. We bought hoodies with their logo on it and ate chowder and laughed so much it was hard to eat, and then we went back to her place and had sex on and off for hours while the rain continued, and we smoked more and watched *2001: A Space Odyssey*, and for almost an hour we deliberated on dinner, half on choosing the place, half on the actual dishes, and when it arrived we ate in silence with only candles lighting the room. After that we read on the couch with our legs intertwined, interrupting each other too often to actually read; I must have gotten through half a *New Yorker* article in an hour. Eventually I became tired in a way I rarely do, the way I imagine other people feel when their head hits the pillow, people who don't question their life choices quite so frequently. When we got in bed we began pushing against each other, practically wrestling, as if to see how much comfort each other's skin could give our own. It was then that I started to feel a firmament of happiness above me, one which I never looked up at, because if I did I knew I'd see it passing slowly, like a cloud. Or maybe it wasn't like a cloud, maybe it was staying exactly where it was and I was the one moving away. That's what it felt like to fall asleep, actually, like someone was pulling at me, relentlessly tugging me to the left, that I could always muster the strength to stay where I was but I knew that they would never stop trying, that inevitably I'd be the one to give up.

I don't know who woke first but by 6 we were having sex again. It was quick and dutiful, Monday-morning efficient. After she took a shower and got ready she made eggs and ate them at the kitchen table. I witnessed this by listening. When she came to say goodbye I pulled her onto the bed. She pretended to protest, she had heels on. We kissed for a long time, long enough that I forgot about the shoes, and when one tore through the sheet it took me a moment to remember that it wasn't mine, the bed, the apartment. We looked at each other, we were both thinking the same thing but I said it first. *I need you in my life.* She started crying, so did I. *I need you too.* Her smell overwhelmed me, this happiness felt irrational, and yet I couldn't imagine it ever leaving. *We'll make this work*, I said. She nodded, we kissed more, we cuddled, she became late for work, and then more so, to break free she practically had to run out the door.

After she left I thought to get up but still I just lolled in bed, mollified, content to kick out my limbs and roll around, smell the pillows which smelled like her, they also smelled like me I'm sure but I can't smell me; what we could each smell of ourselves on the bed was complementary and mutually exclusive. The love I held then was so thorough I didn't even feel it, it was coterminous with my being, no part of me existed outside its bounds and it did not waste itself on any spot where I was not. It didn't matter that she wasn't there with me, the love stayed. That struck me as something worth thinking about, and I carried the thought out of bed over to the kitchen. There was enough coffee in the French press for a cup. It was lukewarm so I microwaved it. I made eggs on the pan, which was dirty with oil and egg film. I wondered if she knew I'd use it or if she no longer cleaned her pan in the morning. I went back to the other thought: she was gone, but the love I had for her was still with me. I felt light, creative. I opened my laptop and put on some music and danced around. I put on my socks to help me glide. *Love is just being loved*, I thought, and then I said it aloud, again and again. It had a nice meter, especially if you put a half beat after *Love* and broke *being* into two words. *Love, is just be-ing loved.* The phrase would be nice in a dance song if it were sung by someone with a deep, celestial voice. I went to my laptop, telling myself I was about to look up train times, but then I opened a Word doc and wrote, *Love, is just be-ing loved.* I wrote it again and again and then realized I might as well copy-and-paste it, and then after I'd done that I copied that big block and pasted it over and over, and then I deleted it all and wrote about when we woke up that morning. I'd never kept a diary but always thought I should, how many times had I questioned my own memory, wished for a more immersive recording of my life? I thought of Gerhard Richter and Googled his work and then went back to the diary. I started to write about the sex we had in great detail, but then decided that wasn't necessary so I just wrote, *We had sex.* The sentences came easy, the process was too natural to be called writing, every time I moved a set of words from my head onto the page the next set took shape, like there was some invisible queue, it was more like reading than writing. Eventually I wrote everything that happened that morning until the present, and then no more words appeared to me.

Suddenly my head was empty, I understood why meditation was a thing, I could think clearly, finally, without all the extra muck, the perpetual guilt, the need to forgive myself for nothing in particular. An impulse: I opened my browser and found the number. Another: I called, but hung up after one ring. The refrigerator started humming, I spun around, facing it. After my heart settled I called the number again, two rings and then, *Tappan, please hold*. I did, I tried not moving my body, as if that's what holding was. A moment later: *How can I help you?* A man, monotone, thoroughly straight. *Yes, hi. I was wondering if Annabelle is available?* White noise, a pixelated song in the background, and then silence, a long silence. *Yeah, hello.* Someone new, an older, hoarse voice. I repeated my question. His tone was casual, belying his actual words: *Get a fucking life. And tell your buddies to get one too. She don't work here anymore, okay? And if one more of you calls or God forbid shows your face I swear to God I'll press charges.* I waited for him to hang up but he didn't, I heard the song in the background, gearing up for the chorus. My hand was shaking. *I—I didn't—I'm calling because someone put her down as a reference. For a job.* I swallowed. He didn't respond, but still he didn't hang up. *Sir? I didn't mean to cause offense, really. I'm just trying to vet a potential candidate.* He sighed. More silence, and then: *Del's. She's working at Del's, in SoHo.* As soon as the sound stopped I let my phone drop to the couch, as if I shouldn't be touching it. I stood up, I started walking circles around the coffee table. Soon my hands wanted to be as busy as my feet, so I put away her clean dishes and then washed the ones in the sink. I rearranged the books on the coffee table by size, a jagged pyramid, and then I made the bed. I went back to the couch and Googled *Del's*, it was two blocks away from the restaurant where Ellis and I met, years ago. I thought to call but thought better of it.

I took a shower, got dressed, and packed my things. I was just out the door when I realized I hadn't looked up train times. My laptop was crammed into my duffel but hers was on the kitchen counter. I took it to the couch. Her password was still the same, so was her desktop: psychotically empty, which made the lone folder, *audio*, impossible to ignore. Austin came to mind—or rather the improbably handsome face my imagination had decided on. I tried to resist, I didn't. Inside were about a dozen mp4s, the first titled *5 21 19*, the last *8 10 19*. I opened one, it was nearly forty-five minutes long. I jumped to the half-way point. It took me a few seconds to identify the voice: her dad's. The volume was too high but I didn't touch it, it made him seem big, like he was filling the room, like I was a fly on the wall. It was hardly ten seconds before any sense of intrigue melted into something else, something that gathered in my stomach like guilt. I thought to turn it off but couldn't, not be-fore I understood what exactly I was listening to, let it fill the shape of what I already knew: *It would surprise me if he remem-bered you at all.* I had believed her, I'd given it a moment's thought, but had I really let myself understand? What I was hearing made sense—he was talking about when he first met his wife, her mom—but the tone didn't, no, he didn't know he was talking to his daughter, a fact I might've tried to ignore but for her own verbal tics, everything she said was bookended with *as your daughter* or *right, Dad*, clues he usually missed but some-times gained a foothold in, reentered his body for long enough to laugh at himself, or, once or twice, explode in frustration. I must have listened for ten minutes when, suddenly, it became too much. As soon as I hit STOP I thought of him, Emmitt, the man I'd once known, an idea I could believe in only by ignoring what I'd just heard, an idea that did not exist in that recording; even when he regained himself it was only to find that person disintegrating. All he could hope for was lucidity, but that itself was the nightmare.

I checked the trains. I did everything short of wiping my fingerprints. I put the laptop back exactly where I found it. I took one last look around, locked myself out, and slid the key through the mail slot. It was a clear day, gray but with no threat of rain. The street was completely dry. It seemed a miracle that it can rain and then all the rain is gone.

I took the G north to the E, which would take me to Penn Station. On the subway I studied the design of the ads—half were for a new startup called Re: POWER that did something I couldn't understand—while I let a small part of my brain do the mental math: yes, if I did just stay on the E, if I went downtown, if I gave myself an hour at the restaurant and not a minute more, I could still catch the last train out.

———

As I approached I slowed my walk, enough to peer inside. It wasn't formal, per se, but intentional. Every detail was thought out. My ensemble was not: the T-shirt I slept in, a dark green JanSport bought before Obama. I thought a belt might help, I stopped around the corner. As I strapped it on I made eye contact with a tourist couple, Eastern Europeans. They were alarmed, curious: Was I one of New York's homeless? I diverted my eyes, walked back to the restaurant. It was almost 11 and there was hardly anyone there. The hostess performed warmth but her eyes wandered to my duffel bag, my chest. She hid her contempt, like the expert she was, and led me to the bar—this despite the fact that all but two tables were available. I hung my duffel on the hook, happy to get it out of view, and took out *The Power Broker*. For the first time I allowed myself a full panorama of the room, which was all but interchangeable with the place where Ellis and I had met—the globe sconces, the baffling play-list; it was Monday brunch and "Just Dance" by Lady Gaga was playing. For the two dining parties there were six or seven serv-ers, huddling together near the kitchen doors. It wasn't until I turned back to my book that I felt the drop in pressure. I waited a moment before looking over again. It came then, the click of recognition, as soft as a clock's second hand. A chill spread from my ribs to the tops of my arms. She was standing in perfect pro-file, her hair darker than it was in the photo but with the same cut. I only realized I was staring when one of her coworkers, a blond woman, noticed me and broke from the pack. I turned back, pretending to be immersed in my reading as she sidled up to the bar. She asked how my morning was going. My nerves obliterated social grace, I forgot to answer the question and or-dered a cappuccino. When she walked away I forced myself to read two pages before lifting my head again. I couldn't find her this time, one of the other servers made a face at me: Did I need something? I shook my head and smiled. Soon the waitress brought the coffee, a four-leaf clover in the foam. I told her it looked nice, my anxiety presented as earnestness, she seemed disarmed, I sensed pity; she thought I was from somewhere that didn't have foam art. After she left I struggled to gather my concentration and just as I did she was back. This time she took a seat. *Do you have everything you need?* The voice was deeper, softer. I turned. Annabelle. I was embarrassed to find I couldn't

keep eye contact, I diverted my gaze to her hands, which held a
pen over a pad, a position I understood was facetious when I finally looked back at her face. I said I was being helped. *I'm sure
you are.* She was glaring at me, I matched her, we continued this
game for a few moments, and when it ended I had the feeling
she'd won. I felt we knew each other through instinct and nothing else, like ex-lovers decades past. *I should introduce myself,* I
said. She made a face; she knew who I was. Maybe she'd researched the book, but enough to recognize the ghostwriter?
Finish your drink and leave, she said. *I don't need an apology. You
don't have to absolve yourself or, you know, make sure I won't sue.*
She thought for a moment. *I can't, I've checked.* I tried to make
sense of things, I couldn't, her eyes widened, I needed to respond, I was afraid that if I spoke it would be the last thing I
ever said to her, it was barely an instinct but I knew I hadn't
gotten what I came for, really. Yes, she was real to me now, yes,
the clay had mass, but I sensed at its center a rock-solid lump,
the very part I needed. Why did she lie to Avi? I could guess, but
I couldn't really, no, I didn't know her, I didn't know the character. She poked her head up, she was being summoned. My
time was limited, I needed more, I threw a Hail Mary, I asked
for her number. She searched for words, she was confused,
recalibrating. *I just need a few minutes,* I said. *That's all, I swear.*
She squinted, looked down. I took out my phone. She said
the digits, once and without stopping. I showed her my screen
and she confirmed. By the time I called it so she'd have my
number she was already standing, signaling my waitress for the
check.

It wasn't until after I left, after I stepped outside, that I began questioning the sudden willingness, the quick nod. Did she even look at the digits on my screen? I gazed back inside; the hostess met my stare. I walked to the end of the block and called the number. No answer, a default voicemail greeting. I texted, *Is this Annabelle?* I checked the time, I could still make the train, easy. I could be in my apartment by dinner, eating the pozole I made days ago, staring at the screen of my laptop, left with nothing but my imagination to break through her core.

———

But she did text back, half an hour later, just as I walked into Grand Central: *At work off @ 3 will call then.*

Re: POWER, it turned out, was a workspace, or the thing that would soon replace workspaces, make them as outdated as the cubicle. *Work-Life Imbalanced* was their motto, which deftly, insanely inverted the concept of work-life balance. Their *POWERstations* were a place to "get work done if it needed to be done," but you could also eat, meet, greet, "make friends, lovers, enemies, frenemies." You could see movies, get buff, get lazy (with CBD drinks on tap), get *Happy* with Pharrell in one of their all-day silent disco rooms. *To live, in other words*, the concierge said as she swiped my credit card. $55 for the day, including snacks, coffee, gym, and showers, not including a tip (20% recommended). I'd stumbled upon the place not two blocks from Grand Central, an attractive mixed-sex couple ushering me in as if my entire life had led me here. I could hardly object, how else would I pass the time?

I'd intended to use those hours grading papers but spent them on an advanced showing of *Joker* and then a Guggenheim-sponsored mini-exhibit featuring the women of Abstract Expressionism. By 3:30 she still hadn't called. I walked out of the building into an unexpected Indian summer, air full of false hope, passersby too happy for fall. I took out my phone, stared at it, succumbed. She picked up on the fifth ring. No salutation, just, *Right, let's talk.* I did, about how thankful I was for her time, how hard it was tracking her down. She was surprised by this, all of the required information was online, it was the only reason she'd given me her number. As the minutes wasted away I continually tried formulating the question, but I couldn't, I knew how easy it would be for her to deflect it, to produce words I couldn't match a face to. I asked to see her in person and she laughed, she didn't mind being harsh. I let myself sound not just a little hurt as I told her that what I wanted to discuss was personal, it was why I'd come all this way, why I'd missed the last train back just to wait for her to be done with work. She didn't respond, the iron was hot, I said if she gave me only a bit of her time I'd need no more of it, I would get out of her life. She sighed. She said she'd be home in a few hours, she was getting drinks with a friend but could meet before, *for thirty minutes, if that.* I thanked her, I said I'd make it up to her. She said she needed nothing made up, she needed nothing at all, only that I should get what I needed and—quoting me—*get out of my life.*

———

I couldn't go back to Sandra's before 9 anyway. When I texted her my change of plans she said she'd be out to dinner with Austin, *our last, I believe*. It struck me that she hadn't mentioned such a meal earlier, but that was fine, a positive even, it relieved me of some of my own guilt. I hadn't fully admitted to myself that I wouldn't tell her I saw Annabelle but I wouldn't, I couldn't. The other lies were easier: Garnett, my classes. For good measure I bought myself another two days, ye old *family emergency*. It didn't feel great, this betrayal of the Socratic Oath, to make up for it I spent the rest of the afternoon grading papers, I was generous with my attention and more so with my marks, I left notes I thought would not only explain my grading but encourage my students to believe they could do better. Actually, it turned out to be a great way to move the hours.

She lived in Chinatown, on Pell Street, a claustrophobic byway stuffed with eateries, salons, massage parlors. We were still an hour or two from sunset but the street was dark, I needed the light of my phone to find which buzzer was hers. I waited a minute and buzzed again and seconds later the door clicked. She was on the fourth floor of a walk-up; by the time I got to the top I regretted not having another coffee. The door was bolted open, when I came in I was immediately overwhelmed, her stuff could've filled three apartments: overlapping oriental rugs, lamps and armchairs from possibly every decade of the twentieth century, stacks of books and magazines, shelves full of East Asian ephemera that also claimed part of the floor and some table space, a folded-up room divider, a liquor cart—for God's sake, a hookah. Through the living room and bedroom I found her on the fire escape, smoking. She was wearing navy-blue shorts and a heathered gray too-large T-shirt. She looked at me and smiled: it was brief, a delicate balance between irritation and mercy.

Neither explained how contrived the whole affair felt, I could even see that the cigarette was full, she must have lit it after buzzing me in. The residue of her smile betrayed it too: She cared what I thought, the impression she made. *Did you borrow those pants from Avi?* I looked down, as if I weren't sure. They were dark blue, rayon, slim, high, cut at the ankle. Her face gave very little but still I sensed I should be intrigued by the comment— had they reunited? I asked her how often they saw each other and she said, *Enough to know his style.* I tried to gauge her opinion of him, if it would be okay to make some slight about his new venture. *So he must've caught you up—* She held up her hand. *You wrote it, I know.* I doubted she had the full story, or at least a truthful version of it, but before I could speak she said, *And you should know that it ruined my life. Not that it—I ruined my life, but the book sure as fuck helped.* She looked right at me, I returned her stare. *That trip was during a rough time for me. I was having doubts about things, and—it doesn't matter, you know what happened. Well, when I got back I came clean, to my fiancé, I mean, my ex, Peter. I'll say we got past it. Actually it could have been the end of the story. For two years it was. We got engaged, we bought an apartment together. And then I heard about the book. I had a publishing friend get me a copy and I read it in one night. I didn't sleep for a week, literally, for five straight days I didn't sleep. I slept only after I gave Peter—* She stopped, collected herself. *Maybe it wasn't meant to be.*

But that was just the beginning. It became a hit, of course it did, I knew it would. What I didn't expect, what I couldn't believe, was that people wanted to fucking find me. They did, Caleb. My name, a picture of me, my number and home address and Tappan's, all on some fucking message board for creeps. Well, creeps and Avi, apparently. He got in touch not too long ago. I didn't want to talk but he insisted. Actually, he was sweeter than he had to be. He offered me a job, at his new thing, food and beverage manager. It would have been a step up. I knew it was just that he felt guilty. He cried when I told him what people did, how they'd call the restaurant, how a few even came in person. She paused, gauging my reaction. *You can't imagine what license people give themselves. Someone even posted a video of me serving them. Eventually my team noticed, that I was some sort of attraction, a niche celebrity. They probably thought I was in porn, which for some reason would have been less embarrassing.*

I'm sorry to hear all that, I said. *And I'm sorry for whatever part I played in it.* She nodded away the formality. *Really, I—I don't know what to say.* I resisted the urge to figure out what story Avi had told her. Instead I let time pass, I measured my words. *I am curious about one thing, though, which is when the two of you reunited, if he—If he also felt a bit betrayed.* Her eyebrows knitted. *By you?* I shook my head, I waited for her to get it, she didn't. *You, well—you told him you were dying.* She started to speak but didn't. Her eyelids lowered, barely. She leaned back and stared at me, happy to sit in the silence. Actually, she was just waiting for me to speak so she could cut me off, the second I opened my mouth she said, *I wonder why you think the book did so well. You're a decent writer, Caleb, but writing doesn't make a book, and neither does fucking. Yeah, I wonder if you ever actually considered what it* meant *to people.* Obviously I had. Many times. And yet the way she looked at me made me feel negligent—or worse, simply uncurious. *I kept thinking about all those skulls you see in old paintings. Those little reminders that there's more to life than money or sex or whatever else. Like your soul, assuming you have one.* I tried to smile at the joke, share a moment, but she didn't care. *Your book, I realized, is the opposite. It says that life is only those things that pass us by.* She squinted at me, making sure her words landed. *Sofia was the story, she gave it life. She was the only reason it had any meaning at all.* She lifted her cigarette but there was nothing left, she picked up the pack only to put it down again. *It amazes me, really, this little pissing match the two of you had, over who really owned the story, as if either of you did. No, you're a couple of straight white men who've been given the world, which is a great gift all things considered but it's given you nothing to say, not these days at least, people are sick of hearing about you.* Her mouth searched for more but apparently that was the end of it; her shoulders fell, her body reinhabited itself, stood like it wanted to.

I scoured her for a single show of pride, anything to give me moral leverage. She had me by, what—one inch? A straight white woman dishing wokeness in the middle of lower Manhattan. God, I wanted to ask what the hell made her life so redeeming. And what gave her the right to assess mine. I didn't need to be reminded I had *nothing to say*, I'd read the fucking drafts, it was why I was here. I swallowed the thought. I looked at her. She was searching for a change of subject, she found it: *Do you want something to eat?* I shook my head. *I'm just making eggs*, she said. *I can't drink on an empty stomach.* A reminder of her plans, that my time was limited. She waited for me to respond, and when I didn't she went inside.

I watched her in the kitchen, rummaging for a pan. Just beyond her was the front door, still ajar. I had now asked the question I'd come to ask. If she hadn't given me an answer she'd still given more of herself than she'd meant to. Yes, it was only when she was knocked off-balance, too angry to keep up a facade, that it felt like I was getting to her, getting the real person. I walked inside. I said that I had something to tell her. She opened the fridge and grabbed a carton of eggs. *I've been writing about you*, I said. *Not you you, but you as a character. A new novel, I mean.* I paused, steadied my pace. *I think it's good, what I'm writing. Better than* Last Resort. She turned around. I didn't realize how close we'd been until we were face-to-face. *Trash it*, she said, waiting for my reaction before turning back. *I'd change the names*, I said. *I'd change everything, it wouldn't take place*—I saw her arm raise, the skillet at its apex, I'd closed my eyes, could only imagine it slamming down on the thin metal of the stove. I had flinched, my back was to her, I saw the eggs on the floor, one yolk broken. I covered my ears but there'd be no more sound, as she walked away it seemed her feet didn't even touch the floor. In her bedroom she turned around, her hands holding the doorframe. She called me a parasite, a coward, at first I couldn't listen, I was concentrating on not smiling, a nervous habit I get from my mom. *Why are you here? To get my permission? You don't need it, legally, as long as you're one fucking millimeter smarter than before. But if you're looking for some sort of moral waiver, then fuck off, truly, I am not your muse, I am not a character, I'm a person.*

That's the point, I said. *You're a person, a very real person.* She laughed at me, through me, it was a laugh she didn't care if I heard. My stomach churned, my face warmed. It was suddenly clear that I might not get what I needed, that the floor beneath me could vanish, that I could find myself back where I started. I saw my life with too much clarity, what kind of person I'd been for the past year, and before I could even feel sad I felt water behind my eyes. The tears were still out of view, I could stop them, but why should I? I let them come, just enough so she could see, and then a bit more after she put her hands on my shoulders and told me she was sorry if she offended me but really I needed to get my shit together. She looked me in the eyes, said I could lie down if I needed to. I nodded, I did need that. She sent me to the bedroom, came in a minute later with a glass of something clear that smelled like turpentine. When I took a sip she pushed my hand up until it all went down. I waited for its effect, it took less than a minute. At a calmer register I told her that she was right about everything, that I had nothing to say. She made a vague attempt to take back her words but she couldn't, they were true. Instead she lay down next to me, her head on my shoulder, her shoulder on my arm. If this was just some consolation prize it was still consoling, unbelievably so, actually it was hard to believe I'd cried at all, that I'd felt anything close to sadness, no, what filled me then was the very opposite, something I won't call love because I know how that sounds but what else could describe such relief? I felt heavy like I never do, heavy like her head, which lent me comfort by its weight alone. I looked at her, she turned too, I hardly had to move as my lips came over hers, it was hardly a moment but it was. We came apart but stayed still, her breath still near, my eyes still closed. Through my lids I was staring at the sun, the red so bright that when I opened my eyes the room was blue, too blue—hazy, mildly opaque, I attributed it to something more spiritual than smoke, which is what it was, seeping into the bedroom from the kitchen. I said her name, she sprang up and tended to the situation, opening windows, turning on a fan.

Alone in her room I became aware of all the items I hadn't noticed before. The lucky cat toy perched on her bookshelf, its back to the room. A framed page torn from a music score. Details I'd need to re-create the scene. Each one was perfect, as if they could be anything less, their only purpose was to reference reality. I turned and saw her in the doorway, watching me. It was then that I came back to myself—her posture, her silhouette, the banality of physical attraction. *I'm seeing someone*, I said, not giving myself the chance to think about it. *Well*, she said. *It was just a kiss.* I searched for a clock but there was none. I asked if she would need to leave soon, I didn't listen to the answer, I stood up, looked around, went out to the fire escape to fetch my things. When I came back in she was in the living room, her hands on her hips, pretending to survey the room. We didn't make eye contact, I let myself out. It was only when I reached her stairwell that I thought to turn, get one last look, but all I saw was her door closing.

I got there before Sandra, by about half an hour. I spent this time trying and failing to fish the key out of the mail slot, and then, well, composing a text to Annabelle. I only wanted to thank her and apologize, and say I appreciated her kindness and patience, and if she'd let me I'd like to meet again, hear more about what she thought of *Last Resort*, what she thought of my new project.

When Sandra came back I could tell her night had been hard, but hard in a good way, she looked happier than I'd seen her in a long time. She ran up the stairs and delivered a kiss I misinterpreted, or wasn't in the state to receive, it was supposed to be wildly romantic whereas I was dying to pee. She let us in, I went to the bathroom, we sat on the couch and drank beer. She told me everything, it was textbook, she said he said he hoped they could *stay friends, like, for a while.*

We drank more beer, our moods converged, we had relatively wild sex I supposed was a proxy for their breakup hookup. It was exactly what I needed, I nearly forgot about the day, right up until she came back from the bathroom and lay in my arms, when a deplorable thought crossed my mind, a chance squiggle that only got airspace because of its shock value: that her body was Annabelle's. I removed myself from the bed but it was too abrupt, she must have sensed something was off. Without a word I walked away, to the living room, where I found my phone lodged in her couch. There were no new messages. When I came back in she was sitting up against the headrest. *I love you, Caleb. That's all I feel I need to say. Everything else, everything that came before and everything we'll have to figure out, it's just—it'll never be as much as I love you.* She looked full, happy. She had filled herself with happiness just by saying words she knew were true and heard. I couldn't help but imagine confessing right then. *I love you too,* I said. I was going to go and kiss her but I heard something from the living room, it took me a second, the couch cushion had muted the buzz. *You can check if you need,* she said, teasing me. I shook the thought away and sat on the bed. I said I thought we should have a sense of things before I went back upstate, we should know what we each expected, and if— Another buzz, but this one was different, it was elsewhere, it was Sandra's and it was continuing. A call. She launched out of bed and scurried to the dining table, mouthing an apology even though she hadn't picked up yet. By the tone of her voice I knew it was work, by her drooping shoulders I knew she was being given more of it. My phone buzzed again. I walked steadily to the living room, grabbed it, and threw myself onto the couch.

The texts were from her, the 917 number; I was glad to have not saved her name. The first: *I'm going away for a while*. The second was just a URL, *flights.app.goo.gl*, followed by a short string of random characters. A buzz, a third: *There are seats left*. I swallowed. I looked at Sandra, who was too immersed in her call to notice my attention. I watched her walk to her bed, surely to get her computer, at which point I grabbed mine, but as soon as I opened it she put down her phone, sighed, and came to the couch. *Something you need to take care of?* I asked. *Yes*, she said. *But this is more important*. She was waiting for me to speak. *I want to be forthright*, I said. *I think things will be difficult as they are now, with me being upstate. This is going to be my last year, and—and I think we should think about some sort of fresh start when we can be in the same place again*. I couldn't look at her. *We're meant for each other*, she said, as if she were reminding me. I thought about how normal it is for completely sane people to say that phrase, people who understand there's no such thing as destiny. *Sandra, I'm just getting out of something. Isn't it healthy to wait?* Her eyes widened, finally something other than sadness. No, disbelief. I'd made a critical error. Yes, just getting out of something might have been fine reasoning, as would waiting until we weren't long-distance, but deploying them both, back-to-back, showed them for what they were: excuses, reverse-engineered. She stood up, grabbed her phone, and walked away. I wanted to say something but had nothing to say, I could only listen as she walked to her bed and began rapping at her keyboard. My laptop was within reach, I moved as smoothly as I could, as if what I was doing were some terrible thing. I pulled it onto my legs and got out my phone and typed the URL into the browser. New York to Auckland, departing Tuesday, tomorrow, at 1:55 p.m., from JFK. Economy seating, $981. It seemed cheap, too cheap. It was too cheap: It was one-way.

I closed my laptop and stood up. I walked to the bookshelf. I looked at a menorah I'd bought Sandra in Tel Aviv, I scanned her books, a photo caught my eye, it was the one of Emmitt and his brother, the one that had prompted our trip to the Rockaways. That grin, bashful just for being happy. It seemed to make me happy too, but not really, not quite—what I felt was more like relief, the untangling of a knot I hadn't noticed. Here was what I'd needed that morning: something to help replace the person I'd heard on that recording, something to remind me of who he actually was.

I shook the thought away, and again.

The flight. Auckland. It was crazy, yes. All I needed was a firm excuse. I found it: My passport, it was upstate, I couldn't get it tomorrow and be back in time. Except wasn't the duffel I had with me the same one I'd taken to the conference in Montreal? And wouldn't I have just left my passport in the outside pocket, given this was the only travel bag I had? I saw it across the room, not five feet from the foot of her bed. I walked over and unzipped the pocket and stuck my hand in, my fingers gliding around the familiar rough plastic. Sandra's typing had since reverted to its normal rhythm, but still when she stopped the silence was jolting.

We made eye contact. She closed her laptop. She asked me what I was doing. It was a good question. A better one would be: Why was I doing it now? Couldn't I have waited, what? A minute? Thirty? I saw myself crouching there, my body open to her, her line of sight unobstructed. No, there was no better time, in this battle against myself I was only playing a few moves ahead.

———

Her alarm went off at 7. She got up immediately, prepared us eggs and coffee. We ate in silence. There was so little eye contact the few glimpses we shared were impossible to bear. Just as she hopped in the shower she told me to get my things ready, I would be leaving the apartment with her, she would be taking the key; she hoped I'd make a careful decision, a deliberate one, but if I didn't she needed the spare.

By the end of the night we had all but devolved into two lawyers—arguing precedent, parsing right and wrong, cataloging each breach of the line between. (I hadn't perjured myself once, nor had I omitted anything of importance—including my visit to Annabelle's apartment, our kiss, and the flight.) The finale consisted of her making an ultimatum: We would be together now and always or never again. There was time given for deliberation—a night of sleep, a morning more of sober thought, as if she could have set any other deadline; I'd told her the time of departure. If we were to be together I was to meet her at her office for lunch, a date that would preclude me from making the flight. She asked only that my decision be final.

Outside, she said, *I'm going this way*, nodding down the

street, implying I was not to follow her, even though I was obviously going that way too. She put her arms around me and allowed herself eye contact. When we kissed it wasn't just both wonderful and painful but the two were always equal in scale. However mad she wanted to be she gave me all of herself; I loved her then as much as I ever had, I told her so through my hands on her back, on her shoulders and her neck. When we came apart she turned away, denying us a proper goodbye. I watched her walk down the street, and after she'd been out of view for a minute I left too. When I got to the subway I worried she'd still be underground, waiting for a train, so I took out my phone. I had a text from Louis: *Just balled with Charlie from Girls.* A pang of guilt. I hadn't gotten in touch, and he lived not far from that Holiday Inn. Guilt wasn't what I needed, to rid myself of it I called him. He picked up, a surprised *Hello?*

I'm in Brooklyn. I just left Sandra's, we're back together, kind of, as long as I don't go to Auckland to follow Annabelle, Sofia, the woman from the book, the one who told Avi Deitsch she was terminally ill. I know if I go—

Too much exposition. How does the narrator feel?

Like I'd be crazy to go.

Because you love Sandra.

Correct.

And love conquers all.

Right.

Though you broke up before. And now you're back together.

This time is different.

Every time is different. A pause. *But yes, you'd be crazy to go.*

Silence. My instinct was to pivot, to ask how he'd been, et

cetera, but our relationship was so good for being past that. *Thanks*, I said, and hung up. I went underground. Sandra wasn't in sight. I took the G south to our old stop, in Fort Greene; there it would be just as easy to take the C to the A to JFK, or walk to Dumbo, to her office.

When I got out I found myself in the middle of the rush-hour stampede and turned around, back north, toward the park. As I approached, the wind pushed against me, the Indian summer had already passed. The trees' leaves shook in that solemn fall way, they were turning fall colors too, as picturesque as a college bro-chure. It seemed not just a bit meaningful that we find beauty in such flagrant displays of death. My walk stopped at the obelisk, where I took a seat on a long granite surface. I wondered about the soldiers of the Revolutionary War for whom the monument was erected, if they'd feel silly for all their effort if they knew the U.S. and Great Britain were best buds now, if they knew how we fawned over Harry and Meghan's wedding, if they knew about the internet, about how we lived and spent our time.

Soon the sun had moved enough that the trees' branches blocked it only intermittently, and the smallest wind was enough to pulsate the light. It made me think of what it would be like to have a seizure. Maybe if I had a seizure I would wake up and realize that everything had been a dream. I looked at my arms expecting them to flail but they just sat there, un-electrocuted. I wondered, if I willed my heart to stop beating, if every cell in my brain colluded against it, whether it would. *Memento mori*, that was what Annabelle was talking about, the skulls in art. It struck me as a bit pedantic to think people need paintings to remind them they'll die. Maybe they did back then, before there was such a thing as old age, before we extended life and found new indignities, before newspapers, and photography, and laptops with microphones built in. I thought of the photograph of Emmitt, and how willfully I'd believed in it, believed that it preserved him, that it encapsulated him, that it was somehow an entire life telescoped into a rectangle. It was so suddenly absurd: to think that an object could ever be consolation for his present state, that objects could be used to survive ourselves. But that hadn't been just wishful thinking. No, it was more, a belief, one that had underwritten my life, defined it. I'd spent some of my best years trying to capture people, capture myself, get my name on cardboard everywhere. But now if— If I flew forward in time, if I found my legs heavy, my thoughts too, if I found myself in a room with an aide staring at me, who in a lucid moment became my daughter, if I realized I was slipping, that the parts of myself were drifting apart, ship-wrecked, what solace could be found in a picture, a book, press clippings? And if suddenly I could go back again, if I could be me again, live my life forward, would I ever care to take my own impression, preserve myself, spend any bit of life capturing it? I had proof that it wasn't impossible, that you could ignore that impulse, in fact you could refuse it outright: Annabelle. It was why she was worth capturing, why I felt what I did when I was with her; she had something I was missing, something I'd spent all this time trying to get closer to: a life that didn't need to survive itself. In her I'd found more than a character, I'd found one who lived off the page, someone who might even make me that way too.

Business or pleasure? Both seemed wrong. It didn't matter. *Pleasure*, I said. He asked me to repeat myself and I did. He handed me back my passport and I picked up my suitcase, ignoring the unidentified grease still on its grip. I'd gone to a café in Fort Greene to buy my ticket, and two doors down was a luggage store. It dispensed Wi-Fi, the bag, "as smart as it looks," which I figured could come in handy. I didn't know where we'd be staying, didn't know anything, really. Not that I expected a full itinerary, but all she'd written back—I'd texted her, *Bought my ticket*, the second it was true—was, *Great!* I took the opportunity to turn my phone off, I was only waiting for her response, by then it was 12:30 and I dreaded a text from Sandra, not an angry tirade—if that would come it would be by email—but something with hope, like *in the lobby*, or, worse, a defensive deployment of humor, *look for the girl in the gray top.* That would shatter me. My conscience hinted that I should tell her as soon as I knew, as soon as I got on the subway and watched the doors close, but, well, I hadn't, I couldn't bear imagining the text traveling through the air, her phone twitching, the instant disappointment, the prickling of skin and warping of sound. She'd know how sorry I was, know that I knew that what I'd done would destroy me and still I'd done it anyway. And anyway, shouldn't my first message come in the form of an email, in a few days, when I fully understood what had happened? I sure as hell didn't yet, didn't feel a drip of pain for breaking the heart of someone I loved and could love for the rest of my life. If I was able to think about it, it was only through metaphor: I'd renewed my vows with a free will, or I'd torn myself away from the Velcro of my life, the latter subpar in that it implied I could reattach to my life again, which I couldn't. Really, I'd burned the loops off the Velcro of my life, which made the case for a less precise metaphor, one that didn't so clearly illustrate how irreversible my choice had been, one that wouldn't make me feel what I was feeling then, which wasn't terror so much as the prelude to it, the sense that everything was darkening, figuratively and literally. The carpet's red and purple tessellations were literally darkening, I'd watched the pattern repeat itself a thousand times and now it was darker. I stopped. My skin became clammy, my forehead cold. I needed to sit down, I went to a restaurant, one with waiters. They told me I had to order or leave. I went to the bathroom and washed my face, and then to a store, I bought *The Economist* and a bottle of water. It was fine, it would be, at least, I just needed to feel more grounded, find new Velcro, I would, it was waiting for me at gate C19, so said the big blue-lit board in front of me. It also said the flight was boarding.

After twenty minutes of security and ten more going the wrong way down Concourse C, I started to run. I hadn't had anything to eat except for the two eggs Sandra had made, and half a coffee, my blood sugar was low, I wished I'd packed a snack and thought of picking something up but soon I heard a muffled announcement, a last call, and I sprinted.

By the time I got to the gate there were just a few elderly couples and one big family, all of them tall and blond with matching black outfits, huddled together as the father took their photo. When the gate agent called me forward I realized I'd stopped walking, I was watching the family. He called me again, I moved but apparently not enough. *Please, sir.* Up close I saw that his face was pockmarked in a way I found beautiful, I had the urge to stay there, stay in his features, actually he had to pull the ticket from my hand. He looked worried so I forced a smile, I made myself sane for him. I continued on through the boarding bridge and when I got to the plane I put my palm against the outside of it, the cold metal, a ritual I'd always performed for good luck or maybe just to remind myself I once believed in it.

I knew she wouldn't be in first class but still I scanned each face, and then all of those I could see in economy. I began accumulating glares, I realized I was the only one standing and took my seat, 14E, in the middle row. To my right was the aisle, to my left a teenager with large headphones who didn't acknowledge me. I imagined how quickly his affected confidence would convert into resentment when I asked him to switch seats with her, but that would be okay. Everything would. I thought that and believed it up until the wheels started moving and they reminded us to turn off our phones. I turned mine on, I needed to text her, I was suddenly full of some unformed fear, it manifested itself irrationally, first as the idea that I'd go looking for her when she was in the bathroom, and then as the even vaguer idea that she had seen me, knew where I was while I couldn't see her. I wrote, *What seat are you?* The wheels gained speed, the engine's whir climbed in pitch, soon we were off the ground. The flight attendants began walking the aisles, checking for seat belts. I tucked my phone into my palm and pretended to watch TV. I felt a buzz, I waited for the flight attendant to pass. *Bon voyage.*

Bon voyage.

If this made sense it did so only superficially; the more I interrogated those words the more they made no sense at all. *Quoi?* I wrote, happy to have remembered the word, to be able to parry with levity. The plane inclined, my body with it, the weight of gravity slid up my legs to my butt and back. I'd been gripping my phone so tightly that when it buzzed the vibrations traveled to the veins of my wrist. *I'm not there Caleb.* I looked at the TV, an action flick, a car chase, an Asian city at night. My mouth was too dry to swallow. Buzz: *& the reason you are has nothing to do with me.*

I heard faint music, it might've been inaudible if it weren't so percussive and violent, it was coming from the kid next to me. His eyes were closed, his arms folded, he looked annoyed, jaded, suddenly well past his years. Before I looked back at the texts I allowed an instant's hope that I'd imagined them. I hadn't, I re-read them, and then again, and again and again, and each new time I felt something cresting higher and higher above me, something I could delay by looking away, and before it could crash I undid my seat belt. I stood up, I started walking forward. It felt good to be moving, to put my legs to use, I got as far as the first-class partition before a flight attendant escorted me back to my seat. She watched as I buckled up again, motioning to someone in the back of the plane. I thought to tell the woman I just needed to see the ground but realized I didn't need her permission, I leaned to my right and looked out the window. Highways, the Rocka-ways, boats against the current. It calmed me more than I thought it would, the steady motion, the fact that it was all receding, or we were. It seemed natural, stable, and continuous, it made me think of centrifugal force, that if you spin around something fast enough you only move farther and farther away from it. It was starting to seem that way, that we were only distancing ourselves from the Earth, that we would never come back to it.

I thought of Auckland. I hadn't looked up a single image. If something came to mind it was just as likely Australia. I laughed, one small peak, *Ha*. The teen looked at me, I pretended not to notice. *What?* he said. He was his age again. He just wanted to know.

Where we're going, I said. *It's nothing I can imagine.*

Acknowledgments

Jonathan Galassi gave this book life. He is a champion, friend, and constant reminder that publishing should be, among other things, fun. Everyone at FSG has been wonderful to work with, including Katie Liptak, Devon Mazzone, and Dave Cole.

Federico Andornino at Weidenfeld and Nicolson is sharp, savvy, and gracious, and his hand greatly benefited these pages.

This book has in it the warmth, wit, and wisdom of Claire Anderson-Wheeler. Thank you for everything, Claire.

Joshua Mikutis has been reading my fiction, for better or worse, for over a decade. I am incredibly lucky to call you a friend.

Gratitude to Gabriel Stutman and Alice Abernathy for inspiration, both on and off the page.

Milena Kazakov made me look in the mirror when things were especially grim.

Ellen Levine and Martha Wydysh answered my many questions and will surely suffer many more.

My mom, dad, and brother, Jeremy, made me who I am. Mom, you always believed in me, nurturing whatever there was to nurture. And Dad: There's much more of you in this book than I realized while I was writing it. There's much more of you in me than I'd ever admit.

Lastly, Mette Lützhøft Jensen made this book possible, in her support and love, her criticism and ideas, and her ability to make me feel free.

Read this excerpt from The Vegan,
the new novel from Andrew Lipstein
Summer 2023

The Vegan
Andrew Lipstein

AUTHOR OF LAST RESORT

'Talent is rare, which is why I let out a big
yippee reading Andrew Lipstein'
The Times

C hirp. Gong. Ding-ding. Ocean waves, ding-ding.

The alerts were coming more frequently now, sounding from the overhead speaker system every few seconds. Something was happening, a lot of activity even for market close. It was perfect timing, a blessing; this barrage of sound was just the kind of quirk Foster might appreciate. I was always looking for ways to underscore our nerdy kind of brilliance, our rejection of the old maxims. In fact I'd had a banner made: *Toto, I've a feeling we're not in Greenwich anymore.* Milosz, my partner, told me to take it down. I knew he was right because he said anything at all. Milosz gave what could be called *an opinion* about twice a year. He spoke only facts, facts that could be backed up with more facts, a chain of unimpeachable logic that I assumed culminated in either the meaning of life or the number zero. They say the best person to start a quantitative hedge fund is someone who can both manage the hell out of other people and master any sort of math thrown their way. Milosz and I were that person, divided in two.

I hurried across the trading floor to the speaker, fiddling with some knobs as Peter, our receptionist, watched patiently. *Do you want me to turn it off?* he asked. I laughed, I couldn't help it, my performance adrenaline was already spiking. *Louder*, I said, and he tapped at his computer.

Chirp, ding-ding. Cash register sound. It was a bit loud, that was okay. But a cash register alert was too on the nose—what did that one stand for, anyway? I told him to change it ASAP.

I turned around and saw Asja, Yuri, and Jake, three of our associate-level researchers, hunched over a table; their posture, their furtive glances, made them look like teens copying homework. I was about to send them back to their desks when I noticed the scrawl on the blackboard. It was a seemingly simple algorithm they'd been discussing for weeks, often for hours at a time, always with a piece of chalk in hand, although they never made a mark lest they disturb such an elegant formulation. *Why don't you three go to the board and have a lively discussion about the, uh*—I drew my finger in a circle until Yuri said, *The Baum-Welch algorithm.* He didn't mind that I could never remember the name, he was glad to teach me something new. *Right*, I said, and smiled. I looked at my watch, 4:01, and then at the door, where I saw Foster standing, his suit jacket over his arm, his hand flattening his hair. I renewed my smile and strode over, pointing to Peter and delivering our tired joke about gearing up the light show. He was game, Peter, his laugh sounded nothing like vocational obligation.

I opened the door and gave him my hand.

Ian? I asked, as if I didn't know what he looked like.

The great Herschel Caine. He didn't wait for an invitation to walk in; actually, I had to move out of his way.

Let's head to my office, I said, stepping past him. I preferred we not loiter, I hardly knew who he was. Well, I knew almost everything about him, I'd scoured the internet—just not what exactly he was doing here. He wanted to invest, that was what he said in his email, but he had a way of phrasing things— *I'll be in the area Monday, might I stop by?*—that suggested conspiracy. And was it just a coincidence that he was also invested in Webber? That part didn't make sense. We had nothing in common with them, the whole point of our firm was to be the antithesis of Webber; in fact Milosz and I often made business decisions by asking ourselves what our old employer *wouldn't* do. Of course I'd never say anything of the sort in a pitch, let alone mention Webber Group, unprovoked, by name. This wasn't just because no investor wanted a David in a sea of Goliaths—they all wanted a Goliath with an excess return slightly higher than that of the other Goliaths—it was because vindication and the associated passions simply weren't the stuff of moneymen. They preferred to hear some- thing more along the lines of *We've discovered a quantitative scheme that, we believe, once perfected, can generate untold wealth.* This line I knew by heart; it was my opener no matter the audience, a nice balance between supper club restraint and carnal greed—Wall Street's stereotypes for WASPs and Jews united at last.

I turned around to find him staring at the floor, as if to make a point of not seeing anything he shouldn't. This only fed my paranoia, that he was so attuned to our need for secrecy. Actually I hoped he'd glimpse enough to see we weren't another Dockers-and-beige-carpet hedge fund, some isolated *campus* with priority parking spots. We had designed our office for creativity, for thinking; we surrounded ourselves with plants: not ferns or cacti but fiddle-leaf figs, variegated strings of pearls, wandering Jews,

Monstera obliqua. We had no dress code, official or implicit; employees were encouraged to come as they were. Yuri was our case in point: he didn't even wear shoes, and I frequently found strands of his long, dry hair around the espresso machine or on the coffee table with the art books. It was with this mindset that we chose to rent three thousand square feet in SoHo, on Wooster off Broome, even though we could have spent the same amount for thirty thousand up Metro-North. It was why we mandated (and paid for) once-a-week therapy for each of our fourteen employees, myself included (Milosz was a harder sell). You had to be careful, though, not to fall on the wrong side of the obnoxious-tech-startup divide, so we forwent the furniture so modern you dared not sit on it, the murals, the liquor (I doubt our researchers even drank), and decided on Vintage seltzer over LaCroix.

Still or sparkling? I asked. He leaned in, he hadn't heard. I told Peter to turn the alerts down and, with my hand on Ian's back, shepherded him into my office.

Some people here think it sounds like a song, I said, walking behind my desk. *Some say it's like listening to a cartoon. But I think if you really pay attention, it starts to sound like language.* He nodded and gave a perfunctory smile—rather, a smile meant to convey that it was perfunctory. Fine, so it wasn't such a profound thought. I would have thought someone with a master's degree in English from Harvard (earned at age forty-two, no less) would appreciate the grace note, but apparently he had more straightforward tastes. *It sounds funny, gimmicky even, and yet, every time you hear, say, a studio audience clapping, that's our algorithm telling us there's a public stock that's more than sixty-two point five percent likely to rise at least two percentage points by market close.*

He gave a more genuine smile now. *If only 62.5 were 100.*

Of course, I said. *And that's why we hear a sound at all. Be- cause we need someone with ears—albeit someone quite smart with ears— to hear that studio audience clapping and walk over to a computer and do something I certainly don't understand, something they could have spent a dissertation on, something that, applied differently, might have made a real difference in the world, but instead it's being used here, in this office, to generate guaranteed profits for people who are already too rich.* I sat down, held my palm out, inviting him to do the same. *Well, that was some kind of introduction. Let's start over.*

Ian Foster, he said. *Nice to meet you. But perhaps I shouldn't waste more of your time. By the sound of it you're basically printing money, and money is all I come with.* He didn't sit. Was he for real? I took him in, matched him against all those preening men I'd met at Webber, at business school—no, surprisingly the best fits were from college; yes, he was a bit immature, insecure, he wasn't at home in the world. He couldn't act natural so he withheld himself, became someone else, covered his unease with affecta-tion—like that hand, his right, which swam in front of him con-stantly.

Well, we're not printing money just yet. We still need to raise enough to buy the printer. But once we've got it, once we can cover the ink and maintenance fees, et cetera, I promise I'll let you walk out of here. In fact I'll stop returning your calls.

Ah, taking a page from the RenTech playbook. Renaissance Technologies was one of the first hedge funds to use quantitative modeling, and still is an industry paragon. Decades ago, their Medallion Fund became so lucrative they kicked out their own investors, and now only employees and executives reap their unprecedented returns. *You know I met Jim Simons*, he said. Who hadn't? I acted impressed. *But let me be a bit more up front. I'm here to invest, yes, but I'm also here as a favor to a friend, Colin Eubanks. You know him, I assume?* I nodded, as if it were some name that fell on my ears now and again—my dentist, my wife's ex-fiancé—and not the Colin Eubanks whose support the firm needed to survive, $220 million, money he'd guaranteed was ours, guaranteed not in a promissory note, which I would have preferred, but with a firm hand on my shoulder and intense eye contact one night at the Harvard Club, a venue I didn't know was taken seriously—let alone by British financiers who hadn't attended Harvard—at least not $220 million seriously. But he was serious. I believed that, I'd already rewritten the clinching line of my boilerplate pitch: *To date we've filled out most of a fund of $400 million*, a line that had helped generate almost the additional $180 mil- lion, though this was all uncommitted, and assumed people wouldn't drop out. They would, I knew how this went, I'd gone through the fundraising cycle end to end four times at Webber. But of course pitching Webber to investors was an entirely different proposition: *In this market? You want tried and true.* Webber had beat the market seventeen years out of the past twenty, and usually by a good margin. We, Atra Arca Capital Management, had beat the market zero years out of zero; we were exactly the kind of risky proposition I'd spent my past life warning investors against: a firm that relied on numbers and numbers only, a quant hedge fund that was truly a quant hedge fund, and not what firms like Webber claimed to be—a quant hedge fund wrapped in rationale. We didn't want rationale, we wanted to build a black box so opaque, so dense with algorithm and data—50 petabytes of it, computed at 105 teraflops, eventually (we already had the servers, $1.5 million worth, so said the insurance we took out on them and

the information they would hold)—that none of it could be explained, not with words or numbers or even overly abstract schemata (the currency of overeducated researchers). Yes, it was sexy, and investors loved to love it, but when it came to putting down a check they wanted to see historical returns, hopefully decades of them. In other words, I was plenty aware of the stigma, and it was my mandate to prove we were not just a room full of PhDs, data servers, and chalk. Hence the name Atra Arca, which means *black box* in Latin, a detail I thought might serve me well in meetings just like this, with people of the Ian Foster sort, the *learned* sort, the sort who, if they didn't know Latin, at least revered it.

Colin, I said. *He's a good man. And I'm intrigued: What's this favor?*

Oh, he said, as if he hadn't guessed I'd ask. *Colin has superb taste, great instincts. But sometimes he needs help pulling the trigger.* *Right*, I said, and smiled. *So you want a bit of due diligence.*

We'd start with an NDA, of course. A bluff of my own. The only nondisclosure agreement we had was for employees; it was needlessly punitive and meant for people who'd know our strategy inside and out—not something that would ever be on offer, even to Colin.

He waited a beat. *No NDA*, he said. *I'm not here for due diligence. I'm not a numbers guy, I trust I know even less than you about*—the hand wave again—*all of this. And I'm not some fink, not that I've never been called that in so many words. It's just that* . . . Now he began talking at great speed, words that were mostly for himself, I could tell by the way he lit up, the self-sneer he couldn't hide, he obviously enjoyed having a captive audience. He spoke about regulation, finance in the eighties, *Den of Thieves* and *Barbarians at the Gate*, books I grew up on that now seemed so outdated I doubt anyone in the office had even heard of them—and he clearly had a keen mind, his sentences were clever, unexpected, I found myself laughing, a real laugh, which I didn't get every day, at least not at work. *And every other character in these books is either tall, thin, and silent, or short, fat, and egregiously loud. No, I don't think things are so cut and dried, and, likewise, I don't know why exactly Colin trusts me. Probably because we think alike, so with me he gets an objective version of himself. So let's say that's why I'm here, to be Colin when Colin's somewhere else. And we'll proceed with that.* He gave a quick nod, an abrupt end to his little soliloquy, and suddenly it felt like our meeting was all but over. Did he only need to be listened to, humored, flattered? That I could do. He smoothed his hair again, looked for his coat and found it already on his arm. I was going to say something, wind the meeting down with some formality, but that didn't seem to be his way; from now on my only purpose with him was deference. He made to leave but stopped at the door. *I have to ask: Why Atra Arca?*

Ah, it means black box. As in—

No, he said. *I know that. But I'd think it would be* Niger *Arca.* Atra *is more . . . gloomy, dismal even.*

Really? I'd used Google Translate. I'd confirmed it with a friend. A Hail Mary: *Do you know why they call economics the dismal science?*

Something about population growth, limited resources—no? Exactly. To profit in any market you have to take from others.

But that predator-prey mindset presumes intent, which we've taken out of the equation. Only our algorithm knows why it does what it does, and so the dismal science is kept in a box.

He laughed. He shook his head. *Herschel*, he said, *that's evil.*